Ninety-Three

Ninety-Three
Victor Hugo

MINT EDITIONS

Ninety-Three was first published in 1874.

This edition published by Mint Editions 2021.

ISBN 9781513291376 | E-ISBN 9781513294223

Published by Mint Editions®

 MINT
EDITIONS

minteditionbooks.com

Publishing Director: Jennifer Newens
Design & Production: Rachel Lopez Metzger
Project Manager: Micaela Clark
Translation by Aline Delano
Typesetting: Westchester Publishing Services

Table of Contents

Part I. At Sea

Book I. The Forest of La Saudraie   11

Book II. The Corvette "Claymore."   22

    I. England and France United   22
    II. Night with the Ship and the Passenger   25
    III. Patrician and Plebeian United   26
    IV. Tormentum Belli   32
    V. Vis Et Vir   34
    VI. The Two Ends of the Scale   38
    VII. He Who Sets Sail Invests in a Lottery   41
    VIII. 9:380   43
    IX. Some One Escapes   47
    X. Does He Escape?   49

Book III. Halmalo   52

    I. Speech is Word   52
    II. A Peasant's Memory is Worth as Much as the
       Captain's Science   56

Book IV. Tellmarch   65

    I. On the Top of the Dune   65
    II. Aures Habet, Et Non Audiet   67
    III. The Usefulness of Big Letters   69
    IV. The Caimand   71
    V. When he Awoke it was Daylight   77
    VI. The Vicissitudes of Civil War   79
    VII. No Mercy! No Quarter!   84

PART II. AT PARIS

BOOK I. CIMOURDAIN   91

    I. The Streets of Paris at that Time   91
    II. Cimourdain   96
    III. A Corner not Dipped into the Styx   102

BOOK II. THE POT-HOUSE OF THE RUE DU PAON   105

    I. Minos, Æacus, and Rhadamanthus   105
    II. Magna Testantur Voce Per Umbras   107
    III. A Quivering of the Inmost Fibres   119

BOOK III. THE CONVENTION   128

    I. The Convention   128
        I   128
        II   129
        III   130
        IV   134
        V   138
        VI   139
        VII   141
        VIII   142
        IX   144
        X   145
        XI   147
        XII   148
    II. Marat in the Green-Room   149

PART III. IN THE VENDÉE

BOOK I. THE VENDÉE   157

    I. The Forests   157
    II. Men   159
    III. Connivance of Men and Forests   160
    IV. Their Life Under Ground   162

V. Their Life in Warfare	164
VI. The Soul of the Earth Passes into Man	168
VII. The Vendée has Ruined Brittany	170

Book II. The Three Children — 173

I. Plus Quam Civilia Bella	173
II. Dol	179
III. Small Armies and Great Battles	184
IV. A Second Time	191
V. A Drop of Cold Water	193
VI. A Healed Breast, but a Bleeding Heart	195
VII. The Two Poles of Truth	200
VIII. Dolorosa	206
IX. A Provincial Bastile	208
I. La Tourgue	208
II. The Breach	209
III. The Oubliette	210
IV. The Bridge-Castle	211
V. The Iron Door	214
VI. The Library	215
VII. The Granary	215
X. The Hostages	216
XI. Terrible as the Antique	220
XII. The Rescue Planned	223
XIII. What the Marquis is Doing	225
XIV. What the Imânus is Doing	227

Book III. The Massacre of Saint Bartholomew — 230

I. The Massacre of Saint Bartholomew	230
I	230
II	232
III	234
IV	236
V	238
VI	239
VII	242

Book IV. The Mother   244

    I. Death Passes   244
    II. Death Speaks   246
    III. Mutterings Among the Peasants   250
    IV. A Mistake   254
    V. Vox in Deserto   256
    VI. The Situation   258
    VII. Preliminaries   260
    VIII. The Speech and the Roar   263
    IX. Titans Against Giants   267
    X. Radoub   270
    XI. The Desperate   276
    XII. The Deliverer   279
    XIII. The Executioner   281
    XIV. The Imânus also Escapes   283
    XV. Never Put a Watch and Key in the Same Pocket   285

Book V. In Dæmone Deus   289

    I. Found, but Lost   289
    II. From the Door of Stone to that of Iron   295
    III. Where the Sleeping Children Wake   296

Book VI. After Victory, Struggle Begins   301

    I. Lantenac Taken   301
    II. Gauvain Meditating   303
    III. The Commander's Hood   313

Book VII. Feudality and Revolution   316

    I. The Ancestor   316
    II. The Court-Martial   322
    III. The Votes   325
    IV. After Cimourdain the Judge, Cimourdain the Master 329
    V. The Dungeon   330
    VI. Still the Sun Rises   338

PART I
AT SEA

Book I

The Forest of La Saudraie

During the last days of May, 1793, one of the Parisian battalions introduced into Brittany by Santerre was reconnoitring the formidable La Saudraie Woods in Astillé. Decimated by this cruel war, the battalion was reduced to about three hundred men. This was at the time when, after Argonne, Jemmapes, and Valmy, of the first battalion of Paris, which had numbered six hundred volunteers, only twenty-seven men remained, thirty-three of the second, and fifty-seven of the third,—a time of epic combats. The battalion sent from Paris into La Vendée numbered nine hundred and twelve men. Each regiment had three pieces of cannon. They had been quickly mustered. On the 25th of April, Gohier being Minister of Justice, and Bouchotte Minister of War, the section of Bon Conseil had offered to send volunteer battalions into La Vendée; the report was made by Lubin, a member of the Commune. On the 1st of May, Santerre was ready to send off twelve thousand men, thirty field-pieces, and one battalion of gunners. These battalions, notwithstanding they were so quickly formed, serve as models even at the present day, and regiments of the line are formed on the same plan; they altered the former proportion between the number of soldiers and that of non-commissioned officers.

On the 28th of April the Paris Commune had given to the volunteers of Santerre the following order: "No mercy, no quarter." Of the twelve thousand that had left Paris, at the end of May eight thousand were dead. The battalion which was engaged in La Saudraie held itself on its guard. There was no hurrying: every man looked at once to right and to left, before him, behind him. Kléber has said: "The soldier has an eye in his back." They had been marching a long time. What o'clock could it be? What time of the day was it? It would have been hard to say; for there is always a sort of dusk in these wild thickets, and it was never light in that wood. The forest of La Saudraie was a tragic one. It was in this coppice that from the month of November, 1792, civil war began its crimes; Mousqueton, the fierce cripple, had come forth from those fatal thickets; the number of murders that had been committed there made one's hair stand on end. No spot was more terrible.

The soldiers forced cautiously. Everything was in full bloom; they were surrounded by a quivering wall of branches, whose leaves diffused a delicious freshness. Here and there sunbeams pierced, these green shades. At their feet the gladiolus, the German iris, the wild narcissus, the wood-daisy, that tiny flower, forerunner of the warm weather, the spring crocus,—all these embroidered and adorned a thick carpet of vegetation, abounding in every variety of moss, from the kind that looks like a caterpillar to that resembling a star.

The soldiers advanced silently, step by step, gently pushing aide the underbrush. The birds twittered above the bayonets.

La Saudraie was one of those thickets where formerly, in time of peace, they had pursued the Houicheba,—the the hunting of birds by night; now it was a place for hunting men.

The coppice consisted entirely of birch-trees, beeches, and oaks; the ground was level; the moss and the thick grass deadened the noise of footsteps; no paths at all, or paths no sooner found than lost; holly, wild sloe, brakes, hedges of rest-harrow, and tall brambles; it was impossible to see a man ten paces distant.

Now and then a heron or a moor-hen flew through the branches, showing the vicinity of a swamp. They marched along at haphazard, uneasy, and fearing lest they might find what they sought.

From time to time they encountered traces of encampments,—a burnt place, trampled grass, sticks arranged in the form of a cross, or branches spattered with blood. Here, soup had been made; there, Mass had been said; yonder, wounds had been dressed. But whoever had passed that way had vanished. Where were they? Far away, perhaps; and yet they might be very near, hiding, blunderbuss in hand. The wood seemed deserted. The battalion redoubled its precaution. Solitude, therefore distrust. No one was to be seen; all the more reason to fear some one. They had to do with a forest of ill-repute.

An ambush was probable.

Thirty grenadiers, detached as scouts and commanded by a sergeant, marched ahead, at a considerable distance from the main body. The vivandière of the battalion accompanied them. The vivandières like to join the vanguard; they run risks, but then they stand a chance of seeing something. Curiosity is one of the forms of feminine courage.

Suddenly the soldiers of this little advanced guard received that shock familiar to hunters, which shows them that they are close upon the lair of their prey. They heard something like breathing in the middle of the thicket, and it seemed as if they caught sight of some commotion among the leaves. The soldiers made signs to each other.

When this mode of watching and reconnoitring is confided to the scouts, officers have no need to interfere; what has to be done is done instinctively.

In less than a minute the spot where the movement had been observed was surrounded by a circle of levelled muskets, aimed simultaneously from every side at the dusky centre of the thicket; and the soldiers, with finger on trigger and eye on the suspected spot, awaited only the sergeant's command to fire.

Meanwhile, the vivandière ventured to peer through the underbush; and just as the sergeant was about to cry, "Fire!" this woman cried, "Halt!"

And turning to the soldiers, "Do not fire!" she cried, and rushed into the thicket, followed by the men.

There was indeed some one there.

In the thickest part of the copse on the edge of one of those small circular clearings made in the woods by the charcoal-furnaces that are used to burn the roots of trees, in a sort of hole formed by the branches,—a bower of foliage, so to speak, half-open, like an alcove,— sat a woman on the moss, with a nursing child at her breast and the fair heads of two sleeping children resting against her knees.

This was the ambush.

"What are you doing here?" called out the vivandière.

The woman raised her head, and the former added angrily,—

"Are you insane to remain there!"

She went on,—

"A little more, and you would have been blown to atoms!" Then addressing the soldiers, she said, "It's a woman."

"Pardieu! That's plain to be seen," replied a grenadier.

The vivandière continued,—"To come into the woods to get oneself massacred. Can you conceive of any one so stupid as that?"

The woman, surprised, bewildered, and stunned, was gazing around, as though in a dream, at these muskets, sabres, bayonets, and savage faces. The two children awoke and began to cry.

"I am hungry," said one.

"I am afraid," said the other.

The baby went on nursing.

The vivandière addressed it.

"You are the wise one," she said.

The mother was dumb with terror.

"Don't be afraid," exclaimed the sergeant, "we are the battalion of the Bonnet Rouge."

The woman trembled from head to foot. She looked at the sergeant, of whose rough face she could see only the eyebrows, moustache, and eyes like two coals of fire.

"The battalion formerly known as the Red-Cross," added the vivandière.

The sergeant continued,—

"Who are you, madam?"

The woman looked at him in terror. She was thin, young, pale, and in tatters. She wore the large hood and woollen cloak of the Breton peasants, fastened by a string around her neck. She left her bosom exposed with the indifference of an animal. Her feet, without shoes or stockings, were bleeding.

"It's a beggar," said the sergeant.

The vivandière continued in her martial yet womanly voice,—a gentle voice withal,—

"What is your name?"

The woman stammered in a scarce audible whisper:

"Michelle Fléchard."

Meanwhile the vivandière stroked the little head of the nursing baby with her large hand.

"How old is this midget?" she asked.

The mother did not understand. The vivandière repeated,—"I ask you how old it is?"

"Oh, eighteen months," said the mother.

"That's quite old," said the vivandière; "it ought not to nurse any longer, you must wean it. We will give him soup."

The mother began to feel more at ease. The two little ones, who had awakened, were rather interested than frightened; they admired the plumes of the soldiers.

"Ah, they are very hungry!" said the mother.

And she added,—

"I have no more milk."

"We will give them food," cried the sergeant, "and you also. But there is something more to be settled. What are your political opinions?"

The woman looked at him and made no reply.

"Do you understand my question?"

She stammered,—

"I was put into a convent when I was quite young, but I married; I am not a nun. The Sisters taught me to speak French. The village was set on fire. We escaped in such haste that I had no time to put my shoes on."

"I ask you what are your political opinions?"

"I don't know anything about that."

The sergeant continued,—

"There are female spies. That kind of person we shoot. Come, speak. You are not a gypsy, are you? What is your native land?"

She still looked at him as though unable to comprehend.

The sergeant repeated,—

"What is your native land?"

"I do not know," she said.

"How is that? You do not know your country?"

"Ah! Do you mean my country? I know that."

"Well, what is your country?"

The woman replied,—

"It is the farm of Siscoignard, in the parish of Azé."

It was the sergeant's turn to be surprised. He paused for a moment, lost in thought; then he went on,—

"What was it you said?"

"Siscoignard."

"You cannot call that your native land."

"That is my country."

Then after a minute's consideration she added,—

"I understand you, sir. You are from France, but I am from Brittany."

"Well?"

"It is not the same country."

"But it is the same native land," exclaimed the sergeant.

The woman only replied,—

"I am from Siscoignard."

"Let it be. Siscoignard, then," said the sergeant. "Your family belong there, I suppose?"

"Yes!"

"What is their business?"

"They are all dead. I have no one left."

The sergeant, who was quite loquacious, continued to question her.

"Devil take it, every one has relations, or one has had them! Who are you? Speak!"

The woman listened bewildered; this "or one has had them" sounded more like the cry of a wild beast than the speech of a human being.

The vivandière felt obliged to interfere. She began to caress the nursing child, and patted the other two on the cheeks.

"What is the baby's name? It's a little girl, isn't it?"

The mother replied, "Georgette."

"And the oldest one? For he is a man, the rogue!"

"René-Jean."

"And the younger one? For he is a man too, and a chubby one into the bargain."

"Gros-Alain," replied the mother.

"They are pretty children," said the vivandière. "They look already as if they were somebody."

Meanwhile the sergeant persisted.

"Come! Speak, madam! Have you a house?"

"I had one once."

"Where was it?"

"At Azé."

"Why are you not at home?"

"Because my house was burned."

"Who burned it?"

"I do not know. There was a battle."

"Were do you come from?"

"From over there."

"Where are you going?"

"I do not know."

"Come, to the point! Who are you?"

"I do not know."

"Don't know who you are?"

"We are people running away."

"To what party do you belong?"

"I do not know."

"To the Blues, or the Whites? Which side are you on?"

"I am with my children."

There was a pause. The vivandière spoke.

"For my part I never had any children. I have not had time."

The sergeant began again.

"But what about your parents? See here, madam, tell me the facts about your parents. Now, my name is Radoub. I am a sergeant. I live on the Rue Cherche-Midi. My father and my mother lived there. I can talk of my parents. Tell us about yours. Tell us who your parents were."

"Their name was Fléchard. That's all."

"Yes. The Fléchards are the Fléchards, just as the Radoubs are the Radoubs. But people have a trade. What was your parents' trade? What did they do, these Fléchards of yours?"[1]

"They were laborers. My father was feeble and could not work, on account of a beating which the lord, his lord, our lord, gave him: it was really a mercy, for my father had poached a rabbit, a crime of which the penalty is death; but the lord was merciful and said, 'You may give him only a hundred blows with a stick;' and my father was left a cripple."

"And then?"

"My grandfather was a Huguenot. The curé had him sent to the galleys. I was very young then."

"And then?"

"My husband's father was a salt smuggler. The king had him hung."

"And what did your husband do?"

"He used to fight in those times."

"For whom?"

"For the king."

"And after that?"

"Ah! For his lord."

"And then?"

"For the curé."

"By all the names of beasts!" cried the grenadier. The woman jumped in terror.

"You see, madam, we are Parisians," said the vivandière, affably.

The woman clasped her hands, exclaiming,—

"Oh, my God and Lord Jesus!"

"No superstitions here!" rejoined the sergeant.

The vivandière sat down beside the woman and drew the oldest child between her knees; he yielded readily. Children are quite as easily reassured as they are frightened, with no apparent reason. They seem to possess instinctive perceptions. "My poor worthy woman of this

---

1. The sergeant makes a pun on the name Fléchard which is untranslatable. Flèche means arrow, and he asks whether the Fléchards made arrows.—Tr.

neighborhood, you have pretty little children, at all events. One can guess their age. The big one is four years, and his brother is three. Just see how greedily the little rascal sucks. The wretch! Stop eating up your mother! Come madam, do not be frightened. You ought to join the battalion. You should do as I do. My name is Housarde. It's a nickname, but I had rather be called Housarde than Mamzelle Bicorneau, like my mother. I am the canteen woman, which is the same as saying, she who gives the men to drink when they are firing grape-shot and killing each other. The devil and all his train. Our feet are about the same size. I will give you a pair of my shoes. I was in Paris on the 10th of August. I gave Westerman a drink. Everything went with a rush in those days! I saw Louis XVI guillotined,—Louis Capet, as they call him. I tell you he didn't like it. You just listen now. To think that on the 13th of January he was roasting chestnuts and enjoying himself with his family! When he was made to lie down on what is called the see-saw, he wore neither coat nor shoes; only a shirt, a quilted waistcoat, gray cloth breeches, and gray silk stockings. I saw all that with my own eyes. The fiacre which he rode in was painted green. Now then, you come with us; they are kind lads in the battalion; you will be canteen number two; I will teach you the trade. Oh, it's very simple! You will have a can and a bell; you are right in the racket, amid the firing of the platoons and the cannons, in all that hubbub, calling out, 'Who wants a drink, my children?' It is no harder task than that. I offer a drink to all, you may take my word for it,—to the Whites as well as to the Blues, although I am a Blue, and a true Blue at that. But I serve them all alike. Wounded men are thirsty. People die without difference of opinions. Dying men ought to shake hands. How foolish to fight! Come with us. If I am killed you will fill my place. You see I am not much to look at, but I am a kind woman, and a good fellow. Don't be afraid."

When the vivandière ceased speaking, the woman muttered to herself,—

"Our neighbor's name was Marie-Jeanne, and it was our servant who was Marie-Claude."

Meanwhile Sergeant Radoub was reprimanding the grenadier.

"Silence! You frighten madam. A man should not swear before ladies."

"I say this is a downright butchery for an honest man to hear about," replied the grenadier; "and to see Chinese Iroquois, whose father-in-law was crippled by the lord, whose grandfather was sent to the galleys by the curé, and whose father was hung by the king, and who fight,—

zounds!—and who get entangled in revolts, and are crushed for the sake of the lord, the curé, and the king!"

"Silence in the ranks!" exclaimed the sergeant.

"One may be silent, sergeant," continued the grenadier; "but it is all the same provoking to see a pretty woman like that running the risk of getting her neck broken for the sake of a calotin."[2]

"Grenadier," said the sergeant, "we are not in the Pike Club. Save your eloquence!" And turning to the woman, "And your husband, madam? What does he do? What has become of him?"

"Nothing; since he was killed."

"Where was that?"

"In the hedge."

"When?"

"Three days ago."

"Who killed him?"

"I do not know."

"How is that? You don't know who killed your husband?"

"No."

"Was it a Blue, or a White?"

"It was a bullet."

"Was that three days ago?"

"Yes."

"In what direction?"

"Towards Ernée. My husband fell. That was all."

"And since your husband died, what have you been doing?"

"I have been taking my little ones along."

"Where are you taking them?"

"Straight along."

"Where do you sleep?"

"On the ground."

"What do you eat?"

"Nothing."

The sergeant made that military grimace which elevates the moustache to the nose. "Nothing?"

"Well, nothing but sloes, blackberries when I found any left over from last year, whortle-berries, and fern-shoots."

"Yes, you may well call it nothing."

---

2. An opprobrious epithet for an ecclesiastic.—TR.

The oldest child, who seemed to understand, said:

"I am hungry."

The sergeant pulled from his pocket a piece of ration bread, and handed it to the mother.

Taking the bread, she broke, it in two and gave it to the children, who bit into it greedily.

"She has not saved any for herself," growled the sergeant.

"Because she is not hungry," remarked a soldier.

"Because she is a mother," said the sergeant.

The children broke in.

"Give me something to drink," said one.

"To drink," repeated the other.

"Is there no brook in this cursed wood?" said the sergeant.

The vivandière took the copper goblet suspended at her belt together with a bell, turned the cock of the can that was strapped across her shoulder, and pouring several drops into the goblet, held it to the children's lips.

The first drank and made a grimace.

The second drank and spit it out

"It is good, all the same," said the vivandière.

"Is that some of the old cut-throat?" asked the sergeant.

"Yes, some of the best. But they are peasants."

She wiped the goblet.

"And so, madam, you are running away?" resumed the sergeant.

"I couldn't help it."

"Across the fields? With no particular object?"

"Sometimes I run with all my might, and then I walk, and once in a while I fall."

"Poor countrywoman!" said the vivandière.

"They were fighting," stammered the woman. "I was in the middle of the firing. I don't know what they want. They killed my husband,—that was all I know about it."

The sergeant banged the butt of his musket on the ground, exclaiming,—

"What a beast of a war! In the name of all that is idiotic!"

The woman continued,—

"Last night we went to bed in an *émousse*."

"All four of you?"

"All four."

"Went to bed?"

"Went to bed."

"Then you must have gone to bed standing." And he turned to the soldiers.

"Comrades, a dead tree, old and hollow, wherein a man can sheathe himself like a sword in a scabbard, is what these savages call an *émousse*. But what would you have? All are not obliged to be Parisians."

"The idea of sleeping in the hollow of a tree,—and with three children!" exclaimed the vivandière.

"And when the little one bawled, it must have seemed queer to the passers-by, who could see nothing, to hear the tree calling out, 'Papa! mamma!'"

"Fortunately, it is summer-time," said the woman, with a sigh.

She looked down resigned, with an expression in her eyes of one who had known surprising calamities.

The silent soldiers surrounded this wretched group. A widow, three orphans, flight, desolation, solitude, the rumblings of war on the horizon, hunger, thirst, no food but herbs, no roof but the sky.

The sergeant drew near the woman and gazed upon the nursing infant. The baby left the breast, turned her head, and looked with her lovely blue eyes on the dreadful hairy face, bristling and fierce, that was bending over her, and began to smile.

The sergeant drew back, and a large tear was seen to roll down his cheek, clinging to the end of his moustache like a pearl.

He raised his voice.

"Comrades, I have come to the conclusion that this battalion is about to become a father. Are you willing? We adopt these three children."

"Hurrah for the Republic!" shouted the grenadiers.

"So be it!" exclaimed the sergeant; and he stretched out both hands over the mother and the children.

"Behold the children of the battalion of the Bonnet-Rouge!" he said.

The vivandière jumped for joy.

"Three heads under one cap!" she cried.

Then she burst out sobbing, and embraced the widow excitedly, saying,—

"She looks like a rogue already, that little girl!"

"Hurrah for the Republic!" repeated the soldiers.

"Come, citizeness," said the sergeant to the mother.

Book II

THE CORVETTE "CLAYMORE."

I

England and France United

IN THE SPRING OF 1793, when France, attacked at one and the same time on all her frontiers, experienced the pathetic diversion of the downfall of the Girondists, the following events were taking place in the Channel Islands. In Jersey, one evening on the first of June, about an hour before sunset, from the lovely little Bay of Bonnenuit, a corvette set sail in that foggy kind of weather dangerous for navigation, and for that very reason better suited for escape than for pursuit. The ship, although it was manned by a French crew, belonged to the English squadron which had been stationed to watch the eastern point of the island. The prince of Tour d'Auvergne, of the house of Bouillon, commanded the English fleet, and it was by his order, and for a special and pressing service, that the corvette had been detached.

This corvette entered at the Trinity House under the name of the "Claymore," and, apparently a freight vessel, was in point of fact a man-of-war. She looked like a heavy and peaceable merchant-ship; but it would not have been wise to trust to that, for she had been built to serve two purposes,—cunning and strength; to deceive if possible, to fight if necessary. For the service on hand that night the freight between decks had been replaced by thirty carronades of heavy caliber. Either for the sake of giving the ship a peaceable appearance, or possibly because a storm was anticipated, these thirty carronades were housed; that is, they were firmly fastened inside by triple chains, with their muzzles tightly braced against the port-holes. Nothing could be seen from the outside. The port-holes were closed. It was as though the corvette wore a mask. These guns were mounted on old-fashioned bronzed wheels, called the "radiating model." The regular naval corvettes carry their guns on the upper deck; but this ship, built for surprise and ambush, had its decks clear, having been arranged, as we have just seen, to carry a masked battery between decks. The "Claymore," although built in a heavy and clumsy fashion, was nevertheless a good sailer, her hull being one of the strongest in the English Navy; and in an engagement she was almost equal to a frigate, although her mizzen-mast was only a small one, with a fore and aft rig. Her rudder, of an odd and scientific shape, had a curved frame, quite unique, which had cost fifty pounds sterling in the Southampton shipyards. The crew, entirely French, was composed of refugee officers and sailors who were deserters. They were experienced men; there was not one among them who was not a good sailor, a good soldier, and a good royalist. A threefold fanaticism possessed them,—for the ship, the sword, and the king.

Half a battalion of marines, which could in case of necessity be disembarked, was added to the crew.

The captain of the "Claymore" was a chevalier of Saint-Louis, Count Boisberthelot, one of the best officers of the old Royal Navy; the first officer was the Chevalier de la Vieuville, who had commanded in the French Guards the company of which Hoche was sergeant; and the pilot, Philip Gacquoil, was one of the most experienced in Jersey.

It was easy to guess that the ship had some unusual work to do. In fact, a man had just stepped on board, who had the look of one starting out for an adventure. He was an old man, tall, upright, and strong, with a severe countenance,—a man whose age it would have been difficult to determine, for he seemed both young and old, advanced in years yet abounding in vigor; one of those men whose eyes flash lightning though the hair is white. Judging from his energy, he was about forty years old; his air of authority was that of a man of eighty.

At the moment when he stepped on board the corvette, his sea-cloak was half-open, revealing beneath wide breeches called *bragoubras*, high boots, and a goat-skin waistcoat embroidered with silk on the right side, while the rough and bristling fur was left on the wrong side,— the complete costume of a Breton peasant. These old-fashioned Breton waist-coats answered two purposes, being worn both on holidays and week-days, and could be reversed at the option of the wearer, with either the hairy or the smooth side out,—fur on a week-day, and gala attire for holidays. And as if to increase a carefully studied resemblance, the peasant dress worn by the old man was well worn on the knees and elbows, showing signs of long usage, and his cloak, made of coarse cloth, looked like the garb of a fisherman. He wore the round hat of the period, tall and broad-brimmed, which when turned down looks countrified, but when caught up on one side by a loop and a cockade has quite a military effect. He wore it turned down, country fashion, with neither loop nor cockade.

Lord Balcarras, the governor of the island, and the Prince de La Tour d'Auvergne had in person escorted him on board. The secret agent of the Prince Gélambre, an old body-guard of the Count d'Artois, himself a nobleman, had personally superintended the arrangement of his cabin, showing his attention and courtesy even so far as to carry the old man's valise. When about to leave him, to return to the land, M. de Gélambre had made a deep bow to this peasant; Lord Balcarras exclaimed, "Good luck to you, general;" and the Prince de La Tour d'Auvergne said, "Au revoir, cousin."

"The peasant" was the name by which the sailors at once called their passenger in the short dialogues which sailors hold among themselves; yet, without further information on the subject, they understood that this peasant was no more a genuine peasant than the man-of-war was a merchantman.

There was scarcely any wind. The "Claymore" left Bonnenuit, passed Boulay Bay, remaining for some time in sight, tacking, gradually diminishing in the gathering darkness, and finally disappeared.

All hour later, Gélambre, having returned home to Saint-Hélier, sent to the Count d'Artois, at the headquarters of the Duke of York, by the Southampton express, the following lines:—

"MY LORD,—The departure has just taken place. Success is certain. In eight days the whole coast, from Granville to St. Malo, will be ablaze."

Four days previously the representative of the Marne, Prieur, on a mission to the army on the coast of Cherbourg, and just then stopping at Granville, received by a secret emissary the following message, in the same handwriting as the previous one:—

"CITIZEN REPRESENTATIVE,—The 1st of June, at high tide, the war corvette 'Claymore,' with a masked battery, will set sail, to land on the coast of France a man who answers to the following description: Tall, aged, gray-haired, dressed like a peasant, and with the hands of an aristocrat. Tomorrow I will send you further details. He will land on the morning of the 2d. Communicate this to the cruiser, capture the corvette, guillotine the man."

II

Night with the Ship and the Passenger

THE CORVETTE, INSTEAD OF SAILING south, in the direction of St. Catherine, headed to the north, then, veering towards the west, had boldly entered that arm of the sea between Sark and Jersey called the Passage of the Déroute. There was then no lighthouse, at any point on either coast. It had been a clear sunset: the night was darker than summer nights usually are; it was moonlight, but large clouds, rather of the equinox than of the solstice, overspread the sky, and, judging by appearances the moon would not be visible until she reached the horizon at the moment of setting. A few clouds hung low near the surface of the sea and covered it with vapor.

All this darkness was favorable. Gacquoil, the pilot, intended to leave Jersey on the left, Guernsey on the right, and by boldly sailing between Hanois and Dover, to reach some bay on the coast near St. Malo, a longer but safer route than the one through Minquiers; for the French coaster had standing orders to keep an unusually sharp lookout between St. Hélier and Granville.

If the wind were favorable, and nothing happened, by dint of setting all sail Gacquoil hoped to reach the coast of France at daybreak.

All went well. The corvette had just passed Gros Nez. Towards nine o'clock the weather looked sullen, as the sailors express it, both wind and sea rising; but the wind was favorable, and the sea was rough, yet not heavy, waves now and then dashing over the bow of the corvette. "The peasant," whom Lord Balcarras had called general, and whom the Prince de La Tour d'Auvergne had addressed as cousin, was a good sailor, and paced the deck of the corvette with calm dignity. He did not seem to notice that she rocked considerably. From time to time he took out of his waistcoat pocket a cake of chocolate, and breaking off a piece, munched it. Though his hair was gray, his teeth were sound.

He spoke to no one, except that from time to time he made a few concise remarks in an undertone to the captain, who listened to him deferentially, apparently regarding his passenger as the commander, rather than himself. Unobserved in the fog, and skilfully piloted, the "Claymore" coasted along the steep shore to the north of Jersey, hugging the land to avoid the formidable reef of Pierres-de-Leeq, which lies in the middle of the strait between Jersey and Sark. Gacquoil, at the helm, sighting in turn Grove de Leeq, Gros Nez, and Plémont, making the corvette glide in among those chains of reefs, felt his way along to a certain extent, but with the self-confidence of one familiar with the ways of the sea.

The corvette had no light forward, fearing to betray its passage through these guarded waters. They congratulated themselves on the fog. The Grande Étape was reached; the mist was so dense that the lofty outlines of the Pinnacle were scarcely visible. They heard it strike ten from the belfry of Saint-Ouen,—a sign that the wind was still aft. All was going well; the sea grew rougher, because they were drawing near La Corbière.

A little after ten, the Count Boisberthelot and the Chevalier de la Vieuville escorted the man in the peasant garb to the door of his cabin, which was the captain's own room. As he was about to enter, he remarked, lowering his voice:—

"You understand the importance of keeping the secret, gentlemen. Silence up to the moment of explosion. You are the only ones here who know my name."

"We will carry it to the grave," replied Boisberthelot.

"And for my part, I would not reveal it were I face to face with death," remarked the old man.

And he entered his state-room.

III

Patrician and Plebeian United

THE COMMANDER AND THE FIRST officer returned on deck, and began to pace up and down side by side, talking as they walked. The theme was evidently their passenger; and this was the substance of the conversation which the wind wafted through the darkness. Boisberthelot grumbled half audibly to La Vieuville,—

"It remains to be seen whether or no he is a leader."

La Vieuville replied,—

"Meanwhile he is a prince."

"Almost."

"A nobleman in France, but a prince in Brittany."

"Like the Trémoilles and the Rohans."

"With whom he is connected."

Boisberthelot resumed,—

"In France and in the carriages of the king he is a marquis,—as I am a count, and you a chevalier."

"The carriages are far away!" exclaimed Vieuville. "We are living in the time of the tumbril."

A silence ensued.

Boisberthelot went on,—

"For lack of a French prince we take one from Brittany."

"For lack of thrushes—No: since an eagle is not to be found, we take a crow."

"I should prefer a vulture," remarked Boisberthelot.

La Vieuville replied,—

"Yes, indeed, with a beak and talons."

"We shall see."

"Yes," replied Vieuville, "it is time there was a leader. I agree with Tinténiac,—a leader and gun-power! See here, commander, I know nearly all the possible and impossible leaders,—those of yesterday, those of today, and those of tomorrow. Not one of them has the head required for war. In this cursed Vendée a general is needed who would be a lawyer as well as a leader. He must harass the enemy, dispute every bush, ditch, and stone; he must force unlucky quarrels upon him, and take advantage of everything; vigilant and pitiless, he must watch incessantly, slaughter freely, and make examples. Now, in this army of peasants there are heroes, but no captains. D'Elbée is a nonentity, Lescure an invalid; Bonchamps is merciful,—he is kind, and that implies folly; La Rochejaquelein is a superb sub-lieutenant; Silz is an officer good for the open field, but not suited for a war that needs a man of expedients; Cathelineau is a simple teamster; Stofflet is a crafty game-keeper; Bérard is inefficient; Boulainvilliers is absurd; Charette is horrible. I make no mention of Gaston the barber. Mordemonbleu! what is the use of opposing revolution, and what is the difference between ourselves and the republicans, if we set barbers over the heads of noblemen! The fact is, that this beastly revolution has contaminated all of us."

"It is the itch of France."

"It is the itch of the Tiers État," rejoined Boisberthelot. "England alone can help us."

"And she will, captain, undoubtedly."

"Meanwhile it is an ugly state of affairs."

"Yes,—rustics everywhere. A monarchy that has Stofflet, the game-keeper of M. de Maulevrier, for a commander has no reason to envy a republic whose minister is Pache, the son of the Duke de Castries' porter. What men this Vendean war brings face to face,—on one side Santerre the brewer; on the other Gaston the hairdresser!"

"My dear La Vieuville, I feel some respect for this Gaston. He behaved well in his command of Guéménée. He had three hundred Blues neatly shot after making them dig their own graves."

"Well enough done; but I could have done quite as well as he."

"Pardieu, to be sure; and I too."

"The great feats of war," said Vieuville, "require noble blood in those who perform them. These are matters for knights, and not for hairdressers."

"But yet there are estimable men in this 'Third Estate,'" rejoined Vieuville. "Take that watchmaker, Joly, for instance. He was formerly a sergeant in a Flanders regiment; he becomes a Vendean chief and commander of a coast band. He has a son, a republican; and while the father serves in the ranks of the Whites, the son serves in those of the Blues. An encounter, a battle: the father captures the son and blows out his brains."

"He did well," said La Vieuville.

"A royalist Brutus," answered Boisberthelot. "Nevertheless, it is unendurable to be under the command of a Coquereau, a Jean-Jean, a Moulin, a Focart, a Bouju, a Chouppes!"

"My dear chevalier, the opposite party is quite as indignant. We are crowded with plebeians; they have an excess of nobles. Do you think the sans-culottes like to be commanded by the Count de Canclaux, the Viscount de Miranda, the Viscount de Beauharnais, the Count de Valence, the Marquis de Custine, and the Duke de Biron?"

"What a combination!"

"And the Duke de Chartres!"

"Son of Égalité. By the way, when will he be king?"

"Never!"

"He aspires to the throne, and his very crimes serve to promote his interests."

"And his vices will injure his cause," said Boisberthelot.

Then, after another pause, he continued,—

"Nevertheless, he was anxious to be reconciled. He came to see the king. I was at Versailles when some one spit on his back."

"From the top of the grand staircase?"

"Yes."

"I am glad of it."

"We called him Bourbon le Bourbeux."

"He is bald-headed; he has pimples; he is a regicide. Poh!"

And La Vieuville added:—

"I was with him at Ouessant."

"On the 'Saint Esprit'?"

"Yes."

"Had he obeyed Admiral d'Orvillier's signal to keep to the windward, he would have prevented the English from passing."

"True."

"Was he really hidden in the bottom of the hold?"

"No; but we must say so all the same."

And La Vieuville burst out laughing.

Boisberthelot continued:—

"Fools are plentiful. Look here, I have known this Boulainvilliers of whom you were speaking; I knew him well. At first the peasants were armed with pikes; would you believe it, he took it into his head to form them into pike-men. He wanted to drill them in crossing pikes and repelling a charge. He dreamed of transforming these barbarians into regular soldiers. He undertook to teach them how to round in the corners of their squares, and to mass battalions with hollow squares. He jabbered the antiquated military dialect to them; he called the chief of a squad a 'cap d'escade'—which was what corporals under Louis XIV were called. He persisted in forming a regiment of all those poachers. He had regular companies whose sergeants ranged themselves in a circle every evening, and, receiving the sign and countersign from the colonel's sergeant, repeated it in a whisper to the lieutenant's sergeant, who repeated it to his next neighbor, who in his turn transmitted it to the next man, and so on from ear to ear until it reached the last man. He cashiered an officer for not standing bareheaded to receive the watchword from the sergeant. You may imagine how he succeeded. This simpleton could not understand that peasants have to be led peasant fashion, and that it is impossible to transform rustics into soldiers. Yes, I have known Boulainvilliers."

They walked along a few steps, each one engrossed in his own thoughts.

Then the conversation was resumed:—

"By the way, has the report of Dampierre's death been confirmed?"

"Yes, commander."

"Before Condé?"

"At the camp of Pamars; he was hit by a cannon-ball."

Boisberthelot sighed.

"Count Dampierre,—another of our men, who took sides with them."

"May he prosper wherever he may be!" said Vieuville.

"And the ladies,—where are they?"

"At Trieste."

"Still there?"

"Yes."

"Ah, this republic!" exclaimed La Vieuville. "What havoc from so slight a cause! To think that this revolution was the result of a deficit of only a few millions!"

"Insignificant beginnings are not always to be trusted."

"Everything goes wrong," replied La Vieuville.

"Yes; La Rouarie is dead. Du Dresnay is an idiot. What wretched leaders are all those bishops,—this Coucy, bishop of La Rochelle; Beaupoil Saint-Aulaire, bishop of Poitiers; Mercy, bishop of Luzon, a lover of Madame de l'Eschasserie—"

"Whose name is Servanteau, you know, commander. Eschasserie is the name of an estate."

"And that false bishop of Agra, who is a curé of I know not what!"

"Of Dol. His name is Guillot de Folleville. But then he is brave, and knows how to fight."

"Priests when one needs soldiers! bishops who are no bishops at all! generals who are no generals!"

La Vieuville interrupted Boisberthelot.

"Have you the 'Moniteur' in your state-room, commander?"

"Yes."

"What are they giving now in Paris?"

"'Adèle and Pauline' and 'La Caverne.'"

"I should like to see that."

"You may. We shall be in Paris in a month." Boisberthelot thought a moment, and then added:

"At the latest,—so Mr. Windham told Lord Hood."

"Then, commander, I take it affairs are not going so very badly?"

"All would go well, provided that the Breton war were well managed."

De Vieuville shook his head.

"Commander," he said, "are we to land the marines?"

"Certainly, if the coast is friendly, but not otherwise. In some cases war must force the gates; in others it can slip through them. Civil war must always keep a false key in its pocket. We will do all we can; but one must have a chief."

And Boisberthelot added thoughtfully,—

"What do you think of the Chevalier de Dieuzie, La Vieuville?"

"Do you mean the younger?"

"Yes."

"For a commander?"

"Yes."

"He is only good for a pitched battle in the open field. It is only the peasant who knows the underbrush."

"In that case, you may as well resign yourself to Generals Stofflet and Cathelineau."

La Vieuville meditated for a moment; then he said,—

"What we need is a prince,—a French prince, a prince of the blood, a real prince."

"How can that be? He who says 'prince'—"

"Says 'coward.' I know it, commander. But we need him for the impression he would produce upon the herd."

"My dear chevalier, the princes don't care to come."

"We will do without them."

Boisberthelot pressed his hand mechanically against his forehead, as if striving to evoke an idea. He resumed,—

"Then let us try this general."

"He is a great nobleman."

"Do you think he will do?"

"If he is one of the right sort," said La Vieuville.

"You mean relentless?" said Boisberthelot.

The count and the chevalier looked at each other.

"Monsieur Boisberthelot, you have defined the meaning of the word. Relentless,—yes, that's what we need. This is a war that shows no mercy. The bloodthirsty are in the ascendant The regicides have beheaded Louis XVI; we will quarter the regicides. Yes, the general we need is General Relentless. In Anjou and Upper Poitou the leaders play the magnanimous; they trifle with generosity, and they are always defeated. In the Marais and the country of Retz, where the leaders are ferocious, everything goes bravely forward. It is because Charette is fierce that he stands his ground against Parrein,—hyena pitted against hyena."

Boisberthelot had no time to answer. Vieuville's words were suddenly cut short by a desperate cry, and at the same instant they heard a noise unlike all other sounds. This cry and the unusual sounds came from the interior of the vessel.

The captain and the lieutenant rushed to the gun-deck, but were unable to enter. All the gunners came running up, beside themselves with terror.

A frightful thing had just happened.

IV

Tormentum Belli

ONE OF THE CARRONADES OF the battery, a twenty-four pound cannon, had become loose.

This is perhaps the most dreadful thing that can take place at sea. Nothing more terrible can happen to a man-of-war under full sail.

A cannon that breaks loose from its fastenings is suddenly transformed into a supernatural beast. It is a monster developed from a machine. This mass runs along on its wheels as easily as a billiard ball; it rolls with the rolling, pitches with the pitching, comes and goes, stops, seems to meditate, begins anew, darts like an arrow from one end of the ship to the other, whirls around, turns aside, evades, rears, hits out, crushes, kills, exterminates. It is a ram battering a wall at its own pleasure. Moreover, the battering-ram is iron, the wall is wood. It is matter set free; one might say that this eternal slave is wreaking its vengeance; it would seem as though the evil in what we call inanimate objects had found vent and suddenly burst forth; it has the air of having lost its patience, and of taking a mysterious, dull revenge; nothing is so inexorable as the rage of the inanimate. The mad mass leaps like a panther; it has the weight of an elephant, the agility of a mouse, the obstinacy of the axe; it takes one by surprise, like the surge of the sea; it flashes like lightning; it is deaf as the tomb; it weighs ten thousand pounds, and it bounds like a child's ball; it whirls as it advances, and the circles it describes are intersected by right angles. And what help is there? How can it be overcome? A calm succeeds the tempest, a cyclone passes over, a wind dies away, we replace the broken mass, we check the leak, we extinguish the fire; but what is to be done with this enormous bronze beast? How can it be subdued? You can reason with a mastiff, take a bull by surprise, fascinate a snake, frighten a tiger, mollify a lion; but there is no resource with the monster known as a loosened gun. You cannot kill it,—it is already dead; and yet it lives. It breathes a sinister life bestowed on it by the Infinite. The plank beneath sways it to and fro; it is moved by the ship; the sea lifts the ship, and the wind keeps the sea in motion. This destroyer is a toy. Its terrible vitality is fed by the ship, the waves, and the wind, each lending its aid. What is to be done with this complication? How fetter this monstrous mechanism of shipwreck? How foresee its comings and goings, its recoils, its halts, its shocks? Any one of those blows may stave in the side of the vessel. How can one guard against these terrible gyrations? One has to do with a projectile that reflects, that has ideas, and changes its direction at any moment. How can one arrest an object in its course, whose onslaught must be avoided? The dreadful cannon rushes about, advances, recedes, strikes to right and to left, flies here and there, baffles their attempts at capture, sweeps away obstacles, crushing men like flies.

The extreme danger of the situation comes from the unsteadiness of the deck. How is one to cope with the caprices of an inclined plane? The ship had within its depths, so to speak, imprisoned lightning struggling for escape; something like the rumbling of thunder during an earthquake. In an instant the crew was on its feet. It was the chief gunner's fault, who had neglected to fasten the screw-nut of the breeching chain, and had not thoroughly chocked the four trucks of the carronade, which allowed play to the frame and bottom of the gun-carriage, thereby disarranging the two platforms and parting the breeching. The lashings were broken, so that the gun was no longer firm on its carriage. The stationary breeching which prevents the recoil was not in use at that time. As a wave struck the ship's side the cannon, insufficiently secured, had receded, and having broken its chain, began to wander threatningly over the deck. In order to get an idea of this strange sliding, fancy a drop of water sliding down a pane of glass.

When the fastening broke, the gunners were in the battery, singly and in groups, clearing the ship for action. The carronade, thrown forward by the pitching, dashed into a group of men, killing four of them at the first blow; then, hurled back by the rolling, it cut in two an unfortunate fifth man, and struck and dismounted one of the guns of the larboard battery. Hence the cry of distress which had been heard.

All the men rushed to the ladder. The gun-deck was empty in the twinkling of an eye.

The monstrous gun was left to itself. It was its own mistress, and mistress of the ship. It could do with it whatsoever it wished. This crew, accustomed to laugh in battle, now trembled. It would be impossible to describe their terror.

Captain Boisberthelot and Lieutenant la Vieuville, brave men though they were, paused at the top of the ladder, silent, pale, and undecided, looking down on the deck. Some one pushed them aside with his elbow, and descended. It was their passenger, the peasant, the man about whom they were talking a moment ago.

Having reached the bottom of the ladder he halted.

V

Vis Et Vir

THE CANNON WAS ROLLING TO and fro on the deck. It might have been called the living chariot of the Apocalypse. A dim wavering of lights and shadows was added to this spectacle by the marine lantern, swinging under the deck. The outlines of the cannon were indistinguishable, by reason of the rapidity of its motion; sometimes it looked black when the light shone upon it, then again it would cast pale, glimmering reflections in the darkness.

It was still pursuing its work of destruction. It had already shattered four other pieces, and made two breaches in the ship's side, fortunately above the water-line, but which would leak in case of rough weather. It rushed frantically against the timbers; the stout riders resisted,—curved timbers have great strength; but one could hear them crack under this tremendous assault brought to bear simultaneously on every side, with a certain omnipresence truly appalling.

A bullet shaken in a bottle could not produce sharper or more rapid sounds. The four wheels were passing and repassing over the dead bodies, cutting and tearing them to pieces, and the five corpses had become five trunks rolling hither and thither; the heads seemed to cry out; streams of blood flowed over the deck, following the motion of the ship. The ceiling, damaged in several places, had begun to give way. The whole ship was filled with a dreadful tumult.

The captain, who had rapidly recovered his self-possession, had given orders to throw down the hatchway all that could abate the rage and check the mad onslaught of this infuriated gun; mattresses, hammocks, spare sails, coils of rope, the bags of the crew, and bales of false assignats, with which the corvette was laden,—that infamous stratagem of English origin being considered a fair trick in war.

But what availed these rags? No one dared to go down to arrange them, and in a few moments they were reduced to lint.

There was just sea enough to render this accident as complete as possible. A tempest would have been welcome. It might have upset the cannon, and with its four wheels once in the air, it could easily have been mastered. Meanwhile the havoc increased. There were even incisions and fractures in the masts, that stood like pillars grounded firmly in the keel, and piercing the several decks of the vessel. The mizzen-mast was split, and even the main-mast was damaged by the convulsive blows of the cannon. The destruction of the battery still went on. Ten out of the thirty pieces were useless. The fractures in the side increased, and the corvette began to leak.

The old passenger, who had descended to the gun-deck, looked like one carved in stone as he stood motionless at the foot of the stairs and glanced sternly over the devastation. It would have been impossible to move a step upon the deck.

Each bound of the liberated carronade seemed to threaten the destruction of the ship. But a few moments longer, and shipwreck would be inevitable.

They must either overcome this calamity or perish; some decisive action must be taken. But what?

What a combatant was this carronade!

Here was this mad creature to be arrested, this flash of lightning to be seized, this thunderbolt to be crushed. Boisberthelot said to Vieuville:—

"Do you believe in God, chevalier?"

"Yes and no, sometimes I do!" replied La Vieuville.

"In a tempest?"

"Yes, and in moments like these."

"Truly God alone can save us," said Boisberthelot.

All were silent, leaving the carronade to its horrible uproar.

The waves beating the ship from without answered the blows of the cannon within, very much like a couple of hammers striking in turn.

Suddenly in the midst of this inaccessible circus, where the escaped cannon was tossing from side to side, a man appeared, grasping an iron bar. It was the author of the catastrophe, the chief gunner, whose criminal negligence had caused the accident,—the captain of the gun. Having brought about the evil, his intention was to repair it. Holding a handspike in one hand, and in the other a tiller rope with the slip-noose in it, he had jumped through the hatchway to the deck below.

Then began a terrible struggle; a titanic spectacle; a combat between cannon and cannoneer; a contest between mind and matter; a duel between man and the inanimate. The man stood in one corner in an attitude of expectancy, leaning on the rider and holding in his hands the bar and the rope; calm, livid, and tragic, he stood firmly on his legs, that were like two pillars of steel.

He was waiting for the cannon to approach him.

The gunner knew his piece, and he felt as though it must know him. They had lived together a long time. How often had he put his hand in its mouth. It was his domestic monster. He began to talk to it as he would to a dog. "Come," said he. Possibly he loved it.

He seemed to wish for its coming, and yet its approach meant sure destruction for him. How to avoid being crushed was the question. All looked on in terror.

Not a breath was drawn freely, except perhaps by the old man, who remained on the gun-deck gazing sternly on the two combatants.

He himself was in danger of being crushed by the piece; still he did not move.

Beneath them the blind sea had command of the battle. When, in the act of accepting this awful hand-to-hand struggle, the gunner approached to challenge the cannon, it happened that the surging sea held the gun motionless for an instant, as though stupefied. "Come on!" said the man. It seemed to listen.

Suddenly it leaped towards him. The man dodged. Then the struggle began,—a contest unheard of; the fragile wrestling with the invulnerable; the human warrior attacking the brazen beast; blind force on the one side, soul on the other.

All this was in the shadow. It was like an indistinct vision of a miracle.

A soul!—strangely enough it seemed as if a soul existed within the cannon, but one consumed with hate and rage. The blind thing seemed to have eyes. It appeared as though the monster were watching the man. There was, or at least one might have supposed it, cunning in this mass. It also chose its opportunity. It was as though a gigantic insect of iron was endowed with the will of a demon. Now and then this colossal grasshopper would strike the low ceiling of the gun-deck, then falling back on its four wheels, like a tiger on all fours, rush upon the man. He—supple, agile, adroit—writhed like a serpent before these lightning movements. He avoided encounters; but the blows from which he escaped fell with destructive force upon the vessel. A piece of broken chain remained attached to the carronade. This bit of chain had twisted in some incomprehensible way around the breech-button.

One end of the chain was fastened to the gun-carriage; the other end thrashed wildly around, aggravating the danger with every bound of the cannon. The screw held it as in a clenched hand, and this chain, multiplying the strokes of the battering-ram by those of the thong, made a terrible whirlwind around the gun,—a lash of iron in a fist of brass. This chain complicated the combat.

Despite all this, the man fought. He even attacked the cannon at times, crawling along by the side of the ship and clutching his handspike and the rope; the cannon seemed to understand his movements, and fled as though suspecting a trap. The man, nothing daunted, pursued his chase.

Such a struggle must necessarily be brief. Suddenly the cannon seemed to say to itself: Now, then, there must be an end to this. And it stopped. A crisis was felt to be at hand. The cannon, as if in suspense, seemed to meditate, or—for to all intents and purposes it was a living creature—it really did meditate, some furious design. All at once it rushed on the gunner, who sprang aside with a laugh, crying out, "Try it again!" as the cannon passed him. The gun in its fury smashed one of the larboard carronades; then, by the invisible sling in which it seemed to be held, it was thrown to the starboard, towards the man, who escaped. Three carronades were crushed by its onslaught; then, as though blind and beside itself, it turned from the man, and rolled from stern to stem, splintering the latter, and causing a breach in the walls of the prow. The gunner took refuge at the foot of the ladder, a short distance from the old man, who stood watching. He held his handspike in readiness. The cannon seemed aware of it, and without taking the trouble to turn, it rushed backward on the man, as swift as the blow of an axe. The gunner, if driven up against the side of the ship, would be lost.

One cry arose from the crew.

The old passenger—who until this moment had stood motionless—sprang forward more swiftly than all those mad whirls. He had seized a bale of the false assignats, and at the risk of being crushed succeeded in throwing it between the wheels of the carronade. This decisive and perilous manoeuvre could not have been executed with more precision and adroitness by an adept in all the exercises given in the work of Durosel's "Manual of Naval Gunnery."

The bale had the effect of a plug. A pebble may block a log; a branch sometimes changes the course of an avalanche. The carronade stumbled, and the gunner, availing himself of the perilous opportunity, thrust his iron bar between the spokes of the back wheels. Pitching forward, the cannon stopped; and the man, using his bar for a lever, rocked it backward and forward. The heavy mass upset, with the resonant sound of a bell that crashes in its fall. The man, reeking with perspiration, threw himself upon it, and passed the slip-noose of the tiller-rope around the neck of the defeated monster.

The combat was ended. The man had conquered. The ant had overcome the mastodon; the pygmy had imprisoned the thunderbolt.

The soldiers and sailors applauded.

The crew rushed forward with chains and cables, and in an instant the cannon was secured.

Saluting the passenger, the gunner exclaimed,—

"Sir, you have saved my life!"

The old man had resumed his impassible attitude, and made no reply.

VI

The Two Ends of the Scale

THE MAN HAD CONQUERED; BUT it might be affirmed that the cannon also had gained a victory. Immediate shipwreck was averted; but the corvette was still in danger. The injuries the ship had sustained seemed irreparable. There were five breaches in the sides, one of them—a very large one—in the bow, and twenty carronades out of thirty lay shattered in their frames. The recaptured gun, which had been secured by a chain, was itself disabled. The screw of the breech-button being wrenched, it would consequently be impossible to level the cannon. The battery was reduced to nine guns; there was a leakage in the hold. All these damages must be repaired without loss of time, and the pumps set in operation. Now that the gun-deck had become visible, it was frightful to look upon. The interior of a mad elephant's cage could not have been more thoroughly devastated. However important it might be for the corvette to avoid observation, the care for its immediate safety was still more imperative. They were obliged to light the deck with lanterns placed at intervals along the sides.

In the mean time, while this tragic entertainment had lasted, the crew, entirely absorbed by a question of life and death, had not noticed what was going on outside of the ship. The fog had thickened, the weather had changed, the wind had driven the vessel at will; they were out of their course, in full sight of Jersey and Guernsey, much farther to the south than they ought to have been, and confronting a tumultuous sea. The big waves kissed the wounded sides of the corvette with kisses that savored of danger. The heaving of the sea grew threatening; the wind had risen to a gale; a squall, perhaps a tempest, was brewing. One could not see four oars' length before one.

While the crew made haste with their temporary repairs on the gun-deck, stopping the leaks and setting up the cannons that had escaped uninjured, the old passenger returned to the deck.

He stood leaning against the main-mast.

He had taken no notice of what was going on in the ship. The Chevalier de la Vieuville had drawn up the marines on either side of the main-mast, and at a signal-whistle of the boatswain the sailors, who had been busy in the rigging, stood up on the yards. Count Boisberthelot approached the passenger. The captain was followed by a man, who, haggard and panting, with his dress in disorder, still wore on his countenance an expression of content.

It was the gunner who had so opportunely displayed his power as a tamer of monsters, and gained the victory over the cannon.

The count made a military salute to the old man in the peasant garb, and said to him:—

"Here is the man, general."

The gunner, with downcast eyes, stood erect in a military attitude.

"General," resumed Count Boisberthelot, "considering what this man has done, do you not think that his superiors have a duty to perform?"

"I think so," replied the old man.

"Be so good as to give your orders," resumed Boisberthelot.

"It is for you to give them; you are the captain."

"But you are the general," answered Boisberthelot.

The old man looked at the gunner.

"Step forward," he said.

The gunner advanced a step.

Turning to Count Boisberthelot, the old man removed the cross of Saint Louis from the captain's breast, and fastened it on the jacket of the gunner. The sailors cheered, and the marines presented arms.

Then pointing to the bewildered gunner he added:

"Now let the man be shot!"

Stupor took the place of applause.

Then, amid a tomb-like silence, the old man, raising his voice, said:—

"The ship has been endangered by an act of carelessness, and may even yet be lost. It is all the same whether one be at sea or face to face with the enemy. A ship at sea is like an army in battle. The tempest, though unseen, is ever present; the sea is an ambush. Death is the fit penalty for every fault committed when facing the enemy. There is no fault that can be retrieved. Courage must be rewarded and negligence punished."

These words fell one after the other slowly and gravely, with a certain implacable rhythm, like the strokes of the axe upon an oak-tree. Looking at the soldiers, the old man added,—

"Do your duty!"

The man on whose breast shone the cross of Saint Louis bowed his head, and at a sign of Count Boisberthelot two sailors went down to the gun-deck, and presently returned bringing the hammock-shroud; the two sailors were accompanied by the ship's chaplain, who since the departure had been engaged in saying prayers in the officers' quarters. A sergeant detached from the ranks twelve soldiers, whom he arranged in two rows, six men in a row. The gunner placed himself between the two lines. The chaplain, holding a crucifix, advanced and took his place beside the man. "March!" came from the lips of the sergeant; and the platoon slowly moved towards the bow, followed by two sailors canning the shroud.

A gloomy silence fell on the corvette. In the distance a hurricane was blowing. A few moments later, a report echoed through the gloom; one flash, and all was still. Then came the splash of a body falling into the water. The old passenger, still leaning against the main-mast, his hands crossed on his breast, seemed lost in thought. Boisberthelot, pointing towards him with the forefinger of his left hand, remarked in an undertone to La Vieuville,—

"The Vendée has found a leader."

VII

He Who Sets Sail Invests in a Lottery

BUT WHAT WAS TO BECOME of the corvette? The clouds that had mingled all night with the waves had now fallen so low that they overspread the sea like a mantle, and completely shut out the horizon. Nothing but fog,—always a dangerous situation, even for a seaworthy vessel.

A heavy swell was added to the mist.

They had improved their time; the corvette had been lightened by throwing into the sea everything that they had been able to clear away after the havoc caused by the carronade,—dismantled cannons, gun-carriages, twisted or loosened timbers, splintered pieces of wood and iron; the port-holes were opened, and the corpses and parts of human bodies, wrapped in tarpaulin, were slid down on planks into the sea.

The sea was running high. Not that the tempest was imminent. On the other hand, it seemed as if the hurricane, that was rumbling afar off on the horizon, and the wind were both decreasing and moving northward; but the waves were still high, showing an angry sea, and the corvette in its disabled condition could with difficulty resist the shocks, so that the high waves might prove fatal to it. Gacquoil, absorbed in thought, remained at the helm. To show a bold front in the presence of danger is the habit of commanders.

La Vieuville, whose spirits rose in time of trouble, addressed Gacquoil.

"Well, pilot," he said, "the squall has subsided. Its sneezing-fit came to naught. We shall pull through. We shall get some wind, and nothing more."

"We can't have wind without waves."

A true sailor, neither gay nor sad; and his reply was charged with an anxious significance. For a leaking ship a high sea means a rapid sinking. Gacquoil had emphasized this prediction by frowning. Perhaps he thought that after the catastrophe with the cannon and the gunner, La Vieuville had been too quick to use light-hearted, almost cheerful, words. Certain things bring ill-luck at sea. The sea is reticent; one never knows its intentions, and it is well to be on one's guard.

La Vieuville felt obliged to resume his gravity.

"Where are we, pilot?" he asked.

"In the hands of God," replied the pilot.

A pilot is a master; he must always be allowed to do what pleases him, and often to say what he chooses. That kind of man is not apt to be loquacious. La Vieuville left him, after asking a question to which the horizon soon replied.

The sea had suddenly cleared.

The trailing fogs were rent; the dusky heaving waves stretched as far as the eye could penetrate into the dim twilight, and this was the sight that lay before them.

The sky was shut in by clouds, although they no longer touched the water. The dawn had begun to illumine the east, while in the west the setting moon still cast a pale glimmering light These two pallid presences in opposite quarters of the sky outlined the horizon in two narrow bands of light between the dark sea and the gloomy sky. Black silhouettes were sketched against them, upright and motionless.

In the west, against the moonlit sky, three high cliffs stood forth, like Celtic cromlechs.

In the east, against the pale horizon of the morning, eight sails drawn up in a row in formidable array came in view. The three cliffs were a reef, the eight sails a squadron. Behind them was Minquiers, a cliff of ill-repute, and in front were the French cruisers. With an abyss on the left hand, and carnage on the right, they had to choose between shipwreck and a battle. The corvette must either encounter the cliffs with a damaged hull, a shattered rigging, and broken masts, or face a battle, knowing that twenty out of the thirty cannons of which her artillery consisted were disabled, and the best of her gunners dead.

The dawn was still feint, and the night not yet ended. This darkness might possibly last for quite a long time, as it was caused mostly by the clouds that hung high in the air, thick and dense, looking like a solid vault.

The wind had scattered the sea-fog, driving the corvette on Minquiers.

In her extreme weakness, and dilapidated as she was, she hardly obeyed the helm as she rolled helplessly along, lashed onward by the force of the waves.

The Minquiers—that tragic reef!—was more dangerous at that time than it is now. Several of the turrets of this marine fortress have been worn away by the incessant action of the sea. The form of reefs changes; waves are fitly likened unto swords; each tide is like the stroke of a saw. At that time, to be stranded on the Minquiers meant certain death. The cruisers composed the squadron of Cancale,—the one that afterwards became so famous under the command of Captain Duchesne, called by Lequinio "Père Duchesne."

The situation was critical. During the struggle with the carronade the ship had wandered unconsciously from her course, sailing more in the direction of Granville than of St. Malo. Even had her sailing power been unimpaired, the Minquiers would have barred her return to Jersey, while the cruisers hindered her passage towards France. Although there was no storm, yet, as the pilot had said, the sea was rough. Rolled by the heavy wind over a rocky bottom, it had grown savage.

The sea never tells what it wants at the first onset. Everything lies concealed in its abyss, even trickery. One might almost affirm that it has a scheme. It advances and recedes; it offers and refuses; it arranges for a storm, and suddenly gives up its intention; it promises an abyss, and fails to keep its agreement; it threatens the north, and strikes the south. All night long the corvette "Claymore" labored with the fog and feared the storm; the sea had disappointed them in a savage sort of way. It had drawn a storm in outline, and filled in the picture with a reef.

It was to be a shipwreck in any event, but it had assumed another form, and with one enemy to supplement the work of the other, it was to combine a wreck on the surf with destruction by battle.

"A shipwreck on the one hand and a fight on the other!" exclaimed Vieuville amid his gallant laughter. "We have thrown double fives on both sides!"

VIII

9:380

THE CORVETTE WAS LITTLE BETTER than a wreck.

A sepulchral solemnity pervaded the dim twilight, the darkness of the clouds, the confused changes of the horizon, and the mysterious sullenness of the waves. There was no sound except the hostile blasts of the wind. The catastrophe rose majestic from the abyss. It looked more like an apparition than an attack. No stir on the rocks, no stir on the ships. The silence was overpowering beyond description. Were they dealing with reality? It was like a dream passing over the sea. There are legends that tell of such visions. The corvette lay, so to speak, between a demon reef and a phantom fleet.

Count Boisberthelot in a low voice gave orders to La Vieuville, who went down to the gun-deck, while the captain, seizing his telescope, stationed himself behind the pilot. Gacquoil's sole effort was to keep up the corvette to the wind; for if struck on her side by the sea and the wind, she would inevitably capsize.

"Pilot, where are we?" said the captain.

"On the Minquiers."

"On which side?"

"On the worst one."

"What kind of bottom?"

"Small rocks."

"Can we turn broadside on?"

"We can always die."

The captain turned his spy-glass towards the west and examined the Minquiers; then turning it to the east he watched the sails that were in sight.

The pilot went on, as though speaking to himself:

"Yonder is the Minquiers. That is where the laughing sea-mew and the great black-hooded gull stop to rest when they migrate from Holland."

Meanwhile the captain had counted the sails.

There were, indeed, eight ships drawn up in line, their warlike profiles rising above the water. In the centre was seen the stately outline of a three-decker.

The captain questioned the pilot.

"Do you know those ships?"

"Of course I do."

"What are they?"

"That's the squadron."

"Of the French?"

"Of the Devil."

A silence ensued; and again the captain resumed his questions.

"Are all the cruisers there?"

"No, not all."

In fact, on the 2d of April, Valazé had reported to the Convention that ten frigates and six ships of the line were cruising in the Channel. The captain remembered this.

"You are right," he said; "the squadron numbers sixteen ships, and only eight are here."

"The others are straggling along the coast down below, on the lookout," said Gacquoil.

Still gazing through his spy-glass the captain murmured,—

"One three-decker, two first-class and five second-class frigates."

"I too have seen them close at hand," muttered Gacquoil. "I know them too well to mistake one for the other."

The captain passed his glass to the pilot.

"Pilot, can you make out distinctly the largest ship?"

"Yes, commander. It is the 'Côte-d'Or.'"

"They have given it a new name. It used to be the 'États de Bourgogne,'—a new ship of a hundred and twenty-eight cannon."

He took a memorandum-book and pencil from his pocket, and wrote down the number "128."

"Pilot, what is the first ship on the port?"

"The 'Expérimentée.'"

"A frigate of the first class; fifty-two guns. She was fitting out at Brest two months ago."

The captain put down on his note-book the number "52."

"What is the second ship to port, pilot?"

"The 'Dryade.'"

"A frigate of the first class; forty eighteen-pounders. She has been in India, and has a glorious military record."

And below the "52" he wrote the number "40." Then, raising his head, he said,—

"Now, on the starboard?"

"They are all second-class frigates, commander; there are five of them."

"Which is the first one from the ship?"

"The 'Résolue.'"

"Thirty-two eighteen-pounders. The second?"

"The 'Richmond.'"

"Same. Next?"

"The 'Athée.'"

"A queer name to sail under. Next?"

"The 'Calypso.'"

"Next?"

"The 'Preneuse.'"

"Five frigates, each of thirty-two guns."

The captain wrote "160" under the first numbers.

"You are sure you recognize them, pilot?" he asked.

"You also know them well, commander. It is something to recognize them; but it is better to know them."

The captain, with his eyes on the note-book, was adding up the column to himself.

"One hundred and twenty-eight, fifty-two, forty, one hundred and sixty."

Just then La Vieuville came up on deck.

"Chevalier," exclaimed the captain, "we are facing three hundred and eighty cannon."

"So be it," replied La Vieuville.

"You have just been making an inspection, La Vieuville: how many guns have we fit for service?"

"Nine."

"So be it," responded Boisberthelot in his turn; and taking the telescope from the pilot, he scanned the horizon.

The eight black and silent ships, though they appeared immovable, continued to increase in size.

They were gradually drawing nearer.

La Vieuville saluted the captain.

"Commander," he said, "here is my report. I mistrusted this corvette 'Claymore.' It is never pleasant to be suddenly ordered on board a ship that neither knows nor loves you. An English ship is a traitor to the French. That slut of a carronade proved this. I have made the inspection. The anchors are good; they are not made of inferior iron, but hammered out of solid bars; the flukes are solid; the cables are excellent, easy to pay out, and have the requisite length of one hundred and twenty fathoms. Plenty of ammunition; six gunners dead; each gun has one hundred and seventy-one rounds."

"Because there are only nine cannon left," grumbled the captain.

Boisberthelot levelled his glass to the horizon. The squadron continued its slow approach. Carronades have one advantage: three men are sufficient to man them. But they also have a disadvantage: they do not carry as far, and shoot with less precision than cannon. It was therefore necessary to let the squadron approach within the range of the carronades.

The captain gave his orders in a low voice. Silence reigned on the ship. No signal to clear the decks for action had been given, but still it had been done. The corvette was as helpless to cope with men as with the sea. They did their best with this remnant of a war-ship. Near the tiller-ropes on the gangway were piled spare hawsers and cables, to strengthen the mast in case of need. The quarters for the wounded were put in order. According to the naval practice of those days, they barricaded the deck,—which is a protection against balls, but not against bullets. The ball-gauges were brought, although it was rather late to ascertain the caliber; but they had not anticipated so many incidents. Cartridge-boxes were distributed among the sailors, and each one secured a pair of pistols and a dirk in his belt. Hammocks were stowed away, guns were pointed, and muskets, axes, and grapplings prepared. The cartridge and bullet stores were put in readiness; the powder-magazine was opened; every man stood at his post. Not a word was spoken while these preparations went on amid haste and gloom; and it seemed like the room of a dying person.

Then the corvette was turned broadside on. She carried six anchors, like a frigate, and all of them were cast,—the spare anchor forward, the kedger aft, the sea-anchor towards the open, the ebb-anchor towards the breakers, the bower-anchor to starboard, and the sheet-anchor to port. The nine uninjured carronades were placed as a battery on the side towards the enemy.

The squadron, equally silent, had also finished its evolutions. The eight ships now stood in a semicircle, of which Minquiers formed the chord. The "Claymore" enclosed within this semicircle, and held furthermore by its own anchors, was backed by the reef,—signifying shipwreck. It was like a pack of hounds surrounding a wild boar, not giving tongue, but showing its teeth.

It seemed as if each side were waiting for something.

The gunners of the "Claymore" stood to their guns.

Boisberthelot said to La Vieuville,—

"I should like to be the first to open fire."

"A coquette's fancy," replied La Vieuville.

IX

Some One Escapes

THE PASSENGER HAD NOT LEFT the deck; he watched all that was going on with his customary impassibility.

Boisberthelot went up to him.

"Sir," he said, "the preparations are completed. We are now clinging to our grave; we shall not relax our hold. We must succumb either to the squadron or to the reef. The alternative is before us: either shipwreck among the breakers or surrender to the enemy. But the resource of death is still left; better to fight than be wrecked. I would rather be shot than drowned; fire before water, if the choice be left to me. But where it is our duty to die it is not yours. You are the man chosen by princes. You have an important mission,—that of directing the Vendean war. Your death might result in the failure of monarchy; therefore you must live. While honor requires us to stand by the ship, it calls on you to escape. You must leave us, General; I will provide you with a boat and a man. You may succeed in reaching the shore, by making a détour. It is not yet daylight; the waves are high and the sea dark. You will probably escape. There are occasions when to flee means to conquer."

The old man bent his stately head in token of acquiescence.

Count Boisberthelot raised his voice.

"Soldiers and sailors!" he called.

Every movement ceased, and from all sides faces were turned in the direction of the captain.

He continued:—

"This man who is among us represents the king. He has been intrusted to our care; we must save him. He is needed for the throne of France. As we have no prince, he is to be,—at least we hope so,—the leader of the Vendée. He is a great general. He was to land with us in France; now he must land without us. If we save the head we save all."

"Yes, yes, yes!" cried the voices of all the crew.

The captain went on:—

"He too is about to face a serious danger. It is not easy to reach the coast. The boat must be large enough to live in this sea, and small enough to escape the cruisers. He must land at some safe point, and it will be better to do so nearer Fougères than Coutances. We want a hardy sailor, a good oars-man and a strong swimmer, a man from that neighborhood, and one who knows the straits. It is still so dark that a boat can put off from the corvette without attracting attention; and later there will be smoke enough to hide it from view. Its size will be an advantage in the shallows. Where the panther is caught, the weasel escapes. Although there is no outlet for us, there may be for a small rowboat; the enemy's ships will not see it, and, what is more, about that time we shall be giving them plenty of diversion. Is it decided?"

"Yes, yes, yes!" cried the crew.

"Then there is not a moment to be lost," continued the captain. "Is there a man among you willing to undertake the business?"

In the darkness, a sailor stepped out of the ranks and said,—

"I am the man."

X

Does He Escape?

A FEW MINUTES LATER, ONE of those small boats called a gig, which are always devoted to the use of the captain, pushed off from the ship. There were two men in this boat,—the passenger in the stern, and the volunteer sailor in the bow. The night was still very dark. The sailor, according to the captain's instructions, rowed energetically towards the Minquiers. For that matter, it was the only direction in which he could row. Some provisions had been placed in the bottom of the boat,—a bag of biscuits, a smoked tongue, and a barrel of water.

Just as they were lowering the gig, La Vieuville, a very scoffer in the presence of destruction, leaning over the stern-post of the corvette, cried out in his cool sneering voice a parting word:—

"Very good for escaping, and still better for drowning."

"Sir, let us joke no more," said the pilot.

They pushed off rapidly, and soon left the corvette far behind. Both wind and tide were in the oars-man's favor, and the small skiff flew rapidly along, wavering to and fro in the twilight, and hidden by the high crests of the waves.

A gloomy sense of expectation brooded over the sea.

Suddenly amid this illimitable, tumultuous silence a voice was heard; exaggerated by the speaking-trumpet, as by the brazen mask of ancient tragedy, it seemed almost superhuman.

It was Captain Boisberthelot speaking.

"Royal marines," he exclaimed, "nail the white flag to the mizzen-mast! We are about to look upon our last sunrise!"

And the corvette fired a shot.

"Long live the King!" shouted the crew.

Then from the verge of the horizon was heard another shout, stupendous, remote, confused, and yet distinct,—

"Long live the Republic!"

And a din like unto the roar of three hundred thunderbolts exploded in the depths of the sea.

The conflict began. The sea was covered with fire and smoke.

Jets of spray thrown up by the balls as they struck the water rose from the sea on all sides.

The "Claymore" was pouring forth flame on the eight vessels; the squadron, ranged in a semicircle around her, opened fire from all its batteries. The horizon was in a blaze. A volcano seemed to have sprung from the sea. The wind swept to and fro this stupendous crimson drapery of battle through which the vessels appeared and disappeared like phantoms. Against the red sky in the foreground were sketched the outlines of the corvette.

The fleur-de-lis flag could be seen floating from the main-mast.

The two men in the boat were silent. The triangular shoal of the Minquiers, a kind of submarine Trinacrium, is larger than the isle of Jersey. The sea covers it. Its culminating point is a plateau that is never submerged, even at the highest tide, and from which rise, towards the northeast, six mighty rocks standing in a line, producing the effect of a massive wall which has crumbled here and there. The strait between the plateau and the six reefs is accessible only to vessels drawing very little water. Beyond this strait is the open sea.

The sailor who had volunteered to manage the boat headed for the strait. Thus he had put Minquiers between the boat and the battle. He navigated skilfully in the narrow channel, avoiding rocks to starboard and port. The cliff now hid the battle from their view. The flaming horizon and the furious din of the cannonade were growing less distinct, by reason of the increased distance; but judging from the continued explosions one could guess that the corvette still held its own, and that it meant to use its hundred and ninety-one rounds to the very last. The boat soon found itself in smooth waters beyond the cliffs and the battle, and out of the reach of missiles. Gradually the surface of the sea lost something of its gloom; the rays of light that had been swallowed up in the shadows began to widen; the curling foam leaped forth in jets of light, and the broken waves sent back their pale reflections. Daylight appeared.

The boat was beyond reach of the enemy, but the principal difficulty still remained to be overcome. It was safe from grape-shot, but the danger of shipwreck was not yet past. It was on the open sea, a mere shell, with neither deck, sail, mast, nor compass, entirely dependent on its oars, face to face with the ocean and the hurricane,—a pygmy at the mercy of giants.

Then amid this infinite solitude, his face whitened by the morning light, the man in the bow of the boat raised his head and gazed steadily at the man in the stern as he said,—

"I am the brother of him whom you ordered to be shot."

Book III

Halmalo

I

Speech is Word

THE OLD MAN SLOWLY LIFTED his head.

He who had addressed him was about thirty years of age. The tan of the sea was upon his brow; there was something unusual about his eyes, as if the simple pupils of the peasant had taken on the keen expression of the sailor; he held his oars firmly in his hands. He looked gentle enough. In his belt he wore a dirk, two pistols, and a rosary.

"Who are you?" said the old man.

"I have just told you."

"What do you wish?"

The man dropped the oars, folded his arms, and replied,—

"To kill you."

"As you please!" replied the old man.

The man raised his voice.

"Prepare yourself."

"For what?"

"To die."

"Why?" inquired the old man.

A silence followed. For a moment the question seemed to abash the man. He continued,—

"I tell you that I mean to kill you."

"And I ask of you the reason."

The sailor's eyes flashed.

"Because you killed my brother."

The old man answered quietly,—

"I saved his life at first."

"True. You saved him first, but you killed him afterwards."

"It was not I who killed him."

"Who was it, then?"

"His own fault."

The sailor gazed on the old man open-mouthed; then once more his brows contracted savagely.

"What is your name?" asked the old man.

"My name is Halmalo, but I can kill you all the same, whether you know my name or not."

Just then the sun rose; a ray struck the sailor full in the face, vividly illumining that wild countenance.

The old man studied it closely. The cannonading, though not yet ended, was no longer continuous. A dense smoke had settled upon the horizon. The boat, left to itself, was drifting to leeward.

With his right hand the sailor seized one of the pistols at his belt, while in his left he held his rosary.

The old man rose to his feet.

"Do you believe in God?" he asked.

"'Our Father who art in heaven.'" replied the sailor.

Then he made the sign of the cross.

"Have you a mother?"

He crossed himself again, saying,—

"I have said all I have to say. I give you one minute longer, my lord."

And he cocked the pistol.

"Why do you call me 'My lord'?"

"Because you are one. That is evident enough."

"Have you a lord yourself?"

"Yes, and a grand one too. Is one likely to be without a lord?"

"Where is he?"

"I do not know. He has left the country. His name is Marquis de Lantenac, Viscount de Fontenay, Prince in Brittany; he is lord of the Sept-Forêts. I never saw him, but he is my master all the same."

"If you were to see him, would you obey him?"

"Of course I should be a heathen were I not to obey him! We owe obedience to God, and after that to the king, who is like unto God, and then to the lord, who is like the king. But that has nothing to do with the question; you have killed my brother, and I must kill you."

The old man replied,—

"Let us say, then, that I did kill your brother; I did well."

The sailor had closed more firmly upon his pistol.

"Come!" he said.

"So be it," said the old man.

And he added composedly,—

"Where is the priest?"

The sailor looked at him.

"The priest?"

"Yes. I gave your brother a priest; therefore it is your duty to provide one for me."

"But I have none," replied the sailor.

And he continued,—

"How do you expect to find a priest here on the open sea?"

The convulsive explosions of the battle sounded more and more distant.

"Those who are dying yonder have their priest," said the old man.

"I know it," muttered the sailor; "they have the chaplain."

The old man went on,—

"If you make me lose my soul, it will be a serious matter."

The sailor thoughtfully bent his head.

"And if my soul is lost," continued the old man, "yours will be lost also. Listen to me; I feel pity for you. You shall do as you like. For my part, I only fulfilled my duty when I first saved your brother's life and afterwards took it from him; and at the present moment I am doing my duty in trying to save your soul. Reflect; for it is a matter that concerns you. Do you hear the cannon-shots? Men are dying over yonder; desperate men, in their last agony, husbands who will never see their wives, fathers who will never see their children, brothers who, like yourself, will never see their brothers. And who is to blame for it? Your own brother. You believe in God, do you not? If so, you know that God is suffering now. He is suffering in the person of his son, the most Christian king of France, who is a child like the child Jesus, and who is now imprisoned in the Temple; God is suffering in his Church of Brittany, in his desecrated cathedrals, in his Gospels torn to fragments, in his violated houses of prayer, in his murdered priests. What were we about to do with that ship which is perishing at this moment? We were going to the relief of the Lord. If your brother had been a trustworthy servant, if he had performed his duties faithfully, like a good and useful man, no misfortune would have happened to the carronade, the corvette would not have been disabled, she would not have got out of her course and fallen into the hands of that cursed fleet, and we should all now be landing in France, brave sailors and soldiers as we were, sword in hand, with our white banner unfurled, a multitude of contented, happy men, advancing to the rescue of the brave Vendean peasants, on our way to save France, the king, and Almighty God. That is what we were intending to do, what we should have done, and what I, the only one remaining, still propose to do. But you intend to prevent me. In this struggle of impious men against priests, in this conflict of regicides against the king, of Satan against God, you range yourself in the ranks of Satan. Your brother was the Devil's first assistant, you are his second. What he began you mean to finish. You are for the regicides against the throne; you take sides with the impious against the Church. You take away the Lord's last resource. For, as I shall not be there,—I, who represent the king,—villages will continue to burn, families to mourn, priests to bleed, Brittany to suffer, the king to remain imprisoned, and Jesus Christ to grieve over his people. And who will have caused all this? You. Well, you are carrying out your own plans. I expected far different things from you, but I was mistaken. It is true that I killed your brother. He played a brave part, for that I rewarded him; he was guilty, therefore I punished him. He failed in his duty; I have not failed in mine. What I did I would do again; and I swear by the great Saint Anne of Auray, who looks down on us, that under like circumstances I would shoot my own son just as I shot your brother. Now you are the master. Indeed, I pity you. You have broken your word to the captain,—you, Christian without faith; you, Breton without honor. I was intrusted to your loyalty, and you accepted the trust meaning to betray it; you offer my death to those to whom you have promised my life. Do you realize whom you are destroying here? It is your own self. You rob the king of my life, and you consign yourself forever to the Devil. Go on, commit your crime. You set a low value on your share in Paradise. Thanks to you, the Devil will conquer; thanks to you, the churches will fall; thanks to you, the heathen will go on turning bells into cannon,—men will be shot with the very instrument that once brought to mind the salvation of their souls. Perhaps at this moment, while I still speak to you, the same bell that pealed for your baptism is killing your mother. Go on with the Devil's work. Do not pause. Yes, I have condemned your brother; but learn this,—I am but a tool in the hands of God. Ah I you pretend to judge God's ways? You will next sit in judgment on the thunderbolt in the heavens. Wretched man, you will be judged by it. Beware what you do. Do you even know whether I am in a state of grace? No. Never mind, go on; do your will. You have the power to hurl me to perdition, and yourself likewise. Your own damnation, as well as mine, rests in your hands. You will be answerable before God. We are alone, face to face with the abyss; complete your work, make an end of it. I am old, and you are young; I have no weapons, you are armed: kill me."

While the old man, standing erect, was uttering these words in a voice that rang above the tumult of the sea, the undulations of the waves showed him now in shadow, now in light. The sailor had turned ghostly pale; large drops of moisture fell from his brow; he trembled like a leaf; now and then he kissed his rosary. When the old man finished, he threw away his pistol and fell on his knees.

"Pardon, my lord! forgive me!" he cried. "You speak like our Lord himself. I have been wrong. My brother was guilty. I will do all I can to make amends for his crime. Dispose of me; command me: I will obey."

"I forgive you," said the old man.

II

A Peasant's Memory is Worth as Much as the Captain's Science

THE PROVISIONS WITH WHICH THE boat had been stocked were far from superfluous; for the two fugitives were forced to make long détours, and were thirty-six hours in reaching the coast. They passed the night at sea; but the night was fine, with more moonlight than is pleasing to people who wish to escape observation.

At first they were obliged to keep away from the French coast, and gain the open sea in the direction of Jersey. They heard the final volley from the unfortunate corvette, and it sounded like the roar of a lion whom the hunters are killing in the forest. Then a silence fell upon the sea.

The corvette "Claymore" perished like the "Vengeur;" but glory has kept no record of its deeds. One can win no laurels who fights against his native land.

Halmalo was a remarkable sailor. He performed miracles of skill and sagacity. The route that he improvised amid the reefs, the waves, and the vigilance of the enemy was a masterpiece. The wind had abated, and the struggle with the sea was over. Halmalo had avoided the Caux des Minquiers, and having rounded the Chaussée aux Boeufs, took refuge there, so as to get a few hours of rest in the little creek formed by the sea at low tide; then rowing southward, he continued to pass between Granville and the Chausey Islands without being noticed by the lookout either of Chausey or Granville. He entered the Bay of

Saint-Michel,—a daring feat, considering that the cruising squadron was anchored at Cancale.

On the evening of the second day, about an hour before sunset, he passed the hill of Saint-Michel, and landed on a shore that is always avoided on account of the danger from its shifting sand.

Fortunately the tide was high.

Halmalo pushed the boat as far as he could, tried the sand, and, finding it firm, grounded the boat and jumped ashore, the old man following, with eyes turned anxiously towards the horizon.

"My lord," said Halmalo, "this is the mouth of the Couesnon. We have Beauvoir to starboard, and Huisnes to port. The belfry before us is Ardevon."

The old man bent over the boat, took from it a biscuit, which he put in his pocket, and said to Halmalo,—

"You may take the rest."

Halmalo put what remained of meat and biscuit in the bag, and hoisted it on his shoulder. Having done this, he said,—

"My lord, am I to lead the way, or to follow you?"

"You will do neither."

Halmalo looked at the old man in amazement.

The latter went on,—

"We are about to separate, Halmalo. Two men are of no use whatever. Unless they are a thousand, it is better for one man to be alone."

He stopped and pulled out of his pocket a knot of green silk resembling a cockade; with a fleur-de-lis embroidered in gold in the centre.

"Can you read?" he asked.

"No."

"That is fortunate. A man who knows how to read is embarrassing. Have you a good memory?"

"Yes."

"Very well. Listen, Halmalo. You will follow the road on the right, and I the one on the left. You are to turn in the direction of Bazouges, and I shall go towards Fougères. Keep your bag, because it makes you look like a peasant; hide your weapons; cut yourself a stick from the hedge; creep through the tall rye; glide behind the hedges; climb over fences and cross the fields: you will thus avoid the passers-by, as well as roads and bridges. Do not enter Pontorson. Ah! you will have to cross the Couesnon. How will you manage that?"

"I shall swim across."

"Excellent. Then you will come to a ford. Do you know where it is?"

"Between Nancy and Vieux-Viel."

"Correct. You are evidently familiar with the country."

"But night is coming on. Where will my lord sleep?"

"I can take care of myself. And where will you sleep?"

"There are plenty of *émousses*. I was a peasant before I was a sailor."

"Throw away your sailor hat; it would betray you. You can surely find some worsted head-covering."

"Oh, a cap is easily found. The first fisherman I meet will sell me his."

"Very well. Now listen. You are familiar with the woods?"

"All of them."

"Throughout this entire neighborhood?"

"From Noirmoutier to Laval."

"Do you know their names too?"

"I know the woods and their names; I know all about them."

"You will forget nothing?"

"Nothing."

"Good. Now mind. How many leagues can you walk in a day?"

"Ten, fifteen, eighteen, twenty, if need be."

"It will have to be done. Do not miss a word of what I am about to tell you. You will go to the woods of Saint-Aubin."

"Near Lamballe?"

"Yes. On the edge of a ravine between Saint-Rieul and Plédéliac there is a large chestnut-tree. You will stop there. No one will be in sight."

"But a man will be there nevertheless. On that I can depend."

"You will give the call. Do you know it?"

Halmalo puffed out his cheeks, turned towards the sea, and there rang the "to-whit-to-hoo" of the owl.

One would have supposed it came from the depths of a forest, so owl-like and sinister was the sound.

"Good!" said the old man. "You have it."

He extended to Halmalo the green silk knot.

"This is my commander's badge. Take it. No one must know my name at present; but this knot is sufficient. The fleur-de-lis was embroidered by Madame Royale in the Temple prison."

Halmalo knelt. Trembling with awe he received the knot

embroidered with the fleur-de-lis, and in the act of raising it to his lips, he paused as if in fear.

"May I?" he asked.

"Yes, since you kiss the crucifix."

Halmalo kissed the fleur-de-lis.

"Rise," said the old man.

Halmalo obeyed him, placing the knot in his bosom.

"Listen carefully to what I am about to say. This is the order: 'Revolt! Give no quarter.' On the edge of the forest of Saint-Aubin you will give the call, repeating it three times. After the third time you will see a man rise from the ground."

"I know, from a hole under the trees."

"That man will be Planchenault, sometimes called Coeur-de-Roi. To him you will show this knot. He will know what it means. Then you are to go by ways that you must discover for yourself to the woods of Astillé, where you will see a cripple surnamed Mousqueton, a man who shows mercy to no human being. You are to tell him that I love him, and that he must stir up the parishes in his neighborhood. Thence you will go to the wood of Couesbon, which is one mile from Ploërmel. When you give the owl-cry, a man will come out of a hole; that will be M. Thuault, seneschal of Ploërmel, who formerly belonged to the Constitutional Assembly, but on the royalist side. You will direct him to fortify the castle of Couesbon, that belongs to the Marquis de Guer, a refugee. Ravines, woods of moderate extent, uneven soil, a good spot. M. Thuault is an able and upright man. From there you will go to Saint-Guen-les-Toits, and speak to Jean Chouan, whom I look upon as the actual leader, and then to the woods of Ville-Anglose, where you will see Guitter, called Saint-Martin; you will tell him to keep his eye on a certain Courmesnil, son-in-law of the old Goupil de Préfeln, and who is the head of the Jacobins of Argentan. Remember all this. I write nothing, because writing must be avoided. La Rouarie made out a list, which ruined everything. Thence you will go to the wood of Rougefeu, where Miélette lives, he who leaps across ravines by the help of a long pole."

"They call it a leaping-pole."

"Do you know how to use it?"

"Am I not a Breton peasant? The leaping-pole is our friend. It makes our arms bigger, our legs longer."

"That is to say, it reduces the enemy and shortens the way. An excellent machine."

"Once, with my leaping-pole, I stood my ground against three salt-tax men armed with sabres."

"When was that?"

"Ten years ago."

"Under the king?"

"Certainly."

"Against whom?"

"I really do not know. I was a salt-smuggler."

"Very good."

"It was called fighting against the collectors of the salt-tax. Is the tax on salt the same thing as the king?"

"Yes, and no. But it is not necessary for you to understand this."

"I ask monseigneur's pardon for having put a question to monseigneur."

"Let us go on. Do you know the Tourgue?"

"Do I know it! I came from there."

"How is that?"

"Why, because I come from Parigné."

"To be sure, the Tourgue borders on Parigné."

"Do I know the Tourgue! The great round castle belongs to the family of my lords. A large iron door separates the old building from the new part, which a cannon could not destroy. In the new building they keep the famous book on Saint-Barthélémy, which people come to see as a curiosity. The grass is full of frogs. When I was a boy I used to play with those frogs. And the underground passage, too. Perhaps I am the only one left who knows about that."

"What underground passage? I don't know what you are talking about."

"That was in old times, when the Tourgue was besieged. The people inside could escape through an underground passage which opened into the woods."

"I know there are subterranean passages of that kind in the châteaux of Jupellière and Hunaudaye, and in the tower of Champéon; but there is nothing like it in the Tourgue."

"But indeed there is, monseigneur. I do not know the passages of which monseigneur speaks; I only know the one in the Tourgue because I belong in the neighborhood; and besides, I am the only one who does know of it. It was never spoken of. It was forbidden, because this passage had been used in the wars of M. de Rohan. My father knew the secret and showed it to me. I know both the secret entrance and the outlet. If I am in the forest I can go into the tower; and if I am in the tower I can go into the forest without being seen, so that when the enemies enter there is no one to be found. That is the passage of the Tourgue. Oh, I know it well."

The old man remained silent for a moment.

"You must be mistaken. If there had been any such secret I should have known it."

"Monseigneur, I am sure of it. There is a stone that turns."

"Oh, yes! You peasants believe in turning-stones, in singing-stones, and in stones that go by night down to a neighboring brook to drink. A pack of idle tales!"

"But when I turned the stone myself—"

"Yes, just as others have heard it sing. My friend, the Tourgue is a Bastille, safe and strong, and easily defended; but he would be a simpleton indeed who depended for escape on a subterranean passage."

"But, monseigneur—"

The old man shrugged his shoulders,—

"Let us waste no more time, but speak of business."

This peremptory tone checked Halmalo's persistence.

The old man resumed:—

"Let us go on. Listen. From Rougefeu you are to go into the wood of Montchevrier, where you will find Bénédicité, the leader of the Twelve. He is another good man. He recites his *Bénédicite* while he has people shot. There is no room for sensibility in warfare. From Montchevrier you will go—"

He broke off.

"I had forgotten about the money."

He took from his pocket a purse and a pocket-book, which he put into Halmalo's hands.

"In this pocket-book you will find thirty thousand francs in paper money, which is worth about three livres and ten sous. The assignats are false, to be sure, but the real ones are no more valuable; and in this purse, mind, you will find one hundred louis d'ors. I give you all I have, because I have no need of anything here, and it is better that no money should be found on me. Now I will go on. From Montchevrier you are to go to Antrain, where you will meet M. de Frotté; from Antrain to Jupellière, where you Will see M. de Rochecotte; from Jupellière to Noirieux, where you will find the Abbé Baudoin. Will you remember all this?"

"As I do my Pater Noster."

"You will see M. Dubois-Guy at Saint-Brice-en-Cogle, M. de Turpin at Morannes, which is a fortified town, and the Prince de Talmont at Château-Gonthier."

"Will a prince speak to me?"

"Am I not speaking to you?"

Halmalo took off his hat.

"You need but to show Madam's fleur-de-lis, and your welcome is assured. Remember that you will have to go to places where there are mountaineers and *patauds*.[1] You will disguise yourself. That is an easy matter, since the republicans are so stupid that with a blue coat, a three-cornered hat, and a cockade, you may go anywhere. The day of regiments and uniforms has gone by; the regiments are not even numbered, and every man is at liberty to wear any rag he fancies. You will go to Saint-Mhervé. You will see Gaulier, called Grand-Pierre. You will go to the cantonment of Parné, where all the men have swarthy faces. They put gravel in their muskets and use a double charge of powder to make more noise. They do well; but be sure and tell them to kill, kill, and kill. You will go to the camp of the Vache-Noire, which is an elevation in the midst of the forest of La Charnie, from Vache-Noire to the camp of l'Avoine, then to the camp Vert, and afterwards to the camp of the Fourmis. You will go to Grand-Bordage, also called Haut-du-Pré, where lives the widow whose daughter married Treton the Englishman; that is in the parish of Quelaines. You will visit Épineux-le-Chevreuil, Sillé-le-Guillaume, Guillaume, Parannes, and all the men in hiding throughout the woods. You will make friends and you will send them to the borders of upper and lower Maine; you will see Jean Treton in the parish of Vaisges, Sans-Regret in Bignon, Chambord in Bonchamps, the Corbin brothers at Maisoncelles, and Petit-Sans-Peur at Saint-Jean-sur-Evre. He is the one who is called Bourdoiseau. Having done this, and uttered the watchwords, 'Revolt!' 'No quarter!' in all these places, you will join the royal and catholic grand army, wherever it may be. You will see d'Elbée, de Lescure, de la Rochejaquelein, and such leaders as may still be living. You will show them my commander's knot. They know what it means. You are only a sailor, but Cathelineau is nothing but a teamster. You will give them this message from me: It is time to join the two wars, the great and the small. The great one makes more noise, but the small

---

1. A name given by the Chouans to the republicans, a corruption of patriot.—Tr.

one does the work. The Vendée does fairly well, but Chouannerie goes farther, and in civil war cruelty is a powerful agent. The success of a war depends on the amount of evil that it causes."

He broke off.

"Halmalo, I tell you all this, not that you can understand the words, but because your perceptions are keen, and you will comprehend the matters themselves. I have trusted you since I saw you managing that boat. Without knowing anything of geometry you execute wonderful sea manoeuvres. He who can pilot a boat can guide an insurrection. Judging from the way in which you managed our affair at sea, I feel sure that you will execute my instructions equally well. But to resume: So you will repeat to the chiefs all that I have told you, or words to the same effect, as near as you can remember; I am confident that you will convey to them my meaning. I prefer the warfare of the forest to that of the open field. I have no intention of exposing one hundred thousand peasants to the grape-shot of the soldiers in blue and the artillery of M. Carnot. In a month's time I expect to have five hundred sharp-shooters hidden in the woods. The republican army is my game. Poaching is one method of warfare. The strategy of the thickets for me! Ah, that is probably another word which you will not understand; but never mind,—you know what I mean when I say, No quarter! and ambushes on every side! Give me more Chouannerie rather than the regular Vendean warfare. You will add that the English are on our side. Let us catch the republic between two fires. Europe helps us: let us put down revolution. Kings are waging a war of kingdoms: we will wage a war of parishes. You will say all this. Do you understand me?"

"Yes: put all to fire and sword."

"That is it,"

"No quarter."

"None whatever. You understand?"

"I will go everywhere."

"And be always on your guard; for in these parts it is an easy matter to lose one's life."

"Death I have no fear of. He who takes his first step may be wearing his last shoes."

"You are a brave fellow."

"And if I am asked monseigneur's name?"

"It is not to be made known yet. You are to say that you do not know it, and you will say the truth."

"Where shall I see monseigneur again?"

"At the place where I am going."

"How shall I know where that is?"

"All the world will know it. Before eight days have gone by you will hear of me. I shall make examples; I shall avenge the king and religion; and you will know well enough that it is I of whom they are speaking."

"I understand."

"Do not forget anything."

"You may rest assured of that."

"Now go, and may God guide you! Go!"

"I will do all you bid me. I will go; I will speak; I will obey; I will command."

"Good."

"And if I succeed—"

"I will make you a knight of Saint-Louis."

"Like my brother. And if I fail, you will have me shot?"

"Like your brother."

"So be it, monseigneur."

The old man bent his head, and seemed to fall into a gloomy reverie. When he raised his eyes he was alone. Halmalo was only a black speck vanishing on the horizon.

The sun had just set; the sea-mews and hooded gulls were flying homeward from the ocean, and the atmosphere was charged with that well-known restlessness that precedes the night; the tree-frogs croaked, the kingfishers flew whistling from the pools, the gulls and rooks kept up their usual evening clamor, and the shore-birds called to each other, but not a human sound was to be heard. It was absolute solitude,—not a sail on the bay, not a peasant in the fields; only a bleak expanse as far as the eye could reach. The tall sand-thistles quivered; the pale twilight sky shed a livid light over all the shore; and the ponds far away on the dark plain looked like sheets of pewter laid flat upon the ground. A sea-wind was blowing.

Book IV

TELLMARCH

I

On the Top of the Dune

THE OLD MAN WAITED UNTIL Halmalo was out of sight; then drawing his sea-cloak more closely around him, he started walking slowly, wrapt in thought. He took the direction of Huisnes; Halmalo had gone towards Beauvoir.

Behind him rose the enormous triangle of Mont Saint-Michel, with its cathedral tiara and its cuirass-like fortress, whose two great eastern towers—the one round, the other square—help the mountain to bear up under the burden of the church and the village. As the pyramid of Cheops is a landmark in the desert, so is Mont-Saint Michel a beacon to the sea.

The quicksands in the bay of Mont Saint-Michel act imperceptibly upon the dunes. At that time between Huisnes and Ardevon there was a very high one, which is no longer in existence. This dune, levelled by an equinoctial gale, was unusually old, and on its summit stood a milestone, erected in the twelfth century in memory of the council held at Avranches against the assassins of Saint Thomas of Canterbury. From its top one could see all the surrounding country, and ascertain the points of the compass.

The old man directed his steps to this dune, and ascended it.

When he reached the summit, he seated himself on one of the four projecting stones, and leaning back against the monument, began to examine the land that lay spread out like a geographical map at his feet. He seemed to be looking for a route in a country that had once been familiar to him. In this broad landscape, obscured by the twilight, nothing was distinctly visible but the dark line of the horizon against the pale sky.

One could see the clustered roofs of eleven hamlets and villages; and all the belfries of the coast were visible several miles away, standing high that they might serve as beacons to the sailors in time of need.

Some minutes later the old man seemed to have found what he was looking for in this dim light; his eye rested on an enclosure of trees, walls, and roofs, partially visible between the valley and the wood: it was a farm. He nodded his head with an expression of satisfaction, like one who says to himself, "There it is!" and began to trace with his finger the outlines of a route across the hedges and the fields. From time to time he gazed intently at a shapeless and somewhat indistinct object that was moving above the principal roof of the farm, and seemed to ask himself what it could be. It was colorless and dim, in consequence of the time of day. It was not a weather-vane, because it was floating; and there seemed to be no reason why it should be a flag.

He felt weary; and grateful to rest on the stone where he was sitting, he yielded to that vague sense of oblivion which the first moment of repose brings to weary men. There is one hour of the day which may be called noiseless,—the peaceful hour of early evening; that hour had come, and he was enjoying it. He gazed, he listened. To what? To perfect tranquillity. Even savage natures have their moments of melancholy. Suddenly this tranquillity was—not exactly disturbed, but sharply defined by the voices of those who were passing below. They were the voices of women and children. It was like a joyous chime of bells heard unexpectedly in the darkness. The group from which the voices came could not be distinguished, on account of the underbrush; but it was evident that the persons were walking along the foot of the dune, in the direction of the plain and the forest. As those clear, fresh voices reached the old man where he sat absorbed in thought, they were so near that he lost not a word.

A woman's voice said,—

"Let us hurry, Flécharde. Is this the way?"

"No; it is over yonder."

And the dialogue went on between the two voices, the one high and shrill, the other low and timid.

"What is the name of this farm where we are living now?"

"Herbe-en-Pail."

"Are we still far from it?"

"Fully a quarter of an hour."

"Let us make haste and get there in time for the soup."

"Yes, I know we are late."

"We ought to run; but your mites are tired. We are only two women, and cannot carry three brats. And then, you, Flécharde, you are carrying one as it is,—a perfect lump of lead. You have weaned that little gormandizer, and you still carry it. That is a bad habit; you had better make it walk. Well, the soup will be cold,—worse luck!"

"Ah, what good shoes you gave me! They fit as though they were made for me."

"It's better than going barefooted."

"Do hurry, René-Jean."

"He is the one who makes us late; he has had to stop and speak to all the little village girls that we meet He behaves like a man already."

"Of course he does; he is going on five years old."

"Tell us, René-Jean, why did you speak to that little girl in the village?"

A child's voice, that of a boy, replied,—

"Because I know her."

"How is that? You know her?" said the woman.

"Yes," answered the boy; "because we played games this morning."

"Well, I must say!" exclaimed the woman. "We have been here only three days; a boy no bigger than your fist, and he has found a sweetheart already!"

And the voices grew fainter in the distance, and every sound died away.

II

Aures Habet, Et Non Audiet

THE OLD MAN SAT MOTIONLESS. He was not consciously thinking, nor yet was he dreaming. Around him was peace, repose, assurance of safety, solitude. Although night had shut down upon the woods, and in the valley below it was nearly dark, broad daylight still rested on the dune. The moon was rising in the east, and several stars pricked the pale blue of the zenith. This man, although intensely absorbed in his own interests, surrendered himself to the unutterable peacefulness of nature. He felt the vague dawn of hope rising in his breast,—if the word "hope" may fitly be applied to projects of civil warfare. For the moment it seemed to him that in escaping from the inexorable sea he had left all danger behind him. No one knew his name; he was alone,—lost, as far as concerned the enemy; he had left no traces behind him, for the surface of the sea preserves no trace; all is hidden, ignored, and never even suspected. He felt unspeakably calm. A little more, and he would have fallen asleep.

It was the deep silence pervading both heaven and earth that lent to the hour a subtle charm to soothe the imagination of this man, stirred as he was by inward and outward agitations.

There was nothing to be heard but the wind blowing in from the sea, a prolonged monotonous bass, to which the ear becomes so used that it almost ceases to be noticed as a sound.

All at once he rose to his feet

His attention was suddenly awakened. An object on the horizon seemed to arrest his glance.

He was gazing at the belfry of Cormeray, at the farther end of the valley. Something unusual was going on in this belfry.

Its dark silhouette was clearly defined against the sky; the tower surmounted by the spire could be seen distinctly, and between the tower and the spire was the square cage for the bell, without a penthouse, and open on the four sides, after the fashion of Breton belfries. Now this cage seemed to open and shut by turns, and at regular intervals; its lofty aperture looked now perfectly white, and the next moment black, the sky constantly appearing and vanishing, eclipse following the light, as the opening and shutting succeeded each other with the regularity of a hammer striking an anvil.

This belfry of Cormeray lay before him at a distance of some two leagues. He looked towards the right in the direction of the belfry of Baguer-Pican, which also rose straight against the horizon, and the cage of that belfry was opening and closing like the belfry of Cormeray. He looked towards the left at the belfry of Tanis; the cage of Tanis opened and closed like that of Baguer-Pican. He examined all the belfries on the horizon, one after another,—the belfries of Courtils, of Précey, of Crollon, and of Croix-Avranchin on his right hand, those of Raz-sur-Couesnon, of Mordray, and of the Pas on his left, and before him the belfry of Pontorson. Every belfry cage was changing alternately from white to black.

What could it mean?

It meant that all the bells were ringing, and they must be ringing violently to cause the light to change so rapidly.

What was it, then? The tocsin, beyond a doubt. They were ringing, and frantically too, from all the belfries, in every parish, and in every village, and yet not a sound could be heard.

VICTOR HUGO

This was owing to the distance, combined with the sea-wind, which, blowing from the opposite direction, carried all sounds from the shore away beyond the horizon.

All these frantic bells ringing on every side, and at the same time this silence; what could be more appalling?

The old man looked and listened.

He could not hear the tocsin, but he could see it. Seeing the tocsin is rather a strange sensation.

Against whom was this fury directed?

Against whom was the tocsin ringing?

III

The Usefulness of Big Letters

SOME ONE WAS SURELY CAUGHT in a trap.

Who could it be?

A shudder shook this man of steel.

It could not be he. His arrival could not have been discovered. It was impossible for the representatives to have learned it already, for he had but just stepped on shore. The corvette had surely foundered with all on board; and even on the corvette Boisberthelot and La Vieuville were the only men who knew his name.

The bells kept up their savage sport. He counted them mechanically, and in the abrupt transition from the assurance of perfect safety to a terrible sense of danger, his thoughts wandered restlessly from one conjecture to another. However, after all, this ringing might be accounted for in many different ways, and he finally reassured himself by repeating, "In short, no one knows of my arrival here, or even my name."

For several minutes there had been a slight noise overhead and behind him,—a sound resembling the rustling of a leaf; at first he took no notice of it, but as it continued, persisted, one might almost say, he finally turned. It was really a leaf,—a leaf of paper. The wind was struggling to tear off a large placard that was pasted on the milestone above his head. The placard had but just been pasted; for it was still moist, and had become a prey to the wind, which in its sport had partly detached it.

The old man had not perceived it, because he had ascended the dune on the opposite side.

He stepped up on the stone where he had been sitting, and placed his hand on the corner of the placard that fluttered in the wind. The sky was clear; in June the twilight lasts a long time, and although it was dark at the foot of the dune, the summit was still light. A part of the notice was printed in large letters; it was yet sufficiently light to read it, and this was what he read:—

THE FRENCH REPUBLIC, ONE AND INDIVISIBLE
We, Prieur of the Marne, representative of the people, in command of the army on the coast of Cherbourg, give notice, That the ci-devant Marquis of Lantenac, Viscount of Fontenay, calling himself a Breton prince, and who has secretly landed on the coast of Granville, is outlawed. A price has been set upon his head. Whoever captures him dead or alive will receive sixty thousand livres. This sum will be paid in gold, and not in paper money. A battalion of the army of the coast guards of Cherbourg will be at once despatched for the apprehension of the former Marquis of Lantenac. The inhabitants of the parishes are ordered to lend their aid.
Given at the Town Hall of Granville the second of June, 1793.

Signed: PRIEUR, DE LA MARNE

Below this name there was another signature written in smaller characters, which the fading light prevented him from deciphering. Pulling his hat down over his eyes, and muffling himself in his sea-cape up to his chin, the old man hastily descended the dune. Evidently it was not safe to tarry any longer on this lighted summit.

Perhaps he had stayed there too long already. The top of the dune was the only point of the landscape that still remained visible.

When he had descended and found himself in the darkness he slackened his pace.

He took the road leading to the farm which he had traced out, evidently believing himself safe in that direction. It was absolute solitude. There were no passers-by at this hour.

Stopping behind a clump of bushes, he unfastened his cloak, turned his waistcoat with the hairy side out, refastened his cloak, that was but a rag held by a string around his neck, and resumed his journey.

It was bright moonlight.

He came to a place where two roads forked, and on the pedestal of the old stone cross which stood there a white square could be distinguished,—undoubtedly another placard like the one he had lately read. As he drew near to it he heard a voice.

"Where are you going?" it said; and turning he beheld a man in the hedge-row, tall like himself, and of about the same age, with hair as white and garments even more ragged than his own,—almost his very double.

The man stood leaning on a long staff.

"I asked you where you were going? he repeated.

"In the first place, tell me where I am," was the reply, uttered in tones of almost haughty composure.

And the man answered,—

"You are in the seigneury of Tanis, of which I am the beggar and you the lord."

"I?"

"Yes, you,—monsieur le marquis de Lantenac."

IV

The Caimand

THE MARQUIS DE LANTENAC (HENCEFORTH we shall call him by his name) replied gravely,—

"Very well. Then deliver me up."

The man continued,—

"We are both at home here,—you in the castle, I in the bushes."

"Let us put an end to this. Do what you have to do. Deliver me to the authorities," said the Marquis.

The man went on,—

"You were going to the farm Herbe-en-Pail, were you not?"

"Yes."

"Don't go there."

"Why not?"

"Because the Blues are there."

"How long have they been there?"

"These three days past."

"Did the inhabitants of the farm and village resist?"

"No; they opened all the doors."

"Ah!" said the Marquis.

The man indicated with his finger the roof of the farm, which was visible in the distance above the trees.

"Do you see that roof, Marquis?"

"Yes."

"Do you see what there is above it?"

"Something waving?"

"Yes."

"It is a flag."

"The tricolor," said the man.

It was the object that had attracted the attention of the Marquis when he stood on the top of the dune.

"Isn't the tocsin ringing?" inquired the Marquis.

"Yes."

"On what account?"

"Evidently on yours."

"But one cannot hear it?"

"The wind prevents it from being heard."

The man continued,—

"Did you see that notice about yourself?"

"Yes."

"They are searching for you."

Then glancing towards the farm, he added,—

"They have a demi-battalion over there."

"Of republicans?"

"Of Parisians."

"Well," said the Marquis, "let us go on."

And he made a step in the direction of the farm. The man seized him by the arm.

"Don't go there!"

"Where would you have me go?"

"With me."

The Marquis looked at the beggar.

"Listen to me, Marquis: My home is not a fine one, but it is safe,—a hut lower than a cellar, seaweed for a floor, and for a ceiling a roof of branches and of grass. Come. They would shoot you at the farm, and at my house you will have a chance to sleep; you must be weary. Tomorrow the Blues start out again, and you can go where you choose."

The Marquis studied the man.

"On which side are you, then?" asked the Marquis. "Are you a royalist, or a republican?"

"I am a beggar."

"Neither royalist nor republican?"

"I believe not."

"Are you for or against the king?"

"I have no time for that sort of thing."

"What do you think of what is transpiring?"

"I think that I have not enough to live on."

"Yet you come to my aid."

"I knew that you were outlawed. What is this law, then, that one can be outside of it? I do not understand. Am I inside the law, or outside of it? I have no idea. Does dying of hunger mean being inside the law?"

"How long have you been dying of hunger?"

"All my life."

"And you propose to save me?"

"Yes."

"Why?"

"Because I said to myself, 'There is a man who is poorer than I, for he has not even the right to breathe.'"

"True. And so you mean to save me?"

"Certainly. Now we are brothers, my lord,—beggars both; I for bread, and you for life."

"But do you know there is a price set on my head?"

"Yes."

"How did you know it?"

"I have read the notice."

"Then you can read?"

"Yes, and write also. Did you think I was like the beasts of the field?"

"But since you can read, and have seen the notice, you must know that he who delivers me up will receive sixty thousand francs."

"I know it."

"Not in assignats."

"Yes, I know,—in gold."

"You realize that sixty thousand francs is a fortune?"

"Yes."

"And that the man who arrests me will make his fortune?"

"Yes; and what then?"

"His fortune!"

"That is exactly what I thought. When I saw you, I said to myself, 'To think that whoever arrests this man will earn sixty thousand francs, and make his fortune! Let us make haste to hide him.'"

The Marquis followed the beggar.

They entered a thicket. There was the beggar's den, a sort of chamber in which a large and ancient oak had allowed the man to take up his abode; it was hollowed out under its roots, and covered with its branches,—dark, low, hidden, actually invisible,—and in it there was room for two.

"I foresaw that I might have a guest," said the beggar.

This kind of subterranean lodging, less rare in Brittany than one might imagine, is called a *carnichot*. The same name is also given to hiding-places built in thick walls. The place was furnished with a few jugs, a bed of straw or sea-weed, washed and dried, a coarse kersey blanket, and a few tallow dips, together with a flint and steel, and twigs of furze to be used as matches.

They stooped, crawling for a moment, and penetrated into a chamber divided by the thick roots of the tree into fantastic compartments, and seated themselves on the heap of dry sea-weed that served as a bed. The space between the two roots through which they had entered, and which served as a door, admitted a certain amount of light. Night had fallen; but the human eye adapts itself to the change of light, and even in the darkness it sometimes seems as if the daylight lingered still. The reflection of a moonbeam illumined the entrance. In the corner was a jug of water, a loaf of buckwheat bread, and some chestnuts.

"Let us sup," said the beggar.

They divided the chestnuts; the Marquis gave his bit of hard-tack; they ate of the same black loaf, and drank in turn out of the same jug of water, meanwhile conversing.

The Marquis questioned the man.

"So it is all one to you, whatever happens?"

"Pretty much. It is for you who are lords to look out for that sort of business."

"But then, what is going on now, for instance—"

"It is all going on over my head."

The beggar added,—

"Besides, there are things happening still higher; the sun rises, the moon waxes and wanes. That is the kind of thing that interests me."

He took a swallow from the jug and said,—

"Good fresh water!"

Then he continued,—

"How do you like this water, my lord?"

"What is your name?" asked the Marquis.

"My name is Tellmarch, but they call me the Caimand."

"I understand. *Caimand* is a local word."

"Which means beggar. I am also called Le Vieux."

He went on,—

"I have been called Le Vieux for forty years."

"Forty years! But you must have been young then!"

"I was never young. You are young still, Marquis. You have the legs of a man of twenty; you can climb the great dune, while I can hardly walk. A quarter of a mile tires me out. Yet we are of the same age; but the rich have an advantage over us,—they eat every day. Eating keeps up one's strength."

After a silence the beggar went on:—

"Wealth and poverty,—there's the mischief; it seems to me that that is the cause of all these catastrophes. The poor want to be rich, and the rich do not want to become poor. I think that is at the bottom of it all, but I do not trouble myself about such matters; let come what may, I am neither for the creditor nor for the debtor. I know that there is a debt, and somebody is paying it; that is all. I would rather they had not killed the king, and yet I hardly know why. And then one says to me, 'Think how they used to hang people for nothing at all! Think of it! For a miserable shot fired at one of the king's deer, I once saw a man hung: he had a wife and seven children.' There is something to be said on both sides."

He was silent again, then resumed:—

"Of course you understand. I do not pretend to know just how matters stand; men go to and fro, changes take place, while I live beneath the stars."

Again Tellmarch became thoughtful, then went on:—

"I know something of bone-setting and medicine. I am familiar with herbs and the use of plants; the peasants see me preoccupied for no apparent reason, and so I pass for a wizard. Because I dream, they think that I am wise."

"Do you belong to the neighborhood?" asked the Marquis.

"I have never left it."

"Do you know me?"

"Certainly. The last time I saw you, you were passing through this part of the country on your way to England; that was two years ago. Just now I saw a man on the top of the dune,—a tall man. Tall men are not common hereabouts; Brittany is a country of short men. I looked more closely; I had read the notice, and I said to myself, 'See here!' And when you came down, the moon was up and I recognized you."

"But I do not know you,"

"You have looked at me, but you never saw me." And Tellmarch the Caimand added,—

"I saw you. The passer-by and the beggar look with different eyes."

"Have I ever met you before?"

"Often, for I am your beggar. I used to beg on the road, below your castle. Sometimes you gave me alms; he who gives takes no notice, but he who receives looks anxiously and observes well. A beggar is a born spy. But though I am often sad, I try not to be a malicious spy. I used to hold out my hand, and you saw nothing but that, into which you threw the alms that I needed in the morning to keep me from dying of hunger at night. Frequently I went twenty-four hours without food. Sometimes a penny means life itself. I am paying you now for the life I owe you."

"True, you are saving my life."

"Yes, I am saving your life, monseigneur."

The voice of Tellmarch grew solemn:—

"On one condition."

"What is that?"

"That you have not come here to do harm."

"I have come here to do good."

"Let us sleep," said the beggar.

They lay down side by side on the bed of sea-weed. The beggar dropped to sleep at once. The Marquis, although much fatigued, remained awake for some time, thinking and watching his companion in the darkness; finally he lay back. Lying upon the bed was equivalent to lying on the earth, and he took advantage of this to put his ear to the ground and listen. He could hear a hollow subterranean rumbling. It is a fact that sound is transmitted into the bowels of the earth; he could hear the ringing of the bells.

The tocsin continued.

The Marquis fell asleep.

V

When he Awoke it was Daylight

THE BEGGAR WAS STANDING UP,—NOT in his den, for it was impossible to stand erect there, but outside on the threshold. He was leaning on his staff, and the sunshine fell upon his face.

"Monseigneur," said Tellmarch, "it has just struck four from the belfry of Tanis. I heard it strike,—therefore the wind has changed; it comes from the land, and as I heard no other sound the tocsin must have ceased. All is quiet at the farm and in the village of Herbe-en-Pail. The Blues are either sleeping or gone. The worst of the danger is over; it will be prudent for us to separate. This is my time for going out."

He indicated a point in the horizon.

"I am going this way;" then pointing in the opposite direction, he said,—

"You are to go that way."

The beggar gravely waved his hand to the Marquis.

"Take those chestnuts with you, if you are hungry," he added, pointing to the remains of the supper.

A moment after he had disappeared among the trees.

The Marquis rose and went in the direction indicated by Tellmarch.

It was that charming hour called in the old Norman peasant dialect the "peep of day." The chirping of the finches and of the hedge-sparrows was heard. The Marquis followed the path that they had traversed the day before, and as he emerged from the thicket he found himself at the fork of the roads marked by the stone cross. The placard was still there, looking white and almost festive in the rising sun. He remembered that there was something at the foot of this notice that he had not been able to read the evening before, on account of the small characters and the fading light. He went up to the pedestal of the cross. Below the signature "Prieur, de la Marne," the notice ended with the following lines in small characters:—

The identity of the ci-devant Marquis of Lantenac having been established, he will be executed without delay.

Signed: GAUVAIN,
Chief of Battalion in Command of
Exploring Column

"Gauvain!" said the Marquis.

He paused, wrapt in deep thought, his eyes fixed on the placard.

"Gauvain!" he repeated.

He started once more, turned, looked at the cross, came back, and read the placard over again.

Then he slowly walked away. Had any one been near, he might have heard him mutter to himself in an undertone:—

"Gauvain!"

The roofs of the farm on his left were not visible from the sunken paths through which he was stealing. He skirted a precipitous hill, covered with blossoming furze, of the species known as the thorny furze. This eminence was crowned by one of those points of land called in this district a *hure*,[1] and at its base the trees cut off the view at once. The foliage seemed bathed in light. All Nature felt the deep joy of morning.

Suddenly this landscape became terrible. It was like the explosion of an ambuscade. An indescribable tornado of wild cries and musket-shots fell upon these fields and woods all radiant with the morning light, and from the direction of the farm rose a dense smoke mingled with bright flames, as though the village and the farm were but a truss of burning straw. It was not only startling but awful,—this sudden change from peace to wrath; like an explosion of hell in the very midst of dawn, a horror without transition. A fight was going on in the direction of Herbe-en-Pail. The Marquis paused.

No man in a case like this could have helped feeling as he did; curiosity is more powerful than fear. One must find out what is going on, even at the risk of life. He climbed the hill at the foot of which lay the sunken path. From there, although the chances were that he would be discovered, he could at least see what was taking place. In a few moments he stood on the *hure* and looked about him. In fact, there was both a fusillade and a fire. One could hear the cries and see the fire. The farm was evidently the centre of some mysterious catastrophe. What could it be? Was it attacked? And if so, by whom? Could it be a battle? Was it not more likely to be a military execution? By the orders of a revolutionary decree the Blues frequently punished refractory farms and villages by setting them on fire. For instance, every farm and hamlet which had neglected to fell the trees as prescribed by law, and had not opened roads in the thickets for the passage of republican cavalry, was

---

1. A head.—Tr.

burned. It was not long since the parish of Bourgon near Ernée had been thus punished. Was Herbe-en-Pail a case in point? It was evident that none of those strategic openings ordered by the decree had been cut, either in the thickets or in the environs of Tanis and Herbe-en-Pail. Was this the punishment thereof? Had an order been received by the advanced guard occupying the farm? Did not this advanced guard form a part of one of those exploring columns called *colonnes infernales*?

The eminence on which the Marquis had stationed himself was surrounded on all sides by a wild and bristling thicket called the grove of Herbe-en-Pail; it was about as large as a forest, however, and extended to the farm, concealing, as all Breton thickets do, a network of ravines, paths, and sunken roads,—labyrinths wherein the republican armies frequently went astray.

This execution, if execution it were, must have been a fierce one, for it had been rapid. Like all brutal deeds, it had been done like a flash. The atrocity of civil war admits of these savage deeds. While the Marquis, vainly conjecturing, and hesitating whether to descend or to remain, listened and watched, this crash of extermination ceased, or, to speak more accurately, vanished. The Marquis could see the fierce and jubilant troop as it scattered through the grove. There was a dreadful rushing to and fro beneath the trees. From the farm they had entered the woods. Drums beat an attack, but there was no more firing. It was like a *battue*; they seemed to be following a scent. They were evidently looking for some one; the noise was wide-spread and far-reaching. There were confused outcries of wrath and triumph, a clamor of indistinct sounds. Suddenly, as an outline is revealed in a cloud of smoke, one sound became clearly defined and audible in this tumult. It was a name, repeated by thousands of voices, and the Marquis distinctly heard the cry,—

"Lantenac, Lantenac! The Marquis of Lantenac!" They were looking for him.

VI

The Vicissitudes of Civil War

AROUND HIM SUDDENLY, FROM ALL directions, the thicket was filled with muskets, bayonets, and sabres, a tricolored banner was unfurled in the dim light, and the cry, "Lantenac!" burst forth on his ears, while at his feet through the brambles and branches savage faces appeared.

The Marquis was standing alone on the top of the height, visible from every part of the wood. He could scarcely distinguish those who shouted his name, but he could be seen by all. Had there been a thousand muskets in the wood, he offered them a target. He could distinguish nothing in the coppice, but the fiery eyes of all were directed upon him.

He took off his hat, turned back the brim, and drawing from his pocket a white cockade, he pulled out a long dry thorn from a furze-bush, with which he fastened the cockade to the brim of his hat, then replaced it on his head, the upturned brim revealing his forehead and the cockade, and in a loud voice, as though addressing the wide forest, he said:—

"I am the man you seek. I am the Marquis de Lantenac, Viscount de Fontenay, Breton Prince, Lieutenant-General of the armies of the king. Make an end of it. Aim! Fire!"

And opening with both hands his goat-skin waistcoat, he bared his breast.

Lowering his eyes to see the levelled guns, he beheld himself surrounded by kneeling men.

A great shout went up,—"Long live Lantenac! Long live our lord! Long live the General!"

At the same time hats were thrown up and sabres whirled joyously, while from all sides brown woollen caps hoisted on long poles were waving in the air.

A Vendean band surrounded him.

At the sight of him they fell on their knees.

Legends tell us that the ancient Thuringian forests were inhabited by strange beings,—a race of giants, at once superior and inferior to men,—whom the Romans regarded as horrible beasts, and the Germans as divine incarnations, and who might chance to be exterminated or worshipped according to the race they encountered.

A sensation similar to that which may have been felt by one of those beings was experienced by the Marquis when, expecting to be treated like a monster, he was suddenly worshipped as a deity.

All those flashing eyes were fastened upon him with a kind of savage love.

The crowd were armed with guns, sabres, scythes, poles, and sticks. All wore large felt hats or brown caps, with white cockades, a profusion of rosaries and charms, wide breeches left open at the knee, jackets of skin, and leather gaiters; the calves of their legs were bare, and they wore their hair long; some looked fierce, but all had frank and open countenances.

A young man of noble bearing passed through the crowd of kneeling men and hastily approached the Marquis. He wore a felt hat with an upturned brim, a white cockade, and a skin jacket, like the peasants; but his hands were delicate and his linen was fine, and over his waistcoat was a white silk scarf, from which hung a sword with a golden hilt.

Having reached the *hure*, he threw aside his hat, unfastened his scarf, and kneeling, presented to the Marquis both scarf and sword.

"Indeed we were seeking for you," he said, "and we have found you. Receive the sword of command. These men are yours now. I was their commander; now am I promoted, since I become your soldier. Accept our devotion, my lord. General, give me your orders."

At a sign from him, men carrying the tricolored banner came forth from the woods, and going up to the Marquis, placed it at his feet. It was the one he had seen through the trees.

"General," said the young man who presented the sword and the scarf, "this is the flag which we took from the Blues who held the farm Herbe-en-Pail. My name is Gavard, my lord. I was with the Marquis de la Rouarie."

"Very well," said the Marquis.

And calm and composed he girded on the scarf.

Then he pulled out his sword, and waving it above his head, he cried,—

"Rise! And long live the king!"

All started to their feet. Then from the depth of the woods arose a tumultuous and triumphant cry,—

"Long live the king! Long live our Marquis! Long live Lantenac!"

The Marquis turned towards Gavard.

"How many are you?"

"Seven thousand."

While they were descending the hill, the peasants clearing away the furze-bushes to make a path for the Marquis de Lantenac, Gavard continued:—

"All this may be explained in a word, my lord: nothing could be more simple. It needed but a spark. The republican placard in revealing your presence has roused the country for the king. Besides, we have been secretly notified by the mayor of Granville, who is one of us,—the same who saved the Abbé Ollivier. They rang the tocsin last night."

"For whom?"

"For you."

"Ah!" said the Marquis.

"And here we are," continued Gavard.

"And you number seven thousand?"

"Today. But we shall be fifteen thousand tomorrow. It is the Breton contingent. When Monsieur Henri de la Rochejaquelein went to join the catholic army they sounded the tocsin, and in one night six parishes—Isernay, Corqueux, Échaubroignes, Aubiers, Sainte Aubin, and Nueil—sent him ten thousand men. They had no munitions of war, but having found at a quarryman's house sixty pounds of blasting-powder, Monsieur de la Rochejaquelein took his departure with that. We felt sure you must be somewhere in these woods, and we were looking for you."

"And you attacked the Blues at the farm Herbe-en-Pail?"

"The wind prevented them from hearing the tocsin, and they mistrusted nothing; the population of the hamlet, a set of clowns, received them well. This morning we invested the farm while the Blues were sleeping, and the thing was over in a trice. I have a horse here; will you deign to accept it, general?"

"Yes."

A peasant led up a white horse with military housings. The Marquis mounted him without accepting Gavard's proffered assistance.

"Hurrah!" cried the peasants. The English fashion of cheering is much in vogue on the Breton coast, for the people have continual dealings with the Channel islands.

Gavard made the military salute, asking, as he did so, "Where will you establish your headquarters, my lord?"

"At first, in the forest of Fougères."

"It is one of the seven forests belonging to you."

"We need a priest."

"We have one."

"Who is it?"

"The curate of the Chapelle-Erbrée."

"I know him. He has made the trip to Jersey." A priest stepped out from the ranks and said,—

"Three times."

The Marquis turned his head.

"Good morning, Monsieur le Curé. There is work in store for you."

"So much the better, Monsieur le Marquis."

"You will have to hear the confessions of such as desire your services. No one will be forced."

"Marquis," said the priest, "at Guéménée, Gaston compels the republicans to confess."

"He is a hairdresser. The dying should be allowed free choice in such a matter."

Gavard, who had gone away to give certain orders, now returned.

"I await your commands, general."

"In the first place, the rendez-vous is in the forest of Fougères. Direct the men to separate and meet there."

"The order has been given."

"Did you not say that the people of Herbe-en-Pail were friendly to the Blues?"

"Yes, general."

"Was the farm burned?"

"Yes."

"Did you burn the hamlet?"

"No."

"Burn it."

"The Blues tried to defend themselves. But they numbered one hundred and fifty, while we were seven thousand."

"What Blues are they?"

"Those of Santerre."

"He who ordered the drums to beat while they were beheading the king? Then it is a Parisian battalion?"

"A demi-battalion."

"What was it called?"

"Their banner has on it, 'Battalion of the Bonnet-Rouge.'"

"Wild beasts."

"What is to be done with the wounded?"

"Put an end to them."

"What are we to do with the prisoners?"

"Shoot them."

"There are about eighty of them."

"Shoot them all."

"There are two women."

"Treat them all alike."

"And three children."

"Bring them along. We will decide what Is to be done with them."
And the Marquis spurred his horse forward.

VII

No Mercy![2] No Quarter![3]

WHILE THESE EVENTS WERE TRANSPIRING in the vicinity of Tanis, the beggar had gone towards Crollon. He plunged into the ravines, under wide leafy bowers, heedless of all things, noticing nothing; as he himself had expressed it, dreaming rather than thinking,—for the thinker has an object, but the dreamer has none; wandering, rambling, pausing, munching here and there a sprig of wild sorrel, drinking at the springs, raising his head from time to time as distant sounds attracted his attention, then yielding again to the irresistible fascination of nature; presenting his rags to the sunlight, hearing human sounds, by chance, but listening to the singing of birds.

He was old and slow; as he told the Marquis of Lantenac, he could not go far; a quarter of a mile fatigued him; he made a short circuit towards Croix-Avranchin, and it was evening when he returned.

A little beyond Macey, the path he followed led him to a sort of elevation, destitute of trees, which commanded a wide expanse of country, including the entire horizon from the west as far as the sea.

A smoke attracted his attention.

There is nothing more delightful than a smoke, and nothing more alarming. There are smokes signifying peace, and smokes that mean mischief. In the density and color of a column of smoke lies all the difference between war and peace, brotherly love and hatred, hospitality and the grave, life and death. A smoke rising among the trees may mean the sweetest thing in all the world,—the family hearth, or the most dreadful of calamities,—a conflagration. And the entire happiness or misery of a human being is sometimes centred in a vapor, scattered by the wind. The smoke which Tellmarch saw was of a kind to excite anxiety.

It was black with sudden flashes of red light, as though the furnace from whence it sprung burned fitfully and was gradually dying out, and

2. Watchword of the Commune.
3. Watchword of the Princes.

it rose above Herbe-en-Pail. Tellmarch hurried along, walking towards the smoke. He was tired, but he wanted to know what it meant.

He reached the top of a hillock, behind which nestled a hamlet and the farm.

Neither farm nor hamlet was to be seen.

A heap of ruins was still burning, all that remained of Herbe-en-Pail.

It is much more heart-rending to see a cottage burn than a palace. A cottage in flames is a pitiful sight. Devastation swooping down on poverty, a vulture pouncing upon an earth-worm,—there is a sense of repugnance about it that makes one shudder.

If we believe the Biblical legend, the sight of a conflagration once turned a human being into a statue. For an instant a similar change came over Tellmarch. The sight before his eyes transfixed him to the spot. The work of destruction went on in silence. Not a cry was heard; not a human sigh mingled with the smoke. That furnace pursued its task of devouring the village with no other sound than the splitting of timbers and the crackling of thatch. From time to time the clouds of smoke were rent, the falling roofs revealed the gaping chambers, the fiery furnace displayed all its rubies, the poor rags turned scarlet, and the wretched old furniture, tinged with purple, stood out amid these dull red interiors; Tellmarch was dazed by the terrible calamity.

Several trees of a neighboring chestnut-grove had caught fire and were in a blaze.

He listened, trying to hear a voice, a call, or some kind of a noise. Nothing stirred but the flames; all was still save the fire. Had all the inhabitants fled?

Where was the community that lived and labored at Herbe-en-Pail? What had become of this little family?

Tellmarch descended the hillock.

A gloomy enigma lay before him. He approached it slowly, gazing at it steadily. He advanced towards the ruin with the deliberation of a shadow, feeling like a ghost in this tomb.

Having reached what had formerly been the door of the farm, he looked into the yard, whose ruined walls no longer separated it from the surrounding hamlet.

What he had seen before was nothing as compared with what he now beheld. From afar he had seen the terror of it; now all its horrors lay before him.

In the middle of the yard was a dark mass, vaguely outlined on one side by the flames, and on the other by the moonlight. It was a heap of men; and these men were dead. Around this mound lay a wide pool, still smoking, whose surface reflected the flames; but it needed not the fire to redden it; it was of blood.

Tellmarch went up to it. He examined, one after another, these prostrate bodies; all were corpses. Both the moon and the conflagration lighted up the scene.

The dead bodies were those of soldiers. Every man had bare feet; both their shoes and their weapons had been taken from them, but they still wore their blue uniforms. Here and there one could distinguish, amid the confusion of the limbs and heads, hats bearing the tricolor cockades riddled with bullets. They were republicans,—the same Parisians who the previous evening had been living, active men, garrisoned at the farm Herbe-en-Pail. The symmetrical arrangement of the fallen bodies proved the affair to have been an execution. They had been shot on the spot, and with precision. They were all dead. Not a sound came from the mass.

Tellmarch examined each individual corpse, and every man was riddled with shot.

Their executioners, doubtless in haste to depart, had not taken time to bury them.

Just as he was about to leave the place, his attention was attracted by the sight of four feet protruding beyond the corner of a low wall in the yard.

These feet were smaller than those which he had previously seen; there were shoes upon them, and as he drew near he perceived that they were the feet of women.

Two women were lying side by side behind the wall, also shot.

Tellmarch stooped over them. One of them wore a kind of uniform; beside her was a jug, broken and empty. She was a vivandière. She had four balls in her head. She was dead.

Tellmarch examined the other, who was a peasant woman. Her eyes were closed, her mouth open, her face discolored; but there were no wounds in her head. Her dress, undoubtedly worn to shreds by long marches, was rent by her fall, exposing her bosom. Tellmarch pushed it still further aside, and discovered on her shoulder a round wound made by a ball; the shoulder-blade was broken. He gazed upon her livid breast.

"A nursing mother," he murmured.

He touched her. She was not cold.

The broken bone and the wound in the shoulder were her only injuries. He placed his hand on her breast, and felt a faint throb. She was not dead.

Tellmarch raised himself, and cried out in a terrible voice,—

"Is there no one here?"

"Is that you, Caimand?" replied a voice, so low that it could scarcely be heard.

At the same time a head emerged from a hole in the ruin, and the next moment a second one peered forth from another aperture.

These were the sole survivors,—two peasants who had managed to hide themselves, and who now, reassured by the familiar voice of the Caimand, crept out of the hiding-places where they had been crouching.

They approached Tellmarch, still trembling violently.

The latter had found strength to utter his cry, but he could not speak; deep emotions always produce this effect.

He pointed to the woman lying at his feet.

"Is she still alive?" asked one of the peasants.

Tellmarch nodded.

"And the other woman,—is she living too?" asked the second peasant.

Tellmarch shook his head.

The peasant who had been the first to show himself continued:—

"All the others are dead, are they not? I saw it all. I was in my cellar. How grateful one is to God, in times like these, to have no family! My house was burned. Lord Jesus! everybody was killed. This woman had children,—three little ones! The children cried, 'Mother!' The mother cried, 'Oh, my children!' They killed the mother and carried away the children. I saw all,—oh, my God! my God! Those who murdered them went off well pleased. They carried away the little ones, and killed the mother. But she is not dead, is she? I say, Caimand, do you think you could save her? Don't you want us to help you carry her to your *carnichot?*"

Tellmarch nodded.

The woods were near the farm. They quickly made a litter with branches and ferns, and placing the woman, still motionless, upon it, they started towards the grove, the two peasants bearing the litter, one at the head, the other at the foot, while Tellmarch supported the woman's arm and constantly felt her pulse.

On the way the two peasants talked; and over the body of the bleeding woman, whose pale face was lighted by the moon, they exchanged their frightened exclamations.

"To kill all!"

"To burn all!"

"Oh, my Lord! Is that the way they are going to do now?"

"It was that tall old man who ordered it."

"Yes; he was the commander."

"I did not see him while the shooting went on. Was he there?"

"No, he was gone. But it was done by his order, all the same."

"Then it was he who did this."

"He said, 'Kill, burn! No quarter!'"

"Is he a marquis?"

"Yes, of course; he is our marquis."

"What is his name?"

"It is Monsieur de Lantenac."

Tellmarch raised his eyes to heaven, murmuring between his teeth,—"Had I but known!"

PART II
AT PARIS

Book I

CIMOURDAIN

I

The Streets of Paris at that Time

PEOPLE LIVED IN PUBLIC; THEY ate at tables spread outside the doors; women sat on the church steps, making lint to the accompaniment of the Marseillaise; the park of Monceaux and the Luxembourg were turned into parade-grounds; at every street-corner there was a gun-maker's shop, where muskets were manufactured before the eyes of the passers-by, to their great admiration. "Patience: this is revolution" was on every lip. People smiled heroically. They went to the theatre as in Athens during the Peloponnesian war. At street-corners were seen such playbills as these, advertising: "The Siege of Thionville;" "A Mother saved from the Flames;" "The Club of Sans-Soucis;" "The oldest of the Popes Joan;" "The Military Philosophers;" "The Art of Love-making in the Village." The Germans were at the gates; it was rumored that the King of Prussia had secured boxes for the opera. Everything was terrible, yet no one was frightened. The grewsome law against the suspected, which was the crime of Merlin de Douai, held a vision of the guillotine suspended over every head. A lawyer, Séran by name, learning that he had been denounced, calmly awaited his arrest, arrayed in his dressing-gown and slippers, playing the flute at his window. No one seemed to have any spare time, every one was in a hurry; all the hats bore their cockades, and the women cried, "Are not red caps becoming to us?" All Paris seemed in the act of changing its abode. The curiosity shops were filled with crowns, mitres, gilded sceptres, and fleur-de-lis, spoils from royal dwellings,—the signs of the destruction of monarchy. Copes and surplices might be seen hanging on hooks offered for sale at the old-clothes shops. At the Porcherons and at Ramponneau's men decked out in surplices and stoles bestrode donkeys caparisoned with chasubles, and drank wine from ecclesiastical ciboria. In the Rue Saint-Jacques barefooted street-pavers once stopped the wheelbarrow of a shoe-pedler and clubbing together bought fifteen pairs of shoes to send to the Convention "for our soldiers." Busts of Rousseau, Franklin, Brutus, and even, be it added, of Marat, abounded. In the Rue Cloche-Perce, below one of Marat's busts, in a black wooden frame under glass, hung a formula of prosecution against Malouet, with facts in support of the charges and the following lines inscribed on the margin:—

These details were given to me by the mistress of Sylvain
Bailly, a good patriot, and who had a liking for me.

Signed: MARAT

The inscription on the Palais Royal fountain, "Quantos effundit in usus!" was hidden under two large canvases painted in distemper, one representing Cahier de Gerville denouncing to the National Assembly the rallying-cry of the "Chiffonistes" of Arles; the other, Louis XVI brought back from Varennes in his royal carriage, and under the carriage a plank fastened by cords bearing on each end a grenadier with levelled bayonet. Very few large shops were open; perambulating carts containing haberdashery and toys, lighted by tallow candles, which, melting, dripped upon the merchandise, were dragged through the streets by women. Ex-nuns adorned with blond wigs kept open shop; this woman, darning stockings in a stall, was a countess; that dressmaker, a marchioness; Madame de Boufflers lived in an attic from which she had a view of her own hotel. Venders ran about offering the news bulletins. People who muffled their chins in their neck-cloths were called "écrouelleux." Street singers swarmed. The crowd hooted Pitou, the royalist song-writer, a brave man, to boot, for he was imprisoned twenty-two times and was brought before the revolutionary tribunal for slapping himself behind when he uttered the word "civism;" seeing that his head was in danger, he exclaimed, "But my head is not the offending member!" which made the judges laugh, and saved his life. This Pitou ridiculed the fashion of Greek and Latin names; his favorite song was about a cobbler and his wife whom he called Cujus and Cujusdam. The Carmagnole was danced in circles; they no longer said "lady" and "gentleman," but "citizen" and "citizeness." They danced in the ruined cloisters, beneath a chandelier made of two sticks fastened crosswise to the vaulted roof, bearing four candles, while the church lamps burned upon the altar, and tombs lay beneath the dancers' feet. They wore "tyrant-blue" waistcoats, and shirt-pins called "liberty's cap," composed of red, white, and blue stones. The Rue de Richelieu was called Rue de la Loi; the Faubourg Saint-Antoine, the Faubourg de Gloire; a statue of Nature stood in the Place de la Bastille. People pointed out to each other well-known personages,—Châtelet, Didier, Nicolas, and Gamier-Delaunay, who mounted guard at the doors of the joiner Duplay; Voullant, who never missed a day of guillotining, and who followed the tumbrils of the condemned, calling it "going to the red mass;" Montflabert, a revolutionary juryman and marquis whom they called *Dix-Août*. They watched the pupils of the École Militaire file past, called "aspirants to the school of Mars" by the decrees of the Convention, and nicknamed by the people "Robespierre's pages." They read the proclamations of Fréron, denouncing those suspected of the crime of "négotiantisime." Young scapegraces gathered about the doors of the mayoralties crowding the brides and grooms as they came in sight, and shouting, "Municipal marriages," in derision of the civil ceremony. The statues of the saints and kings at the Invalides were crowned with Phrygian caps. They played cards on curbstones at the crossings, and the very cards themselves were totally revolutionized; kings were replaced by genii, queens by the Goddess of Liberty, knaves by Equality, aces by emblems of Law. The public gardens were tilled; they ploughed the Tuileries.

With all this was intermingled, especially among the conquered party, an indescribably haughty weariness of living. A man wrote to Fouquier-Tinville, "Be so kind as to lift from me the burden of life. This is my address." Champcenetz was arrested for exclaiming at the Palais Royal: "When are we to have a Turkish revolution? I should like to see the republic *à la Porte.*"[1] Newspapers abounded. Hair-dressers' apprentices curled the women's wigs in public while the master read the "Moniteur" aloud; others, surrounded by listeners, commented with expressive gesticulations on the journal "Entendons nous," of Dubois Crancé, or the "Trompette du père Bellerose." Sometimes a man was both a barber and a pork-dealer; and hams and chitterlings would hang side by side with a golden-haired doll. The wines of the Émigrés were sold by dealers on the streets. One merchant advertised wine of fifty-two different brands; others retailed lyre-shaped clocks and sofas *à la duchesse.* A hairdresser had the following notice printed on his sign: "I shave the clergy; I dress the hair of the nobility; I wait upon the Tiers-État." People went to Martin, at No. 173 in the Rue d'Anjou, formerly called Rue Dauphine, to have their fortune told. Bread, coal, and soap

---

1. A pan meaning a Turkish republic, and the republic expelled.—Tr.

were scarce. Herds of milch-cows on their way from the provinces were constantly passing. At La Vallée, lamb was sold at fifteen francs a pound. An order of the Commune assigned to each person a pound of meat for every ten days. People stood in files at the shop-doors; one file that reached from the door of a grocer's shop in the Rue du Petit-Carreau to the middle of the Rue Montorgueil has become a matter of tradition. Forming a queue was called "holding the string," on account of the long cord held by those who stood in line one behind the other.

In the midst of all this wretchedness women were brave and gentle. They passed whole nights waiting their turn to be served at the baker's. The revolution was successful in its expedients. It alleviated this wide-spread misery by two dangerous measures,—the assignat and the maximum; in other words, the lever and the fulcrum. France was actually saved by empiricism. The enemy, both in Coblentz and in London, speculated in assignats.

Girls went hither and thither offering lavender-water, garters, and false hair, and selling stocks at the same time; there were stock-jobbers on the steps of the Rue Vivienne, with muddy shoes, greasy hair, woollen caps with fox-tails, and the dandies of the Rue de Valois, with their polished boots, a toothpick in their mouths, and beaver hats on their heads, to whom the girls said "thee and thou." The people hunted them down as they did thieves, whom the royalists called "active citizens." Robbery, however, seldom occurred; the fearful destitution was matched by a stoical honesty. With downcast eyes the barefooted and the hungry went gravely past the shop-windows of the jewellers of the Palais Égalité. During a domiciliary visit made by the Section Antoine at Beaumarchais' house, a woman plucked a flower in the garden: the crowd boxed her ears. A cord of wood cost four hundred francs in coin. People were to be seen in the streets sawing up their wooden beds. In the winter the fountains froze, and two pails of water cost twenty sous; every man was his own water-carrier. A gold louis was worth three thousand nine hundred and fifty francs. A ride in a fiacre cost six hundred francs. After a day's ride the following dialogue might be heard: "How much do I owe you, coachman?" "Six thousand livres." The trade of a greengrocer woman amounted to twenty thousand francs a day. A beggar was known to have said: "Help me, for charity's sake! I want two hundred and thirty livres to pay for my shoes." At the entrance of the bridges might be seen colossal figures, sculptured and painted by David, which Mercier insultingly called "enormous wooden

Punchinellos." These figures represented Federalism and Coalition overthrown. No infirmity of purpose among the people. There was a gloomy sense of pleasure in having put an end to thrones. No lack of volunteers ready to lay down their lives: every street furnished a battalion. The flags of the district went hither and thither, each one with its own device. On the banner of the Capuchin District might be read, "No one will shave us;" on another, "No other nobility save that of the heart." On the walls were placards, large and small, white, yellow, green, and red, printed and written, on all which might be read this war-cry: "Long live the Republic!" Little children lisped, "Ça ira."

These little children were the nucleus of a great future.

Later on, a cynical city took the place of the tragical one; the streets of Paris have displayed two distinct revolutionary aspects,—the one preceding the 9th Thermidor, and that which followed it. After the Paris of Saint-Just came the Paris of Tallien. Such are the constant antitheses of Almighty God. Immediately after Sinai, the Courtille appeared.

Paroxysms of popular folly may always be expected. The same thing had taken place eighty years before. After Louis XIV, as well as after Robespierre, the people needed breathing space; hence the Regency at the opening of the century and the Directory at its close, each reign of terror ending in a Saturnalia. France fled from the Puritan as well as from the monarchical cloister with the joy of a nation escaping from bondage.

After the 9th Thermidor, Paris was like one gone mad with gayety. An unwholesome joy prevailed, exceeding all bounds. The frenzy of life followed the frenzy of death, and grandeur eclipsed itself. They had a Trimalcion whom they called Grimod de la Reynière; also an "Almanach des Gourmands." People dined to the accompaniment of trumpets in the entresols of the Palais Royal; the orchestras were composed of women beating drums and blowing trumpets; the "rigadooner," bow in hand, reigned over all; they supped after the Oriental fashion at Méot's, surrounded by censers of perfume. The artist Boze painted his daughters, innocent and charming heads of sixteen, "en guillotinés,"—that is, bare-necked and in red chemises. The wild dances in ruined churches were followed by the balls of Ruggieri, Luquet Wenzel, Mauduit, and the Montansier; to the dignified *citoyennes* making lint, succeeded sultanas, savages, and nymphs; to the bare feet of the soldiers, disfigured by blood, mud, and dust, succeeded the bare feet of women adorned with diamonds; and together with shamelessness came dishonesty,—which had its purveyors in high places, and their imitators in the lower ranks.

Paris was infested by swarms of sharpers, and every man had to watch his "luc," or in other words, his pocket-book. One of the amusements was to go to the Place of the Palais de Justice to see the female acrobats on the tabouret; they were forced to tie their skirts down. At the doors of the theatres street-urchins offered cabs, crying, "Citizen and Citizeness, there is room enough for two." They sold no more copies of "The Old Cordelier" or of "L'Ami du peuple;" but in their stead they offered "Punch's Letter" and "The Rogues' Petition." The Marquis de Sade presided at the section of the Pikes, Place Vendôme. The reaction was both jovial and ferocious. The Dragons of Liberty of '92 were revived under the name of Knights of the Dagger. At the same time there appeared on the stage the type Jocrisse. There were the "Merveilleuses," and after the "Merveilleuses," the "Inconcevables." People swore fantastic oaths by "sa paole victimée" and by "sa paole verte." This was the recoil from Mirabeau to Bobèche. Paris vibrates like an enormous pendulum of civilization; now it touches one pole, now the other,—Thermopylæ and Gomorrah. After '93, Revolution suffered a singular eclipse: the century apparently forgot to finish what it had begun; a strange orgie, interposing, took possession of the foreground, and thrusting the dread Apocalypse behind, it drew a veil over the monstrous vision, and shouted with laughter after its fright; tragedy vanished in parody; and rising from the horizon's edge the smoke of carnival obscured the outlines of Medusa.

But in the year '93 the streets of Paris still retained the imposing and fierce aspect of the beginning. They had their orators, like Varlot for instance, who travelled about in a booth on wheels, from the top of which he harangued the passers-by; their heroes, one of whom was called "the Captain of iron-shod poles;" their favorites, like Guffroy, the author of the pamphlet "Rougiff." Some of these celebrities were mischievous, others exerted a wholesome influence. One among all the rest was honest and filial,—it was Cimourdain.

II

Cimourdain

CIMOURDAIN HAD A PURE BUT gloomy soul. There was something of the absolute within him. He had been a priest, which is a serious matter. A man may, like the heavens, enjoy a gloomy serenity,—it needs only an influence powerful enough to create night within his soul; and the priesthood had done this thing for Cimourdain. To be once a priest is to be a priest forever.

Though there be night within us, we may still possess the stars. Cimourdain was a man of many virtues and truths, but they shone amid the darkness.

His story may be told in a few words. He had been a village curate, and tutor in an influential family; but falling heir to a small legacy, he had thereby gained his freedom.

He was obstinate to the last degree. He employed meditation as the artisan uses his pincers. He believed it wrong to abandon an idea until he had fully developed it. His method of thought was intense. He was familiar with all the European languages, and had some acquaintance with other tongues. His devotion to study was a great help towards the preservation of his chastity. But there is nothing more dangerous than such a system of repression.

Either from pride, circumstances, or loftiness of soul, he had been true to his priestly vows; but his faith he had not been able to keep. Science had crushed it; all his dogmas had gone from him. Then, looking into his own soul, he saw therein a mutilated being, and having no power to rid himself of his priesthood, he tried, after an austere fashion, to remould the man. For want of a family he adopted his country; a wife had been refused him,—he had wedded humanity. There is a certain sense of emptiness in this all-embracing zeal.

His parents, who were peasants, had thought to lift him above the common people by consecrating him to the priesthood; he had returned among them of his own accord, and with a feeling of passionate devotion watched the suffering with intense sympathy. From a priest he had become a philosopher, and from a philosopher an athlete. Even during the life of Louis XV, Cimourdain had vaguely fancied himself a republican. But of what republic? Perhaps of the Republic of Plato, and it might be of Draco also. Forbidden to love, he devoted himself to hating. He detested lies, monarchy, theocracy, and his priestly garb; he hated the present, and eagerly invoked the future; he had a presentiment of what it would be, he foresaw it, he pictured it, both terrible and grand. In order to put an end to this deplorable human misery, he felt the need of a leader who would appear not only as an avenger but also as a liberator. He worshipped the catastrophe from afar.

In 1789 this catastrophe came and found him ready. Cimourdain flung himself into that gigantic scheme for human regeneration on logical principles, which, for a mind constituted like his, is equivalent to saying with inexorable determination. Logic is not a softening influence. He had survived the great revolutionary years, and had been shaken by the blasts thereof,—in '89, the fall of the Bastille, the end of the martyrdom of people; in.'90, on the 19th of June, the end of the feudal system; in '91, Varennes, and the end of royalty; in '92, the birth of the Republic. He had seen the rise of Revolution. He was not the man to fear that giant; on the contrary, the universal growth had given him new life, and though already advanced in years,—for he was fifty, and a priest ages faster than other men,—he too began to develop. From year to year he had watched and kept pace with the progress of events. At first he had feared lest Revolution might fail; he watched it. Since it had both logic and justice on its side, he expected its success, and his confidence increased in proportion to the fear it inspired; he would have this Minerva crowned with the stars of the future,—a Pallas likewise bearing the Gorgon's head for her buckler. In case of need he would have wished an infernal glare to flash from her divine eyes upon the demons, paying them back in their own coin.

Thus he reached '93.

'93 is the war of Europe against France, and of France against Paris. What then is Revolution? It is the victory of France over Europe, and of Paris over France. Hence the immensity of that terrible moment '93, grander than all the rest of the century.

Nothing could be more tragic. Europe attacking France, and France attacking Paris,—a drama with the proportions of an epic.

'93 is a year of intense action. The tempest is there in all its wrath and grandeur. Cimourdain felt himself in his element. This scene of distraction, wild and magnificent, suited the compass of his outspread wings. Like a sea-eagle, he united a profound inward calm with a relish for external danger. Certain winged natures, souls of the tempest, ferocious yet tranquil, seem eminently fitted for combatting the storms of life.

His sense of pity was never kindled, save in behalf of the wretched. He devoted himself to those forms of suffering that are most repulsive. For him nothing was abhorrent. That was his kind of goodness. He was divine in his zeal to relieve the most loathsome sufferers. He searched for ulcers that he might kiss them. Those noble actions which are hideous to look upon are the most difficult to perform; for such he had a preference. One day at the Hôtel-Dieu a man was at the point of death, suffocating with a tumor in the throat,—a putrid, malignant, and perhaps contagious abscess, which must be opened at once. Cimourdain was there; he put his lips to the abscess, sucked it, spitting it out as his mouth filled, emptied the tumor and saved the man. As he still was wearing his priestly garb at the time, some one said to him: "Had you done that for the king you would be made a bishop." "I would not do it for the king," replied Cimourdain. The act and the answer made him popular in the gloomy quarters of Paris to a degree that won for him unbounded influence over the classes that suffer, weep, and struggle for vengeance. When the public indignation, that fruitful source of blunders, rose high against the monopolists, it was Cimourdain who by a word prevented the sacking of a boat laden with soap at the Saint-Nicolas quay, and who dispersed the furious crowds that were stopping the carriages at the barrier Saint-Lazare.

He it was who ten days after the 10th of August marshalled the people who went forth to overthrow the statues of kings, which as they fell cost some of them their lives. On the Place Vendôme, a woman, Reine Violet, pulling at the rope she had fastened around the neck of Louis XIV, was crushed to death beneath its weight. This statue had been standing for a hundred years: it was erected on the 12th of August, 1692; it was overthrown on the 12th of August, 1793. On the Place de la Concorde one Guinguerlot, having called the demolishers "canaille," was butchered on the pedestal of the statue of Louis XV. The statue itself was hacked to pieces; later, it was melted into sous. One arm alone escaped,—the right arm, which Louis XV held outstretched with the gesture of a Roman emperor. By request of Cimourdain the people sent a deputation to offer this arm to Latude, a man who had been buried alive in the Bastille for forty years. When Latude with an iron collar round his neck and a chain round his loins was rotting alive in that prison at the bidding of the king whose statue overlooked Paris, who could have prophesied to him that both prison and statue would fall, and that he would come forth from his tomb,—he, the prisoner, would be the master of that hand of bronze which had signed his warrant, and that nothing would be left of this monarch of clay save his brazen arm?

Cimourdain was one of those men who possess an inward monitor, and who when they appear absent-minded are simply listening to its voice.

Cimourdain was both learned and ignorant. He was versed in science, and knew nothing whatever of life; hence his severity. His eyes were bandaged like those of Homer's Themis: he possessed the blind certainty of an arrow,—that, seeing naught besides, flies straight to the goal. In revolution there is nothing so formidable as the straight line. Cimourdain went straight ahead, with fatal results. He believed that in these social geneses the farthest point is solid ground,—an error common to minds in which logic occupies the place of reason. He went beyond the Convention, beyond the Commune: he belonged to the Évêché.

The society called the Évêché because it held its meetings in a hall of the old episcopal palace was rather a medley of men than a society. There were present, as in the Commune, those silent but important spectators who, as Garat expressed it, "had about them as many pistols as they had pockets." The Évêché was a queer mixture, both cosmopolitan and Parisian,—no contradiction in terms, since Paris is the place where throbs the heart of all nations. There at the Évêché was the great plebeian incandescence. As compared with the Évêché, the Convention was cold and the Commune lukewarm. It was one of those revolutionary formations which partake of the nature of a volcano. The Évêché combined everything,—ignorance, stupidity, honesty, heroism, wrath, and policy. Brunswick had agents therein. It held men worthy of Sparta, and others fit only for the galleys. The greater number of them were mad and honest. The Gironde, speaking in the person of Isnard, temporary president of the Convention, had uttered this appalling prophecy: "Parisians, beware! for in your city not one stone shall be left resting upon another, and the day will come when men will search for the place where Paris once stood." This speech had given Birth to the Évêché. Certain men—and as we have just said, men of all nations—had felt the need of drawing closer to Paris. Cimourdain joined this group.

The party reacted against the reactionists. It sprang from that public necessity for violence which constitutes the formidable and mysterious side of revolutions. Strong in this strength, the Évêché at once defined its position. In the disturbances of Paris it was the Commune that fired the cannon, and the Évêché that sounded the alarm.

In his inexorable sincerity Cimourdain believed that all means are fair when devoted to the service of truth,—a conviction which eminently fitted him for the control of extremists of all parties. Scoundrels perceived him to be honest, and were satisfied. Crime is flattered to feel that virtue has taken it in charge. It is rather embarrassing, but pleasing nevertheless. Palloy the architect, who had taken advantage of the destruction of the Bastille to sell the stones for his own benefit, and who, being appointed to paint the cell of Louis XVI, had in his zeal covered the wall with bars, chains, and iron collars; Gonchon, the suspected orator of the Faubourg Saint-Antoine, whose receipts were found later; the American Fournier, who on the 17th of July fired a pistol-shot at Lafayette,—an act for which, they said, Lafayette himself had paid; Henriot, who had come from Bicêtre, and who had been a lackey, a juggler, a thief, and a spy before he turned general and levelled his guns on the Convention; La Reynie, formerly grand-vicar of Chartres, who had substituted "Père Duchesne" for his breviary,—all these men were respected by Cimourdain, and all that was needed to keep the worst of them from stumbling occasionally was to feel that really formidable and determined candor like a judgment before them. It was thus that Saint-Just terrified Schneider. At the same time the majority in the Évêché, consisting for the most part of poor and violent men, sincere in their purposes, believed in Cimourdain and followed him. His vicar or aide-de-camp, whichever you choose to call him, was Danjou,—that other republican priest, whose lofty stature endeared him to the people, who called him the Abbé Six-Pieds. Cimourdain could have led whithersoever he chose that fearless chief called Général la Pique and the bold Truchon (surnamed Grand-Nicolas), who tried to save Madame de Lamballe, offering her his arm to assist her in leaping over the corpses,—an attempt which would have proved successful had it not been for the barbarous joke of Chariot the barber.

The Commune kept watch over the Convention, and the Évêché over the Commune. Cimourdain, an upright man, despising intrigues, had broken more than one mysterious thread in the hands of Pache, whom Beurnonville called "the black man." At the Évêché, Cimourdain was on good terms with all. He was consulted by Dobsent and Momoro. He spoke Spanish to Gusman, Italian to Pio, English to Arthur, Flemish to Pereyra, German to the Austrian Proly, the bastard of a prince. He reconciled all these discordant elements: hence his strong though obscure position. Hébert feared him.

In those times and over those tragic assemblies Cimourdain possessed the power of the inexorable. He was a faultless man, who believed himself to be infallible. He had never been seen to weep. His was an inaccessible and frigid virtue; a just, but awful, man.

There are no half measures possible for a revolutionary priest. A priest who embarks in an adventure so portentous in its aims, is influenced either by the highest or the lowest motives; he must be either infamous or sublime. Cimourdain was sublime, but isolated in rugged inaccessibility, inhospitably repellent,—sublime in his surrounding of precipices. Lofty mountains possess this forbidding purity.

Cimourdain looked like an ordinary man, clothed in whatever happened to be convenient, rather poor in aspect. In his youth he had received the tonsure, and later in life had become bald. His few remaining locks were gray. Looking upon his forehead, expansive as it was, an observing eye could read his character. Cimourdain had an abrupt way of speaking, at once passionate and solemn; his utterance was rapid, his tone peremptory, the expression of his mouth sad and bitter; his eyes were clear and deep, and his whole face bore the impress of an unspeakable indignation. Such was Cimourdain.

Today his name is unknown.

History possesses these terrible incognitos.

III

A Corner not Dipped into the Styx

WAS SUCH A MAN IN very deed a man? Could the servant of all men feel a personal affection? Was he not too much of a soul to possess a heart? That vast embrace, enfolding everything and everybody, could it be limited to one? Could Cimourdain love? We answer, yes.

In his youth, when he was a tutor in an almost princely family, he had a pupil, the son and heir of the house, whom he loved. It is easy to love a child. What is there that one cannot forgive a child? One forgives him for being a lord, a prince, a king. His innocent age and his weakness make one forget the crimes of his race and the arrogance of his rank. He is so little that one pardons him for being great, the slave forgives him for being the master. The old negro idolizes the white nursling. Cimourdain had conceived a passionate love for his pupil. Childhood is so ineffably charming, it absorbs all love. All the power of loving in Cimourdain's nature had, so to speak, concentrated itself upon that child; the heart, condemned to solitude, fed upon this sweet and innocent creature, which it loved with the combined tenderness of a father, a brother, a friend, and a creator. To him he was indeed a son,—

not of the flesh, but of the soul; he was not his father, the author of his being, but he was his master, and this was his masterpiece. He had made a man of this little lord,—possibly a great man, who knows? Thus run our dreams. Without the knowledge of the family,—for does one require permission to create an intelligence, a well-directed will, and an upright character?—he had communicated to the young viscount, his pupil, all the advanced ideas that he himself held; he had inoculated him with the dread virus of his own virtue; he had infused into his veins his belief, his conscience, his ideal; into the brain of this aristocrat, as into a mould, he had poured the soul of the people. Mind seeks nourishment; intelligence is a breast. There is an analogy between the nurse who gives her milk and the tutor who gives his thought. Sometimes the tutor is more of a father than the actual father himself, just as the nurse is more like a mother than the natural mother. Cimourdain was closely bound to his pupil by the profound paternity of the soul. The very sight of the child touched him.

Let us add this: it was an easy matter to replace the father, since the child had none, he was an orphan; his father and mother were both dead; there was only a blind grandmother, and a great-uncle who did not live at home to watch over him. The grandmother died; the great-uncle, who was the head of the family, was a military man, a member of the high nobility, who held various appointments at Court; he avoided the old family dungeon, living at Versailles, changing his quarters with the army, and leaving the orphan alone in the solitary castle. Thus the preceptor was the master in every sense of the word. Furthermore, let us add, Cimourdain had witnessed the birth of his pupil. When almost a baby, the child had a serious illness; during the crisis Cimourdain had watched over him night and day. The doctor prescribes, but it is the nurse who saves, and Cimourdain had saved the child. Not only was his pupil indebted to him for his instruction, his education, and his knowledge, he also owed him his convalescence and his health; over and above the development of his mind he owed him his very life. We worship those who are indebted to us for everything; hence Cimourdain worshipped the child.

In the course of time the natural separation between them took place. Having finished his education, Cimourdain was obliged to leave the child, who had now become a young man. With what cold and careless cruelty such separations are planned! How calmly do families discharge the tutor, who leaves his soul behind him with the child, and the nurse who leaves her heart's blood! Cimourdain, having received his salary and his dismissal, had left the higher for the lower sphere; the partition that separates the great from the little had closed once more. The young lord, an officer by birth, received a captain's commission at the outset, and had departed to join some garrison. The humble tutor, already a rebellious priest in his secret heart, had lost no time in returning to the obscure ground-floor of the church, among the inferior clergy, and thus lost sight of his pupil.

Revolution came. The recollection still brooding within him of that creature whom he had transformed into a man was by no means lost, although buried beneath the immense accumulation of public affairs.

It is a noble deed to model a statue and breathe into it the breath of life; but to mould an intelligence and inspire it with the spirit of truth is far nobler. Cimourdain was the Pygmalion of a soul.

The mind may possess its offspring.

The only being on earth whom he loved was this pupil,—child and orphan as he was. Is such a man vulnerable to the influence of any affection whatsoever? We shall see.

Book II

THE POT-HOUSE OF THE RUE DU PAON

I

Minos, Æacus, and Rhadamanthus

IN THE RUE DU PAON there was an ale-house called by courtesy a café, and in this café a back-room which has since become famous in history. It was there that from time to time those men, so powerful and so closely watched that they dared not venture to speak to one another in public, held their secret meetings.

It was there, on the 23d day of October, 1792, that the Mountain and the Gironde exchanged their famous kiss. There, too, Garat—although he does not admit it in his memoirs—came for information during that rueful night when, after having placed Clavière in safety in the Rue de Beaune, he stopped his carriage on the Pont-Royal to listen to the tocsin. On the 28th of June, 1793, in this back-room, three men were gathered around a table. Their chairs did not touch. Each man occupied one of the three sides of the table, leaving the fourth one vacant. It was about eight o'clock in the evening. Although it was still light in the street, the back-room was dark, and a lamp—a luxury in those times—hanging from the ceiling threw its light upon the table. The first of those men was pale, young, and grave, with thin lips and a cold unsympathetic expression. There was a nervous twitching in his cheek, which must have been a drawback to the act of smiling. He was powdered and gloved, and his well-brushed and carefully-buttoned light-blue coat fitted him without a wrinkle. He wore nankeen breeches, white stockings, a high cravat, a plaited shirt-frill, and silver buckles on his shoes. Of the two other men, one was, so to speak, a giant, the other a dwarf. The tall man was negligently dressed in a loose coat of scarlet, with his neck bare, and a half-untied cravat hanging carelessly below his shirt-frill; his waistcoat was unfastened for want of buttons; he wore top-boots; and his hair, although dishevelled and bristling, still showed signs of former dressing; his wig looked very much like a mane, and his face was marked by the small-pox. Between his eyebrows was a line betokening a fierce temper, and at the corner of his mouth another, rather suggestive of a kindly nature. His lips were thick, his teeth large; he had the fist of a porter, and flashing eyes. The short personage was a yellow-looking man, who when seated had the effect of one deformed. His head was thrown back, his eyes blood-shot; livid patches covered his face; a handkerchief was tied over his straight, greasy hair; no forehead to speak of, but a monstrous and terrible mouth. He wore long trousers, slippers, a waistcoat that seemed originally to have been made of white satin, and over it a loose jacket, in the folds of which a hard straight line revealed the presence of a poniard. The first of these men was Robespierre, the second Danton, the third Marat.

They were alone in this room. Before Danton stood a bottle of wine covered with dust,—reminding one of Luther's half pint of beer,—a cup of coffee before Marat, and papers were spread in front of Robespierre.

Near the papers stood one of those round, heavy, ridged, leaden inkstands, which will be remembered by all who were schoolboys at the beginning of this century, and a pen had been thrown down beside it. A large brass seal bearing the words "Palloy fecit," and representing an exact miniature model of the Bastille, rested upon these papers. A map of France lay outspread in the middle of the table. Outside the door stood Marat's watchdog, one Laurent Basse, the same who was an agent at No. 18 Rue des Cordeliers, and who on the 13th of July, nearly a fortnight after this 28th of June, was to deal a blow with a chair upon the head of a woman named Charlotte Corday, who at this time was vaguely dreaming at Caen. Laurent Basse was the proof-carrier of "L'Ami du Peuple." On that evening, having been brought by his master to the café of the Rue du Paon, he was ordered to keep the room closed where Marat, Danton, and Robespierre were seated, and to admit no one, unless it were some person from the Committee of Public Safety, the Commune, or the Évêché.

Robespierre would not have it closed against Saint-Just, neither would Danton refuse admittance to Pache, or Marat to Gusman.

The subject of the conference, which had already lasted a long time, lay in the papers spread out on the table, which Robespierre had been reading aloud. The voices were gradually rising higher and higher. Something very like anger was developing between these three men. From without one could catch, from time to time, fragments of excited speech. In those days the custom of public tribunals seemed to have created a certain right to listen. It was at the time when the copying clerk, Fabricius Pâris, watched through the key-hole the proceedings of the Committee of Public Safety; not an act of supererogation, be it observed, for it was this very Pâris who notified Danton on the night of the 31st of March, 1794. Laurent Basse had his ear at the door of the back-room in which Danton, Marat, and Robespierre were seated; he served Marat, but he belonged to the Évêché.

II

Magna Testantur Voce Per Umbras

DANTON HAD JUST RISEN, PUSHING back his chair impetuously. "Listen!" he cried. "There is but one urgent business,—the Republic is in danger. I have but a single purpose, that is, to deliver France from the enemy. And to accomplish this, all means are fair. All! All! All! I have to deal with every form of danger. I employ every variety of expedient, and when all is to be feared, then I venture all. My thought is a lioness. No half measures, no squeamishness in revolution. Nemesis is not a haughty prude. Let us make ourselves terrible and likewise useful. Does the elephant stop to see where he puts his foot? Let us crush the enemy."

Robespierre replied mildly,—

"I am willing."

Then he added,—

"The question is, to learn the whereabouts of the enemy."

"He is without, and it is I who have driven him there," said Danton.

"He is within, and I am watching him," said Robespierre.

"I will drive him out again," replied Danton.

"One cannot so easily expel an internal enemy."

"What, then, is to be done?"

"He must be exterminated."

"I agree to that," said Danton, in his turn.

And he continued,—

"But I tell you he is outside, Robespierre."

"And I tell you that he is within, Danton."

"Robespierre, he is on the frontier."

"He is in the Vendée, Danton."

"Calm yourselves," remarked a third voice; "he is everywhere, and you are lost."

It was Marat who spoke.

Robespierre looked at Marat, and quietly retorted,—

"A truce to generalizations. Let us come to particulars. Here are the facts."

"Pedant!" growled Marat.

Placing his hand on the paper spread out before him, Robespierre continued:—

"I have just read you the despatches of Prieur de la Marne, and also communicated the information given by Gélambre. Listen, Danton; foreign war is as nothing compared with the dangers of civil war. A foreign war is like a scratch on the elbow, but civil war is an ulcer which eats away your liver. Here is the sum and substance of all that I have just read to you: the Vendée, which has hitherto been divided among many chiefs, is about to concentrate its forces. Henceforth it is to have one leader—"

"A sort of central brigand," muttered Danton.

"It is the man who landed near Pontorson on the 2d of June. You have seen what he is. Observe, that this landing was contemporary with the arrest of the representatives, Prieur de la Côte d'Or and Romme, at Bayeux, by that treacherous district of Calvados, which took place on the very same day, the 2d of June."

"And their transfer to the castle of Caen," said Danton.

Robespierre replied:—

"I will proceed to sum up the despatches. They are organizing the warfare of the forest on a vast scale. At the same time an English invasion is in preparation,—Vendeans and Englishmen; Brittany joining hands with Britain. The Hurons of Finistère speak the same language as the Topinambes of Cornwall. I showed you an intercepted letter of Puisaye, where he says that 'twenty thousand red coats distributed among the insurgents will be the means of raising one hundred thousand more.' When the peasant insurrection is fully organized, the English descent will take place. Here is the plan; follow it on the map." And putting his finger on the map, Robespierre continued:—

"The English have the choice of landing place, from Cancale to Paimpol. Craig would prefer the Bay of Saint-Brieuc, Cornwallis the Bay of Saint-Cast. But this is simply a matter of detail. The left shore of the Loire is guarded by the rebel Vendean army, and as to the twenty-eight miles of open country between Ancenis and Pontorson, forty Norman parishes have promised their assistance. The descent will be made at three points, Plérin, Iffiniac, and Pléneuf; from Plérin they will go to Saint-Brieuc, and from Pléneuf to Lamballe; on the second day they intend to reach Dinan, where there are nine hundred English prisoners, thus simultaneously occupying Saint-Jouan and Saint-Méen, where they, are to leave the cavalry; on the third day two columns will march,—one to Jouan on Bédée, the other to Dinan on Becherel, a natural fortress, and where they propose to set up two batteries; on the fourth day they expect to be at Rennes, which is the key to Brittany. Whoever has Rennes is master of the situation. Rennes once taken, Châteauneuf and Saint-Malo are sure to fall. There are one million cartridges and fifty field-pieces at Rennes."

"Which they will sweep away," muttered Danton.

Robespierre continued:—

"To conclude. From Rennes three columns will descend, one upon Fougères, and the second and third upon Vitré and Redon. As the bridges are destroyed, the enemy will be provided, as has already been stated, with pontoons and planks, and they will also have guides for such places as are fordable by cavalry. From Fougères they will diverge to Avranches, from Redon to Ancenis, from Vitré to Laval. Nantes will surrender, Brest likewise. Redon opens the way to Vilaine, as Fougères to Normandy and Vitré to Paris. In fifteen days they will have a brigand army of three hundred thousand men, and the whole of Brittany will belong to the King of France."

"You mean to the King of England," said Danton. "No, to the King of France," replied Robespierre, adding: "the King of France is worse; it takes fifteen days to expel a foreign foe, and eighteen hundred years to destroy a monarchy."

Danton, who had reseated himself with his elbows resting on the table, supported hip head on his hands and remained buried in thought.

"You perceive the danger," said Robespierre. "Vitré opens for the English the way to Paris."

Raising his head, Danton brought his two clenched fists down upon the map as though it were an anvil.

"Robespierre, did not Verdun open the way to Paris for the Prussians?"

"What then?"

"Well, we will drive the English as we drove the Prussians."

And Danton rose again.

Robespierre placed his cold hand on Danton's burning wrist.

"Danton, Champagne did not take sides with the Prussians, as Brittany does with the English. Retaking Verdun was foreign war; but to recapture Vitré will be civil war."

And Robespierre murmured in a cold, sepulchral tone,—

"A serious difference."

Then he continued,—

"Sit down, Danton, and look at the map, instead of battering it with your fists."

But Danton was wholly carried away with his own ideas.

"Well, this goes beyond everything!" he exclaimed; "to be on the alert for a catastrophe in the west, when it is actually in the east! I grant you, Robespierre, that England looms up on the ocean; but Spain rises from behind the Pyrenees, Italy from the Alps, Germany from the Rhine, and the big Russian bear is behind them all. Robespierre, danger surrounds us like a circle, and we are in its centre. Coalition abroad, treason at home. In the south, Servant holds the door of France ajar for the King of Spain; in the north, Dumouriez goes over to the enemy. However, he always threatened Holland less than Paris. Nerwinde has wiped out Jemmapes and Valmy. The philosopher Rabaut Saint-Étienne, a traitor, like the Protestant he is, corresponds with the courtier Montesquiou. The army is decimated. No battalion has now over four hundred men, and the brave regiment of Deux-Ponts is reduced to one hundred and fifty; the camp of Pamars has surrendered; Givet has but five hundred bags of flour left. We are falling back on Landau; Wurmser presses Kléber; Mayence makes a valiant defence; Condé yields ignobly, and Valenciennes likewise, but this in no way alters the fact that their defenders Féraud and Chancel are two heroes, not to mention Meunier, who defended Mayence; but all the others are betraying us. Dharville plays the traitor at Aix-la-Chapelle, Mouton at Brussels, Valence at Bréda, Neuilly at Limbourg, Miranda at Maëstricht; Stengel, Lanoue, Ligonnier, Menou, Dillon, traitors all,—hideous coin of Dumouriez. Examples are needed. I am suspicious of Custine's countermarches. I am inclined to believe that he preferred the lucrative capture of Frankfort to the more useful one of Coblentz. Suppose that Frankfort is able to pay a war indemnity of four millions,—what is that in comparison with crushing a nest of Émigrés? I call it treason. Meunier died on the 13th of June, and Kléber is now alone. Meanwhile Brunswick gains strength and marches onward. He raises the German flag in every French place that he captures. The Margrave of Brandenburg is today the arbiter of Europe; he is pocketing our provinces; you will soon see him appropriating Belgium; one might think that we were working for Berlin; and if this continues, and we take no means to prevent it, the French Revolution will result in the aggrandizement of Potsdam. Its chief consequence will be the advancement of the little State of Frederick II, and we shall have killed the King of France for the benefit of the King of Prussia."

Here Danton, terrible in his wrath, burst into a fit of laughter, which made Marat smile.

"You have each your hobby. Yours, Danton, is Prussia, and yours, Robespierre, is the Vendée. I will also mention a few facts. You do not see the real danger which is centred in the cafés and the gaming-houses: the Café de Choiseul is Jacobin; the Café Patin, royalist; the Café Rendez-Vous attacks the National Guard, and the Café de la Porte Saint-Martin defends it; the Café de la Régence is opposed to Brissot, the Café Corazza favors him; the Café Procope swears by Diderot, and the Café du Théâtre Français by Voltaire; at the Rotonde they tear up the assignats; the Cafés Saint-Marceau are in a state of perfect fury; the Café Manouri is agitating the flour problem; at the Café de Foy there is a perpetual racket and brawling, and at the Perron the hornets of finance are buzzing. All this is a serious matter."

Danton no longer laughed, but Marat still continued to smile. The smile of a dwarf is worse than the laugh of a giant.

"Are you sneering, Marat?" growled Danton.

Marat twitched his hip convulsively,—that motion peculiar to himself which has been so often described,—and his smile died away.

"Ah, I recognize you, Citizen Danton. You are the man who in full convention called me 'that individual Marat.' Listen: I forgive you. We are in times when men play the fool. Sneering, did you say? What kind of a man do you think I am? I have denounced Chazot, Pétion, Kersaint, Mouton, Dufriche-Valazé, Ligonnier, Menou, Banneville, Gensonné, Biron, Lidon, and Chambon. Was I wrong? I scent the treason of the traitor before the deed is done, and I find it useful to denounce the criminal in advance. It is my habit to say in the evening what the rest of you say the next day. I am the man who proposed to the Assembly a complete scheme for criminal legislation. What have I done up to the present moment? I asked to have the sections instructed that they might be disciplined for revolution; I had the seals of thirty-two boxes broken; I reclaimed the diamonds placed in the hands of Roland; I proved that the Brissotins had given to the Committee of General Safety blank warrants; I noted certain omissions in Lindet's report concerning the crimes of Capet; I voted for the execution of the tyrant in the course of twenty-four hours; I defended the battalions of Mauconseil and the Républicain; I prevented the reading of Narbonne's and Malouet's letters; I motioned in favor of the wounded soldiers; I caused the suppression of the Committee of Six; I foresaw the treason of Dumouriez in the affair of Mons; I demanded to have one hundred thousand relatives of the refugees taken as hostages for the commissioners delivered to the enemy; I proposed to declare traitor any representative who crossed the frontier; I unmasked the faction of Roland in the disturbances at Marseilles; I insisted that a price should be set on the head of Égalité's son; I defended Bouchotte; I called for a nominal vote to expel Isnard from the chair.

It was I who instigated the declaration that Parisians had deserved well of their country; that is why Louvet calls me a dancing puppet, and why Finistère demands my expulsion. For this the city of Loudun wishes me to be exiled, and the city of Amiens proposes to muzzle me, Coburg requires my arrest, and Lecointe-Puiraveau suggests to the Convention that it would be well to pronounce me insane. Bah! Citizen Danton, why did you ask me to come to your Conventicle if you did not wish for my advice? Did I ask permission to belong to it? Far from it. I have no inclination for a tête-à-tête with such counter-revolutionists as Robespierre and yourself. However, I might have expected this. You have not understood me,—neither you nor Robespierre. Are there then no statesmen here? You need a spelling lesson in politics, and some one to dot your *i*'s for you. This is the meaning of what I told you,— you are both mistaken. The danger comes neither from London nor from Berlin, as you two believe. It is in Paris. It is in the absence of unity; in the right of every man to pull his own way, beginning with you yourselves; in the levelling of intellects; in the anarchy of will—"

"Anarchy!" interrupted Danton. "Who is it that causes anarchy if not yourself?"

Marat paid no attention.

"Robespierre, Danton, the danger is in this multitude of cafés, in these countless gaming-houses, this crowd of clubs,—Club des Noirs, Club des Fédérés, Club des Dames, Club des Impartiaux (which dates from Clermont-Tonnerre, and which was the Monarchical Club of 1790,—a social circle originated by the priest Claude Fauchet), the Club des Bonnets de Laine, founded by the journalist Prudhomme, etc.; without counting your Jacobin Club, Robespierre, and your Club of Cordeliers, Danton. The danger is in the famine that made the porte-sacs Blin hang François Denis, the baker of Palu market, to the lamp-post of the Hôtel de Ville, and likewise in the justice that hung porte-sacs Blin for hanging baker Denis. The danger lies in the depreciation of the currency. One day on the Rue du Temple an assignat of a hundred francs fell to the ground, and a passer-by, a man of the lower class, remarked, 'It is not worth while to pick it up.' The danger comes from the stock-brokers and the monopolists. Fine progress we have made when we hoist the black flag over the Hôtel de Ville! You have arrested Baron Trenck; but that is not sufficient. I want to see you wring the neck of that old prison intriguer. Do you think that the business is accomplished because the President of the Convention places a civic crown on the head of Labertèche, who received forty-one sabre-thrusts at Jemmapes, and of whom Chénier makes himself the showman? Comedies and idle shows! Ah, you take no heed of Paris! You are looking for danger at a distance, when it is close at hand. Of what use are your police, Robespierre? You have your spies,—Payan in the Commune, Coffinhal at the Revolutionary Tribunal, David in the Committee of Public Safety, Couthon in the Committee of Public Well-being. You perceive that I am well informed. Now, then, learn this: The danger is hanging over your heads and rising beneath your feet. Conspiracies! conspiracies! conspiracies! The people passing along the streets read the papers to one another, and nod their heads significantly; six thousand men having no civic papers—the returned Émigrés, Muscadins, and Mathevons—are hidden in the cellars and garrets and in the wooden galleries of the Palais Royal; they are ranged in files in front of the bake-shops; women stand on the door-sills, and clasping their hands, cry, 'When shall we have peace?' It is of no use to close the doors of the Executive Committee against the public. Every word you utter is known; and as a proof, Robespierre, I will repeat the words you spoke last night to Saint-Just: 'Barbaroux's paunch grows apace; that will inconvenience him in his flight.' Danger, I tell you, lurks on every side, but chiefly in the centre. In Paris, while the ci-devants are weaving their plots the patriots go barefoot; the aristocrats arrested on the 9th of March are already released; the fine private horses that bespatter us with mud in the streets ought to be harnessed to the cannons on the frontier; a loaf of bread weighing four pounds is sold for three francs and twelve sous; indecent plays are given on the stage; and Robespierre will sooner or later send Danton to the guillotine."

"Phew!" exclaimed Danton.

Robespierre was attentively studying the map.

"What we need is a dictator!" cried Marat, fiercely. "You know, Robespierre, that I want a dictator."

Robespierre raised his head. "Yes, I know, Marat, it must be either you or I."

"I or you, you mean," retorted Marat.

"The dictatorship,—I advise you to try it!" grumbled Danton between his closed teeth.

Marat perceived Danton's frown.

"Stop," he said. "Let us make one last effort to come to an agreement. The situation is well worth it. Was there not an understanding for the 31st of May? The question of mutual agreement is even more important than Girondism, which is a matter of detail. There is a certain amount of truth in your statements; but truth itself, the whole truth, the real truth, lies in, I say, Federalism in the south, Royalism in the West, a deadly struggle between the Convention and the Commune in Paris, and on the frontier the backsliding of Custine and the treason of Dumouriez. What will be the result? The end will be nothing less than dismemberment. And what do we require? Unity. Therein lies our salvation. But we have no time to lose. Paris must undertake the control of the Revolution. If we waste one hour, the Vendeans may be in Orleans tomorrow, and the Prussians in Paris. I grant one thing to you, Danton, and another to Robespierre. So be it. And the conclusion must be dictatorship. Let us, we three who represent the Revolution, grasp the dictatorship. We are the three heads of Cerberus. One is a talking head, and that is you, Robespierre; the second head does the roaring, and that is you, Danton—"

"And the other bites, and that is you, Marat," said Danton.

"All three bite," said Robespierre.

For a time there was silence; then this dialogue full of gloomy and violent utterances proceeded.

"Listen, Marat; people should know each other before they marry. How did you find out what I said to Saint-Just yesterday?"

"That is my affair, Robespierre."

"Marat!"

"It is my duty to gain information."

"Marat!"

"I like to know what is going on."

"Marat!"

"Robespierre, I know what you say to Saint-Just, as I know what Danton says to Lacroix; I know what happens on the quay of the Théatins, at the Hôtel Labriffe, a den frequented by the nymphs of the Emigration, as well as I know what is going on at the house of Thilles, near Gonesse, which now belongs to Valmerange, the former administrator of the postal service, where Maury and Cazalès were in the habit of going,—a house which Sieyès and Vergniaud have since frequented, and where at the present time a certain person goes once a week."

In saying a certain person, Marat looked significantly at Danton.

"If I had but two farthings' worth of power, this would be terrible," cried Danton.

"I know what you say, Robespierre," continued Marat, "just as I knew what was going on in the tower of the Temple when they were fattening Louis XVI; and the wolf, the she-wolf, and the cubs, during the month of September alone, devoured eighty-six baskets of peaches. At that time the nation was starving. I know it, as I know that Roland was concealed in a lodging looking out on a back-yard, in the Rue de la Harpe; as I know that six hundred pikes used on the 14th of July were manufactured by Faure, the locksmith of the Duke of Orleans; as I know what they do at the house of Saint-Hilaire, the mistress of Sillery. On the days when there is to be a ball, old Sillery himself chalks the parquet floors of the yellow salon in the Rue Neuve-des-Mathurins; Buzot and Kersaint dined there; Saladin dined there on the 27th, and with whom do you guess, Robespierre? With your friend Lasource."

"Idle talk," muttered Robespierre; "Lasource is not my friend."

He added thoughtfully,—

"In the mean time there are eighteen manufactories of false assignats in London."

Marat went on in a voice calm but somewhat tremulous, an ominous sign with him,—

"You are the faction of the All-Importants. Yes, I know everything, in spite of what Saint-Just calls the silence of State—"

Marat emphasized this word, looked at Robespierre, and continued:—

"I know the conversation that takes place at your table on the days when Lebas invites David to eat the food prepared by his betrothed, Élisabeth Duplay, your future sister-in-law, Robespierre. I am the all-seeing eye of the people, and from the depths of my cave I observe. Yes, I hear, I see, and I know. You are contented with small things. You admire yourself. Robespierre shows himself off before his Madame de Chalabre, the daughter of the Marquis who played whist with Louis XV on the evening of Damiens' execution. Yes, heads are carried high in these days. Saint-Just never unbends; Legendre is a scrupulous devotee to fashion, with his new frock-coat and white waistcoat, and a frill, that people may forget his apron. Robespierre imagines that history will be interested to know that he wore an olive-colored coat *à la Constitution*, and a sky-blue coat *à la Convention*. He hangs his portrait on every wall around his room—"

Robespierre interrupted him in a voice even more quiet than that of Marat himself:—

"And you drag yours through all the sewers, Marat."

They continued this conversation in tones whose very deliberation emphasized the violence of the attacks and retorts, and added a certain irony to the implied threats.

"Robespierre, you called those who are in favor of the abolition of monarchy the Don Quixotes of mankind."

"And you, Marat, after the 4th of August, in No. 559 of your 'Ami du Peuple,'—you see, I remember the number, a useful item,—you requested to have the titles of the nobles restored to them. You said: 'Once a Duke, always a Duke.'"

"Robespierre, in the session of the 7th of December you defended Roland's wife against Viard."

"Just as my brother defended you, Marat, when you were attacked at the Jacobins'. What does that prove? Nothing at all."

"Robespierre! we all know the cabinet at the Tuileries where you said to Garas: 'I am tired of the Revolution.'"

"Marat, in this very ale-house, on the 20th of October, you embraced Barbaroux."

"And you said to Buzot, Robespierre, 'What does the Republic signify?'"

"Marat, you invited three men from Marseilles to breakfast with you here in this ale-house."

"Robespierre, you go about escorted by a strong fellow from the market armed with a club."

"And you, Marat, on the eve of the 10th of August,—you asked Buzot to assist you in escaping to Marseilles disguised as a jockey."

"During the prosecutions of September you took good care to hide yourself, Robespierre."

"And you, Marat, were not backward in making a display of yourself."

"Robespierre, you flung the red cap on the ground."

"Yes, when a traitor hoisted it. Dumouriez defiles Robespierre."

"Robespierre, you refused to throw a veil over the head of Louis XVI when Chateauvieux' soldiers were passing."

"I did better than veil his head; I cut it off."

Danton interposed, but it was like pouring oil upon the flames.

"Robespierre, Marat, calm yourselves," he said. Marat did not like to be mentioned in the second place. He turned round.

"What affair is this of Danton?"

"What affair of mine? I will tell you. There must be no fratricides; we must have no strife between two men, both of whom serve the people. It is enough to have to deal with foreign and civil wars, and it would be too much if we were to have a family conflict. It is I who made the Revolution, and I do not choose to have it destroyed. This is why I feel called upon to interfere."

Marat replied, without raising his voice,—

"You had better be attending to the settlement of your own accounts."

"My accounts!" cried Danton. "Go ask for them in the passes of Argonne, in Champagne delivered, in Belgium conquered, in the armies where I have exposed my breast four times already to the grape-shot! Inquire in the Place de la Révolution, on the scaffold of the 21st of January, of the throne lying on the ground, of the guillotine, that widow—"

Here Marat broke forth, interrupting Danton,—

"The guillotine is a virgin who gives death unto men, but not life."

"What do you know about it? I will make her fruitful."

"We shall see."

And he smiled.

Danton saw the smile.

"Marat," he cried, "you are the man who prefers to hide; I am a man who rejoices in broad daylight, in the open air. I despise the life of a reptile. It would not suit me to be a woodlouse. You live in a cave; I live in the street. You hold no communication with mankind; the chance passer-by may see and speak with me."

"Handsome youth! Will you ascend to my abode?" growled Marat.

And no longer smiling, he continued in a peremptory tone:—

"Danton, give an account of the thirty-three thousand crowns cash, that were paid you by that Montmorin in the name of the king, under the pretext of indemnifying you for the post of solicitor of the Châtelet."

"I belonged to the 14th of July," said Danton, haughtily.

"And the Garde-meuble? And the crown diamonds?"

"I was also of the 6th of October."

"And the thefts of your *alter ego*, Lacroix, in Belgium?"

"I was of the 20th of June."

"And the loans to Montansier?"

"I influenced the people to bring about the return from Varennes."

"And the Opera House built with the money that you furnished?"

"I armed the sections of Paris."

"And the hundred thousand livres in secret funds of the Ministère de la Justice?"

"The 10th of August was my work."

"And the two millions secret expenses of the Assembly, a quarter of which fell to your share?"

"I arrested the progress of the enemy, and barred the road to the allied kings."

"Prostitute!" cried Marat.

Danton was terrible in his wrath.

"Yes," he cried; "you have spoken the word! I have sold my virtue, but I saved the world!"

Robespierre meanwhile continued to bite his nails. He could neither laugh nor smile. He possessed not the lightning-like laughter of Danton, nor the sting of Marat's smile.

Danton continued,—

"I am like the ocean: I have my flood and ebb. When the tide is low you can see the shoals; but at high tide you see only the waves."

"What one might call your froth," said Marat.

"My tempest, rather," replied Danton.

They both sprang to their feet, and Marat burst forth; the adder suddenly assumed the shape of a dragon.

"Ah, Robespierre! ah, Danton!" he exclaimed, "you will not listen to me. I tell you, you are lost! Your policy brings you up against a wall! Every issue is closed to you, and you go on committing deeds that will finally leave you with no outlet save that of the grave."

"In that lies the very essence of our greatness," said Danton, shrugging his shoulders.

Marat went on:—

"Danton, beware! Vergniaud has a wide mouth, thick lips, and frowning brows, like yourself. He is also pitted, like you and Mirabeau.

Yet this did not prevent the 31st of May. Ah, you shrug your shoulders! A shrug of the shoulders has been known to cost a man his head. I tell you, Danton, your loud voice, your loose cravat, your top-boots, your late suppers, your ample pockets,—Louisette will have something to say about all that."

Louisette was Marat's pet name for the guillotine.

He continued:—

"And as for you, Robespierre, you are a Moderate; but that will avail you nothing. Go on; powder and dress your hair, brush your clothes, play the coxcomb, wear fine linen, be a model of propriety, frizzed and bedizened; sooner or later you will go to the Place de Grève; read Brunswick's proclamation, and make up your mind to be treated like the regicide Damiens, and you are arrayed in fine style to be drawn and quartered."

"Echo of Coblentz!" muttered Robespierre between his teeth.

"Robespierre, I echo no one. I am the cry of the whole world. Ah, you are young, both of you! How old are you, Danton? Thirty-four. And you, Robespierre? Thirty-three. Well, as for myself, I have lived from the beginning of time. I am the embodiment of the ancient misery of mankind. I am six thousand years old."

"That is true," replied Danton; "for six thousand years Cain has been preserved in hatred, like a toad in a stone. The stone breaks, and Cain leaps forth among men, to be known as Marat."

"Danton!" cried Marat; and a livid glare shone in his eyes.

"Well, what is it?" said Danton.

Thus conversed these three terrible men,—conflicting thunderbolts!

III

A Quivering of the Inmost Fibres

THE CONVERSATION CEASED FOR A time. Each Titan betook himself to his own reflections.

Lions are disturbed by hydras. Robespierre had grown very pale, and Danton very much flushed. Both shuddered. Marat's wild glare had died out; calmness, imperious calmness, now rested on the face of that man, feared by those who were themselves objects of awe.

Danton felt himself conquered, but was unwilling to yield.

He continued,—

"Marat talks loudly of dictatorship and unity, possessing all the while a talent for destroying."

Robespierre opened his thin lips, and by way of supplementing Danton's speech remarked,—

"I agree with Anacharsis Cloots. Give me neither Roland nor Marat."

"And I," said Marat,—"I say neither Danton nor Robespierre."

He gazed steadily at the two men, and then added:

"Let me advise you, Danton. You are in love, and think of marrying again; let politics alone,—be wise."

And taking a step towards the door, he was about to take his departure, with the ominous salutation,—

"Farewell, gentlemen."

Danton and Robespierre shuddered.

At that moment a voice was heard at the farther end of the room, saying,—

"You are wrong, Marat."

All turned. During Marat's outbreak some one had entered, unperceived, through the door at the back of the room.

"Is that you, citizen Cimourdain?" said Marat "Good-day."

It was Cimourdain.

"I tell you that you are wrong, Marat," he repeated.

Marat turned green, which was his way of growing pale, and Cimourdain added:—

"You are useful, but Robespierre and Danton are indispensable. Why do you threaten them? Let us have union, citizens. The people wish us to be united."

This entrance was like a dash of cold water, or the arrival of a stranger upon the scene of a family quarrel; it produced a calming effect upon the surface, if it did not reach the depths.

Cimourdain advanced towards the table.

Both Danton and Robespierre knew him. They had often noticed, in the public tribunals of the Convention, this obscure but influential man, whom the people greeted with respect. Robespierre, however, always ceremonious, inquired,—

"How did you get in, citizen?"

"He belongs to the Évêché," replied Marat, in an unusually meek tone of voice.

Marat braved the Convention and led the Commune, but he feared the Évêché.

This is a law.

Mirabeau, in some mysterious far-away depth, is conscious of the existence of Robespierre. Marat, too, is aware of Hébert,—Hébert of Babeuf. So long as the subterranean strata remain quiet, the politician can move at his ease. But there is a sub-soil under the most revolutionary, and the boldest men will quail when they feel beneath their feet the movement which they themselves have started overhead.

To be able to distinguish between the disturbance that springs from covetousness and that which is founded on principle, to combat the one and to aid the other, constitutes the genius and merit of great revolutionists.

"Oh, citizen Cimourdain is not unwelcome," he said, as he extended his hand to Cimourdain, adding:

"Parbleu! Let us explain the situation to citizen Cimourdain. He comes in just in time. I represent the Mountain, Robespierre the Committee of Public Safety, Marat the Commune; and Cimourdain represents the Évêché. He will give us the casting vote."

"So be it," replied Cimourdain, in his serious and simple manner. "What is the subject under consideration?"

"The Vendée," replied Robespierre.

"The Vendée," echoed Cimourdain, then went on:

"There lies the great danger. If Revolution expires, the Vendée will have given it its death-blow. One Vendée is more to be feared than ten Germanys. If France is to be saved, we must destroy the Vendée."

These words won Robespierre to his side; but still the latter put the question,—

"Were you not formerly a priest?"

For the priestly aspect had not escaped his observation. He recognized in another what he had within himself.

"Yes, citizen," replied Cimourdain.

"What does that matter?" cried Danton. "When priests are good they are better than other men. In time of revolution priests are melted into citizens, just as bells are melted into sous and cannon. Danjou and Danon are both priests. Thomas Lindet is Bishop of Évreux. At the Convention, Robespierre, you sit side by side with Massieu, Bishop of Beauvais. The Vicar-General Vaugeois belonged to the Insurrection Committee of the 10th of August. Chabot is a capuchin. Dom Gerle devised the oath of the Tennis-Court. The Abbé Audran declared the National Assembly superior to the king; the Abbé Goutte asked the

Legislature to remove the daïs from the chair of Louis XVI, and the Abbé Grégoire instigated the abolition of royalty."

"A motion seconded by the comedian Collot d'Herbois. They two did the business; the priest overturned the throne, the comedian deposed the king!"

"Let us return to the Vendée," said Robespierre.

"Well, what is it?" asked Cimourdain; "what is the Vendée doing now?"

"This," replied Robespierre. "It has found a leader; it will become terrible."

"Who is this leader, citizen Robespierre?"

"He is a ci-devant Marquis de Lantenac, who styles himself a Breton prince."

Cimourdain made a movement.

"I know him," he said. "I was chaplain at his house."

He reflected for a moment, and then continued:

"He was fond of women before he became active in military affairs."

"Like Biron, who was a Lauzun," said Danton. Cimourdain added thoughtfully,—

"Yes, formerly a man devoted to pleasure. He must be terrible."

"Frightful!" said Robespierre. "He burns villages, kills the wounded, massacres prisoners, and shoots women."

"Women?"

"Yes. Among others he ordered a woman to be shot who was the mother of three children. No one knows what became of the children. Moreover, he is really a leader. He understands the art of warfare."

"True," replied Cimourdain. "When he was in the Hanoverian war the soldiers used to say, 'Richelieu above, Lantenac below;' but the latter was the actual general. Ask your colleague Dussaulx about it."

Robespierre remained for a moment absorbed in thought; then the conversation between Cimourdain and himself was renewed.

"Well, citizen Cimourdain, this man is in the Vendée."

"How long since?"

"Three weeks ago."

"He must be outlawed."

"That has been done."

"A price must be set upon his head."

"That also has been done."

"A large sum of money must be offered for his capture."

"The offer has been made,"

"It must not be in assignats."

"Certainly not."

"But in gold."

"It has been so promised."

"And he must be guillotined."

"That shall be done."

"By whom?"

"By you!"

"By me?"

"Yes; you will be delegated by the Committee of Public Safety with ample powers."

"I accept," said Cimourdain.

Robespierre was rapid in his decisions,—a states-manlike quality. He took from the portfolio that lay before him a sheet of white paper, at the head of which the following words were printed: "French Republic, one and indivisible: Committee of Public Safety."

"I accept," continued Cimourdain. "Let the terrible encounter the terrible. Lantenac is ferocious; I will be equally so. It shall be war unto death with that man; I shall rid the Republic of him, if it be God's will."

He stopped, then continued,—

"I am a priest; I believe in God."

"God has grown antiquated," said Danton.

"I believe in God," repeated Cimourdain, unmoved.

Robespierre gloomily nodded his approval, and Cimourdain continued,—

"To whom shall I be delegated?"

Robespierre replied,—

"To the commandant of the exploring division sent against Lantenac. But I give you warning that he is a nobleman."

"That is another thing that excites my contempt," cried Danton. "A nobleman? Well, what of that? It is all the same whether a man be a priest or a nobleman; if he is a good man, he is excellent. Nobility is a prejudice; but we ought to deal impartially with it, granting both its merits and its demerits. Is not Saint-Just a nobleman, Robespierre? Florelle de Saint-Just,—parbleu! Anacharsis Cloots is a baron. Our friend Charles Hesse, who never misses a single session of the Cordeliers, is a prince, brother to the reigning Landgrave of Hesse-Rothenbourg. Montaut, Marat's intimate friend, is Marquis de Montaut. In the revolutionary tribunal there is one juror Vilate, who is a priest, and another Leroy, Marquis de Montflabert. Both are trustworthy men."

"And you forget," added Robespierre, "the foreman of the revolutionary jury—"

"Antonelle!"

"Marquis Antonelle," corrected Robespierre.

"And that Dampierre, who was lately killed before Condé by the Republic," rejoined Danton, "was a nobleman; and Beaurepaire too, who blew his brains out rather than open the gates of Verdun to the Prussians."

"And in spite of all that," grumbled Marat, "on the day when Condorcet exclaimed, 'The Gracchi were nobles!' Danton cried out, 'All nobles are traitors,—beginning with Mirabeau, and ending with thee!'"

Here the serious voice of Cimourdain rose above the others:—

"Citizen Danton, citizen Robespierre, you may perhaps be justified in your confidence; but the nation distrusts, and it has reason to do so. When a priest is charged with the surveillance of a nobleman, the responsibility is a double one, and it is the duty of the priest to be inflexible."

"That is true," said Robespierre.

"And inexorable," added Cimourdain.

"Well said, citizen Cimourdain!" rejoined Robespierre. "It is a young man with whom you will have to deal, and you will have the advantage over him, from the fact that you are twice his age. He must be guided, but with the utmost discretion, that he may not suspect it. It seems that he has military ability; all reports are unanimous on that point. He forms part of a corps which has been detached from the army of the Rhine and sent into the Vendée. He has lately returned from the frontier, where he distinguished himself by his bravery and intelligence, and is now in command of the exploring division, which he handles like an expert. For fifteen days he has held the old Marquis de Lantenac in check. He restrains him, and at the same time compels him to give way. He will end by forcing him to the sea and pitching him into it. Lantenac has the cunning of an old general, while his opponent possesses the boldness of a young captain. This young man has already won for himself enemies and detractors, who are envious of him. Adjutant-General Léchelle is jealous of him."

"This Léchelle wants to be commander-in-chief," interrupted Danton. "He has only a pun in his favor,—it needs a ladder to mount into a cart. Meanwhile, Charette defeats him."

"And he is not willing that any one else should defeat Lantenac," added Robespierre. "The misfortune of the Vendean war is the existence of these rivalries. Our soldiers are heroes led by inferior commanders. Chérin, a mere captain of hussars, enters Saumur with trumpets, playing *Ça ira*; he takes Saumur; he might go on and take Cholet, but having received no orders, he pauses. Every position of command in the Vendée ought to be reconstructed; the garrisons are scattered, the forces dispersed; an army that is scattered is paralyzed; it is like a rock crumbling into dust. Nothing but tents are left at Camp de Paramé. Between Tréguier and Dinan there are a hundred useless little encampments out of which a division could be formed to cover the entire coast. Léchelle, supported by Parrein, robs the northern coast under the pretext of protecting the southern, and thus exposes France to the English. Half a million of peasants in revolt, and a descent of England upon France,—such is Lantenac's plan. The young commander of the exploring column presses his resistless sword against Lantenac's loins, until he forces him to yield, and this without asking leave of Léchelle. Now, Léchelle is his chief, therefore he denounces him. Opinions are divided regarding this young man. Léchelle would like to have him shot, and Prieur de la Marne wishes to make him Adjutant-General."

"He seems to me to possess great qualities," observed Cimourdain.

"But he has one defect!"

This interruption came from Marat.

"And what is that?" asked Cimourdain.

"Clemency," replied Marat; and he went on: "He is firm in the assault, but after the victory he shows his weakness. He grants indulgences, he is too merciful and forgiving, he protects *religieuses* and nuns, he saves the wives and daughters of the aristocrats, he releases prisoners, and lets the priests go free."

"A grave fault," murmured Cimourdain.

"A crime, you would do better to call it," said Marat.

"Sometimes," said Danton.

"Often," said Robespierre.

"Almost always," insisted. Marat.

"Yes, when one has to deal with the enemies of one's country it may always be called a crime," said Cimourdain.

Marat turned towards the latter.

"And what then would you do with a Republican chief who would set a Royalist leader at liberty?" he inquired.

"I should agree with Léchelle; I would have him shot."

"Or guillotined," said Marat.

"He might take his choice," said Cimourdain. Danton began to laugh.

"The one seems to me as good as the other."

"You are quite sure to have one or the other," muttered Marat; and averting his eyes from Danton, he fixed them again on Cimourdain.

"So, citizen Cimourdain, if you caught a Republican chief stumbling, you would have him beheaded?"

"Within twenty-four hours."

"Well," resumed Marat, "I agree with Robespierre; citizen Cimourdain must be sent as a delegate from the Committee of Public Safety to the commander of the exploring division of the coast army. What is this commander's name, by the way?"

Robespierre, beginning to turn over his papers, replied,—

"He is a ci-devant nobleman."

"It is an excellent plan to set a priest to guard a nobleman," said Danton. "Either one of them, singly and alone, I am inclined to distrust; but when taken together, I have no fear of them: they keep a mutual watch over each other, and go on very well."

The expression of indignation peculiar to Cimourdain's face grew more pronounced; but doubtless aware that the observation was based upon truth, he did not turn towards Danton as he lifted his severe voice.

"If the Republican commander intrusted to my care makes a false step, he will suffer the penalty of death."

Robespierre, with his eyes still resting on his portfolio, said:—

"Here is the name; the commander in charge of whom you will be placed, to conduct yourself in his regard at your own discretion, is a former Viscount called Gauvain."

Cimourdain turned pale.

"Gauvain!" he exclaimed.

Marat observed Cimourdain's pallor.

"The Viscount Gauvain!" repeated Cimourdain.

"Yes," said Robespierre.

"Well?" exclaimed Marat, gazing steadfastly at Cimourdain.

There was a brief silence, broken by Marat.

"Citizen Cimourdain, do you accept the appointment of commissioner delegate to the commander Gauvain, with the condition which you yourself have laid down? Is it agreed?"

"It is," replied Cimourdain, with increasing pallor.

Robespierre took the pen that lay beside him, and in his slow and regular handwriting traced four lines on the sheet of paper headed

"Committee of Public Safety." After signing it, he passed the pen and paper to Danton, who signed; and the signature of Marat, who had not once removed his eyes from the pale face of Cimourdain, was added to the others.

Robespierre, taking back the sheet, dated it and gave it to Cimourdain, who read on it the following:—

YEAR II OF THE REPUBLIC
Full powers are granted to citizen Cimourdain, commissioner delegated from the Committee of Public Safety to the citizen Gauvain, in command of the exploring division of the army of the coast.

ROBESPIERRE
DANTON
MARAT

And below the signatures: "June 29, 1793."

The revolutionary calendar, called the civil calendar, had no legal existence at that time, and was only adopted by the Convention on the 5th of October, 1793, in response to the proposition of Romme.

While Cimourdain was reading, Marat continued to watch him. Then, in a tone half-inaudible, as though speaking to himself, he said,—

"All this must be confirmed by a decree from the Convention, or by a special resolution of the Committee of Public Safety. Something still remains to be done."

"Citizen Cimourdain, where do you live?" asked Robespierre.

"Cour du Commerce."

"Indeed! Then you are a neighbor of mine. I live there also," said Danton.

Robespierre continued:—

"There is not a moment to lose. Tomorrow you will receive your formal commission, signed by all the members of the Committee of Public Safety. This is a confirmation of the commission accrediting you specially to the acting representatives Philippeaux, Prieur de la Marne, Lecointre, Alquier, and others. We know you; your powers are unlimited. It rests with you to make Gauvain a general or send him to the scaffold. You will receive your commission tomorrow at three o'clock. When will you start?"

"At four o'clock," said Cimourdain; and they separated.

On returning home, Marat informed Simonne Évrard that he should go to the Convention tomorrow.

Book III

THE CONVENTION

I

The Convention

I

WE ARE APPROACHING THE SUMMIT.

The Convention is before our eyes, and in the presence of this lofty eminence the gaze grows steady.

Nothing more towering ever rose above the human horizon. There is but one Himalaya, but one Convention.

The Convention may perhaps be called the culminating point in history.

During its lifetime—an assembly actually lives—one did not realize what it was. Its supreme grandeur was not appreciated by its contemporaries, who were too much terrified to be dazzled. Mediocrities and moderate hills levy no severe tax on one's admiration; but the majestic inspires a holy horror, whether it be the majesty of genius or of a mountain, an assembly or a masterpiece. Too close proximity excites alarm; every peak seems exaggerated, the ascent is fatiguing, and one loses breath in climbing its sharp acclivities, misses his footing on the slopes, and is wounded by the cragged surfaces, which in themselves are beauties; the foaming torrent indicates the presence of the chasm, the summit is veiled in clouds; whether ascending or descending, it is equally frightful, hence one feels the influence of terror rather than of admiration,—a kind of aversion to grandeur, which is a strange enough sensation. While gazing on the abyss, one cannot always appreciate its sublimity; the monster is more evident than the miracle. It was thus that men first judged the Convention. The purblind undertook to fathom an abyss whose depths could only be sounded by the eagle.

Today we behold it in the perspective outlining the granite profile of the French Revolution against the calm and tragic background of the far-away heavens.

THE 14TH OF JULY SET the nation free.

The 10th of August hurled its thunderbolts.

The 21st of September founded a new era; for the 21st of September was the equinox, the equilibrium, *Libra*,—the balance-scales of Justice. According to the remark of Romme, the Republic was proclaimed beneath this sign of Equality and Justice,—heralded, so to speak, by a constellation.

The Convention is the first avatar of the people. It was the Convention that turned the new and glorious page, introducing the future of today.

Every idea requires a visible embodiment; every principle needs a habitation; a church means the four walls within which the Almighty has his dwelling-place; every dogma must have its temple. When the Convention became a fact, the first problem was to locate it.

At first it was established in the Manège, but afterwards at the Tuileries. Here they raised a platform and arranged scenery, painted in gray, by David; also, rows of benches and a square tribune; there were parallel pilasters, with massive plinths, and long rectangular stems, and square enclosures, into which the multitude crowded, and which were called public tribunes; a Roman velarium, and Grecian draperies; and amid these right angles and straight lines the Convention was installed,—a tempest confined within geometrical limits. On the tribune the red cap was painted in gray. At first the Royalists ridiculed this gray *bonnet-rouge*, this artificial hall, this pasteboard monument, this sanctuary of papier-mâché, this pantheon of mud and spittle. How quickly it was destined to vanish! The pillars were made of barrel-staves, the arches of thin deal boards, the bas-reliefs were mastic, the entablature was of pine, the statues were of plaster, the marble was painted, the walls were of canvas; and in this provisional shelter France has recorded deeds that can never be forgotten.

During the early sessions of the Convention the walls of the Hall of the Manège were covered with the advertisements with which Paris swarmed at the time of the return from Varennes. On one might be read: "The King returns. Whoever applauds him will be chastised; whoever insults him will be hung." On another: "Peace. Keep your hats on your heads. He is about to pass before his judges." On another: "The King took aim at the nation, but his weapon hung fire. Now the nation has its turn." On another: "The law! the law!" It was within these walls that the Convention sat in judgment on Louis XVI.

At the Tuileries, now called the Palais National, where the Convention had held its sessions from the 10th of May, 1793, the Assembly Hall occupied the space between the Pavillon de l'Horloge, called Pavillon Unité, and the Pavillon Marsan, called Pavillon Liberté. The Pavillon de Flore was now called Pavillon-Égalité. The Assembly Hall was accessible by the grand staircase of Jean Bullant. The entire ground-floor of the palace below the first story, occupied by the Assembly, was a kind of long guardroom, littered with the luggage and camp-beds of the various troops mounting guard over the Convention. The Assembly had a special guard of honor, called "the Grenadiers of the Convention."

A tricolored ribbon divided the palace occupied by the Assembly from the garden where the people passed in and out.

III

LET US FINISH OUR DESCRIPTION of the Assembly Hall. Everything concerning this terrible place is of interest. The first object to attract one's attention on entering was a tall statue of Liberty, placed between two large windows. This hall, which was formerly the king's theatre, had now become the stage of Revolution. It was forty-two metres long, ten metres in width, and eleven in height. This elegant and superb hall built by Vigarani for the use of the courtiers was hidden beneath the rude timber-work which served to support the weight of the people in '93. The only point of support upon which this timber-work of the public tribunes rested, was a single post, which well deserves honorable mention. This post consisted of one solid piece, ten metres in circumference, and few caryatides have done an equal amount of work; for years it bore the severe pressure of revolution. It has supported applause, enthusiasm, insult, clamors and tumults, the tremendous chaos of wrath, the fury of insurrection, and never given way beneath its burden. After the Convention it witnessed the council of the Ancients. On the 18th Brumaire it was relieved. At that time Percier replaced this wooden pillar by columns of marble that did not last so long.

An architect's ideal is sometimes peculiar; that of the architect of the Rue de Rivoli was the curved path of a cannon-ball in its flight; the architect of Carlsruhe conceived the ideal of a fan; and the conception of the architect who built the hall where the Convention established itself on the 10th of May, 1793, was apparently a huge bureau drawer, for it was long as well as high and flat. A great semicircle had been added to one of the long sides of the parallelogram; this was the amphitheatre with seats for the representatives, but neither tables nor desks; Garan-Coulon, who wrote a great deal, used to write, resting his paper on his knee; facing the benches was the tribune,—before it the bust of Lepelletier-Saint-Fargeau, and behind it the president's arm-chair. The head of the bust projected slightly above the edge of the tribune, which afterwards was the cause of its removal.

The amphitheatre consisted of nineteen semicircular benches, rising one above the other, some of which had been lengthened in order to fit into the corners, by means of other benches cut off for the purpose.

In the semicircle beneath, at the foot of the tribunal, were the places of the ushers, and on the other side of the tribune hung a placard nine feet high, set in a black wooden frame, and bearing on its two pages, separated by a kind of sceptre, the Declaration of the rights of man. On the other side was an empty space which was afterwards occupied by a similar frame, containing the Constitution of the year II, with the two pages separated by a sword. Above the tribune, over the head of the orator, from a deep loge divided into two compartments and filled with People, floated three immense tricolored banners, arranged in a horizontal position, resting on an altar upon which could be read the following words: "The Law." Behind this altar rose, like the sentinel of freedom of speech, an enormous Roman fasces as tall as a column. Two colossal statues, placed erect against the wall, faced the representatives,—Lycurgus on the president's right hand, Solon on his left, with Plato towering above the Mountain. The statues stood on simple wooden blocks, resting on a long projecting cornice that encircled the hall, separating the people from the Assembly. The spectators leaned their elbows on this cornice.

The black wooden frame enclosing the proclamation of the Rights of Man reached to the cornice, interfering with the symmetry of the entablature,—an infraction of the straight line that made Chabot growl. "It is ugly," he said to Vadier.

The heads of the statues were decorated with wreaths of oak and laurel.

Green curtains, on which similar wreaths were painted in a deeper shade of the same color, fell in heavy folds from the surrounding cornice, draping the entire lower floor of the hall occupied by the Assembly. Above this drapery the wall was white and bare. In this wall, as if carved by a chisel, without moulding or ornament, were two stories of public tribunes, the square ones below, the round ones above; according to the rule-for the influence of Vitruvius was still acknowledge—the archivolts were superimposed upon the architraves. There were ten tribunes on each of the long sides of the hall, and two huge boxes at both ends; twenty-four in all. There sat the assembled crowd.

The spectators in the lower tribunes overflowed their bounds, grouping themselves on every projection along the cornice. A long iron bar, firmly fastened at the point of support, served as a rail to the upper tribunes, and protected the spectators from the pressure of the crowds that ascended the stairs. Once, however, a man who was pitched suddenly into the Assembly below escaped death by falling partly upon Massieu, Bishop of Beauvais; whereupon he exclaimed, "Really, a bishop has his use, then, after all!"

The hall of the Convention was large enough to contain two thousand persons, and on the days of insurrections even three thousand.

The Convention held two sessions,—one during the day and one in the evening.

The back of the president's chair was round, studded with gilt nails. His table was supported by four winged monsters with a single foot, who might have been supposed to have come forth from the Apocalypse to witness the Revolution. They seemed to have been unharnessed from Ezekiel's chariot to drag the tumbril of Samson.

On the president's table stood a huge bell, almost as large as a church-bell, a big copper inkstand, and a parchment portfolio, which contained the record of proceedings. The blood from many a severed head, borne aloft on the end of a pike, has dripped upon this table.

Nine steps led to the tribune. These steps were high, steep, and difficult of ascent; Gensonné once tripped in the act of mounting them. "It is like the staircase of a scaffold!" he said. "It is well to serve your apprenticeship!" cried Carrier.

In the corners of the hall, where the walls seemed rather bare, the architect had placed Roman fasces as ornaments, with the axe bound on the outside.

On the right and left of the tribune pedestals supported two candelabra twelve feet high, each bearing four pairs of Argand lamps. For each public box there was a similar candelabra; and on the pedestals of these candelabra circles were carved, which the people called "guillotine collars."

The seats of the Assembly, rising almost to the cornice of the tribunes, gave the representatives and the people an opportunity to chat with one another.

The exits of the tribunes opened into a labyrinth of corridors, often echoing with wild and tumultuous sounds.

The Convention, outgrowing the limits of the palace, ace, overflowed into the neighboring hotels of Longueville and Coigny. If we may credit Lord Bradford's letter, it was to the Hôtel Coigny that the royal furniture was removed after the 10th of August. It took two entire months to empty the Tuileries.

The committees were lodged in the vicinity of the hall: those of legislation, agriculture, and commerce at the Pavillon-Égalité; those of the navy, the colonies, finance, assignats, and public safety, at the Pavillon Liberté; the Committee of War was at the Pavillon-Unité.

The lodgings of the Committee of General Safety were accessible to those of the Public Safety through a dark corridor, lighted night and day by a lantern,—a passage-way for the spies of all parties, who came and went, talking in whispers.

The bar of the Convention had been changed several times. Usually it was at the right hand of the president.

At both ends of the hall the two vertical partitions that shut off the concentric semicircles of the amphitheatre on the right hand and on the left, allowed space enough between partition and wall for two long and narrow passages closed at either end by square doors, which afforded entrance and exit.

A door opening upon the Terrasse des Feuillants, and leading directly into the hall, served for the admittance of the representatives.

This hall, ineffectually lighted during the day by windows, whose insufficient glimmer was replaced by livid torches when twilight fell, seemed ever shrouded in night. The lamplight sessions were lugubrious, the artificial light seeming really to increase rather than diminish the darkness. No man could see his neighbor; from all parts of the hall indistinct groups of faces seemed to be mocking each other. People passed one another without recognition. One day Laignelot, hastening to the tribune, jostled some one in the descending passage. "I beg pardon, Robespierre," he said. "For whom do you take me?" replied a hoarse voice. "Excuse me, Marat," said Laignelot.

Below, one tribune on either Bide of the president was reserved; for, strange to say, privileged spectators were admitted to the Convention.

The draperies of these tribunes—the only ones thus adorned—were caught back to the middle of the architrave by golden cords and tassels. The tribunes of the people were bare. The general effect was stern, unconventional, and yet correct. The union of propriety and fierceness is the essence of a revolutionary life. The Hall of the Convention presented a perfect example of what artists have since called the "messidor architecture." It was at once massive and frail. The builders of that period mistook symmetry for beauty. The Renaissance had said its last word under Louis XV, and a reaction had set in. The standards of nobility and purity had been so exaggerated that that which was really noble had degenerated into insipidity, and purity itself had become inexpressibly wearisome. Prudery may exist in architecture. After the dazzling orgies of form and color of the eighteenth century, art had begun a system of diet, and allowed itself only a straight line. This style of improvement resulted in ugliness, and art was thereby reduced to a skeleton,—a phenomenal condition which is the drawback to this kind of wisdom and abstinence; the style is so strict that it becomes meagre. Apart from all political emotion, the mere sight of this architecture made one shiver. Dimly recalling the old theatre, with its garlanded boxes, its ceiling of azure and crimson, its chandelier and girandoles with their prismatic reflections glittering like diamonds, its dove-colored upholstery, the profusion of cupids and nymphs on its curtain and draperies,—all that royal and amorous idyl, painted, sculptured, and gilded, which once irradiated this gloomy place with its smile,—and then casting one's eyes upon these severe rectangular lines, cold and sharp as steel, made one think of Boucher guillotined by David.

IV

He who looked upon the Assembly utterly forgot the hall. He who witnessed the drama was oblivious to the theatre. Nothing more misshapen and at the same time sublime. A crowd of heroes, a herd of cowards; wild beasts on the mountain, reptiles in the swamp. There all those combatants, the ghosts of today, swarmed, elbowed each other, quarrelling, threatening, fighting, and living out their lives.

A convocation of Titans!

On the right the Gironde,—a legion of thinkers; on the left the Mountain,—a group of athletes. Here might be seen Brissot, to whom the keys of the Bastille had been delivered; Barbaroux, who ruled the

Marseillais; Kervélégan, who had entire control of the battalion of Brest, quartered in the Faubourg Saint-Marceau; Gensonné, who had established the supremacy of representatives over generals; Gaudet, that man of ill-omen, to whom the Queen one evening at the Tuileries had shown the sleeping Dauphin: Gaudet kissed the child on the forehead, and beheaded the father; the chimerical Salles, who denounced the intrigues of the Mountain with Austria; Sillery, the cripple of the Right, and Couthon, the paralytic of the Left; Lause-Duperret, who, upon being called a "villain" by a certain journalist, invited him to dinner, saying, "Oh, 'villain' simply means a man whose opinions differ from our own;" Rabaut-Saint-Étienne, who began his almanac in 1790 with these words: "The Revolution is over;" Quinette, one of those who hastened the downfall of Louis XVI; the Jansenist Camus, who compiled the civil constitution of the clergy, believed in the miracles of the deacon of Pâris, and prostrated himself every night before an image of Christ seven feet high, nailed to his chamber wall; the priest Fauchet, who, together with Camille Desmoulins, was instrumental in bringing about the 14th of July; Isnard, guilty of saying, "Paris will be destroyed," at the very moment when Brunswick was saying, "Paris will be burned;" Jacob Dupont, who was the first man to proclaim himself "an atheist," and to whom Robespierre replied, "Atheism is aristocratic;" Lanjuinais, a stern, sagacious, and valiant Breton; Ducos, the Euryalus of Boyet-Fonfrède; Rebecqui, the Pylades of Barbaroux, who tendered his resignation because Robespierre had not as yet been guillotined; Richaud, who was opposed to the permanency of Sections; Lasource, who uttered the murderous apothegm, "Woe be unto grateful nations," and who at the foot of the scaffold was to contradict himself by those haughty words, flung to the members of the Mountain,—"We are dying because the nation slumbers; when it awakes your turn will come;" Biroteau, who in abolishing the inviolability of the crown unconsciously forged his own axe and reared his own scaffold; Charles Villatte, who shielded his conscience behind this protest: "I will not vote beneath the axe;" Louvet, the author of "Faublas," who was to end as a librarian at the Palais Royal, with Lodoïska at the desk; Mercier, the author of the "Tableau de Paris," who exclaimed, "Every king felt of his neck on the 21st of January;" Marec, who had the care of the "faction of ancient limits;" the journalist Carra, who at the foot of the scaffold said to the executioner: "It is provoking to die; I should like to have seen the result;" Vigée, who called himself a grenadier of the second battalion of Mayenne-et-Loire, and who when threatened by the public tribunes, cried, "I move that at the first murmur of the tribunes we all withdraw, and, sabre in hand, march upon Versailles;" Buzot, who was doomed to die of hunger, and Valazé, to fall by his own dagger; Condorcet, who was to die at Bourg-la-Reine, or Bourg-Égalité, as it was called at that time, betrayed by a volume of Horace that he carried in his pocket; Pétion, whose fate it was to be adored by the populace in 1792 and devoured by the wolves in 1794; and twenty more besides,—Pontécoulant, Marboz, Lidon, Saint-Martin, Dussaulx, the translator of Juvenal, who had made the Hanover campaign; Boileau, Bertrand, Lesterp-Beauvais, Lesage, Gomaire, Gardien, Mainvielle, Duplantier, Lacaze, Antiboul, and, foremost among them all, Barnave, whom men called Vergniaud.

On the other side, Antoine-Louis-Léon Florelle de Saint-Just, a youth of twenty-three, whose pallid face, low forehead, regular profile, and deep, mysterious eyes conveyed an impression of profound melancholy; Merlin de Thionville, whom the Germans called "Feuer-Teufel"—the fire-devil; Merlin de Douai, the guilty author of the Law of the Suspects; Soubrany, whom the Parisians, in the riot of the first Prairial, demanded for their general; the former curé, Lebon, who now held a sabre in the hand that had once sprinkled holy water; Billaud-Varennes, who foresaw the magistracy of the future, when arbitrators would take the place of judges; Fabre d'Églantine, who chanced upon the happy invention of the republican calendar, and Rouget de Lisle, the composer of the Marseillaise,—no second inspiration ever visited either of these two men; Manuel, the attorney of the Commune, who had said, "A dead king is no less a man;" Goujon, who marched into Tripstadt, Newstadt, and Spire, and who witnessed the flight of the Prussian army; Lacroix, a lawyer transformed into a general and made knight of Saint-Louis six days before August 10; Fréron-Thersite, son of Fréron Zoïle; Ruth, the inexorable searcher of the iron cupboard, predestined to a great republican suicide, who was to kill himself on the day of the death of the Republic; Fouché, with the soul of a demon and the face of a corpse; Camboulas, the friend of Père Duchesne, who used to say to Guillotin, "You belong to the Club of the Feuillants, but your daughter belongs to the Club of the Jacobins;" Jagot, who replied to those who pitied the nakedness of the prisoners in those savage words: "A prison is a dress of stone;" Javogues, the frightful desecrator of the tombs of Saint-Denis; Osselin, himself a proscriber, who sheltered one of the proscribed, Madame Charry, in his own house; Bentabolle, who while presiding over the Assembly gave the tribunes the signal for applause or disapproval; the journalist Robert, Mademoiselle Kéralio's husband, who wrote: "Neither Robespierre nor Marat comes to my house; Robespierre is welcome to come whenever he chooses, Marat never;" Garan-Coulon, who, when Spain interceded on the occasion of the trial of Louis XVI, had haughtily requested that the Assembly should not condescend to read the letter of one king pleading for another; the bishop Grégoire, who in the earlier part of his career was worthy to have belonged to the primitive church, but who afterwards, during the period of the Empire, renounced his Republican principles; Amar, who said, "The whole earth condemns Louis XVI; to whom then shall we appeal for judgment? To the planets;" Rouyer, who on the 21st of January opposed the firing of the cannon of the Pont-Neuf, saying, "A king's head ought to make no more noise in falling than the head of any other man;" Chénier, brother of the poet André; Vadier, one of those who placed a pistol on the tribune; Tanis, who used to say to Momoro, "I want Marat and Robespierre to embrace at my table."

"Where do you live?" "At Charenton." "It would have surprised me had you said elsewhere," was Momoro's reply; Legendre, who was the butcher of the French Revolution, as Pride had been of the English Revolution. "Come and be slaughtered!" he cried to Lanjuinais. To which the latter replied: "First pass a decree that I am an ox, if you please;" Collot d'Herbois, that gloomy comedian, wearing, as it were, the antique mask with the double mouth, one of which said "Yes," while the other said "No," approving on the one hand and blaming on the other, defaming Carrier in Nantes and deifying Châlier in Lyons, sending Robespierre to the scaffold and Marat to the Pantheon; Génissieux, who asked that the penalty of death should be imposed on whosoever should be found wearing a medal that bore the inscription, "Louis XVI martyred;" Léonard Bourdon, the schoolmaster, who had offered his house to the old man of Mount Jura; Topsent, the sailor; Goupilleau, the lawyer; Laurient Lecointre, merchant; Duhem, the doctor; Sergent, the sculptor; David, the artist; and Joseph Égalité, the prince; and others besides,—Lecointe Puiraveau, who called for a formal decree pronouncing Marat "insane;" Robert Lindet, the troublesome author of that devilfish whose head was the Committee of Public Safety, and whose twenty-one thousand arms embraced France in the shape of revolutionary committees; Leboeuf, on whom Girey-Dupré, in his "Noël des faux-Patriotes," wrote this line:—

"Leboeuf vit Legendre et beugla."

Thomas Paine, the benevolent American; Anacharsis Cloots, the millionnaire, a German baron, who although an atheist was still a man of sincere purpose, and a follower of Hébert; the upright Lebas, a friend of the Duplays; Rovère, one of those men whom one occasionally meets, who indulge in wickedness for its own sake, a variety of amateur more common than we might imagine; Charlier, who wished to address aristocrats with the familiar "vous;" the elegiac and cruel Tallien, who was to bring about the 9th Thermidor out of pure love of it: Cambacérès, a lawyer, who finally became a prince; Carrier, another lawyer, who turned into a tiger; Laplanche, who once exclaimed, "I demand priority for the alarm-gun;" Thuriot, who wished the jurors of the Revolutionary Tribunal to vote aloud; Bourdon de l'Oise, who provoked Chambon to challenge him, denounced Paine, and in his turn was denounced by Hébert; Fayau, who proposed to despatch an incendiary army into the Vendée; Tavaux, who on the 13th of April acted as a sort of mediator between the Gironde and the Mountain; Vernier, who suggested that the leaders of the Gironde and the Mountain should be sent to serve as common soldiers; Rewbell, who shut himself up in Mayence; Bourbotte, whose horse was killed under him at Saumur; Guimberteau and Jard-Panvilliers, the commanders of the army of the Cherbourg coast and that of La Rochelle; Lecarpentier, who was in charge of the squadron of Cancale; Roberjot, for whom the ambush of Rastadt was lying in wait; Prieur de la Marne, who wore in camp his former major's epaulettes; Levasseur de la Sarthe, who by a single word induced Serrent, commander of the Battalion of Saint-Armand, to kill himself; Reverchon, Maure, Bernard de Saintes, Charles Richard, Lequinio, and towering above them all a Mirabeau whom men called Danton.

Belonging to neither of these parties, and yet holding both in awe, rose the man Robespierre.

V

Below crouched dismay, which may be noble, and fear, which cannot fail to be contemptible. Beneath all these passions, this heroism and devotion, this rage, might be seen the gloomy multitude of the anonymous. The shoals of the Assembly were called the Plain, comprising the entire floating element,—men who are in doubt, who hesitate, retreat, temporize, mistrustfully watching one another. The Mountain and the Gironde were the chosen few, the Plain was the crowd. The Plain was summed up and expressed in Sieyès.

Sieyès was a man of a naturally profound mind, full of chimerical projects. He had paused at the Third Estate, and had never been able to rise as high as the people. Certain minds are constituted to rest midway. Sieyès called Robespierre a tiger, who returned the compliment by calling him a mole. He was a philosopher who had attained prudence if not wisdom. He was a courtier, rather than the servant of the Revolution. He took a spade and went to work with the people in the Champs de Mars, hauling the same cart with Alexander de Beauharnais. He urged others to energetic labors which he never performed himself. He said to the Girondists: "Put the cannon on your own side." There are philosophers who are natural wrestlers, and they like Condorcet joined the party of Vergniaud, or like Camille Desmoulins that of Danton. There are philosophers who value their lives, and those who belonged to this class followed Sieyès.

The best vats have their dregs. Still lower even than the Plain was the Marsh, whose stagnation was hideous to look upon, revealing as it did transparent egotism. There shivered the timid in silent expectation. Nothing could be more wretched. Ignominious to the last degree, and yet feeling no shame, hiding their indignation, living in servitude, cherishing covert rebellion, possessed by a certain cynical terror, they had all the desperation peculiar to cowardice; they really preferred the Gironde, and yet they chose the Mountain; when the final result depended on them, they went over to the successful side; they surrendered Louis XVI to Vergniaud, Danton to Robespierre, and Robespierre to Tallien. They put Marat in the pillory during his lifetime, and deified him after his death. They showed themselves the partisans of the very cause which they suddenly turned against. They seemed to possess an instinct for jostling the infirm. Since they had joined the cause with the understanding that it was a strong one, any sign of wavering seemed to them equivalent to treason. They were the majority, the power, and the fear. Hence springs the audacity of the base.

Hence the 31st of May, the 11th Germinal, the 9th Thermidor,— tragedies where dwarfs untied the knots of giants.

VI

AND AMONG THESE PASSIONATE MEN were to be found others, fanciful dreamers. Utopia was there in all its varied forms,—from the warlike, which admitted the scaffold, to the mild, which would fain abolish the penalty of death; a spectre or an angel, according as one viewed it from the throne or from the side of the common people. Men eager for the fray stood face to face with others who were contented to brood over their dreams of peace. The brain of Carnot created fourteen armies while Jean Debry was revolving in his head a scheme of universal democratic federation. Amid this furious eloquence, amid these howling and thundering voices, some men there were who preserved a fruitful silence. Lakanal was silent, preoccupied with his system for national public education; Lanthenas held his peace, absorbed in his plans for primary schools; Revellière-Lepaux was silent, dreaming of philosophy when it should attain the dignity of religion. Others busied themselves with matters of minor importance and the details of every-day life. Guyton-Morveaux was interested in the improvement of the sanitary condition of hospitals; Maire in the abolishment of existing servitudes; Jean-Bon-Saint-André in the suppression of arrest and imprisonment for debt; Romme in Chappe's proposition; Duböe in the filing of the archives; Coren-Fustier in the foundation of the Cabinet of Anatomy and the Museum of Natural History; Guyomard in the navigation of rivers and the damming of the Scheldt. Men were fanatical about art, even monomaniacs on the subject; on the 21st of January, at the very time when the head of monarchy was falling on the Place de la Révolution, Bézard, the representative of the Oise, went to see a picture of Rubens which had been found in a garret in the Rue Saint-Lazare. Artists, orators, and prophets, giants like Danton, and men as childlike as Cloots, gladiators and philosophers, were all straining for the same goal,—progress. Nothing disconcerted them. The greatness of the Convention consisted in its efforts to discover what degree of reality there might be in that which men call the impossible. At one end stood Robespierre with his eyes fixed upon the Law, and at the other Condorcet gazing with equal steadiness on Duty.

Condorcet was a man enlightened, but given to dreaming. Robespierre possessed executive ability; and sometimes, in the final crises of worn-out conditions, execution signifies extermination. Revolutions have two slopes,—the one ascending, the other descending,—whereon we meet at different stages each season in its turn, from the freezing to the flowery; and each zone produces men suited to the climate, from those who live under the hot rays of the sun, to those who dwell with the thunderbolt.

PEOPLE POINTED OUT TO EACH other the bend in the left-hand passage, where Robespierre whispered to Clavière's friend Garat that terrible epigram, "Clavière a conspiré partout où il a respiré." In this same bend, well adapted for privacy and suppressed indignation, Fabre d'Églantine quarrelled with Romme, reproaching him for having disfigured his calendar by changing Fervidor into Thermidor. People pointed out the corner where, elbow to elbow, sat the seven representatives of Haute-Garonne, who, being the first called upon to pronounce their verdict upon Louis XVI, had thus answered, one after the other: Mailhe, "death;" Delmas, "death;" Projean, "death;" Calès, "death;" Ayral, "death;" Julien, "death;" Desaby, "death,"— eternal reverberation that fills all history, and since the birth of human justice has continued to send forth a funereal echo from the walls of the tribunal. Amid this stormy sea of faces one man would point out to another the individuals whose tragic votes had caused that fearful din: Paganel, who cried, "Death. A king serves no purpose save by his death." Millaud, who said, "If death had never been known, we must today have invented it." Old Raffron du Trouillet, who exclaimed, "A speedy death!" Goupilleau, who cried, "The scaffold, at once. Delay but aggravates the pain of death." Sieyès, who with solemn brevity uttered the single word, "Death." Thuriot, who, rejecting the appeal to the people proposed by Buzot, said, "What! The primary assemblies! forty-four thousand tribunals! an endless trial! The head of Louis XVI would have time to grow gray before it fell." Augustin-Bon-Robespierre, who exclaimed, after his brother, "I ignore that humanity which massacres the people and pardons despots! Death! The demand for a reprieval means a substitution of the appeal to tyrants for the appeal to the people." Foussedoire, who took the place of Bernardin-de-Saint-Pierre, saying, "The shedding of human blood is abhorrent to me; but the blood of a king is not human blood. Death!" Jean-Bon-Saint-André, who said, "No nation can be free until the tyrant dies." Lavicomterie, who expressed himself in this formula: "So long as the tyrant breathes, liberty is strangled. Death!" Châteauneuf-Randon, who cried, "The death of Louis the Last!" Guyardin, who suggested, "Let him be executed at the Barrière-Renversée." The Barrière-Renversée was the Barrière du Trône. Tellier, who said, "Let us forge a cannon of the calibre of Louis XVI's head, to fire upon the enemy." And among those inclined to mercy, Gentil was one, who said, "I vote for imprisonment. He who makes a Charles I makes a Cromwell likewise." Bancal, who said, "Exile. I should like to see the first king of the earth sentenced to earn his living at a trade." Albouys, who said, "Exile. Let this living spectre wander round among the thrones." Zangiacomi, who said, "I vote for imprisonment; let us keep Capet alive for a scarecrow." Chaillon, who said, "Let him live! I do not approve of killing a man for Rome to canonize." While sentences like these fell one after the other from these severe lips, making their way into history, bedizened women in low-necked dresses sat in the boxes, and with list in hand counted the votes as they were given, pricking each name with a pin.

Where tragedy has entered in, horror and pity remain. To see the Convention, at whatsoever epoch of its reign, was to witness anew the judgment of the last of the Capets; the legend of the 21st of January seemed to be interwoven with all its acts; the formidable Assembly was composed of those men whose fatal breath put out the ancient torch of monarchy, which had burned for eighteen centuries; the decisive trial of all kings in the person of one seemed to be the starting-point of the great war which it waged against the past. At whatsoever session of the Convention one might be present, the shadow cast by the scaffold of Louis XVI never failed to make itself evident. The spectators told each other about the resignations of Kersaint and Roland, and also about Duchâtel the deputy of the Deux-Sèvres, who, being ill, caused himself to be carried to the Assembly, and on his death-bed voted against the execution of the king,—an act which excited Marat to laughter. People looked for the representative forgotten today, who, after a session that had lasted thirty-seven hours, overcome by fatigue, fell asleep on his bench, and being roused by the usher when his turn came to vote, half-opened his eyes, murmured, "Death," and fell asleep again.

At the time when the death-sentence of Louis XVI was passed, Robespierre had eighteen months to live, Danton fifteen, Vergniaud nine, Marat five months and three weeks, and Lepelletier-Saint-Fargeau one day! Brief and terrible was the breath of life in those days.

VIII

THE PEOPLE HAD A WINDOW, opening on the Convention in the shape of the public tribunes, and when this window proved inadequate, they opened the door, and the street-population poured in upon the Assembly. The invasions of the crowd into this senate presented one of the most striking spectacles known to history. Generally these irruptions were amicable. The street fraternized with the curule chair. But friendship with a people who had once, in the course of three hours, taken the cannon of the Invalides and forty thousand muskets besides, was a somewhat formidable relationship. At every moment a procession interrupted the session. There were deputations admitted to the bar, petitions, expressions of respect, offerings. The pike of honor of the Faubourg Saint-Antoine was brought in, borne by women. The English offered twenty thousand pairs of shoes for our barefooted soldiers. "Citizen Arnoux," said the "Moniteur," "the curé of Aubignan, in command of the battalion of the Drôme, requests permission to march to the frontier, and begs that his parish may be kept for him." The delegates from the Sections came, bringing in wheelbarrows, dishes, patens, chalices, monstrances, heaps of gold, silver, and gilt, offerings to the country from this ragged crowd, who asked, as a reward, permission to dance the Carmagnole before the Convention.

Chenard, Narbonne, and Vallière came to sing stanzas in honor of the Mountain. The section of Mont-Blanc brought the bust of Lepelletier, and a woman placed a red cap on the head of the president, who embraced her; "the citoyennes of the section du Mail" strewed flowers "before the legislators;" the "pupils of the country," escorted by music, came to thank the Convention for having "paved the way for the prosperity of the century;" the women of the section of the Gardes-Françaises brought roses; the women of the section of the Champs-Élysées presented a crown of oak-leaves; the women of the section of the Temple came to the bar and took an oath "to wed only true Republicans;" the section of Molière presented a medal of Franklin which, by a formal decree, was suspended from the wreath of the statue of Liberty; the Foundlings, who had been declared the Children of the Republic, filed by, dressed in the national uniform; young girls of the ninety-third section came arrayed in long white gowns, and the next day the "Moniteur" contained this line: "The president receives a bouquet from the innocent hands of a fair young girl." The orators saluted the crowds and sometimes flattered them, saying to the multitude; "Thou art infallible; thou art irreproachable; thou art sublime." The lower classes are childlike; they are fond of sugar-plums. Sometimes a riot would invade the Assembly, entering in a fury and departing pacified, like the Rhone flowing through Lake Leman, which is muddy enough on its entrance, but flows out as blue as the sky.

If it continued turbulent, Henriot would now and then order his furnaces for heating the bullets to be brought up to the entrance of the Tuileries.

IX

WHILE THIS ASSEMBLY WAS THROWING off the shackles of revolution, it was also promoting civilization. It was a furnace, to be sure, but it was likewise a forge. In this caldron where terror was bubbling, progress also fermented. From that chaos of shadows and tempestuous whirlwind of clouds spread immense rays of light parallel with the eternal laws,—rays that have since rested on the horizon, forever visible in the sky of the nations, and which are called justice, tolerance, goodness, reason, truth, and love. The Convention proclaimed this grand axiom: "The liberty of one citizen ends where that of another begins;" thus summing up in two lines the essence of social science. It proclaimed the sanctity of the poor, as well as of the infirm in the persons of the blind, and of the mutes, whose guardianship had been assumed by the State; it honored maternity in the person of the girl-mother, whom it comforted and lifted up, childhood in the orphans adopted by the State, and innocence in the accused, who was indemnified by the government after his acquittal. It branded the traffic in blacks and abolished slavery. It proclaimed civil consolidation. It decreed gratuitous instruction. It organized national education by the establishment of the normal school in Paris, the central school in the cities, and the primary school in the communes. It founded conservatories and museums. It systematized the Code as well as the weights and measures, and the method of calculation by decimals. It established the finances of France upon a firm basis, and brought about an era of public credit after the long monarchical bankruptcy. It established communication by telegraph, it provided almshouses for old age and the improved hospitals for sickness; it gave the Polytechnic School to the cause of education, the Bureau of Longitude to science, and the Institute to the domain of human intellect. It was at once cosmopolitan and national. Of the eleven thousand two hundred and ten decrees issued by the Convention, the proportion of philanthropic as compared with the political was as two to one. It proclaimed universal morality to be the basis of society, and universal conscience the basis of the law. And it must be remembered that all these reforms—the abolition of slavery, the proclamation of universal brotherhood, the protection of humanity, the elevation of the human conscience, the law of labor changed into a privilege, thus transforming the burden into a comfort, the consolidation of the national wealth, the enlightenment and protection of children, the dissemination of knowledge and science, a light set upon all the mountain-tops, help proffered to the suffering, and the promulgation of all principle—were accomplished by the Convention, with the Vendée gnawing like hydra at its entrails, and the kings of the world leaping like tigers upon its shoulders.

X

ASTONISHING ASSEMBLY! THE HUMAN, THE inhuman, and the superhuman,—every type in short might be found there. An epic accumulation of antagonisms,—Guillotin avoiding David, Bazire insulting Chabot, Gaudet mocking Saint-Just, Vergniaud despising Danton, Louvet attacking Robespierre, Buzot denouncing Égalité, Chambon branding Pache: all hating Marat. And how many more names might yet be registered! Armonville,—called Bonnet-Rouge, because at the sessions he invariably wore a Phrygian cap,—a friend of Robespierre, who demanded that the latter should be "guillotined after Louis XVI" to restore the equilibrium; Massieu, a colleague and counterpart of the kindly Lamourette, the bishop, destined to leave his name to a kiss; Lehardy du Morbihan, stigmatizing the priests of Brittany; Barère, the man of majorities, who presided when Louis XVI appeared at the bar, and who bore the same relation to Paméla as Louvet to Lodoïska; the orator Daunou, who said, "Let us gain time;" Dubois-Crancé, who listened to Marat's whispered confidences; the Marquis de Châteauneuf; Laclos; Herault de Séchelle, who fell back before Henriot, crying, "Gunners, to your pieces!" Julien, who compared the Mountain to Thermopylæ; Gamon, who demanded that a public tribune should be reserved exclusively for women; Laloy, who awarded the honors of the session to Bishop Gobel, who came to the Convention to exchange his mitre for the red cap; Lecomte, who cried, "So we pay homage to the priest who unfrocks himself;" Féraud, whose head was saluted by Boissy-d'Anglas, leaving to history the solution of the query, "Did Boissy-d'Anglas salute the victim in the person of the head, or the assassins in the form of the pike?" the two brothers Duprat, one a member of the Mountain, the other a Girondist, who hated each other, as did the two brothers Chénier.

Many a word has been uttered in this tribune in moments of excitement which has sometimes unconsciously to the speaker aroused the fatal spirit of revolution, and so influenced the existing circumstances that a sense of discontent and passion suddenly sprang to life. As if displeased with what they heard, events seemed to take offence at the words of men, and catastrophes were precipitated by human speech. The reverberation of a voice in the mountain is sufficient to start an avalanche. The utterance of one superfluous word may be followed by a landslide, which might not have happened had no word been spoken. One might almost fancy that events develop a certain irascibility.

Thus a mistaken word falling by chance from the lips of an orator cost Mme. Élisabeth her head.

Intemperance of language was the rule at the Convention. In the discussions threats flew back and forth, crossing one another, like sparks from a conflagration.

Pétion. "Come to the point, Robespierre."

Robespierre. "You are the point, Pétion. I shall come; you need have no fear."

A Voice. "Death to Marat!"

Marat. "When Marat dies, the city of Paris will be no more; and when Paris is gone, there is an end to the Republic."

Billaud-Varennes rose to say, "We wish to—"

Barère interrupted him: "You speak in the plural, like a king."

And another day:—

Philippeaux. "One of the members drew his sword upon me."

Audouin. "President, call the assassin to order."

The President. "Wait."

Panis. "President, I call you to order,"—a sally followed by an outburst of rude laughter.

Lecointre. "The Curé of Chant-de-Bout complains that his Bishop Fauchet forbids him to marry."

A Voice. "I see no reason why Fauchet, who has mistresses, should try to prevent other men from having wives."

Another Voice. "Priest, take to thyself a wife."

The tribunes mingled in the conversation, and said "Thou" to the members.

One day the representative Ruamps mounted to the tribune, and, one of his hips being much larger than the other, a spectator called out to him: "Turn that one towards the Right, since you have a cheek *à la David!*"

Such were the liberties that the people took with the Convention. Once, however, during the uproar of the 11th of April, 1793, the president caused a disorderly person in the tribunes to be arrested.

One day, during a session at which the venerable Buonarotti was present, Robespierre had the floor, and spoke for two hours, never removing his eyes from Danton,—sometimes looking straight at him, which was unpleasant enough, but when he looked at him sideways, it was even more disagreeable. His thunders of eloquence were not without effect, ending by an indignant outburst full of ominous words: "We know the intriguers, and those who strive to corrupt, as well as those who are corrupted; we know the traitors also. They are present in this Assembly. They hear our voice, our eyes are upon them, and our gaze pursues them. Let them look above their heads, and they will discover the sword of the law; let them look into their conscience, and there behold their own infamy. Let them beware!" When Robespierre had finished, Danton, with his half-closed eyes turned upwards and one arm hanging over the back of his chair, threw himself back and began to hum,—

"Cadet Roussel fait des discours
Qui ne sont pas longs quand ils sont courts."

Imprecations fell thick on every side,—"Conspirator!" "Assassin!" "Scoundrel!" "Seditious!"

"Moderate!" They denounced one another in the presence of the bust of Brutus standing there. Exclamations, insults, challenges! Angry glances interchanged, much shaking of fists, flashing of pistols and half-drawn daggers. An awful outblazing from the tribune. Some talked as if they were pushed up against the guillotine. Heads waved to and fro, frightened yet terrible. The multitude was like a volume of smoke blown all ways at once,—men of the Mountain, Girondists, Feuillantists, Moderates, Terrorists, Jacobins, Cordeliers, and the eighteen regicide priests.

All these men!—a mass of smoke driven about in every direction.

XI

SPIRITS AT THE MERCY OF the wind,—but a wind of preternatural power!

It might be truthfully said, even of the chief among them, that to be a member of the Convention was like being a wave of the ocean.

The impetus came from above. There was an inherent force in the Convention, which might be called a will,—not in the sense of an individual quality, but belonging to the Assembly as a body; and this will was an idea, indomitable and boundless, which from the heavens above descended into the darkness below. Men called it Revolution, and wherever it passed, some men were overthrown and others exalted; one would be scattered like foam, while another was dashed to pieces against the rocks. It kept its goal well in mind as it drove the maelstrom before it. To impute revolution to men is like attributing the tides to the waves.

Revolution is a manifestation of the unknown. You may call it good or evil, according as you aspire to the future or cling to the past; but leave it to its authors. It would seem to be the joint product of great events and great individualities, but is in reality the result of events alone. Events plan the expenditures for which men pay the bills. Events dictate, men sign. The 14th of July was signed by Camille Desmoulins, the 10th of August by Danton, the 2d September by Marat, the 21st of September by Grégoire, and the 21st of January by Robespierre; but Desmoulins, Danton, Marat, Grégoire, and Robespierre are merely clerks. The majestic and mysterious compiler of those grand pages was Almighty God, wearing the mask of destiny. Robespierre believed in God,—he did indeed.

Revolution is one form of the eternal phenomenon that circumscribes us on all sides, and which we call Necessity.

In the presence of this mysterious complication of benefits and wretchedness rises the wherefore of history.

Because. This answer may be the reply of one who knows nothing, as well as that of one who knows all.

In the presence of these monstrous catastrophes which both devastate and revivify civilization, one hesitates to sit in judgment on the details. To blame or to praise men on account of the result is very much like praising or criticising the ciphers on account of the sum total. The inevitable is sure to happen; if the wind is to blow, it will blow, but the eternal serenity remains untouched by these blasts. Like the starlit sky above the tempest, truth and justice sit enthroned above all revolutions.

XII

Such was this immeasurable Convention, like an intrenched encampment of the human race attacked simultaneously by all the powers of darkness; the camp-fires of an army of ideas besieged by its foes, an immense bivouac of human intellect on the slope of a precipice. Nothing in history can be compared to this Assembly, which contained within itself senate and people, conclave and street-crossing, Areopagus and public square, tribunal and accused.

The Convention always yielded to the wind; but this wind came from the mouth of the people, and it was the breath of God.

And today, after the lapse of eighty years, every time the Convention presents itself to the mind of any man whomsoever, whether philosopher or historian, he cannot but pause and meditate; since no man can be indifferent to that grand procession of shadows.

II

Marat in the Green-Room

ON THE DAY FOLLOWING THE interview in the Rue du Paon, Marat, according to the intention which he had announced to Simonne Évrard, went to the Convention.

There chanced to be present a certain marquis, Louis de Montaut, an admirer of Marat,—the same who afterwards presented to the Convention a decimal clock surmounted by a bust of Marat.

Just as Marat entered, Chabot approached Montant. "Ci-devant—" he said.

Montaut looked up.

"Why do you call me ci-devant?"

"Because that's what you are."

"I?"

"Of course, since you were once a marquis."

"Never!"

"Nonsense!"

"My father was a soldier; my grandfather was a weaver."

"What folly is this, Montaut?"

"My name is not Montaut."

"What is it, then?"

"My name is Maribon."

"Very well," declared Chabot; "it is all one to me."

And he added, between his teeth,—

"Every man, nowadays, pretends that he is no marquis."

Marat stopped in the left-hand corridor and looked at Montaut and Chabot.

Whenever he came in, a murmur would pass through the crowd, but always at a respectful distance; it was quiet in his immediate vicinity. Marat paid no attention whatever. He scorned the croaking of the frogs.

In this dim shadow obscuring the lower benches, Conpé de l'Oise, Prunelle, Villars,—a bishop who afterwards became a member of the French Academy,—Boutroue, Petit, Plaichard, Bonet, Thibaudeau, Valdruche, pointed him out to one another.

"Look! There is Marat!"

"He is not ill, then?"

"Probably he is, since he is here in a dressing-gown."

"In a dressing-gown?"

"Certainly."

"What liberties he allows himself!"

"That he should dare to come to the Convention in such a garb!"

"Since he came one day crowned with laurels, he might be expected to appear in a dressing-gown."

"With his face of copper, and teeth of verdigris."

"His dressing-gown seems new."

"What is it made of?"

"A kind of rep."

"Striped?"

"Just see the lapels!"

"They are made of fur."

"Tiger-skin?"

"No, ermine."

"Imitation."

"He has stockings on."

"Remarkable!"

"And shoes with buckles."

"Silver buckles!"

"Camboulas' sabots will not soon forgive him that."

On the opposite benches they pretended not to see Marat, but continued to talk of other matters. Santhonax accosted Dussaulx.

"Have you heard, Dussaulx?"

"What?"

"The ci-devant Count de Brienne."

"The one who was at La Force with the ci-devant Duke de Villeroy?"

"Yes."

"I knew them both. What about them?"

"You know they were so frightened that they saluted all the red caps of the turnkeys, and one day refused to take a hand at *piquet* because a pack of cards with kings and queens was offered them."

"Well?"

"They were guillotined yesterday."

"Both of them?"

"Yes."

"Well, how did they behave in prison?"

"Like cowards!"

"And what sort of a figure did they cut on the scaffold?"

"Intrepid."

Whereupon Dussaulx exclaimed,—

"It's easier to die than to live."

Barère had begun to read a report on the subject of the Vendée. Nine hundred men from Morbihan had started with cannon to relieve Nantes. Redon was threatened by the peasants, and Paimboeuf had been attacked. A fleet was cruising in the vicinity of Maindrin to prevent invasions. From Ingrande to Maure the entire left bank of the Loire bristled with Royalist batteries. Three thousand peasants had taken possession of Pornic. They cried: "Vive les Anglais!" Barère read a letter from Santerre to the Convention ending with the following words:

"Seven thousand peasants attacked Vannes. We repulsed them, and they retreated, leaving four cannon in our hands."

"And how many prisoners?" interrupted a voice. Barère went on,—

"Postscript. We have no prisoners, because we have ceased to take them."[1]

Marat, as usual, stood motionless, paying no attention to what was going on, apparently absorbed in deep preoccupation.

---

1. Moniteur, vol. xix. p. 81.

He held a paper in his hand, crumpling it between his fingers. Had it been unfolded, certain words in the handwriting of Momoro, in answer, no doubt, to some question of Marat, might have been read:—

"Nothing can be done in opposition to the supreme authority of the delegated commissioners, especially those of the Committee of Public Safety. Although Génissieux said in the session of May 6th, 'Each commissioner is more than a king,' it had no effect. Life and death are in their hands. Massade at Angers, Trullard at Saint-Amand, Nyon with General Marcé, Parrein in the army of the 'Sables,' Millier in the army of Niort, are all-powerful. The Jacobin Club has gone so far as to appoint Parrein brigadier-general. Circumstances excuse everything. A delegate of the Committee of Public Safety may hold in check a commander-in-chief."

Marat ceased crumpling the paper, put it in his pocket, and walked slowly towards Montaut and Chabot, who had continued their conversation and had not seen him enter.

Chabot was just saying,—

"Maribon, or Montaut, listen to this: I have just left the Committee of Public Safety."

"And what are they doing there?"

"They are setting a priest to watch a noble."

"Ah!"

"A noble like yourself—"

"I am not a noble," said Montaut.

"To be watched by a priest—"

"Like you."

"I am not a priest," said Chabot.

And both men began to laugh.

"Please give us a more definite account."

"Well, here is the tale: a priest, Cimourdain by name, has been delegated with full powers to a Viscount Gauvain, who is in command of the exploring division of the army of the coast. Now, the difficulty is, to prevent the nobleman from cheating and the priest from betraying."

"There will be no trouble about that. You have only to make death the third party."

"That is what I came for," said Marat They looked up.

"Good-day, Marat," said Chabot; "we seldom see you at our sessions."

"My doctor has ordered baths," replied Marat.

"Ah, you had better beware of baths," continued Chabot. "Seneca died in a bath."

Marat smiled.

"There is no Nero here, Chabot."

"I should say there was, since you are here," said a gruff voice.

It was Danton, who was passing on his way towards his seat.

Marat did not turn round.

He thrust his head in between the faces of Montaut and Chabot.

"Listen, I have come on serious business; one of us three must propose the draft of a decree to the Convention today."

"I am not the man," said Montaut. "They pay no attention to me; I am a marquis."

"Neither will they listen to me; I am a Capuchin," said Chabot.

"Nor to me, for I am Marat"

A silence ensued.

Marat, absorbed in his own thoughts, was not accessible to questions; still, Montaut ventured upon one.

"What decree would you like the Assembly to pass, Marat?"

"A decree inflicting the penalty of death on any military chief who allows a rebel prisoner to escape."

Chabot interposed.

"There is such a decree already; it was made a law at the end of April."

"That amounts to nothing whatever," said Marat. "Everywhere throughout the Vendée prisoners are helped to escape, and any man may shelter them with impunity."

"That is because the decree is no longer in force, Marat."

"It must be revived, Chabot."

"No doubt it needs to be revived."

"And to accomplish this we must address the Convention."

"There will be no need to do that, Marat; the Committee of Public Safety will suffice."

"The object will be attained," added Montaut, "if the Committee of Public Safety order the decree to be placarded in every Commune of the Vendée, and make two or three suitable examples."

"Of men in authority," rejoined Chabot. "Of the generals."

Marat mumbled between his teeth, "Yes, I suppose that will answer."

"Marat," continued Chabot, "go and say that to the Committee of Public Safety yourself."

Marat gazed steadily at him, which was not pleasant, even for a Chabot.

"Chabot," he said, "the Committee of Public Safety meets at Robespierre's house; I do not visit Robespierre."

"Then I will go myself," said Montaut.

"Very well," replied Marat.

The next day a mandate from the Committee of Public Safety was sent in all directions, ordering the authorities of the cities and villages of the Vendée not only to publish, but also strictly to execute, a decree awarding the penalty of death to all who were known to aid and abet the escape of brigands and rebel prisoners.

This decree was but the first step. The Convention was to go still farther than that. Several months later, on the 11th Brumaire, in the year II (November, 1793), when Laval opened its gates to the Vendean fugitives, it decreed that every city that sheltered rebels should be demolished and destroyed.

The princes of Europe, on their side, in the manifesto of the Duke of Brunswick, suggested by the Émigrés and drawn up by the Marquis of Linnon, steward to the Duke of Orleans, declared that every Frenchman taken with arms in his hand should be shot, and if but a hair fell from the head of the king, Paris should be razed to the ground.

Cruelty against barbarity.

PART III
IN THE VENDÉE

Book I

The Vendée

I

The Forests

THERE WERE IN BRITTANY AT that time seven much-dreaded forests. The Vendean war was a rebellion among priests, and the forest was their auxiliary. The spirits of darkness help one another.

The seven Black Forests of Brittany were the forest of Fougères, which bars the passage between Dol and Avranches; the forest of Princé, eight miles in circumference; the forest of Paimpont, abounding in ravines and brooks, and almost inaccessible in the direction of Baignon, with an easy retreat towards Concornet, which was a Royalist town; the forest of Rennes, whence could be heard the tocsin of the Republican parishes, always numerous in the neighborhood of cities,—there it was that Puysaye lost Focard; the forest of Machecoul, where Charette dwelt like a wild beast; the forest of La Garnache, belonging to the Trémoilles, the Gauvains, and the Rohans; and the forest of Brocéliande, that had been appropriated by the fairies.

One nobleman in Brittany was called the *Seigneur des Sept-Forêts*, and he was the Viscount de Fontenay, a Breton prince.

For the Breton prince was a creation quite distinct from the French prince. The Rohans were Breton princes. Gamier de Saintes, in his report to the Convention of the 15th Nivôse, year II, thus describes the Prince de Talmont,—"That Capet of brigands, the sovereign of Maine and Normandy."

The events that transpired in Breton forests from 1792 to 1800 would form a history in themselves, blending like a legend with the stupendous affair of the Vendée.

There is truth in legend as well as in history, but the nature of legendary truth differs from that of historic truth. The former may be invention; but its result is reality. Both, however, have the same aim, inasmuch as each strives to depict the eternal type of mankind under the transitory specimen.

The Vendée cannot be fully understood unless legend is allowed to supplement history; history must present the total effect, legend describe the details.

We cannot refuse to acknowledge that the Vendée is well worth the trouble, for it is a prodigy.

That War of the Ignorant, so dull and yet so splendid, so detestable and at the same time so magnificent, was at once the despair and the pride of the nation. In the act of wounding France, the Vendée covered her with glory. There are times when human society presents enigmas whose meaning becomes evident to the wise, while for the ignorant it remains obscure, signifying nothing more than violence and barbarism. A philosopher is slow to accuse. He takes into consideration the disturbances caused by these problems, which never pass without casting a shadow like a cloud.

He who would understand the Vendée must picture the antagonism of the French Revolution on the one hand, and the Breton peasant on the other.

Face to face with these unparalleled events,—this tremendous promise of every advantage at once, this fit of rage on the part of civilization, this excess of infuriated progress, to be accompanied by an improvement that could neither be measured nor understood,—stands this serious and peculiar savage, this man with the keen eyes and long hair, who lives on milk and chestnuts; whose ideas are bounded by his roof, by his hedge, and by his ditch; who can distinguish each village by the sound of its bells; who drinks nothing but water, yet wears a leather waistcoat worked with silken arabesques,—a man uncultivated, dressed in embroidered garments, who tattoes his clothes as his ancestors the Celts used to tattoo their faces; who respects his master in the person of his executioner; who speaks a dead language, which is equivalent to keeping his mind in a tomb, goading his oxen, sharpening his scythe, hoeing his black grain, kneading his buckwheat cake; reverencing, first his plough, and secondly his grandmother; believing in the Blessed Virgin, and in the White Lady no less; worshipping before the altar, and also before the tall mysterious stone set up in the midst of the moor,—a laborer in the plain, a fisherman on the coast, a poacher in the thicket, devoted to his kings, his priests, his lords, and to his very lice; a man of pensive mood, often standing motionless for hours on the wide deserted shore, listening gloomily to the sounding sea.

Is it then strange that this blind man failed to appreciate the light?

II

Men

THE PEASANT HAS CONFIDENCE IN the field that nourishes him, no less than in the wood that serves to hide him. It is no easy matter to conceive an idea of the forests of Brittany. They were cities in themselves. Nothing could be more secret, more silent, or more impenetrable than those tangled thickets of briers and branches offering shelter, repose, and silence. No solitude could seem more death-like and sepulchral; if one could, like a flash of lightning, have felled the entire forest at a single stroke, a swarm of human beings would have stood forth revealed within those shades.

Concealed on the outside by coverings of stones and branches were wells, round and narrow, sinking at first vertically and then horizontally, widening under the ground like funnels, and ending in dark chambers. Wells like these discovered by Westermann in Brittany were also found in Egypt by Cambyses,—with this difference, that while the Egyptian caves in the desert held dead men only, those in the forests of Brittany contained living human beings. One of the wildest glades in the woods of Misdon, intersected by subterranean passages and cells, wherein a mysterious population moved to and fro, was called "la Grande Ville." Another glade, just as deserted above ground, and no less populous below, was called "la Place Royale."

This subterranean life in Brittany had existed from time immemorial. Man had there sought refuge from his brother man. Hence these hiding-places, like the dens of reptiles, hollowed out under the trees. They dated from the times of the Druids, and some of the crypts were as old as the dolmens. All the evil spirits of legend and the monsters of history passed over this gloomy land,—Teutates, Cæsar, Hoël, Néomène, Geoffrey of England, Alain of the iron glove, Pierre Mauclerc, the French house of Blois and the English house of Montfort, kings and dukes, the nine barons of Brittany, the judges of the Great Days, the counts of Nantes who wrangled with the counts of Rennes, highwaymen, banditti, Free Lances, René II, the Viscount de Rohan, the king's governors, the "good Duke de Chaulnes" who hung the peasants under the windows of Madame de Sévigné, the seignorial butcheries in the fifteenth century, religious wars in the sixteenth and seventeenth, and the thirty thousand dogs trained to hunt men in the eighteenth. During this wild trampling, the people made up their minds that it would be better for them to disappear. One after the other, the troglodytes seeking to escape from the Celts, the Celts from the Romans, the Bretons from the Normans, the Huguenots from the Catholics, and the smugglers from the excise officers, had sought refuge first in the forests, then underground. It is thus that tyranny forces the nations to the last resource of the hunted beast. For two thousand years had despotism, in all its varied forms,—of conquest, vassalage, fanaticism, and taxation,—hunted down this unfortunate and distracted Brittany; it was like an inexorable *battue* constantly changing its method of attack. Men disappeared underground. While that terror which is a sort of rage was brooding in human souls, and the dens in the forests were in waiting for them, the French Republic sprang into existence. Brittany, thinking this compulsory deliverance but a new form of oppression, broke into open rebellion,—a mistake usually made by enslaved peoples.

III

Connivance of Men and Forests

THUS THE TRAGIC FORESTS OF Brittany once more resumed their ancient rôle of servant and accomplice to revolution.

The subsoil of such a forest was like a madrepore pierced and intersected in all directions by a secret labyrinth of mines, cells, and galleries. Each of these hidden cells was large enough to shelter five or six men; the only difficulty was in breathing. Certain mysterious ciphers have been preserved that give us a clew to this powerful organization of the peasant rebellion. In Ille-et-Vilaine, in the forest of Pertre, where the Prince de Talmont had taken refuge, not a breath could be heard, not a trace of human life was visible; and yet Focard had there mustered six thousand men. In Morbihan, in the forest of Meulac, not a man of all the eight thousand there was to be seen. These two forests, le Pertre and Meulac, are not, however, to be reckoned among the great Breton forests. It would have been dangerous walking over their explosive soil. These treacherous copses, with their multitudes of combatants lurking in a sort of subterranean labyrinth, were like great black sponges, from which, beneath the pressure of Revolution's giant foot, civil war gushed forth. Invisible battalions were lying in wait. This army, unknown to the world, wound its way along under the feet of the Republican armies, leaping out of the ground at times in vast numbers, and disappearing as suddenly,—possessing the power of vanishing at will no less than the gift of ubiquity. It was like the descending avalanche that leaves but a cloud of dust behind, colossi with a marvellous genius for contraction, giants in warfare, dwarfs in flight, jaguars with the habits of moles. Moreover, there were woods as well as forests. As the village ranks below the city, so the woods, bear a similar relation to the forests, which they serve to connect after the fashion of a labyrinth. Old castles, fortresses once upon a time, hamlets that had been camps, farms covered with ambushes and snares, divided by ditches and fenced in by trees, formed the meshes of the net in which the Republican armies were caught.

All this was called the Bocage.

There was the wood of Misdon, with a pond in its midst, held by Jean Chouan; the wood of Gennes, held by Taillefer; the wood of La Huisserie, held by Gouge-le-Bruant; the wood of La Charnie, held by Courtillé-le-Bâtard, called the apostle Saint Paul, chief of the camp of the Vache-Noire; the wood of Burgault, in possession of that enigmatical Monsieur Jacques, who was to meet with a mysterious death in the vault of Juvardeil; the wood of Charreau, where Pimousse and Petit-Prince, when attacked by the garrison of Châteauneuf, captured the grenadiers from the ranks of the Republicans in a hand-to-hand encounter; the wood of La Heureuserie, which witnessed the defeat of the military post of Longue-Faye; the wood of L'Aulne, whence the road between Rennes and Laval could be watched; the wood of La Gravelle, won by a Prince of La Tremoille in a bowling-match; the wood of Lorges in the Côtes-du-Nord, where Charles de Boishardy succeeded Bernard de Villeneuve; the wood of Bagnard, near Fontenay, where Lescure offered battle to Chalbos,—a challenge accepted by the latter although they were five to one against him; the wood of La Durondais, over which Alain le Redru and Hérispoux, sons of Charles the Bald, quarrelled in former times; the wood of Croque-loup, on the edge of that moor where Coupereau used to shear the prisoners; the wood of La Croix-Bataille, witness to the Homeric insults hurled against each other by Jambe d'Argent and Morière; the wood of La Saudraie, which the reader will remember was reconnoitred by the Paris battalion; and many others besides.

In several of these forests and woods there were not only subterranean villages grouped around the burrow-like headquarters of the chief, but actual hamlets composed of low cabins hidden under the trees in such numbers that the forest was often filled with them. Sometimes the smoke betrayed their presence. Two among these hamlets in the forest of Misdon have become famous,—Lorrière, near Létang, and the group of huts called La Rue-de-Bau, in the direction of Saint-Ouen-les-Toits.

The women lived in the huts, and the men in the caves. The galleries of the fairies and the old Celtic mines were utilized for purposes of warfare. Food was conveyed to the dwellers underground, and some there were who, forgotten, died of hunger. They, however, were awkward fellows, who had not sense enough to uncover their wells. This cover, usually made of moss and branches, and arranged so skilfully that it was impossible to distinguish it on the outside from the surrounding grass, was yet easily opened and closed from the inside. A den like this, known under the name of "la loge," was hollowed out with great care, and the earth taken therefrom thrown into some neighboring pond. The inside walls and the floor were afterwards lined with ferns and moss. It was fairly comfortable, save for the lack of light, fire, bread, and air.

To rise from underground and appear among the living without due precaution, possibly to disinter themselves at an inappropriate moment, would be a serious business. They might chance to encounter an army on the march. Those were dangerous woods, snares with a double trap. The Blues dared not enter, and the Whites dared not come out.

IV

Their Life Under Ground

THE MEN, WEARIED OF LIVING in these beasts' lairs, would sometimes venture to come out by night and dance on the neighboring moor; or else they said prayers, by way of killing time. "Jean Chouan made us say our beads from morning till night," says Bourdoiseau.

It was almost impossible, when the season arrived, to prevent the men of Bas-Maine from going to the Fête de la Gerbe. They clung to their own ideas. Tranche-Montagne says that Denys disguised himself as a woman, to go to the play at Laval; after which he returned to his den.

All at once they would rush out in search of death, changing one tomb for another.

Sometimes they would lift the cover of their grave and listen for any chance sounds of battle in the distance, following it with their ears, guided by the steady fire of the Republicans and the intermittent shots of the Royalists. When the platoon-firing suddenly ceased, they knew that the Royalists had lost the day; but if the scattering shots continued, receding into the distance, it was a sign that the victory was theirs. The Whites always pursued; the Blues never did so, because the country was against them.

These underground belligerents were wonderfully well-informed. Nothing could be more rapid or more mysterious than their means of communication. The bridges and wagons had all been destroyed, yet they found means to keep one another informed of all that went on, and to send timely warning. Messenger-stations of danger were established from forest to forest, from village to village, from hut to hut, from bush to bush.

A stupid-looking peasant might be seen passing along; he carried despatches in his hollow staff.

Furnished by Boétidoux, a former constituent, with the modern Republican passport, in which a blank space is left for the name, bundles of which were in the possession of that traitor, they were enabled to travel from one end of Brittany to the other.

It was impossible to take them by surprise. Puysaye[1] states that "secrets confided to upwards of four thousand individuals have been religiously kept."

It seemed as though this quadrilateral, closed on the south by the line from Sables to Thouars, on the east by that from Thouars to Saumur as well as by the river of Thoué, on the north by the Loire, and on the west by the ocean, possessed a system of nerves in common, and that no single part of the ground could stir without shaking the whole. In the twinkling of an eye, they learned in Luçon what was going on in Noirmoutier, and the camp of La Loué knew what was passing in the camp La Croix-Morineau. It was as if the birds had carried the news. On the 7th Messidor, in the year III, Hoche wrote: "One might have supposed they had telegraphs."

They formed clans, as in Scotland, and each parish had its own captain. My father fought in this war, and I know whereof I am speaking.

---

1. Vol. ii. p. 35.

V

Their Life in Warfare

MANY OF THEM HAD NOTHING but pikes; but good hunting-rifles were plentiful, and no marksmen were more expert than the poachers of the Bocage and the smugglers of Loroux. They were eccentric, terrible, and intrepid fighters. The proclamation of a decree to levy three hundred thousand men was the signal for ringing the tocsin in six hundred villages. The flames burst forth in all directions at once. Poitou and the Anjou revolted on the same day. Let us remark that the first rumbling was heard on the 8th of July, 1792, a month previous to the 10th of August, on the moor of Kerbader. Alain Redeler, whose name is now forgotten, was the forerunner of La Rochejaquelein and Jean Chouan. The Royalists forced all able-bodied men to march, under penalty of death. They confiscated harnesses, wagons, and provisions. Sapinaud at once assembled three thousand soldiers, Cathelineau ten thousand, Stofflet twenty thousand, and Charette took possession of Noirmoutier. The Viscount de Scépeaux roused the Haut-Anjou, the Chevalier de Dieuzie the Entre-Vilaine-et-Loire, Tristan l'Hermite the Bas-Maine, the barber Gaston the city of Guéménée, and the Abbé Bernier all the others.

It required but little to excite the masses. A great black cat was placed in the tabernacle of a priest who had taken the civil oath,—a "priest-juror," as he was called,—whence it suddenly leaped forth in the middle of the Mass. "It's the Devil!" cried the peasants, and a whole district rose in revolt. Sometimes flames would be seen issuing from the confessionals. For assailing the Blues and crossing the ravines, they had sticks fifteen feet long, called the "ferte,"—a weapon of defence, which was likewise available for flight. In the very heat of the conflict, when the peasants were attacking the Republican squares, if they chanced to see on the battlefield a cross or a chapel, all fell on their knees and said their prayers under the fire of the enemy; and after finishing the rosary, those who had not been killed rushed upon the enemy. Alas! what giants were these! They loaded their muskets on the run; that was their special talent. They could be made to believe anything. Their priests showed them other priests whose necks had been reddened by a tightly drawn cord, saying to them: "These are the guillotined come to life again." They had their fits of chivalrous emotion; they paid military honors to

Fesque, a Republican standard-bearer, who had allowed himself to be sabred without once losing hold of his banner. These peasants were at times derisive; they called the married Republican priests "sans-calottes devenus sans-culottes."[2] At first they stood in awe of the cannon; but after a while they dashed upon them with no other weapons than their sticks, and captured several. The first one they took was a fine bronze cannon, which they baptized "le Missionnaire;" another gun, dating from the times of the Catholic wars, and which had Richelieu's arms and an image of the Virgin engraved upon it, they named Marie-Jeanne. When they lost Fontenay, they lost Marie-Jeanne, around which six hundred peasants fell fighting with unflinching courage.

Later, they recaptured Fontenay in order to recover Marie-Jeanne, which they brought back under the fleur-de-lis flag, covering it with flowers, and making the women who passed by kiss it. But two cannon were insufficient. It was Stofflet who had captured Marie-Jeanne; Cathelineau, envying him, left Pin-en-Mange, attacked Jallais, and took possession of a third one. Forest fell on Saint-Florent and captured a fourth. Two other commanders, Chouppes and Saint-Paul, were still more successful. They manufactured imitation-cannon from the trunks of trees, using manikins for gunners; and with this artillery, over which they made merry, they forced the Blues to retreat to Mareuil. At that time they were in the height of their glory. Later, when Chalbos defeated La Marsonnière, the peasants left behind them on the dishonored battlefield two cannon, bearing the arms of England. At that time the French princes were paid by England, who, as Nantiat writes on the 10th of May, 1794, "remitted funds to Monseigneur because Mr. Pitt was told that it was the proper thing to do." Mellinet, in a report of the 31st of March, says: "The cry of the rebels is, 'Long live the English!'" The peasants tarried for purposes of pillage, for these devotees were thieves. Savages have their vices, and it is to these that civilization appeals. Puysaye says: "Several times I have saved the town of Plélan from pillage." And again he says that he refrained from entering Montfort: "I made a circuit in order to avoid the sacking of the houses of the Jacobins."[3] They pillaged Cholet; they sacked Chalans; passing by Granville, they robbed Ville-Dieu. They called the country-people who joined the Blues the "Jacobin herd," and exterminated them

2. The uncapped become unbreeched.—Tr.

3. Puysaye, vol. ii. pp. 187, 434.

more fiercely than they did their other foes. They enjoyed carnage like soldiers, and revelled in massacre like brigands. To shoot the *patauds* was their delight. They called it breaking their fast.

At Fontenay one of their priests, named Barbotin, killed an old man with a blow from his sabre. At Saint-Germain-sur-Ille[4] one of their captains, a nobleman, shot the solicitor of the Commune, and took his watch. At Machecoul for the space of five weeks they made a practice of slaughtering the Republicans at the rate of thirty a day. Each string of thirty they called a rosary. Behind this row of men there was a trench prepared, into which the men fell back as they were shot; and when, as sometimes happened, a man was still alive, he was buried as if he were dead. Such acts have been witnessed in our own times. Joubert, president of the district, had his wrists sawed off. They had handcuffs for the Blues made expressly to cut the flesh. They slaughtered them in the public squares, sounding the halloo. Charette, who signed himself, "Fraternity, Chevalier Charette," and who, like Marat, wore a handkerchief knotted around his brows, burned the city of Pornic, with the inhabitants in their dwellings.

Meanwhile Carrier was frightful. Terror answered unto terror. The Breton rebel looked very much like the Greek insurgent, clad as he was in a short jacket, with a gun slung across his shoulders, leggings, wide trousers of a material not unlike fustian. The lads resembled a Greek klepht. Henri de la Rochejaquelein went into this war at the age of twenty-one, armed with a pair of pistols and a stick. There were one hundred and fifty-four divisions in the Vendean army. They laid regular sieges. The city of Bressuire was invested by them for three days. On a Good Friday ten thousand peasants bombarded the city of des Sables with red-hot cannon-balls. They succeeded in destroying in one day the fourteen Republican cantonments from Montigné to Courbeveilles. On the high wall at Thouars the following astonishing dialogue was heard between La Rochejaquelein and a lad: "Fellow!" "Here I am."—"Lend me your shoulders to climb up on." "Take them."—"Give me your gun." "Here it is." And La Rochejaquelein leaped into the city, and thus without the aid of scaling-ladders they captured the very towers once besieged by Duguesclin. They valued a cartridge far beyond a gold louis. They burst into tears whenever they lost sight of their village belfry. To run away seemed to them the simplest affair in the world. At such times

---

4. Ibid., p. 35.

their leaders would exclaim, "Throw away your sabots, but keep your guns!" When munitions failed, they said their beads, and proceeded to take the powder from the caissons of the Republican artillery; and afterwards d'Elbée demanded powder from the English. On the approach of the enemy they concealed their wounded in the tall grain, or among the brakes, and came back for them after the engagement was over. They wore no uniform, and their clothing was falling to pieces. Noblemen as well as peasants wore any rags that came to hand. Roger Mouliniers was arrayed in a turban and dolman taken from the wardrobe of the Théâtre de La Flèche; the Chevalier de Beauvilliers had a barrister's gown, and a lady's bonnet over a woollen cap. All wore the white belt and scarf. The different grades were indicated by a knot. Stofflet wore a red knot, La Rochejaquelein a black one. Wimpfen, a semi-Girondist, and who moreover had never been out of Normandy, wore the armlets of the Carabots of Caen.

They had women in their ranks,—Madame de Lescure, who afterwards became Madame de la Rochejaquelein; Thérèse de Mollien, mistress of La Rouarie, she who burned the list of parishes; Madame de la Rochefoucauld, young and beautiful, who sabre in hand rallied the peasants at the foot of the Tower of the Château Puy-Rousseau; and Antoinette Adams, styled the Chevalier Adams, so brave that when captured she was shot standing, out of respect for her courage. This epic period was a cruel one. Men behaved like maniacs. Madame de Lescure deliberately walked her horse over the Republicans who lay disabled on the battle-ground. She said they were dead, but very possibly they may have been only wounded. There was occasionally a traitor among the men, but never among the women. It is true, Mademoiselle Fleury of the French Theatre forsook La Rouarie for Marat; but that was for love's sake. The commanders were often as ignorant as the soldiers. M. de Sapinaud could not spell correctly; he wrote, "Nous *orions* de notre *cauté*."

The leaders hated one another. The captains of the Marais cried, "Down with the Mountaineers!" Their cavalry was few in numbers, and difficult to form. Puysaye writes: "A man who would cheerfully give me his two sons grows cool when I ask for one of his horses." Poles, pitchforks, scythes, muskets, old and new, poacher's knives, spits, iron-pointed cud-gels studded with nails,—such were their weapons. Some carried a cross made of two human bones. They rushed to the attack with shouts, springing up at once from all quarters,—from woods, hills, underbrush, and hollow roads,—ranging themselves in a circle, killing, exterminating, striking terror, and then disappearing. Whenever they passed a Republican town they cut down the liberty-pole, set it on fire, and forming in a circle, danced around it. All their activity was displayed by night. The rule of the Vendean is to be always unexpected. They would march fifteen leagues in utter silence, without so much as stirring a blade of grass. At night, their chiefs having determined in a council of war at what point the Republican posts were to be surprised the next day, they loaded their muskets, mumbled their prayers, and taking off their sabots, filed through the woods in long columns, barefoot across the heather and moss, noiseless, without uttering a sound or drawing a breath, like a procession of cats in the darkness.

VI

The Soul of the Earth Passes into Man

THE NUMBER OF THE REBELS in the Vendée, including men, women, and children, cannot be estimated at less than five hundred thousand. Tuffin de la Rouarie states the sum total of the combatants to have been half a million.

The federalists helped them, and the Vendée had the Gironde on its side also. Lozère sent thirty thousand men into the Bocage. Eight departments formed a coalition: five in Brittany, three in Normandy. Évreux, who fraternized with Caen, was represented in the rebellion by Chaumont, its mayor, and Gardembas, a man of note. Buzot, Gorsas, and Barbaroux at Caen, Brissot at Moulins, Chassan at Lyons, Rabaut-Saint-Étienne at Nismes, Meillan and Duchâtel in Brittany, all fanned the flames of the furnace. There were two Vendées,—the great army fighting in the forests, and the smaller one carrying on the war in the bushes. And this marks the difference between Charette and Jean Chouan. The little Vendée was simple-minded and true; the great Vendée was corrupt. The little Vendée was the better of the two. The rank of Marquis, lieutenant-general of the king's armies, was bestowed upon Charette, and he received the grand cross of Saint-Louis. Jean Chouan remained Jean Chouan. Charette resembles a bandit, Jean Chouan is more like a paladin of old.

As to those magnanimous chiefs, Bonchamps, Lescure, La Rochejaquelein, they were mistaken; the great Catholic army was an insane attempt, upon whose heels disaster was sure to follow; imagine a crowd of peasants storming Paris, a coalition of villages besieging the Pantheon, a chorus of Christmas hymns and prayers striving to drown the Marseillaise, a cohort of rustics rushing upon a legion of enlightened minds. Mans and Savenay chastised this folly. The Vendée could not cross the Loire; that was a stride beyond its power. Civil war can make no conquests. Crossing the Rhine confirms the power of Cæsar and adds to that of Napoleon; crossing the Loire kills La Rochejaquelein. The genuine Vendée is the Vendée at home: there it is more than invulnerable; it is unconquerable. At home the Vendée is smuggler, laborer, soldier, shepherd, poacher, sharpshooter, goat-herd, bell-ringer, peasant, spy, assassin, sacristan, and wild beast.

La Rochejaquelein is only an Achilles, while Jean Chouan is a Proteus.

The Vendée failed. Other revolts have been successful, that in Switzerland for instance. The difference between mountain insurgents like the Swiss and forest insurgents like the Vendean, exists in the fact that almost invariably, owing to some fatal influence of his surroundings, the former fights for an ideal, while the latter fights for a prejudice. The one soars, the other crawls. The one fights for humanity, the other for solitude; the one demands liberty, the other isolation; the one defends the commune, the other the parish. "The Commons! The Commons!" cried the heroes of Morat. The one has to do with precipices, the other with quagmires; the one is the man of torrents and foaming streams, the other of stagnant pools whence fever rises; one has the blue sky above his head, the other a thicket; one is on the mountain-top, the other among the shadows.

An education that is gained upon the heights is quite a different affair from that of the shallows.

A mountain is a fortress; a forest is an ambush; the former inspires courage, the latter teaches trickery. The ancients placed their gods upon a pinnacle, and their satyrs within copses. The satyr is a savage, half man, half beast. Free countries have their Apennines, Alps, Pyrenees, an Olympus. Parnassus is a mountain. Mont Blanc was the gigantic auxiliary of William Tell. Looking beyond and above those titanic contests between human intellect and the darkness of night, which form the subjects of the poems of India, one sees Himalaya towering overhead. Greece, Spain, Italy, Helvetia have the mountains for their inspiration. Cimmeria, whether it be Germany or Brittany, has but the woods. The forest tends to barbarism.

The formation of the soil influences man in many of his actions. It is more of an accomplice than one might imagine. When we consider certain wild scenery, we feel tempted to exonerate man and accuse Nature; we are conscious of an occult provocation on the part of Nature; the desert has sometimes an unwholesome influence upon the conscience, especially on one that is not enlightened. A conscience may be gigantic,—take for example Socrates or the Christ; it may be dwarf-like, in which case we find Atreus and Judas. A narrow conscience soon displays the attributes of the reptile; it delights to haunt the dim forests, it is attracted by the brambles, the thorns, the marshes underneath the branches, and absorbs the evil influences of the place. Optical illusions, mysterious mirages, the terrors of the hour and the place, inspire a man with that sort of half-religious, half-animal fear which in every-day life begets superstition, and in times of wild excitements degenerates into brutality. Hallucination holds the torch that lights the path to murder. A vertigo seizes the brigand. Nature, marvellous as she is, holds a double meaning that dazzles great minds and blinds the savage soul. When man is ignorant, and the desert is alive with visions, the gloom of solitude is added to the blindness of the intelligence; hence the abyss that sometimes yawns in the human soul. There are certain rocks, ravines, copses, weird spaces between the trees, revealing the blackness of the night, that incite man to mad and cruel deeds. One might say that the evil fiend possesses such spots. What tragic scenes has not the gloomy hill between Baignon and Plélan beheld!

Wide horizons tend to enlarge the mind; limited horizons, on the contrary, circumscribe it; hence men naturally kind-hearted, such, for instance, as Jean Chouan, grow narrow-minded.

It is the hatred of narrow minds for liberal ideas that fetters the march of progress. The Vendean war, a quarrel between the local and the universal idea, the contest of peasant and patriot, may be summed up in two words,—the village community and the fatherland.

VII

The Vendée has Ruined Brittany

BRITTANY IS AN OLD REBEL. In all her revolts in the past two thousand years she has had the right on her side until now; in her last rebellion she was wrong. And yet, after all, whether she was fighting against revolution or against monarchy, against the acting representative or against the ruling dukes and peers, against the financial resource of the assignats or the oppression of the salt-tax,—whoever might be fighting, whether it were Nicolas Rapin, François de La Noue, Captain Pluviaut, and The Lady of La Garnache, or Stofflet, Coquereau, and Lechandelier de Pierreville, and whether they were fighting under M. de Rohan against the king, or under M. de La Rochejaquelein for the king, it was practically the same war, that of local government against centralization.

These ancient provinces might be compared with a pond; stagnant water is not inclined to flow; the wind, instead of rousing it to life, simply irritates it. France ended at Finistère; that was the limit of the space granted to man, and there the forward march of generations ceased. "Pause!" cries the ocean to the land, and barbarism to civilization. Whenever it feels the influence of any excitement in Paris, whatever may be the occasion thereof, monarchy or republic, despotism or liberty, it is an innovation, and Brittany bristles with alarm, and says, "Let us alone! What do you want of us?" The Marais seizes its pitchfork, and the Bocage grasps its musket. All our attempts at reform in matters of education and legislation, our philosophical systems, our men of genius, our triumphs, fail before the Houroux; the tocsin of Bazouges holds the French Revolution in awe; the moor of Faou defies the stormy assemblies on our public squares; and the belfry of Haut-des-Près declares war against the Tower of the Louvre. Terrible blindness!

The Vendean insurrection was a melancholy misunderstanding.

An affray on a gigantic scale, wrangling among Titans, a colossal rebellion, fated to bequeath but one word to history, *The Vendée*,—a glorious though melancholy word, devoting itself to death for the absent, sacrificing itself to egotism, squandering its dauntless courage, offering itself in the cause of cowards, with neither foresight nor strategy, without tactics, plan, or aim, following no leader, accepting no responsibility, showing how powerless the human will may become, uniting the spirit of chivalry with the deeds of the savage, absurdity at its height, darkness screening itself from the light, ignorance offering a determined resistance to truth, justice, right, reason, and deliverance, the terror of eight years, the devastation of fourteen departments, the ravages in the fields, the destruction of crops, the burning of villages, the ruin of cities, the massacre of women and children, the torch applied to the thatch, the sword plunged into the heart, the terror of civilization, the hope of Mr. Pitt,—such was this war, an unreasoning attempt at parricide.

On the whole, the Vendée has served the cause of progress by showing the necessity of scattering the ancient shadows of Brittany by discharging into its thickets all the arrows of enlightenment Catastrophes have a gloomy way of settling affairs.

Book II

THE THREE CHILDREN

I

Plus Quam Civilia Bella

THE SUMMER OF 1792 HAD been a very rainy one; but that of 1793 was so extremely warm that, although the civil war had gone far towards ruining the roads in Brittany, the people—thanks to the fine weather—were able to travel from place to place, for a dry soil makes the best road.

At the close of a clear July day, about an hour after sunset, a man on horseback, riding from the direction of Avranches, stopped before the little inn called the Croix-Blanchard, situated at the entrance of Pontorson. For some years its sign had borne the following inscription: "Good cider obtained here." The day had been a very warm one, but now the wind was beginning to rise.

The traveller was wrapped in an ample cloak that fell over his horse's back. He wore a broad-brimmed hat, ornamented with a tricolored cockade, which was rather a bold thing to do in a country like this, with its hedges and sharpshooting, for which a cockade offered an excellent target. The cloak fastened around his neck was pushed back, leaving his arms free, and revealing at the same time a tricolored belt and the butts of two pistols protruding from it, while a sabre hung down below the cloak. At the sound of the horses hoofs stopping before the inn the door opened, and the landlord came out, holding a lantern in his hand. It was just at twilight, when it is still light out of doors, although dark within.

The host glanced at the cockade.

"Do you mean to stop here, citizen?"

"No."

"Where are you going, then?"

"To Dol."

"In that case, you would do better to return to Avranches, or else remain at Pontorson."

"Why so?"

"Because they are fighting at Dol."

"Ah!" said the rider; then he continued, "Give my horse some oats."

The host, having brought the trough and poured the oats into it, proceeded to unbridle the horse, which began at once snuffing and champing, while the dialogue went on.

"Is this one of the requisition horses, citizen?" "No."

"Does it belong to you?"

"Yes. I bought him and paid for him."

"Where do you come from?"

"From Paris."

"Not directly?"

"No."

"I should say not. The roads are blocked; but the post still runs."

"As far as Alençon. I left it there."

"Ah, it will not be long before we shall have no more posts in France. The horses are all gone; one worth three hundred francs costs six hundred, and the price of fodder is beyond all reason. I used to be a postmaster; and now, you see, I keep a tavern. Out of thirteen hundred and thirteen postmasters, two hundred have resigned. Have you been travelling according to the new tariff, citizen?"

"You mean the tariff of the 1st of May? Yes."

"Twenty sous a post for a carriage, twelve for a gig, five for a van. Did you not buy this horse at Alençon?"

"Yes."

"And you have been travelling all day?"

"Yes, since dawn."

"And yesterday?"

"And the day before."

"I should think so. You came by the way of Domfront and Mortain."

"And Avranches."

"You had better take my advice, and rest, citizen. Are you not tired? Your horse certainly is."

"Horses may be tired, but men have no right to give way to fatigue."

Again the host gazed at the traveller, whose face, grave, calm, and severe, was framed by gray hair.

Casting a glance along the road, that was deserted as far as the eye could reach, he said,—

"And so you are travelling alone."

"I have an escort."

"Where is it?"

"My sabre and pistols."

The innkeeper went for a pail of water; and while he was watering the horse he contemplated the traveller, saying to himself, "He looks like a priest, all the same."

The rider continued,—

"You say there is fighting at Dol?"

"Yes. They are just about ready to begin."

"Who is fighting?"

"One ci-devant against another."

"How is that?"

"I mean that the ci-devant who is a Republican is fighting against another who takes sides with the king."

"But there is no longer a king."

"There is the little fellow. But the strangest part is that the two ci-devants are related to each other."

Here the rider listened attentively, while the innkeeper continued:—

"One is a young man, and the other an old one. It is the grand-nephew fighting against his great-uncle. The uncle is a Royalist, while the nephew is a patriot; the uncle commands the Whites, the nephew the Blues. Ah! they will show no mercy to each other, you may be sure! It is a war to death!"

"Death?"

"Yes, citizen. Perhaps you might like to see the polite speeches they fling at each other's head. Here is a placard, which the old man has managed to post on all the houses and trees, and which I found had been stuck on my very door."

The host held up his lantern to a square bit of paper glued upon one of the panels of his door, and as it was written in very large characters, the rider was able to read it as he sat in his saddle:—

"The Marquis de Lantenac has the honor to inform his grand-nephew the Viscount Gauvain that if the Marquis is so fortunate as to take him prisoner, M. le Viscount may rest assured that he will be speedily shot."

"And here is the reply," continued the innkeeper.

He turned so as to throw the light of his lantern upon a second placard on the other panel of the door, directly opposite the first one.

"Gauvain warns Lantenac that if he catches him he will have him shot."

"Yesterday the first placard was posted on my door," said the host, "and this morning came the second. He was not kept waiting for his answer."

The traveller, in an undertone, as though speaking to himself, uttered certain words which the innkeeper caught without fully understanding their meaning:—

"Yes, this is more than waging war against one's native land; it is carrying it into the family. And it must needs be done; great regenerations are only to be purchased at this price."

And the traveller, with his eyes still riveted to the second placard, lifted his hand to his hat and saluted it.

The host continued:—

"You see, citizen, this is the way matters stand. In the cities and in larger towns we are in favor of revolution, but in the country they are opposed to it; which amounts to saying that we are Frenchmen in the cities, and Bretons in the villages. It is a war between the peasants and the townspeople. They call us *patauds*,[1] and we call them *rustauds*.[2] They have the nobles and the priests on their side."

"Not all of them," interrupted the rider.

"That is true, citizen, for here we have a Viscount fighting against a Marquis; and I verily believe," he added aside, "that I am speaking to a priest at this minute."

"Which of the two is likely to gain the day?"

"I should say the Viscount, so far. But he has a hard time of it. The old man is a tough customer. They belong to the Gauvains, a noble family in these parts, of which there are two branches; the Marquis de Lantenac is the head of the older, and the Viscount Gauvain of the younger branch. Today the two branches are fighting each other. You never see this among trees, but often among men. This Marquis de Lantenac is all-powerful in Brittany; the peasants regard him as a prince. On the very day he landed he rallied eight thousand men; in a week three hundred parishes had risen. If he had only been able to establish a foothold on the coast, the English would have made a descent. Luckily Gauvain, who, strange to say, is his grand-nephew, was on the spot. He is a Republican commander, and has got the upper hand of his great-uncle. And then, as good luck would have it, this

1. A corruption of the word "patriot."—Tr.
2. Rustics.

Lantenac at the time of his arrival, when he was massacring a multitude of prisoners, gave orders to have two women shot, one of whom had three children, who had been adopted by a Paris battalion. This roused the rage of the battalion, which is called the Bonnet-Rouge. There are but few of the original Parisians left, but they are desperate fighters. They have been incorporated into Commandant Gauvain's division. Nothing can resist them. Their great object is to avenge the women and recapture the children. No one knows what the old Marquis did with the little ones, and that is what infuriates the Parisian grenadiers. Had not these children been mixed up in it, this war would not have been what it is. The Viscount is a good and brave young fellow; but the old man is a terrible Marquis. The peasants call this the war of Saint Michel against Beelzebub. You know, maybe, that Saint Michel is the patron of these parts. There is a mountain named after him in the middle of the bay. They give him credit for conquering the Devil and burying him under another hill not far away, called Tombelaine."

"Yes," murmured the rider. "Tumba Beleni,—the tomb of Belenus, Belus, Bel, Belial, Beelzebub."

"I see that you are well informed." And the host said to himself,—

"He knows Latin; surely he must be a priest." Then he added:—

"Well, citizen, this war is beginning all over again for the peasants. No doubt they think the Royalist general is Saint Michel, and the patriot commander Beelzebub; but if there is a devil it is Lantenac, and Gauvain is an angel if there ever was one. Will you take nothing, citizen?"

"I have my gourd and a bit of bread. But you have not told me what is going on at Dol."

"To be sure; well, Gauvain is in command of the exploring division of the coast. Now, Lantenac's plan was to stir up a general insurrection, to bring Lower Normandy to the aid of Lower Brittany, to throw open the door to Pitt, and to lend a helping hand to the great Vendean army in the shape of twenty thousand English and two hundred thousand peasants. Gauvain has checkmated this plan. He holds the coast and drives Lantenac back into the interior and the English into the sea. Lantenac was here, but Gauvain dislodged him, recaptured Pont-au-Beau, drove him out from Avranches and Villedieu, and prevented him from reaching Granville. He is manoeuvring now to force him to retreat into the forest of Fougères, and there to surround him. Yesterday everything was favorable, and Gauvain was here with his division. All at once, mind you, the old man, who is a shrewd one, made a point; the news came that he had marched on Dol. If he should take it, and succeeds in establishing a battery on Mont-Dol,—for he has artillery,— that will give the English a chance to land, and then all is lost. That is the reason why Gauvain, who has a head on his shoulders, knowing there was not a moment to be lost, consulted no one; nor did he wait for orders, but giving the signal to saddle, and harnessing his artillery, he collected his troops, drew his sabre, and while Lantenac is hurrying towards Dol, Gauvain is all ready to pounce upon Lantenac; and Dol is to be the place where these two Breton heads will clash, and a famous crash it will be. They are at it now."

"How long does it take to reach Dol?"

"For troops with artillery carriages, at least three hours; but they are there now."

The traveller, as he listened, said,—

"You are right; I think I can hear the cannon." The host, too, was listening.

"Yes, citizen, and the firing is steady. You had better spend the night here. There is nothing to be gained by going over there."

"I cannot stop. I must continue my journey."

"You are wrong. I do not know anything about your business, but the risk is great, and unless all that you hold dearest in the world is at stake—"

"That is precisely the state of things," replied the rider.

"Now, supposing your son—"

"You are very near the truth," said the rider.

The innkeeper raised his head as he said to himself,—

"And yet I thought this citizen was a priest." Then, after a moment's reflection, he added: "But a priest may have children, after all."

"Put the bridle back on my horse," said the traveller. "How much do I owe you?"

After receiving his pay, the host put the trough and bucket against the wall, and came back to the traveller.

"Since you are determined to go, take my advice. You must be going to Saint-Malo. Now, then, do not go by the way of Dol. There are two roads,—one leading through Dol, and the other along the coast. There is very little difference in their length. The road along the coast passes through Saint-Georges-de-Brehaigne, Cherrueix, and Hirelle-Vivier. You leave Dol to the south, and Cancale to the north, and at the end of this street, citizen, you will come to a place where the two roads fork,—that of Dol to the left, that of Saint-Georges-de-Brehaigne to the right. Mark my words: if you go to Dol, you will plunge headlong into the massacre; so do not take the left-hand turning, but keep to the right."

"Thank you," said the traveller.

And he set spurs to his horse.

As it was now quite dark, he soon vanished in the gloom, and the innkeeper lost sight of him.

When the traveller reached the end of the street where the two roads forked, he heard the voice of the innkeeper calling to him from the distance,—

"Turn to your right!"

He turned to the left.

II

Dol

DOL, A FRANCO-SPANISH CITY IN Brittany, as the old records call it, is not really a city; it is a street,—a grand old Gothic street, with rows of houses supported by pillars on both sides of it. These houses are not built in straight lines, but stand irregularly, now and then elbowing into the street, which is, to be sure, a very wide one. The rest of the town is a mere network of lanes, all leading into this great diametrical street,— emptying into it, one might say, like streams into a river, with Mont-Dol towering above it. The city, with neither gates nor walls, could not have withstood a siege; but the street was quite capable of sustaining one. The houses, like promontories, which but fifty years ago were still standing, and the two pillared galleries bordering the street, made it a strong and well-nigh impregnable redoubt. Each of the houses was a fortress in itself, and the enemy would have found himself forced to capture them one by one. Almost in the middle of the street stood the old market.

The innkeeper of the Croix-Branchard had told the truth; a furious battle was raging in Dol even while he was speaking. A nocturnal duel between the Whites who arrived in the morning and the Blues who appeared at night had burst suddenly upon the town. The forces were unequal, the Whites numbering six thousand, while the Blues were only fifteen hundred; but they fought with equal fury. Surprising as it may seem, it was the fifteen hundred who attacked the six thousand.

A mob pitted against a phalanx. On one side were six thousand peasants, with images of the Sacred Heart upon their leathern waistcoats, white ribbons on their round hats, Christian emblems on their leather cuffs, rosaries hanging from their belts, carrying pitchforks oftener than sabres, and carbines without bayonets, dragging along cannon by means of ropes, wretchedly equipped, undisciplined, with no suitable weapons, yet mad with rage. On the other side were fifteen thousand soldiers, wearing three-cornered hats with the tricolored cockade, long-tailed coats, with broad lapels, and shoulder-belts crossed, short sabres with copper hilts, muskets with long bayonets, well-drilled and disciplined, obedient though savage, knowing how to obey like men who could at need command, volunteers like the others, but patriots withal, although barefooted and in rags; paladins in the shape of peasants fighting in defence of Monarchy; barefooted heroes in the ranks of the Revolution; while the life and soul of both Royalists and Republicans was centred in their leaders,—Lantenac, the man advanced in years, and the young Gauvain.

Standing side by side in the Revolution with young giants like Danton, Saint-Just, and Robespierre, were the ideal and youthful forms of Hoche and Marceau, and like unto them was Gauvain.

Gauvain was thirty years of age, with the chest of Hercules, the solemn eye of a prophet, and the laugh of a child. He never smoked; he neither drank nor swore. He carried a dressing-case with him throughout the entire war, and took great care of his nails, his teeth, and his luxuriant brown hair. Whenever they halted, it was his habit carefully to shake his commander's uniform, riddled with balls and whitened with dust as it was. Though always rushing headlong into the thickest of the fray, he had never been wounded. His voice, unusually melodious, could assume at need the imperative ring of command. He set the example of sleeping on the ground, in the wind, the rain, and the snow, wrapped in his cloak, with his charming head resting on a stone. His was a heroic and innocent soul. Let him but take a sabre in his hand, he was straightway transformed. He had that effeminate aspect that changes to something formidable in battle.

A thinker and philosopher withal; in short, a youthful sage. Beautiful to look upon as Alcibiades, his speech showed the wisdom of Socrates.

In that grand improvisation which men called the French Revolution, this young man at once became a leader.

The division which he had formed was like a Roman legion; an army on a small scale, complete in itself; it consisted of infantry and cavalry; it had its scouts, its pioneers, its sappers, its engineers; and as the Roman legion had its catapults, this army had its cannon. Three well-mounted pieces strengthened the division, while leaving it easy to handle.

Lantenac was also a military leader, but a more accomplished one,— more cautious, and at the same time more daring. The veritable old hero is cooler than a younger man, because he is farther removed from the heyday of life, and more daring from the consciousness that he is nearer death. What has he to lose? So slight a matter. This explains the bold and yet scientific manoeuvres of Lantenac. Yet on the whole, in this obstinate wrestling-match between the old and the young, Gauvain almost always had the advantage, and he owed this rather to chance than to anything in himself. Every sort of good-fortune, even though it may be terrible, falls to the lot of youth. Victory has something feminine in its nature.

Lantenac was exasperated with Gauvain; first, because his nephew had defeated him, and second, because he was his nephew. What possessed him to be Jacobin?—a Gauvain! Unruly youngster that he was. His heir,—for the Marquis had no children,—a great-nephew, almost a grandchild! "Ah!" cried this quasi grandfather, "if he falls into my hands, I will kill him like a dog."

The Republic, moreover, had good reason to feel uneasy about this Marquis de Lantenac. He had no sooner landed than its terror began. The mere utterance of his name was like a powder-train spread through the Vendean insurrection, of which he straightway became the centre. In a revolt of this kind, where each one is jealous of his neighbor, where each has his bush or his ravine, if a superior leader appears, the separate chiefs who have been on a level will rally round him and submit themselves to his authority. Nearly all the forest captains had joined Lantenac, and whether near or remote, they all obeyed him. Only Gavard, who had been the first to join him, had departed. And why was this? Because he had enjoyed the confidence of the Republic and been in a position of authority. Gavard had held all the secrets and had adopted the old-fashioned system of civil war, which Lantenac had come to change and replace. A successor can hardly agree with a man of that stamp. The shoe of La Rouarie was not a fit for Lantenac, and so Gavard had gone to join Bonchamp.

Lantenac belonged to the military school of Frederic II; he understood the art of warfare, which consists of combining the greater with the lesser; he favored neither the great Catholic and Royal army, that "mass of confusion" destined to be crushed, nor the guerilla troops scattered through the thickets and hedges, useful to harass, but powerless to crush. There is either no end to guerilla warfare, or else it comes to an unfortunate one: it begins by attacking the Republic and ends by robbing a diligence. Lantenac did not propose to carry on the Breton war altogether in the open country like La Rochejaquelein, nor yet in the forest like Chouan. He neither approved of the Vendée nor of the Chouannerie; he believed in real warfare; he was willing to use the peasant, but he wished to support him by the soldier. He required bands for strategy and regiments for tactics. The village armies so easily disbanded he considered excellent for an attack, an ambush, or a surprise, but he felt that they lacked solidity; they were like water in his hands; he sought a solid foundation for this unstable and diffusive warfare; to the savage army of the forest he proposed to add regular troops as a sort of pivot about which to manoeuvre the peasants. Had this scheme, deep-laid and terrible as it was, proved successful, the Vendée would never have been conquered.

But where could regular troops be found? Where look for soldiers? Where seek for regiments, and find a ready-made army? In England. Hence Lantenac's determination that the English should effect a landing. Thus do parties compromise with their consciences. He quite lost sight of the red coat, eclipsed as it was by the white cockade. Lantenac had but one idea,—first to seize upon some point on the coast, and then to deliver it into the hands of Pitt. It was with this object that, seeing Dol unprotected, he had thrown himself upon it, knowing that once in possession of Dol, he could readily gain Mont-Dol, and by means of the latter gain a footing on the coast.

The spot was well chosen. From Mont-Dol the cannon would sweep Fresnois on one side; and Saint-Brelade, on the other, would keep the fleet of Cancale at a distance, and leave the whole beach, from Raz-sur-Couesnon to Saint-Mêloir-des-Ondes, open to an attack.

In order to insure success, Lantenac had brought with him six thousand of the most active men in the regiment at his disposal, together with all his artillery,—ten sixteen-pound culverins, one demi-culverin, and one four-pounder. He proposed to establish a strong battery on Mont-Dol, on the principle that a thousand shots fired from ten cannon do more execution than fifteen hundred fired from five cannon.

With six thousand men, he felt sure of success. In the direction of Avranches they had nothing to fear but Gauvain with his fifteen hundred men. Towards Dina there was Léchelle, to be sure, with twenty-five thousand; but he was twenty leagues away. In regard to the latter, Lantenac felt quite safe, the distance offsetting the numbers; and as for Gauvain though he was quite near, his force was very small. WE may here remark that Léchelle was a fool, who afterwards allowed his twenty-five thousand men to be slaughtered on the moors of Croix-Bataille,—a mistake for which he strove to atone by suicide.

So Lantenac felt quite safe. His entrance into Dol had been sudden and stern. The Marquis de Lantenac enjoyed a hard reputation; and knowing him to be merciless, the terrified inhabitants shut themselves up in their houses without attempting resistance, and the six thousand Vendeans installed themselves in the city after the disorderly fashion of a band of rustics. It was almost like a market-ground; in default of quartermasters, they chose their own quarters, camping at haphazard, cooking, in the open air, dispersing hither and yonder through the churches, dropping their muskets to take up their rosaries. Lantenac, accompanied by a few artillery officers, proceeded without delay to reconnoitre Mont-Dol, leaving Gouge-le-Bruant, whom he had appointed field-sergeant, in command. This Gouge-le-Bruant has left but an indistinct trace in history. He had two nicknames,—*Brise-Bleu* in token of his massacre of the patriots, and *Imânus*, because there was something indescribably horrible about him. *Imânus* is derived from *immanis*, and old Low-Norman word, which expresses a superhuman degree of ugliness, almost godlike in its terror,—a demon, a satyr, an ogre. An old manuscript says, "With my own eyes I beheld Imânus." Today the old people in Brittany no longer know who Gouge-le-Bruant was, nor what Brise-Bleu means; but they have a vague idea of the Imânus, whose name is interwoven with all the local superstitions. He still is spoken of in Trémorel and Plumaugat,—the two villages where Gouge-le-Bruant has left the impress of his ill-omened footstep. In the Vendée, where all the inhabitants were savages, Gouge-le-Bruant was the barbarian. He was a sort of Cacique tattooed all over with crucifixes and fleurs-de-lis. Upon his face was the hideous, almost supernatural glow of a soul unlike that of any other human being. He was as brave in battle as Satan himself, and atrociously cruel when the battle was over.

His heart, full of mysterious determinations, now urged him to acts of devotion, now to deeds of wildest fury. Did he use his reason? Yes, after a serpentine fashion. Heroism was his starting-point, murder his goal. It was impossible to conceive how his resolutions, often grand in their very monstrosity, could have entered his mind. He was capable of any horror, when least expected. His ferocity was on a scale of epic grandeur.

Hence his peculiar surname, Imânus.

The Marquis de Lantenac relied upon his cruelty; but while none could dispute the fact that he excelled in cruelty, in matters of strategy and tactics he was less efficient, and it may perhaps have been a mistake on the part of the Marquis when he made him his field-sergeant. But however that may be, he left him behind in charge, with the injunction to look after matters in general.

Gouge-le-Bruant was more of a fighter than a soldier, and guarding a town was not so much in his line as massacring a clan would have been; still, he posted sentries. When at nightfall the Marquis, having decided upon the position of his battery, was returning to Dol, he suddenly caught the sound of cannon. Looking in the direction of the sound, he saw a red smoke rising from the street. This meant a surprise, an invasion, an attack; fighting was going on in the town.

Although not easily taken by surprise, he was now utterly amazed, for he had anticipated nothing of the sort. What could it mean? Evidently not Gauvain, for a man would hardly attack an enemy outnumbering him four to one. Could it be Léchelle? But was it possible for him to have made such a forced march? Léchelle was improbable, Gauvain impossible.

Lantenac urged on his horse. On the way he met some of the inhabitants in the act of flight; but when he questioned them, they seemed beside themselves with terror, crying, "The Blues! the Blues!" And on his arrival he found the situation a bad one.

This is what had happened.

III

Small Armies and Great Battles

ON THEIR ARRIVAL AT DOL, the peasants, as we have seen, had dispersed through town, each man guided by his own fancy, as it often happens when "on obéit d'amitié," as the Vendeans expressed it,—a form of obedience that may produce heroes, but not well-disciplined soldiers. They had stored their artillery, together with the baggage, under the arches of the old market, and feeling weary, when they had eaten and drunk and said their beads, they stretched themselves out in the middle of the principal street, that was encumbered rather than guarded. As night came on most of them fell asleep, pillowing their heads on their knapsacks, some having their wives beside them; for it often happened that the peasant women followed the men. In the Vendée, women about to become mothers frequently acted as spies. It was a mild July night The constellations shone forth against the deep-blue sky. The entire bivouac, which might have been mistaken for the halt of a caravan rather than for a military encampment, gave itself up to quiet slumber. Suddenly by the glimmering twilight those who were still awake perceived three cannon levelled at the entrance of the principal street.

It was Gauvain. He had surprised the guard, had entered the town, and with his division held the entrance of the street.

A peasant started up, crying, "Who goes there?" and fired off his musket. A cannon-shot, followed by a terrific volley of musketry, was the reply. The whole sleeping crowd sprang up with a start. It was a rude shock to be roused by a volley of grape-shot from a peaceful sleep beneath the stars.

The first moment was terrific. There is nothing more tragic than the confusion of a panic-stricken crowd. They snatched their weapons. Many fell as they ran yelling to and fro. Confused by the unexpected assault, the lads lost their heads and fired madly at one another. The townspeople, bewildered by all this confusion, rushed in and out of their houses, shouting to each other as they wandered helplessly about,—a dismal struggle in which women and children played a part. The balls whistling through the air left streaks of light in the darkness behind them. Amid the smoke and tumult a constant firing issued from every dark corner. The entanglement of the baggage-wagons and cannon-carriages was added to the general confusion. The horses, rearing, trampled upon the wounded, whose groans could be heard on every side. Some were horror-stricken, others stupefied. Officers were looking for their men, and soldiers for their officers. In the midst of all this some there were who displayed a stolid indifference. One woman, seated on the fragment of a wall, was nursing her new-born babe, while her husband, with bleeding wounds and a broken leg, leaned against it as he calmly loaded his musket and fired at random in the darkness, killing or not, as it happened. Men lying flat on the ground fired between the spokes of the wagon-wheels. At times there rose a hideous din of clamors, and again the thundering voice of the cannon would overwhelm all. It was frightful,—like the felling of trees when one falls upon the other.

Gauvain from his ambush aimed with precision, and lost but few men. But at last the peasants, intrepid in spite of the disaster, ended by taking the defensive. They fell back on the market, which was like a great dark fortress, with its forest of stone pillars. There they made a stand; anything that resembled a forest inspired them with courage. The Imânus did his best to atone for the absence of Lantenac. They had cannon; but, to the great surprise of Gauvain, they made no use of them. This was due to the fact that the artillery officers had gone with the Marquis to reconnoitre Mont-Dol, and the peasants did not know how to manage the culverins and demi-culverins; but they riddled with balls the Blues who cannonaded them. The peasants answered the grape-shot by a volley of musketry. They now had the advantage of a shelter, having heaped up the drays, the carts, the baggage, and all the small casks that were lying about in the old market, thus improvising a high barricade, with openings through which they could pass their muskets, and from which they opened a deadly fire. So rapidly had they worked, that in a quarter of an hour the market presented an impregnable front.

Matters were beginning to look serious for Gauvain. The sudden transformation of a market into a fortress, and the peasants assembled in a solid mass within, was a condition of affairs which he had not anticipated. He had taken them by surprise, it is true; but he had not succeeded in routing them. He had dismounted, and holding his sword by the hilt, he stood with folded arms, gazing steadfastly into the gloom, his own figure distinctly revealed by the flame of the torch that lighted the battery,—a target for the men of the barricade; of which fact he took no heed, as he stood there lost in thought, while a shower of balls from the barricade fell around him.

He set his cannon against their rifles; and victory is ever on the side of the cannon-ball. He who has artillery is sure to win the day, and his well-manned battery gave him the advantage.

Suddenly a flash of lightning burst forth from the dark market; there came a report like a peal of thunder, and a bullet went crashing through a house over Gauvain's head.

The barricade was paying him back in his own coin.

What was going on? This was a new development. The artillery was no longer confined to one side.

A second ball followed the first, embedding itself in the wall close to Gauvain; and a third ball knocked off his hat.

These balls were of a calibre so heavy that they must have been fired from a sixteen-pounder.

"They are aiming at you, commander," cried the gunners, as they put out the torch; and Gauvain, still absorbed in his reverie, stooped to pick up his hat.

Some one was indeed aiming at Gauvain, and it was Lantenac.

The Marquis had just reached the barricade from the opposite side.

The Imânus hastened to meet him.

"Monseigneur, we have been taken by surprise."

"By whom?"

"I do not know."

"Is the road to Dinan open?"

"I believe so."

"We must begin to retreat."

"We have done so. Many have already fled."

"I am not speaking of flight, but of retreat. Why did you not use the artillery?"

"The men were beside themselves, and then the officers were absent."

"I was to be here."

"Monseigneur, I sent everything I could on to Fougères,—the women, the baggage, and all useless incumbrances; but what is to be done with the three little prisoners?"

"Do you mean the children?"

"Yes."

"They are our hostages. Send them on to the Tourgue."

So saying, the Marquis started for the barricade, and directly after his arrival things took on another aspect. The barricade was not well constructed for artillery; there was room for but two cannon; the Marquis placed in position the two sixteen-pounders for which embrasures were made. As he was leaning on one of the cannon, watching the enemy's battery through the embrasure, he caught sight of Gauvain.

"It is he!" he cried.

Then, taking the swab and the ramrod, he loaded the piece, adjusted the sight, and took aim.

Three times he aimed at Gauvain and missed him, but the third shot knocked off his hat.

"Bungler!" murmured Lantenac. "A little lower, and I should have had his head."

Suddenly the torch went out, and he had only darkness before him.

"Well, let it go," he said.

And turning to the peasant gunners, he exclaimed:

"Let them have the grape-shot!"

Gauvain for his part was also in deadly earnest. The situation had become a serious one since the development of this new phase of the conflict, and the barricade was now cannonading him. Who could tell how soon it might pass from the defensive to the offensive? The enemy numbered at least five thousand, even allowing for the dead and the fugitives, while he had no more than twelve hundred service-able men at his command. What would happen to the Republicans if the enemy should become aware of their limited number? Their rôles would soon be reversed; from playing the part of assailants, he would become the object of assault. If the barricade were to make a sortie, all would be lost.

What was to be done? It was out of the question to think of attacking the barricade in front; an attempt to capture it by main strength would be folly; twelve hundred men could not dislodge five thousand. Imperative as it was to make an end of it, knowing as he did that delay was fatal, still he realized that to force the enemy's hand would be impossible. What was he to do?

Gauvain belonged to this neighborhood; he was familiar with the town, and knew that behind the old market, where the Vendeans were intrenched, was a labyrinth of narrow and crooked streets.

He turned to his lieutenant, the brave Captain Guéchamp, who afterwards became famous for clearing the forest of Concise, where Jean Chouan was born, and who prevented the capture of Bourgneuf by cutting the rebels off from the highway that led to the pond of La Chaine.

"Guéchamp," said Gauvain, "I intrust you with the command. Fire as rapidly as possible. Riddle the barricade with cannon-balls, and keep them busy over yonder."

"I understand," said Guéchamp.

"Mass the whole column with their guns loaded, and hold them in readiness for an attack."

He whispered a few words in Guéchamp's ear.

"It shall be done," said the latter.

Gauvain continued,—

"Are all our drummers ready?"

"Yes"

"We have nine. Keep two and give me seven."

The seven drummers silently ranged themselves in front of Gauvain.

"Step forward, battalion of the Bonnet-Rouge!" exclaimed Gauvain.

Twelve soldiers, one of whom was a sergeant, stepped from the ranks.

"I called for the whole battalion," said Gauvain.

"Here it is," replied the sergeant.

"Are there but twelve?"

"Only twelve of us left."

"Very well," said Gauvain.

This sergeant was that very Radoub, the rough and kindly soldier who in the name of the battalion had adopted the three children found in the forest of La Saudraie.

It will be remarked that only half that battalion was massacred at Herbe-en-Pail, and Radoub, by good luck, was not among them.

A forage-wagon was standing near, and Gauvain pointed it out to the sergeant.

"Let your men weave ropes of straw and bind them around their muskets to deaden the noise when they clash against each other."

A minute went by; the order was silently executed in the darkness.

"It is done," said the sergeant.

"Take off your shoes, soldiers," continued Gauvain.

"We have none," replied the sergeant.

Including the drummers, they numbered nineteen men; Gauvain was the twentieth.

"Follow me, in single file!" cried Gauvain. "Let the drummers go before the battalion. You will command the battalion, sergeant!"

He placed himself at the head of this column, and while the cannonading still continued on both sides, these twenty men glided along like shadows and plunged into the deserted lanes.

Thus they proceeded for some time, skirting along the fronts of the houses. It seemed as though the whole town were dead; the citizens had taken refuge in their cellars. Every door was barred and every shutter closed. Not a light was to be seen anywhere.

But through this silence they still heard the awful din on the principal street: the cannonading went on; the Republican battery and the Royal barricade spit out their grape-shot with unabated fury.

After marching twenty minutes, winding in and out, Gauvain, who had led the way unerringly through this darkness, reached the end of a lane that led into the principal street; they were now, however, on the other side of the market.

The position was changed. On that side there was no intrenchment,—a common mistake of barricade builders; the market was open, and one could walk in under the pillars, where several baggage-wagons stood ready to leave. Gauvain and his nineteen men were in the presence of the five thousand Vendeans as before, only instead of facing them they found themselves in their rear.

Gauvain whispered to the sergeant; the straw was unwound from the muskets, and the twelve grenadiers ranged themselves in a line behind the corner of the lane, while the seven drummers, with uplifted drumstick, waited for the signal.

The artillery firing was intermittent, when suddenly, during the interval between two discharges, Gauvain raised his sword, and in a voice that rang out like a clarion upon the silence, exclaimed,—

"Two hundred men to the right, two hundred to the left, the rest in the centre."

The drums beat and the twelve musket-shots were fired.

Then Gauvain uttered the formidable battle-cry of the Blues,—

"Charge! Bayonets!"

The effect was wonderful.

All this crowd of peasants finding themselves assailed in the rear, imagined that another army had come up from behind. At the same time, on hearing the beating of the drums, the column which held the upper part of the street and was commanded by Guéchamp began to move, sounding the charge in its turn, and starting on the run, attacked the barricade; the peasants saw themselves between two fires. A panic magnifies, and at such moments a pistol-shot sounds like the report of a cannon; imagination distorts every sound, and the barking of a dog seems like the roar of a lion. Let us add, moreover, that the peasant takes fright as easily as a thatch catches fire, and as quickly as a burning thatch becomes a conflagration, a panic among peasants grows into a rout; and on this occasion the flight was beyond description.

In a few moments the market was deserted; the terrified lads scattered in all directions, and the officers were helpless. The Imânus killed two or three of the fugitives, but it was of no avail. Nothing could be heard save the cry, "Sauve qui peut," and with the rapidity of a cloud driven onward by a hurricane, the entire army scattered through the streets as through the meshes of a sieve and vanished into the country.

Some fled towards Châteauneuf, some towards Plerguer, and others in the direction of Antrain.

The Marquis de Lantenac, who was the last man to leave the scene, spiked the guns with his own hands, and then quietly and calmly took his departure, saying as he went,—

"It is evident that the peasants cannot be depended upon to stand their ground. We need the English."

IV

A Second Time

THEY HAD WON THE VICTORY, and, turning to the men of the battalion of the Bonnet-Rouge, Gauvain exclaimed, —

"Though you are but twelve, you are equal to a thousand."

One word from the chief in times like these was as good as the cross of honor.

Guéchamp, who had been sent by Gauvain outside the city in pursuit of the fugitives, captured many of them.

Torches were lighted, and the town was searched.

All those who had not been able to escape, surrendered themselves. The principal street, illuminated by *pots-à-feu*, was strewn with the dead and the wounded. The fierce struggle that always terminates a battle was still continued by a few groups of desperate fighters, who, however, on being surrounded, threw down their arms and surrendered.

Gauvain had observed amid the wild tumult of the flight a fearless man, vigorous and agile as a faun, who stood his own ground while covering the flight of the others. This peasant, after handling his musket like an expert, alternately firing: and Rising the butt as a club, until he had broken it, now stood grasping a pistol in one hand and a sabre in the other, and no man dared approach him. Suddenly Gauvain saw him reel, and lean against one of the pillars of the principal street. He was evidently wounded, but he still held his sabre and his pistols. Gauvain put his sword under his arm and came up to him. As he called upon him to surrender, the man gazed steadily at him, while the blood oozing from his wound formed a pool at his feet.

"You are my prisoner," said Gauvain. "What is your name?"

"Danse-à-l'Ombre," was the reply.

"You are a brave fellow," said Gauvain, extending his hand.

"Long live the King!" cried the man.

Then gathering all his strength, and raising both hands simultaneously, he fired his pistol at Gauvain's heart, at the same time aiming a blow at his head with the sabre.

This movement, tiger-like in its rapidity, was yet forestalled by the action of another. A horseman had appeared on the scene; he had been there for some moments without attracting attention, and when he saw the Vendean lift his sabre and pistol, he threw himself between the latter and Gauvain, intercepting the sabre-thrust by his own person, while his horse was struck by the pistol-shot, and both horse and rider fell to the ground. Thus Gauvain's life was saved. All this took place as quickly as one would utter a cry.

The Vendean also sank to the pavement.

The blow from the sabre struck the man full in the face; he lay on the ground in a swoon. The horse was killed.

Gauvain drew near, asking, as he approached, if any could tell who he was.

On looking at him more closely he saw that the blood was gushing over the face of the wounded man, covering it as with a red mask, and rendering it impossible to distinguish his features. One could see that his hair was gray.

"He has saved my life," said Gauvain. "Does any one here know him?"

"Commander," said a soldier, "he has but just arrived in town. I saw him coming from the direction of Pontorson."

The surgeon-in-chief of the division hurried up with his instrument-case.

The wounded man was still unconscious, but after examining him the surgeon said,—

"Oh, this is nothing but a simple cut. It can be sewed, and in eight days he will be on his feet again. That was a fine sabre-cut."

The wounded man wore a cloak and a tricolored belt, with pistols and a sabre. They placed him on a stretcher, and after undressing him, a bucket of water was brought, and the surgeon washed the wound. As the face began to appear, Gauvain studied it attentively.

"Has he any papers about him?" he asked.

The surgeon felt in his side pocket and drew out a pocket-book, which he handed to Gauvain.

Meanwhile the wounded man, revived by the cold water, was regaining his consciousness. His eyelids quivered slightly.

Gauvain was looking over the pocket-book, in which he discovered a sheet of paper folded four times; he opened it and read,—

"Committee of Public Safety. Citizen Cimourdain—"

"Cimourdain!" he cried; whereupon the wounded man opened his eyes.

Gauvain was beside himself.

"It is you, Cimourdain! For the second time you have saved my life."

Cimourdain looked at Gauvain, while a sudden burst of joy, impossible to describe, lit up his bleeding face.

Gauvain fell on his knees before him, exclaiming:

"My master!"

"Thy father!" said Cimourdain.

V

A Drop of Cold Water

It was many a year since last they met, but their hearts had never been separated, and they knew each other again as if they had parted but yesterday.

A hospital had been improvised in the town hall of Dol, and Cimourdain was placed on a bed in a small room adjoining the large hall devoted to the other wounded men. The surgeon who had sewed up his wound put a stop to all exciting conversation between the two men, considering it wiser to leave Cimourdain to sleep. Besides, Gauvain was called away by the thousand duties and cares incident to victory. Cimourdain was left alone, but he could not sleep, excited as he was by the double fever of his wound and of his joy.

He knew he was not sleeping, and yet he hardly felt sure that he was awake. Could it be possible that his dream had come to pass? Cimourdain was one of those men who have no faith in good luck, and yet it had fallen to his lot. He had found Gauvain. He had left him a child, he found him a man,—a grand, brave, awe-inspiring conqueror, and that in the cause of the people. In the Vendée, Gauvain was the pillar of the Revolution, and it was really Cimourdain himself who had bestowed this support upon the Republic. This conqueror was his pupil. Cimourdain beheld his own thought illumining the youthful countenance of this man, for whom a niche in the Republican Pantheon was perhaps reserved; his disciple, the child of his mind, was a hero from this time forth, and would soon become famous; it seemed to Cimourdain like seeing his own soul transformed into a genius. As he watched Gauvain in the battle he had felt like Chiron watching Achilles. There is a certain analogy between the priest and the Centaur, since a priest is but half a man.

The incidents of this day's adventure, added to the sleeplessness caused by his wound, filled Cimourdain with a strange sort of intoxication. He seemed to see a youthful destiny rising before him in all its splendor, and the knowledge of his own absolute control of this destiny contributed to increase his deep joy. It needed but one more triumph like that which he had just witnessed, and at a word from Cimourdain, the Republic would place Gauvain at the head of an army. Nothing dazzles one so much as an unexpected success. This was the epoch of military dreams. Every man had a longing to create a general; Westermann was the hero of Danton's dream, Rossignol of Marat's, Ronsin of Hébert's; and Robespierre would have liked to ruin them all. So why not Gauvain? Cimourdain asked himself; and thereupon he proceeded to lose himself in dreams. There were no limits to his imaginings; as he passed from one hypothesis to another, all obstacles vanished before him. For this is a ladder on which, having once set foot, one never pauses; the ascent is a long one, starting from man and ending at the stars. A great general is only the commander of an army; a great captain is also a leader of thought; Cimourdain pictured Gauvain as a great captain. It seemed to him—for fancies travel fast—that he saw him on the sea, pursuing the English; on the Rhine, driving before him the kings of the North; in the Pyrenees, repulsing Spain; on the Alps, setting the signal for insurrection before the eyes of Rome. Cimourdain was a man who possessed two distinct natures,—the one tender, the other gloomy,—both of which were satisfied; for since the inexorable was his ideal, it gratified him to see Gauvain at once glorious and terrible. Cimourdain thought of all he had to pull down before he could build up. "And certainly," he said to himself, "this is no time to indulge in tender emotions. Gauvain will be up *à la hauteur*,"[3]—an expression of the day. Cimourdain pictured Gauvain to himself with a sword in his hand, girded in light, a flaming meteor on his brow, spreading the grand ideal wings of justice, right, and progress, and, like an angel of extermination, crushing the darkness beneath his heel.

Just at the crisis of this reverie, which one might almost have called an ecstasy, through the half-open door he heard men talking in the great ambulance-hall adjoining his room, and he recognized Gauvain's voice, which, in spite of years of absence, had always rung in his ears; for the voice of the man often retains something of its childish tones. He listened. There was a sound of footsteps, and he heard the soldiers saying,—

"Here is the man who fired at you, commander. He had crawled into a cellar when no one was watching; but we found him, and here he is."

Then Cimourdain heard the following conversation between Gauvain and the man:—

"Are you wounded?"

"I am well enough to be shot."

"Put this man to bed, dress his wounds, take good care of him until he recovers."

"I want to die."

"But you are going to live. You tried to kill me in the name of the King; I pardon you in the name of the Republic."

A shadow crossed Cimourdain's brow. He seemed to wake as with a start, and whispered to himself in a tone of gloomy dejection,—

"Yes, he has a merciful nature, there can be no doubt."

VI

A Healed Breast, but a Bleeding Heart

A GASH IS QUICKLY HEALED; but there was elsewhere one more seriously wounded than Cimourdain. This was the woman who had been shot, and whom the beggar Tellmarch had rescued from the great pool of blood at the farm Herbe-en-Pail.

Michelle Fléchard was in a more critical condition than Tellmarch had supposed. There was a wound in the shoulder-blade corresponding to that above her breast; one ball had broken her collar-bone, while

---

3. Equal to the occasion.

another had entered her shoulder; but as the lung was uninjured, she might recover. Tellmarch was what in peasant language is called a "philosopher," that is to say, a combination of doctor, surgeon, and wizard. Upon the bed of seaweed in his underground den he nursed the wounded woman, using those mysterious remedies called "simples;" end thanks to his care, she lived.

The collar-bone knitted together, the wounds in the breast and the shoulder closed, and after a few weeks the wounded woman became convalescent.

One morning she was able to walk out of the *carnichot*, leaning on Tellmarch; she seated herself under the trees, in the sun. Tellmarch knew very little about her; for a wound in the breast necessitates silence, and during the death-like agony which preceded her recovery she had hardly spoken a word. Whenever she seemed about to open her lips, Tellmarch would prevent her; but he could not control her thoughts, and he observed by the expression in her eyes the heart-rending nature of her ever-recurring fancies. This morning she felt strong, and could almost walk alone. The doctor who has cured his patient enjoys a sense of fatherhood; and as he watched her, Tellmarch felt happy. The good old man began to smile as he addressed her.

"Well, it seems we are up; our wounds are healed."

"All but those of the heart."

And presently she added,—

"Then you don't know where they are?"

"Whom do you mean?" asked Tellmarch.

"My children."

The word "then" revealed a whole world of meaning; it seemed to say: "Since you do not speak of them to me, since you have been with me for so many days without opening your lips to me on the subject, since you silence me every time I try to speak, since you seem to fear that I am going to talk about them,—it must mean that you have nothing to tell me." During the course of her fever she had often noticed that whenever, in her delirious ramblings, she had called for her children (the perceptions of delirium are sometimes acute), the old man would make no reply.

The truth was that Tellmarch did not know what to tell her. It is not easy to speak to a mother of her lost children; and besides, what did he know? Nothing at all, in fact,—that a mother had been shot, that he had found this mother on the ground, that when he had lifted her up she was nearly dead, that this dying woman had three children, and lastly, that the Marquis de Lantenac, after ordering the mother to be shot, had carried away the children; and here his information ceased. What had become of the children? Were they still living? Having made inquiries, he had learned that there were two boys, and a little girl barely weaned; and this was the extent of his knowledge. He asked himself more questions than he could answer in regard to this unhappy family; but the neighbors whom he had asked only shook their heads. M. de Lantenac was a man of whom no one cared to talk.

They were equally reluctant either to speak about Lantenac or to talk to Tellmarch. Peasants have their own peculiar superstitions. They disliked Tellmarch. Tellmarch le Caimand was a perplexing man. Why was he always looking up at the sky? What was he doing, what could he be thinking about, when he stood motionless for hours at a time? Surely he must be a very odd sort of man. While the district was in a state of combustion and conflagration, when warfare, devastation, and carnage were the sole occupations of life, when every man was doing his best to burn houses, murder families, massacre outposts, and plunder villages, thinking of nothing but setting ambushes and traps and killing one another, here was this hermit absorbed in nature, enjoying absolute peace of mind, gathering plants and herbs, interested only in flowers, birds, and stars,—of course he was a dangerous character! He must be insane. He never hid behind a bush to fire at his fellow-men. "The man is mad!" said the passers-by. Hence he inspired a certain awe, and men avoided him, thus increasing the isolation of his life.

They asked him no questions, and seldom vouchsafed replies; therefore he had been unable to get the information he wanted. The conflict had been transferred to other districts, and the fighting was more remote. The Marquis de Lantenac had vanished from the horizon; and war must set its foot on a man of Tellmarch's character before he becomes aware of its existence.

After hearing these words, "My children!" Tellmarch ceased to smile, and the mother sank into deep thought. What was passing in her soul? She seemed to have plunged into the depths. Suddenly she looked up at Tellmarch, and repeated her demand almost angrily,—

"My children!"

Tellmarch bent his head like a culprit.

He was thinking of the Marquis de Lantenac, who, so far from returning his thought, had probably forgotten his very existence. He realized the fact as he said to himself, "When a nobleman is in danger he reckons you among his acquaintance; but let the danger pass, and he forgets that he ever saw you."

And he asked himself, "Why, then, did I save him?" To which question he made reply, "Because he was a man."

For some moments he dwelt upon this thought; then he resumed the thread of his meditations,—

"Am I sure of this?"

And presently he repeated those bitter words: "Had I but known!"

This whole experience gave him a sense of oppression, for his own action in the affair was enigmatical to him. His thoughts were sad, since a sense of guilt had crept into them. A kindly act may prove in the end to have been an evil one. He who saves the wolf kills the sheep; he who sets the vulture's wing is responsible for his talons. The unreasoning anger of this mother was therefore justified.

Still he felt a certain consolation in the knowledge that he had saved the mother, which partly balanced his regret for having saved the Marquis.

"But the children?"

The mother was also thinking; and these two currents of thoughts moved side by side, perhaps to mingle unawares in the shadowy land of reverie.

Meanwhile her eyes, gloomy as the night, rested again on Tellmarch.

"We cannot go on like this," she said.

"Hush!" rejoined Tellmarch, putting his finger on his lips.

She continued,—

"I am angry with you for saving me; you did wrong. I would rather have died, for then I should surely see them and know where they are. They would not see me, but I should be near them. The dead must have power to protect."

He took her by the arm, and felt her pulse.

"You must calm yourself, or you will have a relapse."

She asked him almost harshly,—

"When can I go away?"

"Go away?"

"Yes. When shall I be fit for tramping?"

"Never, if you are unreasonable; tomorrow, if you are good."

"What do you call being good?"

"Trusting in God."

"God? What has He done with my children?"

She seemed to be wandering. Her voice had grown very gentle.

"You must see," she went on to say, "that I cannot stay like this. You never had any children; but I am a mother: that makes a difference. One cannot judge of a thing unless he knows what it is like. Did you ever have any children?"

"No," replied Tellmarch.

"But I have. Can I live without my children? I should like to be told why my children are not here. Something is happening, but what it is I cannot understand."

"Come," said Tellmarch, "you are feverish again. You mustn't talk any more."

She looked at him and was silent.

And from that day she kept silence again.

This implicit obedience was more than Tellmarch desired. She spent hour after hour crouching at the foot of the old tree, like one stupefied. She pondered in silence,—that refuge of simple souls who have sounded the gloomy depths of woe. She seemed to give up trying to understand. After a certain point despair becomes unintelligible to the despairing.

As Tellmarch watched her, his sympathy increased. The sight of her suffering excited in this old man thoughts such as a woman might have known. "She may close her lips," he said to himself, "but her eyes will speak, and I see what ails her. She has but one idea; she cannot be resigned to the thought that she is no longer a mother. Her mind dwells constantly on the image of her youngest, whom she was nursing not long ago. How charming it must be to feel a tiny rosy mouth drawing ones soul from out one's body, feeding its own little life on the life of its mother!"

He too was silent, realizing the impotence of speech in the presence of such sorrow.

There is something really terrible in the silence of an unchanging thought, and how can one expect that a mother will listen to reason? Maternity sees but one side. It is useless to argue with it. One sublime characteristic of a mother is her resemblance to a wild animal. The maternal instinct is divine animalism. The mother ceases to be a woman; she becomes a female, and her children are her cubs.

Hence we find in the mother something above reason and at the same time below it,—a something which we call instinct. Guided as she is by the infinite and mysterious will of the universe, her very blindness is charged with penetration.

However anxious to make this unfortunate woman speak, Tellmarch could not succeed. One day he said to her:—

"Unfortunately I am old, and can no longer walk. My strength is exhausted before I reach my journey's end. I would go with you, only that my legs give out in about fifteen minutes and I have to stop and rest. However, it may be just as well for you that I cannot walk far, as my company might be more dangerous than useful. Here, I am tolerated; but the Blues suspect me because I am a peasant, and the peasants because they believe me to be a wizard."

He waited for an answer, but she did not even raise her eyes.

A fixed idea ends either in madness or heroism. But what heroism can be expected from a poor peasant woman? None whatever. She can be a mother, and that is all. Each day she grew more and more absorbed in her reverie. Tellmarch was watching her.

He tried to keep her busy. He bought her needles, thread, and a thimble, and to the delight of the poor Caimand, she really began to busy herself with sewing; she still dreamed, it is true, but she worked also,—a sure sign of health,—and by degrees her strength returned. She mended her underwear, her dress, and her shoes, her eyes all the while preserving a strange, far-away look. As she sewed she hummed to herself unintelligible songs. She would mutter names, probably children's names, but not distinctly enough for Tellmarch to understand. Sometimes she paused and listened to the birds, as though she expected a message from them. She watched the weather, and he could see her lips move as she talked to herself in a low voice. She had made a bag and filled it with chestnuts, and one morning Tellmarch found her gazing vaguely into the depths of the forest, and he saw that she was all ready to start.

"Where are you going?" he asked.

And she replied,—

"I am going to look for them."

He made no effort to detain her.

VII

The Two Poles of Truth

AFTER A FEW WEEKS, CROWDED with the vicissitudes of civil war throughout the district of Fougères, the talk ran for the most part upon two men, wholly unlike in character, who were nevertheless engaged in the same work, fighting side by side in the great revolutionary struggle. The savage duel still continued, but the Vendée was losing ground,— especially in Ille-et-Vilaine, where, thanks to the young commander who at Dol had so opportunely confronted the audacity of six thousand Royalists with that of fifteen hundred patriots, the insurrection, if not suppressed, was at least far less active, and restricted to certain limits. Several successful attacks had followed that exploit, and from these repeated victories a new state of affairs had sprung into existence. Matters had assumed a different aspect, but a singular complication had arisen.

That the Republic was in the ascendant throughout this region of the Vendée was beyond a doubt; but which Republic? Amidst the dawning of triumph, two republics confronted each other,—that of terror, determined to conquer by severity, and that of mercy, striving to win the victory by mildness. Which was to prevail? The visible representatives of these two forms, one of which was conciliatory and the other implacable, were two men, each possessing influence and authority,—one a military commander, the other a civil delegate. Which of the two would win the day? The delegate was supported by a tremendous influence; he came bringing with him the threatening watchword from the Paris Commune to the battalion of Santerre: "No mercy, no quarter!" As a means of compelling implicit obedience to his authority, he had the decree of the Convention reading as follows: "Penalty of death to whomsoever shall set at liberty or connive at the escape of a rebel chief," and also full powers from the Committee of Public Safety, with an injunction commanding obedience to him as a delegate, signed by Robespierre, Danton, and Marat. The soldier, for his part, had but the power that is born of pity.

His weapons of defence were his right arm to chastise the enemy, and his heart to pardon them. As a conqueror, he felt that he had a right to spare the conquered.

Hence a conflict, deep but as yet unacknowledged, between these two men. They lived in different atmospheres, both wrestling with rebellion,—the one armed with the thunderbolts of victory, the other with those of terror.

Throughout the Bocage, men talked of nothing else; and the extreme intimacy of two men of such utterly opposite natures contributed to increase the anxiety of those who were watching them on every side. These two antagonists were friends. Never were two hearts drawn together by a deeper or a nobler sympathy. The man of ungentle nature had saved the life of him who was merciful; the scar on his face bore witness to the fact. These men represented in their own persons the images of death and of life, embodying the principle of destruction and that of peace, and they loved each other. Conceive, if you can, Orestes merciful and Pylades pitiless. Try to imagine Arimanes the brother of Ormus!

Let us also add that of these two men, the one who was called ferocious showed himself at the same time the most brotherly of men. He dressed wounds, nursed the sick, spent his days and nights in the ambulances and hospitals, took pity on the barefooted children, kept nothing for himself, but gave all he had to the poor. He never missed a battle,—always marching at the head of the columns; was ever in the thickest of the fight,—armed, it is true, for he always wore in his belt a sabre and two pistols, yet practically unarmed, for no one had ever seen him draw his sword or raise his pistols. He faced blows, but never returned them. It was said that he had been a priest.

These two men were Gauvain and Cimourdain,—at variance in principles, though united in friendship: it was like a soul cleft in twain; and Gauvain had in truth received the gentler half of Cimourdain's nature. One might say that the latter has bestowed the white ray upon Gauvain, and kept the black one for himself. Hence a secret discord. Sooner or later this suppressed disagreement could hardly fail to explode; and one morning the contest began as follows.

Cimourdain said to Gauvain,—

"What have we accomplished?"

To which the latter replied,—

"You know as well as I. I have dispersed Lantenac's bands. He has but a few men left, and has been driven to the forest of Fougères. In eight days he will be surrounded."

"And in fifteen?"

"He will be captured."

"And then?"

"You have seen my notice?"

"Yes; and what then?"

"He is to be shot."

"A truce to clemency. He must be guillotined."

"I approve of a military death."

"And I of a revolutionary one."

Looking Gauvain full in the face, Cimourdain said,—

"Why did you order those nuns of the convent of Saint-Marc-le-Blanc to be set at liberty?"

"I do not wage war against women," replied Gauvain.

"Those women hate the people; and when there is a question of hatred, one woman is equal to ten men. Why did you refuse to send that band of fanatical old priests, whom you took at Louvigné, before the revolutionary tribunal?"

"Neither do I wage war against old men."

"An old priest is worse than a young one. The rebellion that is advocated by white hair is so much the more dangerous. People have faith in wrinkles. Do not indulge in false pity, Gauvain. The regicide is the true liberator. Keep your eye on the tower of the Temple."

"The Temple Tower! I would have the Dauphin out of it. I am not making war against children."

Cimourdain's eye grew stern.

"Learn then, Gauvain, that one must make war on a woman when her name is Marie-Antoinette, on an old man if he happens to be Pope Pius VI, and upon a child who goes by the name of Louis Capet."

"I am no politician, master."

"Try, then, not to be a dangerous man. Why was it that during the attack of the post of Cossé, when the rebel Jean Treton, repulsed and defeated, rushed alone, sabre in hand, against your entire division, you cried, 'Open the ranks! Let him pass through!'"

"Because it is not fit that fifteen hundred men should be allowed to kill one man."

"And why at Cailleterie d'Astillé, when you saw that your soldiers were about to kill the Vendean Joseph Bézier, who was wounded and just able to drag himself along, did you cry, 'Forward! leave this man to me!' and directly afterwards fire your pistol in the air?"

"Because one shrinks from killing a fallen enemy."

"There you were wrong. Both of these men are leaders at this present moment. Joseph Bézier is known as Moustache, and Jean Treton as Jambe-d'Argent. By saving their lives you presented the Republic with two enemies."

"I should prefer to make friends for her rather than enemies."

"After the victory of Landéan, why did you not shoot the three hundred peasant prisoners?"

"Because Bonchamp pardoned the Republican prisoners, and I wished it to be known that the Republic pardons the Royalist prisoners."

"Then I suppose you will pardon Lantenac if you take him?"

"No."

"Why not,—since you pardoned three hundred peasants?"

"The peasants are only ignorant men. Lantenac knows what he is about."

"But Lantenac is your kinsman."

"And France nearer than he."

"Lantenac is an old man."

"To me Lantenac is a stranger; he has no age. He is ready to summon the English, he represents invasion, he is the country's enemy, and the duel between us can only be ended by his death or mine."

"Remember these words, Gauvain."

"I have said them."

For a while both men remained silent, gazing at each other; then Gauvain continued,—

"This will be a bloody year,—this '93."

"Tate care," cried Cimourdain. "There are terrible duties to be performed, and we must beware of accusing the innocent instrument. How long since we have blamed the doctor for his patient's illness? Yes, the chief characteristic of this stupendous year is its pitiless severity. And why is this? Because it is the great revolutionary year,—the year which is the very incarnation of revolution. Revolution feels no more pity for its enemy, the old world, than the surgeon feels for the gangrene against which he is fighting. The business of revolution is to extirpate royalty in the person of the king, aristocracy in that of the nobleman, despotism in that of the soldier, and superstition and barbarism in the persons of the priest and the judge,—in one word, of every form of tyranny in the image of the tyrant. The operation is a fearful one, but revolution performs it with a steady hand. As to the amount of sound flesh that must be sacrificed, ask a Boerhave what he thinks of it. Do you suppose it possible to remove a tumor without loss of blood? Can a conflagration be extinguished without violent efforts? These terrible necessities are the very condition of success. A surgeon may be compared to a butcher, or a healer may seem like an executioner. Revolution is devoted to its fatal work. It mutilates that it may save. What! can you expect it to take pity on the virus? Would you have it merciful to poison? It will not listen. It holds the past within its grasp, and it means to make an end of it. It cuts deeply into civilization, that it may promote the health of mankind. You suffer, no doubt; but consider for how short a time it will endure,—only so long as the operation requires; and after that is over you will live. Revolution is amputating the world; hence this hemorrhage,—'93."

"A surgeon is calm," said Gauvain, "and the men I see are violent."

"Revolution requires the aid of savage workmen," replied Cimourdain; "it repulses all trembling hands; it trusts only such as are inexorable. Danton is the impersonation of the terrible, Robespierre of the inflexible, Saint-Just of the immovable, and Marat of the implacable. Take note of it, Gauvain. We need these names. They are worth as much as armies to us. They will terrify Europe."

"And possibly the future also," replied Gauvain. He paused, and then continued,—

"But really, master, you are mistaken. I accuse no one. My idea of revolution is that it shall be irresponsible. We ought not to say this man is innocent, or that one is guilty. Louis XVI is like a sheep cast among lions. He wishes to escape, and in trying to defend himself he would bite if he could; but one cannot turn into a lion at will. His weakness is regarded as a crime; and when the angry sheep shows his teeth, 'Ah, the traitor!' cry the lions, and they proceed straightway to devour him, and afterwards fall to fighting among themselves."

"The sheep is a brute."

"And what are the lions?"

This answer set Cimourdain thinking.

"The lions," he replied, "represent the human conscience, principles, ideas."

"It is they who have caused the Reign of Terror."

"Some day the Revolution will justify all that."

"Take care lest Terror should prove the calumny of the Revolution."

Gauvain continued,—

"Liberty, equality, fraternity,—these are the dogmas of peace and harmony. Why give them so terrible an aspect? What are we striving to accomplish? To bring all nations under one universal republic. Well, then, let us not terrify them. Of what use is intimidation? Neither nations nor birds can be attracted by fear. We must not do evil that good may come. We have not overturned the throne to leave the scaffold standing. Death to the king, and life to the nations. Let us strike off the crowns, but spare the heads. Revolution means concord, and not terror. Schemes of benevolence are but poorly served by merciless men. Amnesty is to me the grandest word in human language. I am opposed to the shedding of blood, save as I risk my own. Still, I am but a soldier; I can do no more than fight. Yet if we are to lose the privilege of pardoning, of what use is it to conquer? Let us be enemies, if you will, in battle; but when victory is ours, then is the time to be brothers."

"Take care!" repeated Cimourdain for the third time; "take care, Gauvain! You are dearer to me than a son."

And he added, thoughtfully,—

"In times like these pity may be nothing less than treason in another form."

Listening to these two men, one might have fancied himself hearing a dialogue between a sword and all axe.

VIII

Dolorosa

Meanwhile the mother was searching for her little ones, walking straight onward; and how she subsisted we cannot tell, since she did not know herself. She walked day and night, begging as she went, often living on herbs and sleeping upon the ground in the open air, among the bushes, under the stars, and sometimes mid the rain and the wind. Thus she wandered from village to village and from farm to farm, making inquiries as she went along, but, tattered and torn as she was, never venturing beyond the threshold. Sometimes she found a welcome, sometimes she was turned away; and when they refused to let her come in, she would go into the woods.

Unfamiliar as she was with the country beyond Siscoignard and the parish of Azé, and having nothing to serve as guide, she would retrace her steps, going over and over the same ground, thus wasting both time and strength. Sometimes she followed the highway, sometimes the cart-ruts, and then again she would turn into the paths in the woods. In this wandering life she had worn out her wretched garments. At first she had her shoes, then she went barefoot, and it was not long before her feet were bleeding.

Unconsciously she travelled on, mid bloodshed and warfare, neither hearing, seeing, nor trying to shield herself, simply looking for her children. As the entire country was in rebellion, there were no longer any gendarmes, or mayors, or authorities of any kind. Only such persons as she encountered on the way would she stop to ask.

"Have you seen three little children anywhere?"

And when the passers-by lifted their heads she would say,—

"Two boys and a girl," and go on to name them:

"René-Jean, Gros-Alain, Georgette. Have you not seen them?"

And again,—

"The oldest one was four and a half and the youngest twenty months."

Presently she would add,—

"Do you know where they are? They have been taken from me."

People gazed at her, and that was all.

Perceiving that she was not understood, she would explain,—

"It is because they are mine. That is the reason."

And then seeing the passers-by continue their way, she would stand speechless, tearing her breast with her nails. One day, however, a peasant stopped to listen to her. The worthy man set his wits at work.

"Let us see. Did you say three children?" he asked.

"Yes."

"Two boys?"

"And a girl."

"And you are looking for them?"

"Yes."

"I was told that a nobleman had carried off three little children and keeps them with him."

"Where is that man? Where are they?" she cried.

"You must go to the Tourgue," answered the peasant.

"And shall I find my children there?"

"Very likely you will."

"What did you say the name was?"

"The Tourgue."

"What is the Tourgue?"

"It is a place."

"Is it a village, a castle, or a farm?"

"I never was there."

"Is it far?"

"I should say so."

"In what direction?"

"In the direction of Fougères."

"Which way shall I go?"

"You are now at Ventortes," replied the peasant. "You will leave Ernée on your left and Coxelles on your right; you must pass through Longchamps, and cross the Leroux."

The peasant raised his hand and pointed westward.

"Keep straight ahead, facing the sunset."

She had already started before he had time to lower his arm.

He called out to her.

"You must be careful; they are fighting over there."

She never turned to reply, but walked straight ahead without pausing.

IX

A Provincial Bastile

I

La Tourgue

THE TRAVELLER WHO FORTY YEARS ago entered the forest of Fougères from the direction of Laignelet and came out towards Parigné, might have beheld on the edge of this dense forest a sinister sight, for emerging from the thicket he would come directly upon the Tourgue, and not the living Tourgue, but the dead one.

The Tourgue cracked, battered, scarred, dismantled. A ruin may be called the ghost of an edifice. Nothing could be more lugubrious than the aspect of the Tourgue. A high circular tower stood alone like a malefactor on the edge of the wood, and rising as it did from a precipitous rock, its severe and solid architecture gave it the appearance of a Roman structure, combining within itself the elements of power and of decay. In fact, it might in one sense be called Roman, since it was Romance. It was begun in the ninth century and finished in the twelfth, after the time of the third crusade. The style of the imposts of its embrasures indicated its period. If one approached it and cared to climb the slope, he might perceive a breach in the wall; and if he ventured to enter in, he would find a vacant space and nothing more. It was not unlike the inside of a stone trumpet set upright on the ground. From top to bottom there were no partitions, and neither ceilings nor floors; here and there arches and chimneys had evidently been torn away, and falconet embrasures were still seen; at different heights, rows of granite corbels and a few cross-beams covered with the ordure of the night birds marked the separate stories; a colossal wall, fifteen feet thick at its base and twelve at its summit; cracks here and there, and holes which once were doors, and through which one caught glimpses of staircases within the gloomy walls. One who passing by at evening might venture in, would hear the cry of the wood-owl, the goat-suckers, and the night-herons; would find brambles, stones, and reptiles beneath his feet; and overhead, through a dark circular opening at the top of the tower which looked like the mouth of an enormous well, he might see the stars.

Local tradition relates that there were secret doors in the upper stories of this tower, like those in the tombs of the kings of Judah, composed of one large stone turning on a pivot, which when closed could not be distinguished from the wall itself,—a fashion in architecture brought home by the crusaders, together with the pointed arch. When these doors were closed, it was impossible to discover them, so skilfully were they fitted into the rest of the stones. Such doors can be found today in those mysterious Libyan cities which escaped the earthquakes that buried the twelve cities in the time of Tiberius.

II

The Breach

THE BREACH BY WHICH ONE gained access to the ruin was the opening of a mine. A connoisseur familiar with Errard, Sardi, and Pagan would have appreciated the skill with which this mine was planned. The fire-chamber, in the shape of a biretta, was of a size accurately proportioned to the strength of the keep which it was intended to destroy. It was capable of containing at least two hundred-weight of powder. The winding passage which led to it was more effective than a straight one. The saucisse, laid bare among the broken stones as the result of the crumbling caused by the mine, was seen to have the requisite diameter of a hen's-egg. The explosion had made a deep rent in the wall, by which the assailants were enabled to enter. It was evident that this tower must have sustained formal sieges from time to time. It was riddled with balls, and these were not all of the same epoch; every missile has its own special way of marking a rampart, and each one, from the stone bullets of the fourteenth century to the iron ones of the eighteenth, had left a scar upon this donjon-keep.

The breach opened into what must have been the ground-floor; and directly opposite, in the wall of the tower, was the gateway of a crypt, cut in the rock and extending under the hall of the lower floor throughout the foundation of the tower.

This crypt, three-fourths filled up, was cleared out in 1835, under the direction of Auguste Le Provost, the antiquary of Bernay.

III

The Oubliette

THIS CRYPT WAS THE OUBLIETTE. Every keep possessed one, and this, like many other penal dungeons of the same period, had two stories. The first story, accessible through the gate, consisted of a good-sized vaulted chamber, on a level with the hall of the ground-floor. On the walls of this room might be seen two vertical furrows, parallel with each other, reaching from wall to wall and passing along the vault, where they had left a deep rut, reminding one of wheel-tracks,—and such in fact they were; for these two furrows were hollowed out by two wheels. In old feudal times men had been torn limb from limb here in this very room, by a process less noisy than that of being drawn and quartered. They had a pair of wheels so large and powerful that they filled the entire room, touching both walls and ceiling, and to each wheel was attached an arm and a leg of the victim; and when these wheels were turned in opposite directions, the man was torn asunder. It required great power; hence the ruts worn in the stone by the grazing of the wheels. A room of this kind may be seen at Vianden.

Above this room there was another, the actual oubliette, whose only entrance was a hole which served the purpose of a door; the victim, stripped of his clothes, was let down, by means of a rope tied under his armpits, into the room below, through an opening made in the middle of the flagging of the upper room. If he persisted in living, food was thrown to him through this aperture. A similar hole may still be seen at Bouillon.

This chamber below, excavated under the hall of the ground-floor to such a depth that it reached water, and constantly swept by an icy wind, was more like a well than a room. But the wind so fatal to the prisoner in the depths was, on the other hand, favorable to the one overhead, groping about beneath the vault, who could breathe the easier on account of it; indeed, all the air he had, came up through this hole. But then any man who entered, or rather fell, into this tomb, never came out again. It behooved the prisoner to look out for himself in the darkness, for it needed but one false step to change the scene of his sufferings. That, however, was his own affair. If he were tenacious of life, this hole was his danger; but if he were weary of it, it was his resource. The upper story was the dungeon, the lower one the tomb,—a superposition not unlike that of the society of the period.

This is what our ancestors called a moat-dungeon; but since the thing itself has disappeared, the name has no longer any meaning for us. Thanks to the Revolution, we can listen with indifference to the sound of these words. On the outside of the tower, and above the breach, which forty years ago was its only entrance, might be seen an embrasure somewhat wider than the other loopholes, from which hung an iron grating, loosened and broken.

IV

The Bridge-Castle

A STONE BRIDGE WHOSE THREE arches were but slightly damaged, was connected with this tower on the side opposite to the breach. This bridge had once supported a building whose few remaining fragments bore the traces of a conflagration; it was only the framework that was left standing, and as the light shone through its interstices as it rose side by side with the tower, it had the effect of a skeleton beside a phantom.

Today this ruin is utterly demolished, leaving no trace whatever behind. A single peasant can destroy in one day structures that kings have labored for centuries to erect. La Tourgue, a peasant abbreviation, signifies La Tour-Gauvain, just as La Jupelle stands for La Jupellière, and Pinson le Tort, the name of a hunchback leader, for Pinson le Tortu.

La Tourgue, which even forty years ago was a ruin, and which today is but a shadow, was a fortress in 1793. It was the old Bastile of the Gauvains, and served to guard, towards the west, the entrance of the forest of Fougères, which is now little more than a grove.

This fortress was built on one of those great blocks of slate which are found in abundance between Mayence and Dinan, scattered in all directions among the copses and along the heath like the missiles of some Titanic combat. The tower composed the entire fortress; and below the tower stood the rock at whose base flowed one of those water-courses which swells into a torrent in January and dries up in June.

Simple as were its means of defence, this tower was almost impregnable in the Middle Ages, but the bridge had proved a source of weakness. The Gauvains of Gothic times had built it without a bridge. It was formerly accessible by means of one of those swinging bridges that could be instantly severed by the stroke of an axe. So long as the Gauvains remained Viscounts it pleased them just as it was, and they were satisfied with it. But when they became Marquises and exchanged the keep for the Court, they spanned the stream with three arches and thus offered access in the direction of the plain very much as they had yielded to the advances of the king. The marquises of the seventeenth century and the marchionesses of the seventeenth no longer prided themselves on their impregnability. They abandoned the traditions of their ancestors to follow the fashions of Versailles.

Facing the tower towards the west was a somewhat elevated plateau adjoining two plains; this plateau was very near the tower, only separated from it by a deep ravine through which flowed a stream tributary to the Couesnon. The bridge that connected the fortress with the plateau stood on lofty piles, and on these piles was constructed as at Chenonceaux a building in the Mansard style of architecture, but more comfortable than the tower. Customs were still very rude, and the lords continued to occupy chambers in the keep that were more like dungeons than bedrooms. As to the building on the bridge, which was a diminutive kind of castle, a long corridor had been added to it, by way of entrance, which was called the hall of the guards. Over this hall, which was like an entresol, was the library, and above that a granary. Separated by pillars stood the long windows with their small panes of Bohemian glass; medallions were sculptured on the walls. The fortress was three stories high; halberds and muskets were to be found below, books in the middle, and over all the bags of oats,—a somewhat barbarous arrangement, but princely to the last degree.

The tower loomed above this coquettish building presenting a stern and gloomy contrast.

The platform offered a point of attack from which the bridge could be destroyed.

Between these two buildings there was no harmony whatsoever; the roughness of the one jarred against the elegance of the other. It would seem as if two semicircles ought to be identical; yet no two styles have less in common than that of a Roman semicircle and a classic archivolt. That tower, a worthy companion for the forest, was a strange neighbor for the bridge, which might have come from Versailles. Fancy Louis XIV leaning on the arm of Alain Barbe-Torte. There was something appalling in this juxtaposition. An inexpressible spirit of terror pervaded the combined majesty of these structures.

Let us repeat, that from a military point of view the bridge went far towards betraying the tower; for while it added to its beauty it diminished its strength, ornamenting it on the one hand and weakening it on the other; by placing it on a level with the plateau, it had exposed it to attacks from that direction, although it still remained impregnable in the direction of the forest. Formerly it had commanded the plateau, but matters were now reversed. An enemy installed on the plain would speedily become master of the bridge. The library and the granary were advantageous to the besiegers rather than to the besieged, since the contents of both are of a combustible nature. For an assailant who knows how to avail himself of fire as a means of assault, it matters but little whether it be a Homer or a bundle of hay, provided it burns. The French offered a proof of this fact to the Germans when they burned the library at Heidelberg, as did the Germans in burning that of Strasbourg. In short, this bridge built on to the Tourgue was a strategic mistake; but in the seventeenth century, under Colbert and Louvois, the Princes Gauvain, like the Princes de Rohan or La Tremoille, believed themselves henceforth safe from assault. Still, the builders of the bridge had taken certain precautions. In the first place, anticipating the chances of fire, they had fastened crosswise below the three windows looking towards the stream, by iron clamps which no longer than fifty years ago were still to be seen, a strong ladder, equal in length to the height of the first two stories of the bridge,—a height surpassing that of three ordinary stories; secondly, foreseeing the possibility of a siege, they had isolated the bridge from the tower by means of a low and heavy iron door, arched at the top and locked with a large key, whose hiding-place was known to the master alone; once closed, it could defy the battering-ram and almost brave the cannon-ball.

One must cross the bridge to reach this door, which was the only means of access to the tower.

The Iron Door

AS A RESULT OF THE elevation of this castle on the bridge by means of piles, its second story was on a level with the corresponding story of the tower; and here, for greater safety, the iron door had been placed.

This iron door led from the bridge into the library, and from the tower into a large vaulted hall with a pillar in the centre. As already stated, this hall was in the second story of the keep. Like the tower itself, it was circular in its form, and was lighted by deep embrasures overlooking the fields. The stones of its rough and naked walls, unhidden from the view, were, however, symmetrically adjusted. This hall was reached by a spiral staircase built in the wall,—quite a simple matter when walls are fifteen feet thick. In the Middle Ages they used to capture a city by streets, a street by houses, and a house by rooms; and thus a fortress was besieged story by story. In this respect La Tourgue was very skilfully arranged, and very difficult to cope with. An uncomfortable staircase connected one story with another; the doors were sloping, and not high enough to admit a man unless he bent his head; and where at every door the besieged stood in waiting for their assailants, a bowed head was certain death.

Below the circular hall with the pillar were two similar rooms, composing the first story and the ground-floor, and above these three more. The tower was closed, so to speak, by a platform which rested on these six rooms like a stone cover, and a narrow watch-tower led up to the platform.

As they were obliged to pierce this wall in which the iron door was sealed to a depth of fifteen feet, it was thereby framed in a deep archway, which when the door was closed formed a porch six or seven feet deep, towards the bridge as well as towards the tower, and when it was open these two porches united to form the entrance arch. Set in the wall under the porch, towards the bridge, was a low gate with a Saint-Gilles bolt, leading into the corridor of the first story under the library. This was another difficulty for the besiegers. That side of the castle on the bridge looking towards the plateau ended in a perpendicular wall, and there the bridge was severed. The drawbridge set up against a low gate to connect it with the plateau, and which on account of the height of the latter could only be lowered like an inclined plane, led into the long corridor called the guard-room. The besiegers who found themselves in possession of this corridor would have been obliged to carry by main force the Saint-Gilles winding stairway that led to the second story, in order to reach the iron gate.

VI

The Library

As to the library, it was an oblong room of the same length and width as the bridge, with a single door, and that the iron one. A false folding-door covered with green cloth, which only needed to be pushed, concealed within the entrance arch of the tower. The walls of the library were lined from floor to ceiling with glass bookcases in the fine taste of the seventeenth century cabinet-work, and lighted by six large windows, three on a side,—that is, one over each arch. Through these windows the interior of the room was visible from the height of the platform. Between the windows stood six marble busts on pedestals of carved oak,—Hermolaüs of Byzantium, the grammarian Athenæus of Naucratis, Suidas, Casaubon, Clovis, King of France, and his chancellor, Anachalus,—who for that matter was no more a chancellor than Clovis was a king.

There were various books in the library. One has remained famous. It was an ancient quarto, enriched with prints, with the title "Saint Bartholomew" in large letters, together with the sub-title, "Gospel according to Saint Bartholomew, preceded by a dissertation by Pantoenus, Christian philosopher, on the question as to whether this Gospel should be considered apocryphal, and whether Saint Bartholomew is identical with Nathanal." This book, supposed to be a unique copy, was placed on a reading-desk in the middle of the library. In the last century people came to see it as a curiosity.

VII

The Granary

As for the granary, which, like the library, followed the oblong form of the bridge, it was merely the space under the woodwork of the roof. It consisted of a large room filled with hay and straw, and lighted by six Mansard windows, with no other ornament than the statue of Saint Barnabas sculptured on the door, and below it the following verse:—

"Barnabus sanctus falcem jubet ire per herbam."

A lofty and massive tower, six stories in height, pierced here and there by a few embrasures, its sole means of entrance and egress an iron door opening into a bridge-castle closed by a drawbridge; behind the tower a forest, before it a heath-covered plateau, higher than the bridge, lower than the tower; below the bridge, between the tower and the plateau, a deep narrow ravine filled with underbrush, a torrent in winter, a stream in the springtime, and a rocky bed in summer,—such was the Tour-Gauvain, called La Tourgue.

X

The Hostages

JULY PASSED AWAY, AND AUGUST came. A blast, fierce and heroic, had swept over France; two spectres had but just crossed the horizon,— Marat with a dagger in his side, and Charlotte Corday headless: events looked threatening. As to the Vendée, defeated in her grand strategic schemes, she turned her attention to others on a smaller scale, which, as we have already said, were likely to prove more dangerous. This war had now become one monstrous battle scattered about in the woods: the disasters of the grand army, Royal and Catholic, so called, had begun. A decree had been passed to send the army of Mayence into the Vendée; eight thousand Vendeans were killed at Ancenis; they were repulsed from Nantes, dislodged from Montaigu, expelled from Thouars, driven out of Noirmoutier, pitched headlong out of Cholet, Mortagne, and Saumur; they had evacuated Parthenay, abandoned Clisson, and lost ground at Châtillon; at Saint-Hilaire their flag was captured; they were defeated at Pornic, Sables, Fontenay, Doui, Château-d'Eau, and Ponts-de-Cé; they were checkmated at Luçon, retreated from Châtaigneraye, and were routed at the Roche-sur-Yon; at present, while they threatened La Rochelle on the one hand, on the other an English fleet riding in the waters of Guernsey, commanded by General Craig, and carrying several regiments of the English army, together with some of the best officers of the French navy, was only waiting for the signal of the Marquis de

Lantenac to disembark,—a descent which might once more turn the tide of victory in favor of the Royalists. Pitt was but a political malefactor. As the dagger to an armament, even so is treason to political warfare. Pitt stabbed our country, and betrayed his own, since to dishonor is to betray. Through his influence and under his administration England waged Punic warfare. She spied, cheated, and deceived. Poacher and forger, she stopped at nothing, stooping to the petty details of hatred. She established a monopoly of tallow that cost five francs a pound. A letter from Prigent, Pitt's agent in the Vendée, which was seized on the person of an Englishman at Lille, contained the following lines: "I beg you to spare no money. In regard to the assassinations, we hope that prudence will be exercised; disguised priests and women are the most suitable for this work. Send sixty thousand livres to Rouen, and fifty thousand to Caen." This letter was read by Barère at the Convention on the first day of August. As a retaliation for these acts of treachery witness the cruelties of Parrein, and still later the atrocities of Carrier. The Republicans of Metz and those of the South were eager to march against the rebels. A decree was passed ordering the formation of twenty-four companies of sappers, who were to burn the fences and enclosures of the Bocage. Here was a crisis without parallel. War was suspended in one direction only to break out in another. "No mercy! No prisoners!" was the war-cry of both parties. Dark and terrible shadows fall across the pages of history in these times.

In this very month of August the Tourgue was besieged.

One evening, just as the stars were rising in the calm twilight peculiar to dog-day weather, when not a leaf stirred in the woods, nor a blade of grass quivered on the plain, the sound of a horn was heard through the silence of the approaching night. It came from the summit of the tower.

This peal was answered by the ring of a clarion from below. On the top of the tower stood an armed man, and in the shadow below lay a camp.

In the obscurity around the Tour-Gauvain one could dimly distinguish the moving to and fro of dark figures. This was the bivouac. A few fires had been kindled beneath the forest-trees and among the heather of the plateau, their shining points of light pricking through the darkness here and there, as if earth as well as sky would deck itself out with stars, though it were but with the lurid stars of war. Towards the plateau the bivouac stretched as far as the plain, and in the direction of the forest it extended into the thicket. The Tourgue was invested.

The extent of the besiegers' bivouac indicated a numerous force.

The camp pressed hard upon the fortress, reaching to the rock in the direction of the tower, and as far as the ravine on the side of the bridge.

Another peal from the horn was heard, followed by a second blast from the clarion.

The horn asked the question, and the clarion made reply.

The horn was the voice of the tower asking the camp, "May we speak with you?" To which the clarion, speaking for the camp, answered, "Yes."

At that time the Convention did not regard the Vendeans in the light of belligerents, and it being forbidden by a decree to exchange flags of truce with "the brigands," they supplemented as best they could the usual means of communication which international law authorizes in ordinary warfare, but interdicts in civil conflicts. Consequently in time of need a certain understanding existed between the peasant horn and the military clarion. The first call simply broached the subject; the second asked the question, "Will you listen?" If the clarion made no reply to the second question, it meant refusal. If, on the other hand, the clarion replied, it was consent, and signified a truce for a few minutes.

When the clarion answered this second call, the man who stood on the top of the tower spoke, and these were his words:—

"Be it known to all ye who hear me, I am Gouge-le-Bruant, surnamed Brise-Bleu because I have killed many of your people, and also surnamed the Imânus because I mean to kill many more; in the attack at Granville, while my finger rested on the barrel of my gun, it was chopped off by a sabre-stroke; at Laval you guillotined my father, my mother, and my eighteen-year-old sister Jacqueline. And now you know me.

"I speak to you in the name of my master, Monseigneur le Marquis Gauvain de Lantenac, Vicomte de Fontenay, Breton Prince, and owner of the Seven Forests.

"It is well for you to learn that before shutting himself up in this tower, where you hold him blockaded, Monsieur le Marquis distributed the command among six chiefs, his lieutenants. To Delière he assigned the country between the woods of Brest and Erneé; to Treton, that which lies between the Roë and Laval; to Jacquet, called Taillefer, the border of the Haut-Maine; to Gaulier, called Grand-Pierre, Château-Gontier; to Lecomte, Craon; to Monsieur Dubois-Guy, Fougères; and to Monsieur de Rochambeau, all Mayenne; so that the capture of this fortress by no means ends the war for you, and even were Monsieur le Marquis to die, the Vendée of God and the king will still live.

"I say this for your information. Monseigneur is here beside me; I am but his mouthpiece. Silence, besiegers!

"It will be well for you to consider my words.

"Remember that the war you are waging against us is unjust; we are men living in our own land and fighting honestly. Submissive to the will of God, we are as simple and upright as the grass beneath the dew. It is the Republic who has attacked us: she comes to trouble us in our fields; she has burned our houses and our harvests and destroyed our farms, and our women and children have been forced to run barefoot in the woods while the hedge-sparrow was still singing.

"You who are down there listening to me,—you have pursued us through the forest and surrounded us in this tower; you have killed or scattered our allies; you have cannon, and you have added to your division the garrisons and the posts of Mortain, Barenton, Teilleul, Landivy, Evran, Tinténiac, and Vitré,—which gives you four thousand five hundred men with which to attack us.

"We, who are nineteen for the defence, are supplied with provisions and munitions.

"You have succeeded in undermining and blowing up a part of our rock and wall, thus making a breach at the foot of the tower, through which you can enter, although it is not open, while the tower stands strong and upright, forming an arch above it.

"Now you are preparing for the assault.

"And we—first of all, Monseigneur le Marquis, who is a Breton prince and the secular prior of the Abbey of Sainte-Marie de Lantenac, where a daily Mass was instituted by Queen Jeanne, and the other defenders of this tower, who are: Monsieur l'Abbé Turmeau, whose military name is Grand-Francoeur; my comrades, Guinoiseau, captain of the Camp-Vert; Chante-en-Hiver, captain of the camp of Avoine; Musette, captain of the camp Fourmis; and myself, a peasant, born in the town of Daon, through which runs the brook Moriandre,—we have one thing to tell you.

"Listen, now, ye men at the foot of this tower!

"We hold three prisoners,—the same children who were adopted by one of your battalions, and they are yours. We offer to give them back to you on one condition,—that we be allowed to go free.

"If you refuse,—listen to this. There are but two points of attack,— either the breach or the bridge, according as you advance from the fortress or the plateau. There are three stories in the building on the bridge; in the lower one I, the Imânus, who speak to you, have placed six casks of tar and one hundred bundles of dry heather; there is straw in the upper, and there are books and papers in the middle story; the iron door communicating with the tower is closed, and monseigneur carries the key on his person; I have made a hole under the door, through which is passed a sulphur slow-match; one end of it is in a cask of tar, and the other within reach of my hand, inside the tower; I can set it on fire whenever I choose. If you refuse to let us go free, the children will be placed on the second floor of the bridge, between the story where the sulphur-match ends in the barrel and the one which is filled with straw, and the iron door will be closed on them. If you attack us by way of the bridge, you will be the ones to set the building on fire; if by the breach, it will be left to us; and if you attack us from both sides at once, we shall both be kindling the fire at the same instant; at all events, the three children will perish.

"It rests with you, now, either to accept or refuse.

"If you accept, we depart; if you refuse, the children die.

"I have finished,"

And the man who had been speaking from the top of the tower was silent.

"We refuse!" cried a voice from below, in tones abrupt and severe. Another voice, quite as firm, although less harsh, added,—

"We give you twenty-four hours to surrender at discretion."

A silence ensued, and then the same voice continued,—

"If tomorrow at this hour you have not surrendered, we begin the assault."

"And give no quarter," resumed the first speaker; and then a voice from the top of the tower made reply to the savage one. Between two battlements a tall figure, in which, by the light of the stars, one might have recognized the awe-inspiring form of the Marquis de Lantenac, leaned forward; his glance, piercing the shadows, seemed searching for some one.

"Ah, it is thou, priest!" he cried.

"Yes, it is I, traitor!" replied the harsh voice from below.

XI

Terrible as the Antique

THIS IMPLACABLE VOICE WAS IN truth the voice of Cimourdain; the younger and less imperative one was that of Gauvain.

The Marquis de Lantenac had not been mistaken in his recognition of the Abbé Cimourdain.

In this district, ensanguined by civil war, Cimourdain, as we have said, had in a few weeks become famous. No man had won a more baleful notoriety. Men would say: "Marat in Paris, Châlier at Lyons, Cimourdain in the Vendée." All the veneration which the Abbé Cimourdain had formerly enjoyed was now turned to his dishonor. This is what a priest who unfrocks himself may fairly expect.

Cimourdain excited a feeling of horror. The austere are unfortunate, inasmuch as their own acts seem to condemn them. Could their consciences be revealed, men might perhaps absolve them. A Lycurgus misunderstood may seem like a Tiberius. However, the fact remains that these two men—the Marquis de Lantenac and the Abbé Cimourdain—were equally matched in regard to the hatred they inspired. The maledictions hurled at Cimourdain by the Royalists were counterbalanced by the execrations which the Republicans heaped upon Lantenac. Each of those men seemed a monster in the eyes of the opposite camp. In fact, by a singular coincidence it chanced that while Prieur de la Marne at Granville had set a price on the head of Lantenac, Charette at Noirmoutier had likewise set one on that of Cimourdain.

We may observe that these two men—the Marquis and the priest—represented in a certain degree one and the same man. The bronze mask of civil war has a double profile, one of which looks towards the past, the other towards the future. Lantenac wore the former, Cimourdain the latter; only the bitter sneer of Lantenac was shrouded in darkness, whereas on Cimourdain's fatal brow might be discerned a glimmer of the dawn.

Meanwhile the besieged Tourgue was enjoying a respite.

Thanks to the intervention of Gauvain, they had agreed upon a sort of truce for twenty-four hours.

The Imânus had indeed been well informed. In consequence of Cimourdain's requisitions Gauvain was now in command of four thousand five hundred men, national guards as well as troops of the line, with which he surrounded Lantenac in the Tourgue, and could, moreover, bring to bear against the fortress a masked battery of six cannon, planted on the edge of the forest towards the tower, together with an open battery of six on the plateau towards the bridge. He had succeeded in springing the mine, and a breach had been made at the foot of the tower.

Thus on the expiration of the twenty-four hours' truce, the struggle would begin again under the following conditions:—

On the plateau and in the forest were four thousand five hundred men against nineteen in the tower.

History may find the names of the nineteen besieged in the placards posted against outlaws. We may possibly come across them.

It would have pleased Cimourdain had Gauvain consented to accept the rank of adjutant-general, in order to command these four thousand five hundred men, which was practically an army. But the latter refused, saying: "We will consider that matter after Lantenac is taken; I have won no promotion as yet."

These important commands, held by officers of subordinate rank, were, moreover, in accordance with Republican customs. Bonaparte, later on, while as yet only a colonel of artillery, was at the same time commander-in-chief of the army of Italy.

It was a strange fate for the Tour-Gauvain to be attacked by one Gauvain, while defended by another member of the same family. Hence a certain reluctance in the attack, but none in the defence; for M. de Lantenac was a man who spared nothing. Accustomed as he had been to live at Versailles, he had no feeling of regard for the Tourgue, which he scarcely knew. He had sought refuge there, simply because he had no other resource; but he would have destroyed it without a scruple. Gauvain felt more respect for it.

The bridge was the weak point of the fortress, but in the library above it were the family records. Now, if the assault began there, the burning of the bridge would be inevitable, and it seemed to Gauvain that to burn the records would be like attacking his ancestors. The Tourgue was the ancestral manor of the Gauvain family; from this tower started all their fiefs of Brittany, as those of France from the tower of the Louvre. It was the centre round which clustered the family associations of the Gauvains. He himself was born there; and now, led by the tortuous chances of fate, the grown man had come to attack the venerable walls that had protected his childhood.

Was it an impious act to lay this dwelling in ashes? Perhaps his own cradle was stored away in some corner of the granary over the library. Certain trains of thought assume the nature of emotions. Before the old family mansion Gauvain felt himself deeply moved, and it was in consequence of this feeling that he had spared the bridge. Contenting himself with making it impossible for the enemy to sally forth or attempt an escape at this point of egress, he held the bridge in check by a battery, and chose the opposite side for the attack. Hence the mining and sapping at the foot of the tower.

Cimourdain had allowed him to take his own course, meanwhile reproaching himself; for these Gothic antiquities were odious to his severe soul, and he was no more indulgent towards buildings than towards human beings. Sparing a castle was the first step in the direction of mercy; and he knew that mercy was Gauvain's weak point. Cimourdain, as we are aware, kept watch over him, and arrested his progress down this slope, so fatal in his eyes. And yet even he—and he acknowledged it to himself with a sort of indignation—had been unable to see the Tourgue again without a secret emotion: he was affected by the sight of that schoolroom containing the first books in which he had taught Gauvain to read. He had been the curé of the neighboring village Parigné; had occupied an upper room in the castle on the bridge; it was in the library that he held little Gauvain between his knees, and taught him the alphabet; within these four old walls he had seen his beloved pupil, the child of his soul, growing up to manhood, and watched the development of his mind. Was he about to burn and destroy this library, this castle, these walls, wherein he had so often blessed the child? He had spared them, but it had not been done without compunction.

He had allowed Gauvain to begin the siege from the opposite point. The tower might have been called the savage side of the Tourgue, and the library its civilized side. Cimourdain had allowed Gauvain to make the breach only in the former.

This ancient castle in the midst of the Revolution had, after all, only resumed its feudal customs, in being at the same time attacked and defended by a Gauvain. The history of the Middle Ages is but a record of wars between kinsmen. Étéocles and Polynices are Gothic as well as Grecian; and Hamlet but repeats in Elsinore what Orestes did in Argos.

XII

The Rescue Planned

THE ENTIRE NIGHT WAS SPENT by both parties in preparations. As soon as the gloomy parley to which we lately listened was over, Gauvain's first act was to summon his lieutenant.

Guéchamp, with whom we must become acquainted, was a man of the secondary order, honest, brave, commonplace, a better soldier than commander, strictly intelligent up to the point when it becomes a duty not to understand, never moved to tenderness, proof against corruption in whatsoever shape it might present itself,—whether in the form of bribery, that taints the conscience, or in that of pity, that corrupts justice. As the eyes of a horse are shaded by his blinders, so were his heart and soul protected by the two screens of discipline and the order of command, and he walked straight ahead in the space they allowed him to see. His course was direct, but his path was narrow.

A man to be depended on, withal,—stern in command, exact in obedience.

Gauvain spoke in rapid tones,—

"We need a ladder, Guéchamp."

"We have none, commander."

"One must be found."

"For scaling?"

"No; for rescue."

After a moments reflection, Guéchamp replied,—

"I understand. But to serve your purpose a very long one is needed."

"The length of three stories."

"Yes, commander, that's about the height."

"It ought to be longer than that, for we must be sure of success."

"Certainly."

"How is it that you have no ladder?"

"Commander, you did not think it best to besiege the Tourgue from the plateau; you were satisfied to blockade it on that side; you planned the attack by way of the tower, and not from the bridge. So we gave our attention to the mine, and thought no more about the scaling. That is why we have no ladder."

"Have one made at once."

"A ladder of the length of three stories cannot be made at once."

"Then fasten several short ones together."

"But we must first get our ladders."

"Find them."

"There are none to be found. All through the country the peasants destroy ladders, just as they break up the carts and cut the bridges."

"True, they intend to paralyze the Republic."

"They mean that we shall neither transport baggage, cross a river, nor scale a wall."

"But I must have a ladder, in spite of all that."

"I was thinking, commander, that at Javené, near Fougères, there is a large carpenter's shop. We might get one there."

"There is not a moment to lose."

"When do you want the ladder?"

"By this time tomorrow, at the latest."

"I will send a messenger at full speed to Javené to carry the order for a requisition. A post of cavalry stationed there will furnish an escort. The ladder may be here tomorrow before sunset."

"Very well; that will answer," said Gauvain; "only be quick about it. Go!"

Ten minutes later, Guéchamp returned, and said to Gauvain,—

"The messenger has started for Javené."

Gauvain ascended the plateau, and for a long time stood gazing intently on the bridge-castle across the ravine. The gable of the castle, with no other opening than the low entrance closed by the raised drawbridge, faced the escarpment of the ravine. In order to reach the plateau at the foot of the bridge one roust climb down the face of the ravine, which might be accomplished by clinging to the bushes. But once in the moat, the assailants would be exposed to a shower of missiles from the three stories. Gauvain became convinced that at this stage of the siege the proper way to attack was through the breach of the tower.

He took every precaution to render flight impossible; he perfected the strict blockade of the Tourgue. Drawing the meshes of his battalions more and more closely, so that nothing could pass between them, Gauvain and Cimourdain divided the investment of the fortress between them,—the former reserving for himself the forest side, and leaving the plateau to Cimourdain. It was agreed that while Gauvain, aided by Guéchamp, should conduct the assault through the mine, Cimourdain, with all the matches of the upper battery lighted, should watch the bridge and the ravine.

XIII

What the Marquis is Doing

WHILE ALL THESE PREPARATIONS FOR the attack were going on outside, they were also making ready for resistance inside the tower.

A tower may be entered by a mine as a cask is bored by an auger; hence a tower is sometimes called a *douve*,[4] and it was the fate of the Tourgue to have its walls pierced by a bung-hole.

The powerful boring of two or three hundred-weight of powder had driven a hole through the mighty wall from one side to the other. Beginning at the foot of the tower, it had made a breach in the thickest part of the wall, in a sort of shapeless arch in the lower story of the fortress, and in order to make this hole more practicable for assault from without, the besiegers had enlarged it by cannon-shot.

The ground-floor where this breach had penetrated was a large, empty hall of a circular form, with a pillar in the centre, supporting the keystone of the vaulted ceiling. The hall, which was the largest in the keep, was no less than forty feet in diameter. Each story of the tower had a similar room, only on a smaller scale, with guards to the embrasures of the loop-holes. The hall on the ground-floor had neither embrasures, ventilators, nor dormer windows. There was about as much air and light in it as in a tomb.

The door of the oubliettes, the greater part of which was iron, was in the lower hall. Another door opened on a staircase leading to the upper rooms. All the staircases were built in the wall itself.

It was to the lower hall that the besieged had gained access by the breach they had made; but even after gaining possession of it, the tower would still remain to be taken.

One could scarcely breathe in this lower hall, and formerly no one could remain in it twenty-four hours without suffocating; but now, thanks to the breach, one could exist there.

For this reason the besieged had not closed the breach. Besides, what purpose would it have served? The guns would have reopened it.

They had fastened an iron torch-holder into the wall, wherein they set a torch, and that lighted the lower floor.

But how were they to defend themselves?

To stop up the hole would have been easy enough, but useless. A *retirade* would be more effective. A *retirade* is an intrenchment with a retreating angle,—a kind of barricade composed of rafters, by means of which the fire may be concentrated on the assailants, and which while leaving the breach open from without closes it from within. There was

---

4. Stave, cask.

no lack of materials, and they proceeded to construct a barricade of this description with clefts for the passage of gun-barrels. The corner of the *retirade* was supported by the middle pillar, the two wings touching the walls on either side. Having completed this they placed *fugades* in safe places.

The Marquis directed everything. Inspirer, commander, guide, and master,—a terrible spirit!

Lantenac was one of those soldiers of the eighteenth century who save cities at the age of eighty. He resembled the Count d'Alberg, who, when almost a centenarian, drove the King of Poland from Riga.

"Courage, friends!" he said; "in 1713, at the beginning of this century, Charles XII, shut up in a house at Bender, with three hundred Swedes, held his own against twenty thousand Turks."

They barricaded the two lower stories, fortified the chambers, converted the alcoves into battlements, supported the doors with beams driven in by a mallet, thus forming buttresses; but the spiral staircase connecting the different stories they were obliged to leave free, since if they blockaded it against the besieger, their own passage would be obstructed. Thus a fortification always has its weak point.

The Marquis, indefatigable, vigorous as a young man, set example for the others by putting his own hands to the work, raising beams and carrying stones; he gave his orders, helped, fraternized, and laughed with this savage band, yet always remaining their lord and master, haughty even while familiar, elegant although fierce.

He allowed no one to contradict him. Once he said: "If half of you were to revolt, I would have you shot by the other half, and still defend the place with the rest."

This is the sort of thing for which men worship a commander.

XIV

What the Imânus is Doing

WHILE THE MARQUIS OCCUPIED HIMSELF with the breach and tower, the Imânus attended to the bridge. At the beginning of the siege the escape-ladder suspended crosswise below the windows of the second story had been removed by order of the Marquis and placed by the Imânus in the library. Probably this was the very ladder whose place Gauvain wished to supply. The windows of the entresol on the first story, called the guard-room, were defended by a triple bracing of iron bars set in the stones, so that one could neither come nor go that way.

The library windows, which were high, had no bars.

The Imânus was accompanied by three men as resolute and daring as himself. These men were Hoisnard, called Branche-d'Or, and the two brothers Pique-en-Bois. Taking with him a dark-lantern, he opened the iron door, and made a careful inspection of the three stories of the bridge-castle. Hoisnard Branche-d'Or, whose brother had been killed by the Republicans, was as implacable as the Imânus. The latter investigated the upper story, filled with hay and straw, as well as the lower one, into which he had several *pots-à-feu* brought, which he placed near the tar-barrels; he ordered bundles of dry heather to be so arranged that they would touch the tar-casks, after which he made sure that the sulphur-match, one end of which was on the bridge and the other in the tower, was in good working order. Over the floor, under the casks and the bundles, he poured a pool of tar into which he dipped the end of the sulphur-match; then he ordered his men to bring into the library, between the ground-floor and the attic, with tar beneath and straw overhead, three cradles containing René-Jean, Gros-Alain, and Georgette, who were all sound asleep. The cradles were brought in very gently, that the children might not be roused.

They were simple little village cribs, something like an osier basket, which when placed on the floor were low enough for a child to climb in and out without help. Beside each cradle the Imânus ordered them to place a porringer of soup, together with a wooden spoon. The escape-ladder, taken off its hooks, was laid on the floor against the wall, and the three cradles were placed end to end along the opposite wall, facing the ladder; then, thinking that a current of air might be useful, he flung wide open the six windows of the library. It was a warm and clear summer night.

He sent the brothers Pique-en-Bois to open the windows in the stories above and below. On the eastern façade of the building he had observed a large ivy, old and withered, about the color of tinder, which entirely covered one side of the bridge, framing the windows of the three stories, and thought that this ivy would do no harm. After bestowing a last glance on everything, the Imânus and his men left the châtelet and returned into the keep. Double locking the heavy iron door, he examined attentively this immense and awe-inspiring lock, nodded approvingly at the sulphur-match, passed through the hole he had drilled, which was henceforth the only channel of communication between the tower and the bridge. This match, starting from the round room, passed beneath the iron door and entered under the arch, coiled snake-like over the spiral stairs, crept across the floor of the corridor below, and ended in the pool of tar under the dry heath. The Imânus had calculated that it would take a quarter of an hour from the time this sulphur-match was lighted from the interior of the tower, to set on fire the pool of tar under the library. Having completed and reviewed all these preparations, he carried the key of the iron door to the Marquis de Lantenac, who put it in his pocket.

Every movement of the besiegers must be watched; so with his cowherd horn in his belt he stood sentinel in the watch-tower of the platform on the summit of the tower. While keeping his eye on both the forest and the plateau, he had beside him in the embrasure of the watch-tower a powder-horn, and a canvas bag filled with good-sized balls and old newspapers, which he tore up to make cartridges. When the sun rose, it revealed in the forest eight battalions, with sabres at their sides, cartridge-boxes on their backs, and fixed bayonets, ready for the assault; on the plateau a battery with caissons, cartridges, and boxes of grape-shot; within the fortress nineteen men loading their muskets, pistols, and blunderbusses, and three children asleep in their cradles.

Book III

The Massacre of Saint Bartholomew

I

The Massacre of Saint Bartholomew

I

THE CHILDREN AWOKE.

The little girl was the first to open her eyes.

The waking of children is like the opening of flowers; and like the flowers, these pure little souls seem to exhale fragrance.

Georgette, the youngest of the three, who last May was but a nursing infant, and now only twenty months old, lifted her little head, sat up in her cradle, looked at her toes, and began her baby-talk.

A ray of light fell upon the crib; it would have been difficult to say which was the rosier,—Georgette's foot, or the dawn.

The other two children still slept,—boys always sleep more soundly than girls,—while Georgette, contented and peaceful, began to prattle.

René-Jean's hair was brown, Gros-Alain's auburn, and Georgette's blond,—all shades peculiar to their ages, which would change as the children grew older. René-Jean looked like an infant Hercules as he lay there on his stomach fast asleep, with his two fists in his eyes. Gros-Alain had thrust his legs outside his little bed.

All three were in rags. The clothes given them by the battalion of the Bonnet-Rouge were in tatters; they had not even a shirt between them. The two boys were almost naked, and Georgette was bundled up in a rag which had formerly been a petticoat, but which now served the purpose of a jacket. Who had taken care of these little ones? It would be impossible to tell. Certainly not a mother. Those savage peasants who had carried them along as they fought their way from forest to forest, gave them their share of the soup, and nothing more. The little ones lived as best they could; they had masters in plenty, but no father. Yet childhood is enveloped by an atmosphere of enchantment that lends a charm to its very rags; and these three tiny beings were delightful.

Georgette chattered away.

The child prattles as the bird sings; but it is always the same hymn,—indistinct, inarticulate, and yet full of deep meaning; only the child, unlike the bird, has the dark fate of humanity before it. None can listen to the joyous song of a child without a sense of sadness. The lisping of a human soul from the lips of childhood may well be called the most sublime of earthly songs. This confused murmuring of thought, which is as yet mere instinct, contains an unconscious appeal to eternal justice. Perhaps it is a protest uttered on the threshold of life,—an unconscious protest, distressing to hear; ignorance, smiling on the infinite, seems to make all creation responsible for the fate allotted to a weak and defenceless being. Should misfortune befall, it would seem like an abuse of confidence.

The prattle of a child is more and less than speech; it is a song without notes, a language without syllables, a murmur that begins in heaven but is not to end on earth. As it began before birth, so it will go on after death. As the lispings are the continuance of what the child said when he was an angel, they are likewise a foreshadowing of what he will say in eternity. The cradle has its Yesterday, as the grave has its Morrow; and the double mystery of both mingles with this unintelligible babble. There is no such proof of God, of eternity, of responsibility, and of the duality of destiny, as is this awe-inspiring shadow which we see resting upon a bright young soul.

Still, there was nothing melancholy about Georgette's chatter, for her sweet face was wreathed in smiles. Her mouth, her eyes, the dimples in her cheeks, all smiled in concert; and by this smile she seemed to show her delight in the morning. The human soul believes in sunshine. The sky was blue, the weather warm and beautiful; and this frail creature, neither knowing nor comprehending the meaning of life,—living in a dream, as it were,—felt safe amid the loveliness of Nature, with its friendly trees and its pure verdure, the serene and peaceful landscape, with the noises of birds, springs, insects, and leaves, and above all, the intense purity of the sunshine.

René-Jean, the oldest of the children, a boy over four years old, was the next one to wake. He stood up, jumped out of his cradle like a little man, discovered his porringer, as the most natural thing that could happen, seated himself on the floor, and began to eat his soup.

Georgette's prattle had not roused Gros-Alain, but at the sound of the spoon in the porringer he started and opened his eyes. Gros-Alain was the three-year-old boy. He too saw his bowl, and as it was within reach of his arm, he seized it, and without getting out of bed, with his dish on his knees and his spoon in his fist, he straightway followed the example of René-Jean.

Georgette did not hear them; the modulations of her voice seemed to keep time with the cradling of a dream. Her large eyes, gazing upward, were divine; however gloomy may be the vault over a child's head, heaven is always reflected in its eyes.

When René-Jean had finished, he scraped the bottom of the porringer with the spoon, sighed, and remarked with dignity,—

"I have eaten my soup."

This roused Georgette from her dreaming.

"Thoup," said she.

And seeing that René-Jean had finished his, and that Gros-Alain was still eating, she took the bowl of soup which stood beside her, and began to eat, carding the spoon quite as often to her ear as she did to her mouth.

From time to time she renounced civilization and ate with her fingers.

When Gros-Alain had scraped the bottom of his porringer he jumped out of bed and trotted after his brother.

II

SUDDENLY FROM BELOW RANG THE blast of a clarion, stern and loud, coming from the direction of the forest, to which a trumpet from the summit of the tower made reply.

This time the clarion called, and the trumpet answered. And again came the summons from the clarion, followed by the reply of the trumpet.

Then from the edge of the forest rose a voice, distant but clear, shouting distinctly,—

"Brigands, a summons! If by sunset you have not surrendered at discretion, we shall begin the assault."

A voice that sounded like the roar of a wild beast answered from the top of the tower,—

"Attack."

The voice from below replied,—

"A cannon will be fired as a last warning half an hour before the assault."

And the voice from above repeated,—

"Attack."

VICTOR HUGO

The children did not hear these voices, but the clarion and the horn echoed louder and more distinctly, and at the first sound Georgette craned her neck and ceased eating; she had dropped her spoon into the porringer, and at the second blast from the clarion she lifted the tiny forefinger of her right hand, and alternately raising and letting it fall, she marked the time of the trumpet, that was prolonged by the second call of the horn; when the horn and the clarion were silent, with her finger still uplifted, she paused dreamily, and then murmured to herself, "Muthic."

She probably meant "music,"

The two older ones, René-Jean and Gros-Alain, had paid no attention to the horn and the clarion; they were absorbed by another object. Gros-Alain, who had spied a woodlouse in the act of crawling across the library floor, exclaimed,—

"A creature!"

René-Jean ran up to him.

"It pricks," continued Gros-Alain.

"Don't hurt it," said René-Jean.

And both the children set themselves to watch the traveller.

Meanwhile Georgette, having finished her soup, was looking about for her brothers, who, crouching in the embrasure of a window, hung gravely over the woodlouse, their heads so close together that their hair intermingled; holding their breath, they gazed in astonishment at the creature, which, far from appreciating so much admiration, had stopped crawling, and no longer attempted to move.

Georgette, seeing that her brothers were watching something, desired to know what it might be. It was no easy matter to reach them, but she undertook it nevertheless. The journey fairly bristled with difficulties; all sorts of things were scattered over the floor,—stools turned upside down, bundles of papers, packing-cases which had been opened and left empty, trunks, all sorts of rubbish,—around which she had to make her way: a very archipelago of reefs; but Georgette took the risk. Her first achievement was to crawl out of the crib; then she plunged among the reefs. Winding her way through the straits, and pushing aside a footstool, she crawled between two boxes and over a bundle of papers, climbing up on one side, rolling down on the other, innocently exposing her poor little naked body, and finally reached what a sailor would call the open sea,—that is to say, quite an expanse of floor unencumbered by rubbish and free from perils. Here she made a rush, and with the agility of a cat she crept across the room on all fours as far as the window, where she encountered a formidable obstacle in the shape of the long ladder, which lying against the wall ended at this window, reaching a little beyond the corner of the embrasure, thus forming a sort of promontory between Georgette and her brothers. She paused, and seemed to consider the subject; and when she had solved the problem to her satisfaction, she resolutely clasped her rosy fingers about one of the rungs, which, as the ladder rested on its side, were not horizontal but vertical, and tried to pull herself up on to her feet; and when, after two unsuccessful attempts, she at last succeeded, she walked the entire length of the ladder, catching one rung after the other. On reaching the end her support failed, she stumbled and fell; but, nothing daunted, she caught at the end of one of its enormous poles with her tiny hands, pulled herself up, doubled the promontory, looked at René-Jean and Gros-Alain, and burst out laughing.

III

Just then René-Jean, satisfied with the result of his investigations of the woodlouse, raised his head and affirmed,—

"It is a female."

Georgette's laughter made René-Jean laugh, and Gros-Alain laughed because his brother did.

Georgette having effected her object and joined her brothers, they sat round upon the floor as in a sort of diminutive chamber, but their friend the woodlouse had vanished.

It had taken advantage of Georgette's laughter and hidden itself away in a crack.

Other events followed the visit of the woodlouse.

First some swallows flew by.

Their nests were probably under the eaves. They flew quite close to the window, somewhat startled at the sight of the children, describing great circles in the air, and uttering their sweet spring note. This made the three children look up, and the woodlouse was forgotten.

Georgette pointed her finger at the swallows, crying,—

"Biddies!"

René-Jean reprimanded her,—

I "You mustn't say 'biddies,' missy; you must say 'birds.'"

"'Bir's,'" said Georgette.

And, all three watched the swallows.

Then a bee flew in.

Nothing reminds one of the human soul more than the bee, which goes from flower to flower as a soul from star to star, gathering honey as the soul absorbs the light.

This one came buzzing in with an air of great stir, as if it said: "Here I am; I have just seen the roses, and now I have come to see the children. What is going on here, I should like to know?"

A bee is a housekeeper, scolding as it hums.

As long as the bee stayed, the children never once moved their eyes from it.

It explored the entire library, rummaging in every corner, flying about quite as if it were at home in its hive; winged and melodious, it darted from case to case, peering through the glass at the titles of the books, just as if it had a brain, and having paid its visit, it flew away.

"It has gone home," said René-Jean.

"It is an animal," remarked Gros-Alain.

"No," replied René-Jean, "it is a fly."

"A f'y,'" said Georgette.

Then Gros-Alain, who had just found a string on the floor with a knot in the end, took the other end between his thumb and his forefinger, and having made a sort of windmill of the string, he was deeply absorbed in watching its whirling.

Georgette on her part, having returned to her former character of quadruped, and started again on her capricious journeys across the floor, had discovered a venerable arm-chair, with moth-eaten upholstery, from which the horse-hair was falling out in several places. She had stopped before this arm-chair, and was carefully enlarging the holes and pulling out the horse-hair.

Suddenly she raised her finger to attract her brothers' attention and make them listen.

They turned their heads.

A vague far-away sound could be heard outside: probably the attacking camp executing some strategic manoeuvre in the forest; there was a neighing of horses, a beating of drums, a rolling to and fro of caissons, a clanking of chains, and military calls and responses echoed on every side,—a confusion of wild sounds, whose combination resulted in a sort of harmony; the children listened in delight.

"It is the good God who does that," said Gros-Alain.

IV

THE NOISE CEASED.

René-Jean had fallen into a dream.

How are ideas formed and scattered in those little minds? What is the mysterious action of those memories, so faint and evanescent? In this dreamy little head there was a confused vision of the good God, of prayer, of clasped hands, of a certain tender smile that had once rested on him, and which now he missed, and René-Jean whispered half-aloud, "Mamma!"

"Mamma," said Gros-Alain.

"Mma," repeated Georgette.

Thereupon René-Jean began to jump, and Gros-Alain lost no time in following his example, imitating all the movements and gestures of his brother; not so Georgette. Three years may copy four, but twenty months preserves its independence.

Georgette remained seated, uttering a word now and then; she had as yet achieved no success in sentences.

She was a thinker, and only uttered monosyllabic apothegms. After a few moments, however, she succumbed to the influence of example, and began her attempts to imitate her brothers, and these three pairs of naked little feet began to dance, run, and totter about in the dust that covered the old oaken floor, under the serious eyes of the marble busts, towards which Georgette from to time threw an uneasy glance, whispering,—

"The Momommes!"

In the language of Georgette a "momomme" was anything that looked like a man without really being one. Living beings are strangely confused with ghosts in the minds of children.

As Georgette tottered along after her brothers she was always on the verge of descending to all fours.

Suddenly René-Jean, who had gone near the window, raised his head, but dropped it the next moment, and ran to hide in a corner formed by the embrasure of the window. He had caught sight of some one looking at him. It was one of the Blues, a soldier from the encampment on the plateau, who, taking advantage of the armistice and perhaps somewhat infringing thereon, had ventured to the edge of the escarpment from whence he had gained a view of the interior of the library. Seeing René-Jean hide, Gros-Alain hid also; he cuddled down close by his brother's side, and Georgette hid herself behind them, and there they stayed silent and motionless, Georgette laying her finger on her lips. After a few moments René-Jean ventured to put out his head, but finding the soldier still there, he quickly drew it back, and the three children hardly dared to breathe. This lasted for quite a long time, but finally Georgette grew tired of it; she plucked up the courage to look out, and behold the soldier had gone, and once more they began to run and play.

Gros-Alain, although an imitator and admirer of René-Jean, possessed a talent peculiarly his own, that of making discoveries; and his brother and sister now beheld him prancing in wild delight, dragging along a little four-wheeled cart, which he had unexpectedly discovered.

This doll-carriage had been lying there for years, forgotten in the dust, side by side with works of genius and the busts of sages. Perhaps Gauvain may have played with it when he was a child.

Gros-Alain had converted his bit of string into a whip, which he cracked with great exultation. Thus it is with discoverers. If one cannot discover America, one can at least find a small cart. It amounts to much the same thing.

But he must share his treasure; René-Jean was eager to harness himself to the wagon, and Georgette tried to get in and sit down.

René-Jean was the horse, Gros-Alain the coachman.

But the coachman did not know his business, and the horse felt obliged to give him a few lessons.

"Say, 'Get up!'" cried René-Jean.

"'Get up!'" repeated Gros-Alain.

The carriage upset, and Georgette fell out, whereupon she proceeded to make it known that angels can shriek,—and after that she had half a mind to cry.

"You are too big, missy," said René-Jean.

"I big," stammered Georgette; and her vanity seemed to console her for her fall.

The cornice under the windows was very wide, and the dust of the fields from the heath-covered plateau had collected there. After the rains had changed this dust into soil, among the seeds wafted thither by the wind was a bramble, which, making the most of this shallow soil, had taken root therein; it was of the hardy variety known as the fox-blackberry, and now in August it was covered with berries, and one of its branches, pushing its way through the window, hung down almost to the floor.

Gros-Alain to the discovery of the string and the cart added that of the blackberry-vine. He went up to it, picked off a berry, and ate it.

"I am hungry," said René-Jean. And Georgette, galloping on her hands and knees, lost no time in making her appearance on the scene.

The three together soon stripped the branch and devoured all the fruit; staining their faces and hands with the purple juices and laughing aloud in their glee, these three little seraphs were speedily turned into three little fauns, who would have horrified Dante and charmed Virgil.

Occasionally the thorns pricked their fingers. Every pleasure has its price.

Pointing to the bush, and holding out her finger, on which stood a tiny drop of blood, Georgette said to René-Jean,—

"Prick."

Gros-Alain, who had also pricked himself, looked suspiciously at the bush, and cried out,—

"It is a beast."

"No, it's a stick," replied René-Jean.

"Sticks are wicked, then," remarked Gros-Alain.

Again Georgette would have liked to cry, but she decided to laugh.

V

Meanwhile René-Jean, jealous perhaps of the discoveries of his younger brother Gros-Alain, had conceived a grand project. For some time past, while he had been gathering the berries and pricking his fingers, his eyes had turned frequently towards the reading-desk, which, raised on a pivot, stood alone like a monument in the middle of the library. On this desk was displayed the famous volume of Saint Bartholomew.

It was really a magnificent and remarkable quarto. It had been published at Cologne by Bloeuw, or Coesius, as he was called in Latin, the famous publisher of the Bible of 1682. It was printed, not on Dutch paper, but on that fine Arabian paper, so much admired by Édrisi, manufactured from silk and cotton, which always retains its whiteness; the binding was of gilded leather, and the clasps of silver; the fly-leaves were of that parchment which the Parisian parchment-sellers swore to buy at the hall Saint-Mathurin "and nowhere else." This volume was full of wood-cuts, engravings on copper, and geographical maps of many countries; it contained a preface consisting of a protest from the printers, paper-manufacturers, and book-sellers against the edict of 1635, which imposed a tax on "leather, beer, cloven-footed animals, sea-fish, and paper," and on the back of the frontispiece was a dedication to the Gryphs, who rank in Lyons with the Elzévirs in Amsterdam. And all this had combined to produce a famous copy almost as rare as the "Apostol" of Moscow.

It was a beautiful book, and for that reason René-Jean gazed at it—too long, perhaps. The volume lay open just at the large engraving which represented Saint Bartholomew carrying his skin on his arm. This print could be seen from below, and when the berries were eaten, René-Jean gazed steadily at it with all his longing and greedy eyes; and Georgette, whose eyes had taken the same direction, spied the engraving, and exclaimed,—

"Picsure."

This word seemed to decide René-Jean. Then to the unbounded surprise of Gros-Alain a most remarkable proceeding took place.

In one corner of the library stood a large oaken chair. René-Jean went up to this chair, seized it, and dragged it across the room all alone by himself to the desk, then pushing it close up to the latter, he climbed upon it and put both his fists on the book.

Having reached the height of his ambition, he felt that it behooved him to be generous; so taking the "picsure" by the upper corner he carefully tore it in two,—the tear crossing the saint diagonally, which was a pity; but that was no fault of René-Jean. The entire left side, one eye, and a fragment of the halo of this old apocryphal evangelist were left in the book; he offered Georgette the other half of the saint and the whole of his skin. Georgette, as she received it, remarked,—

"Momomme."

"Me too!" cried Gros-Alain.

The tearing out of the first page is like the first shedding of blood in battle; it decides the carnage.

René-Jean turned over the page; next to the saint came the commentator, Pantoenus; he bestowed Pantoenus upon Gros-Alain.

Meanwhile, Georgette had torn her large piece into two smaller ones, and then the two into four; thus it might have been recorded in history that Saint-Bartholomew, after being flayed in Armenia, was quartered in Brittany.

VI

THE EXECUTION FINISHED, GEORGETTE HELD out her hand to René-Jean for more.

After the saint and his commentator came the frowning portraits of the glossarists. First came Gavantus; René-Jean tore him out and placed him in Georgettes hand.

A similar fate befell all the commentators of Saint-Bartholomew.

The act of giving imparts a sense of superiority. René-Jean kept nothing for himself. He knew that Gros-Alain and Georgette were watching him, and that was enough for him; he was satisfied with the admiration of his audience. René-Jean, inexhaustible in his magnificent generosity, offered Fabricius and Pignatelli to Gros-Alain, and Father Stilting to Georgette; Alphonse Tostat to Gros-Alain, *Cornelius a Lapide* to Georgette; Gros-Alain had Henry Hammond, and Georgette Father Roberti, together with an old view of the city of Douai, where the latter was born in 1619; Gros-Alain received the protest of the paper-manufacturers, while Georgette obtained the dedication to the Gryphs. And then came the maps, which René-Jean also distributed. He gave Ethiopia to Gros-Alain, and Lycaonia to Georgette; after which he threw the book on the floor.

This was an awful moment. With mingled feelings of ecstasy and awe, Gros-Alain and Georgette saw René-Jean frown, stiffen his limbs, clench his fists, and push the massive quarto off the desk. It is really quite tragical to see a stably old book treated with such disrespect. The heavy volume, pushed from its resting-place, hung a moment on the edge of the desk, hesitating, as if it were trying to keep its balance; then it fell, crumpled and torn, with disjointed clasps and loosened from its binding, all flattened out upon the floor. Luckily, it did not fall on the children.

They were startled, but not crushed. The results of conquest have sometimes proved more fatal.

Like all glories, it was accompanied by a loud noise and a cloud of dust.

Having upset the book, René-Jean now came down from the chair.

For a moment, silence and dismay prevailed; for victory has its terrors. The three children clung to one another's hands and gazed from a distance upon the ruins of this monstrous volume.

After a brief pause, However, Gros-Alain went up to it with an air of determination and gave it a kick.

This was quite enough; the appetite for destruction is never sated. René-Jean gave it a kick too, and Georgette gave it another, which landed her on the floor, but in a sitting position, of which she at once took advantage to throw herself on Saint Bartholomew. All respect was now at an end. René-Jean and Gros-Alain pounced upon it, jubilant, wild with excitement, triumphant, and pitiless, tearing the prints, slashing the leaves, tearing out the markers, scratching the binding, detaching the gilded leather, pulling the nails from the silver corners, breaking the parchment, defacing the noble text,—working with hands, feet, nails, and teeth; rosy, laughing, and fierce, they fell upon the defenceless evangelist like three angels of prey.

They annihilated Armenia, Judea, and Benevento, where the relics of the saint are to be found; Nathanael, who is supposed by some authorities to be the same as Bartholomew; Pope Gelasius, who declared the Gospel of Nathanael-Bartholomew apocryphal; and every portrait and map. Indeed, they were so utterly engrossed in their pitiless destruction of the old book, that a mouse ran by unobserved.

It might well be called extermination.

To cut to pieces history, legend, science, miracles true or false, ecclesiastical Latin, superstition, fanaticism, and mysteries,—thus to tear a whole religion to tatters,—might be considered a work of time for three giants. And even for three children it was no small matter; they labored for hours, but at last they conquered, and nothing remained of Saint-Bartholomew.

When they came to the end, when the last page was detached and the last print thrown on the floor, when all that was left in the skeleton binding were fragments of text and tattered portraits, René-Jean rose to his feet, looked at the floor all strewn with scattered leaves, and clapped his hands in triumph.

Gros-Alain immediately did the same.

Georgette rose, picked up a leaf from the floor, leaned against the window-sill, that was just on a level with her chin, and began to tear the big page into tiny bits and throw them out of the window.

When René-Jean and Gros-Alain saw what she was doing, they were at once eager to follow her example; and picking up the pages, they tore them over and over again, page by page, and threw the fragments outside the window as she had done. Thus almost the whole of that ancient book, torn by those destructive little fingers, went flying to the winds. Georgette dreamily watched the fluttering groups of tiny white papers blown about by every wind, and cried,—

"Butterflies."

And here ended the massacre, its last traces vanishing in thin air.

Thus for the second time was Saint Bartholomew put to death,—he who had already suffered martyrdom in the year of our Lord 49.

Meanwhile the evening was drawing on, and as the heat increased a certain drowsiness pervaded the atmosphere. Georgette's eyes were growing heavy; René-Jean went to his crib, pulled out the sack of straw that served him for a mattress, dragged it to the window, and stretching himself out upon it, said, "Let us go to bed."

Gros-Alain leaned his head against René-Jean, Georgette laid hers on Gros-Alain, and thus the three culprits fell sound asleep.

Warm breezes stole in at the open windows; the scent of wild-flowers borne upon the wind from the ravines and hills mingled with the breath of evening; Nature lay calm and sympathetic; radiance, peace, and love pervaded the world; the sunlight touched each object with a soft caress; and one felt in every pore of his being the harmony that springs from the profound tenderness of inanimate things. Infinity holds within itself the essence of motherhood; creation is a miracle in full bloom, whose magnitude is perfected by its benevolence. One seemed to be conscious of an invisible presence exercising its mysterious influence in the dread conflict between created beings, protecting the helpless against the powerful; beauty meanwhile on every side, its splendor only to be equalled by its tenderness. The landscape, calm and peaceful, displayed the enchanting hazy effects of light and shade over the fields and river; the smoke rose upwards to the clouds, like reveries melting into dreams; flocks of birds circled above the Tourgue; the swallows peeped in at the windows, as much as to say, "We have come to see if the children are sleeping comfortably." And pure and lovable they looked as they lay motionless, prettily grouped, like little half-naked Cupids, their united ages amounting to less than nine years. Vague smiles hovered round their lips, reflecting dreams of Paradise. Perchance Almighty God was whispering in their ears, since they were of those whom all human tongues unite to call the weak and the blessed. Theirs was the innocence that commands veneration. All was silent, as if the breath that stirred those tender bosoms were the business of the universe, and all creation paused to listen; not a leaf rustled, not a blade of grass quivered. It seemed as if the wide starry universe held its breath lest these three lowly but angelic slumberers should be disturbed;

and nothing could be more sublime than the impressive reverence of Nature in the presence of this insignificance.

The declining sun had nearly reached the horizon, when suddenly, amid this profound peace, lightning flashed from the forest, followed by a savage report. A cannon had just been fired. The echoes seized this sound, and magnified it to a dreadful din, and so frightful was the prolonged reverberation from hill to hill that it roused Georgette.

She raised her head a little, lifted her finger, listened, then said,—
"Boom!"

The noise ceased, and silence returned again. Georgette put her head back on Gros-Alain, and fell asleep again.

Book IV

THE MOTHER

I

Death Passes

THAT EVENING THE MOTHER, WHOM we have seen wandering onward with no settled plan, had walked all day long. This was, to be sure, a matter of every-day occurrence. She kept on her way without pause or rest; for the sleep of exhaustion in some chance corner could no more be called rest than could the stray crumbs that she picked up here and there like the birds be considered nourishment. She ate and slept just enough to keep her alive.

She had spent the previous night in a forsaken barn,—a wreck such as civil wars leave behind them. In a deserted field she had found four walls, an open door, a little straw, and the remains of a roof, and on this straw beneath the roof she threw herself down, feeling the rats glide under as she lay there, and watching the stars rise through the roof. She slept several hours; then waking in the middle of the night, she resumed her journey, so as to get over as much ground as possible before the excessive heat of the day came on. For the summer pedestrian midnight is more favorable than noon.

She followed as best she could the brief directions given her by the Vautortes peasant, and kept as far as possible toward the west. Had there been any one near, he might have heard her incessantly muttering half aloud, "La Tourgue." She seemed to know no other word, save the names of her children.

And as she walked she dreamed. She thought of the adventures that had befallen her, of all she had suffered and endured, of the encounters, the indignities, the conditions imposed, the bargains offered and accepted, now for a shelter, now for a bit of bread, or simply to be directed on her way. A wretched woman is more unfortunate than a wretched man, inasmuch as she is the instrument of pleasure. Terrible indeed was this wandering journey! But all this would count for nothing if she could but find her children.

On that day her first adventure was in a village through which her route lay; the dawn was barely breaking, and the dusk of night still shrouded all the surrounding objects; but in the principal village street a few doors were half open, and curious faces peeped out of the windows. The inhabitants seemed restless like a startled hive of bees,—a disturbance due to the noise of wheels and the clanking of iron, which had reached their ears.

On the square in front of the church, a frightened group was staring at some object that was descending the hill towards the village. It was a four-wheeled wagon drawn by five horses, whose harness was composed of chains, and upon which could be seen something that looked like a pile of long joists, in the middle of which lay an object whose vague outlines were hidden by a large canvas resembling a pall. Ten horsemen rode in front of the wagon, and ten behind. They wore three-cornered hats, and above their shoulders rose what seemed like the points of naked sabres. The whole procession advanced slowly, its dark outlines sharply defined against the horizon; everything looked black,—the wagon, the harness, and the riders. On entering the village they approached the square with the pale glimmer of the dawn behind them.

It had grown somewhat lighter while the wagon was descending the hill, and now the escort was plainly to be seen,—a procession of ghosts to all intents, for no man uttered a word.

The horsemen were gendarmes; they really were carrying drawn sabres, and the canvas that covered the wagon was black.

The wretched wandering mother, entering the village from the opposite direction, just as the wagon and the gendarmes reached the square, approached the crowd of peasants and heard voices whispering the following questions and answers,—

"What is that?"

"It's the guillotine."

"Where does it come from?"

"From Fougères."

"Where is it going?"

"I don't know. They say it is going to some castle near Parigné."

"Parigné!"

"Let it go wherever it will, so that it does not stop here."

There was something ghostlike in the combination of this great wagon with its shrouded burden, the gendarmes, the clanking chains of the team, and the silent men, in the early dawn.

The group crossed the square and passed out from the village, which lay in a hollow between two hills. In a quarter of an hour the peasants who had stood there like men petrified saw the funereal procession reappear on the summit of the western hill. The great wheels jolted in the ruts, the chains of the harness rattled as they were shaken by the early morning wind, the sabres shone; the sun was rising, and at a bend of the road all vanished from the sight.

It was at this very moment that Georgette woke up in the library beside her still sleeping brothers, and wished her rosy feet good-morning.

II

Death Speaks

THE MOTHER HAD WATCHED THIS dark object as it passed by, but she neither understood nor tried to understand it, absorbed as she was in the vision that pictured her children lost in the darkness.

She too left the village soon after the procession which had just passed, and followed the same road at some distance behind the second squad of gendarmes. Suddenly the word "guillotine" came back to her, and she repeated it to herself; now, this untaught peasant woman, Michelle Fléchard, had no idea of its meaning, but her instinct warned her; she shuddered involuntarily, and it seemed dreadful to her to be walking behind it,—so she turned to the left, quitting the highway, and entered a wood, which was the Forest of Fougères.

After roaming about for some time she spied a belfry and the roofs of houses,—evidently a village on the edge of the forest; and she went towards it, for she was hungry.

It was one of those hamlets where the Republicans had established a military outpost.

She went as far as the square in front of the mayoralty-house.

Here, too, there was agitation and anxiety. A crowd had gathered in front of the flight of steps leading to the hall, and here, standing on one of these steps was a man accompanied by soldiers, who held in his hand a large unfolded placard. A drummer stood on his right, and on his left a bill-sticker, with his brush and paste-pot. Upon the balcony, over the door, stood the mayor, wearing a tricolored scarf over his peasant's dress.

The man with the placard was a public crier.

He wore a shoulder-belt from which hung a small wallet, in token that he was going from village to village proclaiming certain news throughout the district.

Just as Michelle Fléchard arrived, he had unfolded the placard and was beginning to read in a loud voice,—

"THE FRENCH REPUBLIC ONE AND INDIVISIBLE."

The drum beat. There was a stir in the crowd. A few took off their caps, others jammed their hats more firmly on their heads; in those times one could almost recognize a man's political views, throughout that district, by the fashion of his head-gear; hats were worn by Royalists, caps by Republicans. The confused murmur of voices ceased, and all listened as the crier proceeded to read:—

"By virtue of the orders given to as, and of the authority vested in us by the Committee of Public Safety,—"

Again the drum beat, and again the crier continued:—

"—and in execution of the decree of the National Convention, that outlaws all rebels taken with arms in their hands, and declares that capital punishment shall be inflicted on any man who harbors them or aids and abets in their escape,—"

One peasant whispered to his neighbor,—
"What does capital punishment mean?"
"I don't know," the neighbor replied.
The crier waved the placard:—

"—in accordance with Article 17 of the law of the 30th of April, that gives to the delegates and sub-delegates full authority over the rebels,—"

Here he made a pause, then resumed:—

"—the individuals designated under the following names and surnames are declared outlawed:—"

The audience listened with a close attention.
The voice of the crier sounded like thunder:—

"—Lantenac, brigand,—"

"That's Monseigneur," muttered a peasant.
And the whisper ran through the crowd, "It's Monseigneur."
And the crier pursued,—

"—Lantenac, ci-devant Marquis, brigand; the Imânus, brigand;—"

Two peasants looked askance at each other.
"That's Gouge-le-Bruant."
"Yes; that's Brise-Bleu."
The crier went on reading the list:—

"Grand-Francoeur, brigand;—"

A murmur ran through the crowd.
"He's a priest."
"Yes,—the Abbé Turmeau."
"I know; he is a curé somewhere near the forest of La Chapelle."
"And a brigand," added a man in a cap.
The crier went on:—

"—Boisnouveau, brigand; the two brothers Pique-en-bois, brigands; Houzard, brigand;—"

"That's Monsieur de Quélen," said a peasant.

"—Panier, brigand;—"

"That's Monsieur Sepher."

"—Place-Nette, brigand;—"

"That's Monsieur Jamois."
Paying no heed to these remarks, the crier continued:—

"—Guinoiseau, brigand; Chatenay, called Robi, brigand;—"

One peasant whispered, "Guinoiseau is the same person we call Le Blond; Chatenay comes from Saint-Ouen."

"—Hoisnard, brigand;—" continued the crier.

"He is from Ruillé," some one in the crowd was heard to say.
"Yes, that's Branche-d'Or."
"His brother was killed at the attack of Pontorson."
"Yes, Hoisnard-Malonnière."
"A fine-looking fellow of nineteen."
"Attention!" called out the crier; "here is the end of the list:—

"—Belle-Vigne, brigand; La Musette, brigand; Sabre-tout, brigand; Brin-d'Amour, brigand;—"

Here a lad jogged the elbow of a young girl; she smiled.
The crier continued,—

"—Chante-en-hiver, brigand; Le Chat, brigand—"

"That's Moulard," said a peasant.

"—Tabouze, brigand.—"

"That's Gauffre," said another.
"There are two of the Gauffres," added some woman.
"Good fellows, both of them," muttered a lad.
The crier waved the placard, the drum beat to command silence, and then he resumed the reading:

"—And the above-named, wheresoever they may be taken, as soon as their identity is proved, will be put to death upon the spot;—"

There was a movement in the crowd.
The crier pursued,—

"—and any man who protects them, or aids them to escape, will be brought before a court-martial and forthwith put to death. Signed—"

The silence grew intense.

"—Signed: Delegate of the Committee of Public Safety,
"CIMOURDAIN."

"A priest," said a peasant.

"The former curé of Parigné," remarked another.

"Turmeau and Cimourdain," added a townsman,—"a White priest and a Blue one."

"And both of them black," remarked another townsman.

The mayor, who stood on the balcony, lifted his hat as he cried,—

"Long live the Republic!"

A roll of the drum made it known that the crier had not yet finished. He waved his hand.

"Listen," he said, "to the last four lines of the Government proclamation. They are signed by the chief of the exploring column of the Côtes-du-Nord, Commander Gauvain."

"Listen," cried voices in the crowd.

The crier read,—

"Under penalty of death,—"

All were silent.

"—it is forbidden, in pursuance with the above, to lend aid or succor to the nineteen rebels herein named, who are at present shut up and besieged in the Tourgue."

"What's that?" cried a voice.

It was a woman's voice,—the voice of the mother.

III

Mutterings Among the Peasants

MICHELLE FLÉCHARD HAD MINGLED WITH the crowd. She had not listened, but some things one may hear without listening. She had heard the word "Tourgue," and raised her head.

"What's that? Did he say La Tourgue?"

People looked at her. The ragged woman seemed like one dazed.

Voices were heard to murmur, "She looks like a brigand."

A peasant woman, carrying a basket of buckwheat cakes, went up to her and whispered,—

"Keep still."

Michelle Fléchard stared stupidly; again she had lost all power of comprehension. That name, "La Tourgue" passed like a flash of lightning, and night closed once more. Had she no right to ask for information? What made the people look at her so strangely?

Meanwhile the drum had beaten for the last time, the bill-poster pasted up the notice, the mayor went back into the house, the crier started for some other village, and the crowd dispensed.

One group was still standing in front of the notice. Michelle Fléchard drew near.

They were commenting on the names of the outlaws.

Both peasants and townsmen were there; that is to say, both Whites and Blues.

"After all, they have not caught everybody," said a peasant. "Nineteen is just nineteen, and no more. They have not got Riou, nor Benjamin Moulins, nor Goupil from the parish of Andouillé."

"Nor Lorieul, of Monjean," remarked another.

And thus they went on:—

"Nor Brice-Denys."

"Nor François Dudouet."

"Yes, they have the one from Laval."

"Nor Huet, from Launey-Villiers."

"Nor Grégis."

"Nor Pilon."

"Nor Filleul."

"Nor Ménicent."

"Nor Guéharrée."

"Nor the three brothers Logerais."

"Nor Monsieur Lechandellier de Pierreville."

"Idiots!" exclaimed a stern-looking, white-haired man. "They have them all, if they have Lantenac."

"They have not got him yet," muttered one of the young fellows.

"Lantenac once captured, the soul is gone. The death of Lantenac means death to the Vendée," said the old man.

"Who is this Lantenac?" asked a townsman.

"He is a ci-devant," replied another.

And another added,—

"He is one of those who shoot women."

Michelle Fléchard heard this, and said,—

"That's true."

When people turned to look at her she added,—

"Because he shot me."

It was an odd thing to say; as if a living woman were to call herself dead. People looked at her suspiciously.

And truly she was a startling object, trembling at every sound, wild-looking, shivering, with an animal-like fear; so terrified was she that she frightened other people. There is a certain weakness in the despair of a woman that is dreadful to witness. It is like looking upon a being against whom destiny has done its worst. But peasants are not analytical; they see nothing below the surface. One of them muttered, "She might be a spy."

"Keep still and go away," whispered the kind-hearted woman who had spoken to her before.

"I am doing no harm," replied Michelle Fléchard; "I am only looking for my children."

The kind woman winked at those who were starring at Michelle Fléchard, and touching her forehead with her finger, said,—

"She is a simpleton."

Then drawing her aside, she gave her a buckwheat cake.

Without even stopping to thank her, Michelle Fléchard began to devour the cake like one ravenous for food.

"You see, she eats just like an animal: she must be a simpleton;" and one by one the crowd gradually dispersed.

After she had eaten, Michelle Fléchard said to the peasant woman,—

"Well, I have finished my cake; now, where is the Tourgue?"

"There she is at it again!" cried the peasant woman.

"I must go the Tourgue. Show me the road to La Tourgue."

"Never!" cried the peasant woman. "You would like to be killed, I suppose; but whether you would or not, I don't know the way myself. You must surely be insane. Listen to me, my poor woman. You look tired; will you come to my house and rest?"

"I never test," replied the mother.

"And her feet are all torn," muttered the peasant woman.

"Didn't you hear me telling you that my children were stolen from me, one little girl and two little boys? I came from the *carnichot* in the forest. You can ask Tellmarch le Caimand about me, and also the man I met in the field down yonder. The Caimand cared me. It seems I had something broken. All those things really happened. Besides, there is Sergeant Radoub; you may ask him; he will tell you, for it was he who met us in the forest. Three,—I tell you there were three children, and the oldest one's name was René-Jean: I can prove it to you; and Gros-Alain and Georgette were the two others. My husband is dead; they killed him. He was a farmer at Siscoignard. You look like a kind woman. Show me the way. I am not mad, I am a mother. I have lost my children, and am looking for them. I do not know exactly where I came from. I slept last night on the straw in a barn. I am going to the Tourgue. I am not a thief. You can't help seeing that I am telling you the truth. You ought to help me to find my children. I don't belong to this neighborhood. I have been shot, but I do not know where it happened."

The peasant woman shook her head, saying,—

"Listen, traveller; in times of revolution you must not say things that cannot be understood, for you might be arrested."

"But the Tourgue," cried the mother; "madam, for the love of the Infant Jesus and of the Blessed Virgin in Paradise I pray you, I beg of you, I beseech you, madam, tell me how I can find the road to the Tourgue!"

Then the peasant woman grew angry.

"I don't know! And if I did, I would not tell you! It is a bad place. People don't go there."

"But I am going there," said the mother.

And once more she started on her way.

The woman, as she watched her depart, muttered to herself:—

"She must have something to eat, whatever she does;" and running after Michelle Fléchard, she put a dark-looking cake in her hand, saying,—

"There is something for your supper."

Michelle Fléchard took the buckwheat-cake, but she neither turned nor made reply as she pursued her way.

She went forth from the village, and just as she reached the last houses she met three little ragged and barefooted children trotting along. She went up to them and said,—

"Here are two boys and a girl;" and when she saw them looking at her bread, she gave it to them.

The children took the bread, but they were evidently frightened.

She entered the forest.

IV

A Mistake

MEANWHILE, ON THIS VERY DAY, before dawn, amid the dim shadows of the forest, the following scene took place on the bit of road that leads from Javené to Lécousse.

All the roads of the Bocage are shut in between high banks, and those enclosing the one that runs from Javené to Parigné by way of Lécousse are even higher than usual; indeed the road, winding as it does, might well be called a ravine. It leads from Vitré, and has had the honor of jolting Madame de Sévigné's carriage. Shut in as it is by hedges on the right and on the left, no better spot for an ambush could well be found.

That morning, one hour before Michelle Fléchard, starting from a different part of the forest, had reached the first village, where she beheld the funereal apparition of the wagon escorted by the gendarmes, a crowd of unseen men, concealed by the branches, crouched in the thickets through which the road from Javené runs after it crosses the bridge over the Couesnon. They were, peasants dressed in coats of skin, such as were worn by the kings of Brittany in the sixteenth century and by the peasants in the eighteenth. Some were armed with muskets, others with axes. Those who had axes had just built in a glade a kind of funeral pile of dry fagots and logs, which was only waiting to be set on fire. Those who had muskets were posted on both sides of the road, in the attitude of expectancy. Could one have seen through the leaves, he might have discovered on every side fingers resting on triggers and guns aimed through the openings made by the interlacing of the branches. These men were lying in wait. All the muskets converged towards the road, which had begun to whiten in the rising dawn.

Amid this twilight low voices were carrying on a dialogue:—

"Are you sure of this?"

"Well, that's what they say."

"She is about to go by?"

"They say she is in this neighborhood."

"She must not leave it."

"She must be burned."

"We three villages have come out for that very purpose."

"And how about the escort?"

"It is to be killed."

"But will she come by this road?"

"So they say."

"Then she is coming from Vitré."

"And why shouldn't she?"

"Because they said she was coming from Fougères."

"Whether she comes from Fougères or from Vitré, she certainly comes from the devil."

"That is true."

"And she must go back to him."

"I agree to that."

"Then she is going to Parigné?"

"So it seems."

"She will not get there."

"No."

"No, no, no!"

"Attention!"

It was the part of prudence to be silent now, since it was growing quite light.

Suddenly these men lurking in ambush held their breath, as they heard the sound of wheels and horses' feet. Peering through the branches, they caught an indistinct glimpse of a long wagon, a mounted escort, and something on the top of the wagon, all of which was coming towards them along the hollow road.

"There she is," cried the one who appeared to be the leader.

"Yes, and the escort too," said one of the men who lay in wait.

"How many are there?"

"Twelve."

"It was said that there were to be twenty."

"Twelve or twenty, let us kill them all."

"Wait till they are within our reach."

A little later and the wagon with its escort appeared at a turn of the road.

"Long live the King!" cried the peasant leader; and as he spoke, a hundred muskets were fired at the same instant. When the smoke scattered, the escort was scattered likewise. Seven horsemen had fallen, and the other five had made their escape. The peasants rushed to the wagon. "Hallo! this is not the guillotine," cried the leader; "it's a ladder."

In fact, there was nothing whatever in the wagon but a long ladder.

The two wounded horses had fallen, and the driver had been killed by accident.

"There is something suspicious about a ladder with an escort, all the same," said the leader. "It was going in the direction of Parigné. No doubt it was intended for scaling the Tourgue."

"Let us burn the ladder," cried the peasants.

As to the funereal wagon for which they were watching, it had taken another road, and was already two miles farther away, in the village where Michelle Fléchard had seen it pass at sunrise.

V

Vox in Deserto

AFTER LEAVING THE THREE CHILDREN to whom she had given her bread, Michelle Fléchard started at random through the woods.

Since no one would show her the way, she must find it without help. From time to time she paused, and sat down to rest; then up and away again. She was overcome by that intense weariness which one feels first in the muscles, then in the bones,—like the fatigue of a slave. And a slave indeed she was,—the slave of her lost children. They must be found; each passing moment might be fatal to them. A duty like this debars one from the right to breathe freely; yet she was very weary. When one has reached this stage of fatigue it becomes a question whether another step can be taken. Could she do it? She had been walking since morning without finding either a village or a house. When she first started she had followed the right path, but soon wandered into the wrong one, and at last quite lost her way among the thick branches, where one tree looked just like another. Was she drawing near her goal? Were her sufferings almost over? She was following the way of the Cross, and felt all the languor and exhaustion of the final station. Was she doomed to fall dead on the road? At one time it seemed to her impossible to take another step: the sun was low, the forest dark, the paths no longer visible in the grass, and God only knew what was to become of her. She began to call, but there was no reply.

Looking around, she perceived an opening among the branches, and no sooner had she started in that direction than she found herself out of the wood.

Before her lay a valley no wider than a trench, across whose stony bottom flowed a slender stream of clear water. Then she realized that she was excessively thirsty, and approaching it knelt to drink; and while thus kneeling she thought she would say her prayers.

When she rose she tried to get her bearings, and crossed the brook.

As far as the eye could reach on the farther side of the little valley stretched a limitless plain overgrown with a stubbly underbrush, which rose from the brook like an inclined plane, occupying the entire horizon. If the forest were a solitude, this plateau might be called a desert. In the forest there was a chance that one might encounter a human being behind any bush; but across the plateau not an object could be descried within reach of human vision. A few birds were flying across the heather, as if making an effort to escape.

Then, in the presence of this utter desolation, feeling her knees give way beneath her, the poor bewildered mother cried out amid the solitude, like one suddenly gone mad,—

"Is there no one here?"

She paused for an answer, and the answer came.

A deep and muffled voice burst forth from the distant horizon, caught and repeated by echo upon echo. It was like a thunderbolt; but it might have been the firing of a cannon, or a voice answering the mother's question, and replying, "Yes."

Then silence reigned once more.

The mother rose with renewed energy. She felt reassured by a sense of companionship. Having quenched her thirst and said her prayers, her strength returned, and she began to climb the plateau in the direction from whence the voice of distant thunder had reached her ears. Suddenly she caught sight of a lofty tower looming up against the far-away horizon. It stood alone amid this wild landscape, and a ray of the setting sun cast a crimson glow across it. It was more than a league away. Beyond it stretched the forest of Fougères, its vast expanse of verdure half hidden by the mist.

Could it have been this tower that made the noise?—for it seemed to her to stand on the very spot whence came the thundering sound that had rung in her ears like a call.

Michelle Fléchard had now reached the summit of the plateau, and the plain alone lay before her.

VI

The Situation

THE MOMENT HAD FINALLY COME when Cimourdain held Lantenac in his grasp. The inexorable had conquered the pitiless. The old rebel Royalist was caught in his own lair, with no possible chance of escape; and Cimourdain had determined to behead the Marquis in the home of his ancestors, on his own estate, upon his very hearthstone, so to speak, that the feudal mansion might look upon the downfall of its feudal lord, and thus present an example not soon to be forgotten.

For this reason he sent to Fougères for the guillotine, which we saw on its way.

To kill Lantenac was to kill the Vendée; the death of the Vendée meant safety for France. Cimourdain was a man utterly calm in the performance of duty, however ferocious it might be, and not for a moment did he hesitate.

In regard to the ruin of the Marquis he felt quite at ease; but he had another cause for anxiety. The struggle would no doubt be a fearful one; Gauvain would direct the assault, and perhaps take part in it. This young chief had all the fire of a soldier; he was the very man to throw himself headlong into this hand-to-hand encounter. And what if he were killed,—Gauvain, his child, the only being on earth whom he loved! Gauvain had been fortunate thus far; but fortune sometimes grows weary. Cimourdain trembled. Strange enough was his destiny, thus placed between these two Gauvains, longing for the death of the one, and praying for the life of the other.

The cannon that had started Georgette in her cradle and summoned the mother from the depths of the woods, did more than that. Whether by accident or intentionally on the part of the man who pointed the gun, the ball, though intended only as a warning, struck, broke, and partly wrenched away the iron bars that defended and closed the great loop-hole on the first floor of the tower, and the besieged had had no time to repair this damage.

The truth was that, in spite of their loud boasting, their ammunition was nearly exhausted; and their situation, let it be remembered, was more critical than the besiegers suspected. Their dream had been to blow up the Tourgue when the enemy was once fairly within the walls; but their store of powder was running low,—not more than thirty rounds left for each man. They had plenty of muskets, blunderbusses, and pistols, but few cartridges. All the guns were loaded, that they might keep up a steady fire. But how long could this last? To keep up the firing and economize their resources at one and the same time would be a somewhat difficult combination. Fortunately (a gloomy kind of fortune) it would be for the most part a hand-to-hand encounter, in which the cold steel of sabre and dagger would take the place of firearms. They would have a chance to hack the enemy in pieces, and therein lay their chief hope.

The interior of the tower seemed impregnable. In the low hall where the breach had been made the entrance was defended by that barricade so skilfully constructed by Lantenac, called that *retirade*. Behind it stood a long table covered with loaded weapons, blunderbusses, carbines, muskets, sabres, hatchets, and daggers. Having been unable to make use of the oubliette prison communicating with the lower hall, for the purpose of blowing up the tower, the Marquis had ordered the door of this dungeon to be closed. Above the hall was the round chamber of the first story, which could only be reached by a very narrow spiral staircase. This room, provided like the lower hall with a table covered with weapons ready for use, was lighted by the wide embrasure whose grating had just been crushed by a cannon-ball. Below this room the spiral staircase led to the round chamber on the second story, from which the iron door opened into the bridge-castle. This room on the second floor was called indiscriminately "the room with the iron door," or "the mirror room", on account of the numerous little mirrors hung from rusty old nails against the naked stone walls,—an odd medley of elegance and barbarism. As there were no means by which the upper rooms could be successfully defended, this mirror-room was what Manesson-Mallet, the authority on fortifications, calls "the last post where the besieged may capitulate." The object was, as we have already stated, to prevent the besiegers from reaching it.

This round chamber on the second floor was lighted by embrasures, but a torch was burning there also. This torch, stuck in an iron torch-holder, like the one in the lower hall, had been lighted by the Imânus and placed quite near the end of the sulphur-match. Appalling solicitude.

At the end of the hall, on a long board raised on trestles, food had been placed as in a Homeric cavern; great dishes of rice, a porridge of some kind of dark grain, hashed veal, a boiled pudding made of flour and fruit, and jugs of cider. Whoever wished to eat and drink could do so.

The cannon had set them all on the alert, and now they had but half an hour of repose before them.

From the top of the tower the Imânus kept watch of the enemy's approach. Lantenac had given orders that the besiegers should be allowed to advance unmolested.

"They are four thousand five hundred," he said; "it would be useless to kill them outside. Wait till they are within the walls, where we shall be equal to them." And he added, laughing, "Equality, Fraternity."

It had been agreed that when the enemy began to advance, the Imânus should give warning on his horn.

Posted behind the *retirade* and on the steps of the staircase, they waited in silence, with a musket in one hand and a rosary in the other.

The situation might be summed up as follows:—

On one side of the besiegers a breach to scale, a barricade to carry, three rooms in succession, one above the other, to be taken by main force, two spiral staircases to be climbed, step by step, under a shower of bullets; the besieged meanwhile standing face to face with death.

VII

Preliminaries

GAUVAIN ON HIS SIDE WAS preparing for the attack. He had given his last instructions to Cimourdain, who, it will be remembered, was to guard the plateau, taking no part in the action, as well as to Guéchamp, who with the main body of the army was to be stationed in the forest camp. It was agreed that neither the lower battery of the wood nor the higher one of the plateau was to fire, unless a sortie or an attempt to escape were made. Gauvain reserved for himself the command of the storming column, and this it was that troubled Cimourdain.

The sun had just set.

A tower in the open country is like a ship in mid-ocean, and must be attacked in the same way. It is more like boarding than assaulting. Cannon is of no avail, for of what use would it be to cannonade walls fifteen feet thick? A port-hole through which men struggle to force a way, while others defend the entrance with axes, knives, pistols, fists, and teeth,—this was the kind of combat that might be expected, and Gauvain knew that by no other means could the Tourgue be taken. Nothing can be more deadly than an attack where the combatants can look into one another's eyes. He was familiar with the formidable interior of the tower, having lived there as a child.

He stood wrapped in deep thought.

A few paces from him, his lieutenant, Guéchamp, with a spy-glass in his hand, was scanning the horizon in the direction of Parigné. Suddenly he cried,—

"Ah! At last!"

This exclamation roused Gauvain from his reverie.

"What is it, Guéchamp?"

"The ladder is coming, commander."

"The escape-ladder?"

"Yes."

"Is it possible that it has not arrived till now?"

"No, commander; and I felt anxious about it. The courier whom I sent to Javené returned."

"I am aware of that."

"He reported that he had found in a carpenter-shop at Javené a ladder of the required dimensions, that he had taken possession of it, and having had it put on a wagon, demanded an escort of twelve horsemen; that he had waited to see them set out for Parigné,—the wagon, the escort, and the ladder,—and had then started for home at full speed."

"And reported the same to us, adding that the team was a good one and had started about two o'clock in the morning, and would therefore be here before sunset. Yes, I know all that. What else?"

"Well, commander, the sun has just set and the wagon that is to bring the ladder has not yet arrived."

"Is it possible? But we must begin the attack. The hour has come. If we are late, the besieged will think that we have retreated."

"We can attack, commander."

"But we must have the escape-ladder."

"Certainly."

"But we have not got it"

"Yes, we have."

"How is that?"

"That's what made me say, 'Ah! at last!' As the wagon had not arrived, I took my spy-glass and have been watching the road from Parigné to the Tourgue, and now I am content; for the wagon and the escort are yonder descending the hill. You can see them."

Gauvain took the spy-glass and looked.

"Yes, there it is. It is hardly light enough to see it all distinctly, but I can distinguish the escort; it is certainly that. Only it seems to me larger than you said, Guéchamp?"

"Yes, it does."

"They are about a quarter of a league distant."

"The escape-ladder will be here in a quarter of an hour, commander."

"Then we can attack."

It was indeed a wagon approaching, but not the one they supposed it to be.

As he turned, Gauvain saw behind him Sergeant Radoub standing with downcast eyes, in the attitude of military salute.

"What is it, Sergeant Radoub?"

"Citizen commander, we, the men of the battalion of the Bonnet-Rouge, have a favor to ask of you."

"What is it?"

"To be killed."

"Ah!" exclaimed Gauvain.

"Will you grant us this favor?"

"Well, that depends," said Gauvain.

"It is just this, commander. Since the affair at Dol, you have been too careful of us. There are twelve of us still."

"Well?"

"It humiliates us."

"You are the reserved force."

"We would rather be in the vanguard."

"I need you to insure success at the close of the engagement. That is why I keep you back."

"There is too much of this keeping back."

"It is all the same. You are in the column. You march."

"In the rear. Paris has a right to march at the head."

"I will consider the matter, Sergeant Radoub."

"Consider it today, commander. The occasion is at hand. Hard knocks will be given on both sides; it will be lively work. He who lays a finger on the Tourgue will get himself burned; we request the favor of being in the thick of it."

The sergeant paused, twisted his moustache, and continued in a changed voice:—

"And then you know, commander, our little ones are in this tower.

Our children are there,—the children of the battalion, our three children. That abominable wretch Brise-Bleu, called the Imânus, that Gouge-le-Bruand, Bouge-le-Gruand, Fouge-le-Truand, that thundering devil of a man, threatens our children,—our children, our puppets, commander! No harm must come to them, whatever convulsion shakes the Tourgue. Do you understand that, commander? We will not endure it. Just now I took advantage of the truce, and climbing up the plateau, I looked at them through the window. Yes, they are certainly there,—you can see them from the edge of the ravine; I saw them, and frightened the darlings. Commander, if a single hair falls from the heads of those little cherubs,—I swear it by the thousand names of all that is sacred,—I, Sergeant Radoub, will demand an account of God Almighty! And this is what the battalion says: we want the babies to be saved, or else we all want to be killed. We have a right to ask it. Yes, that every man of us be killed! And now I salute you, and present my respects."

Gauvain held out his hand to Radoub as he exclaimed:—

"You are brave fellows! You will join the attacking column. I shall divide you into two parties; six of you I shall place in the vanguard to insure the advance, and six in the rear-guard to prevent a retreat."

"And am I still to command the twelve?"

"Of course."

"Thank you, commander. In that case, I join the vanguard."

Radoub made the military salute, and returned to the ranks. Gauvain drew out his watch, whispered a few words to Guéchamp, and the attacking column began to form.

VIII

The Speech and the Roar

Meanwhile, Cimourdain who had not yet taken his position on the plateau, and who stood beside Gauvain, approached a trumpeter.

"Sound the trumpet!" he said to him.

The clarion sounded, the horn replied.

Again the clarion and the trumpet exchanged calls.

"What does that mean?" asked Gauvain of Guéchamp. "What does Cimourdain want?"

Cimourdain, with a white handkerchief in his hand, approached the tower; and as he drew near, he cried aloud,—

"You men in the tower, do you know me?"

And the voice of the Imânus made answer from the heights,—

"We do."

These two voices were now heard exchanging question and reply as follows:—

"I am the ambassador of the Republic,"

"You are the former curé of Parigné."

"I am a delegate of the Committee of Public Safety."

"You are a priest."

"I am a representative of the law."

"You are a renegade."

"I am a commissioner of the Revolution."

"You are an apostate."

"I am Cimourdain."

"You are a demon."

"Do you know me?"

"We abominate you."

"Would you like to have me in your power?"

"There are eighteen of us here who would give our heads to have yours."

"Well, then, I have come to give myself up to you."

A burst of savage laughter rang out from the top of the tower, with the derisive cry,—

"Come!"

A deep silence of expectancy reigned in the camp.

Cimourdain continued,—

"On one condition."

"What is that?"

"Listen."

"Speak."

"You hate me?"

"Yes."

"And I love you; I am your brother."

The voice from above replied,—

"Yes—our brother Cain."

Cimourdain went on, with a peculiar inflection of voice,—soft, but penetrating:—

"Insult me, if you will, but listen to my words. I come here protected by a flag of truce. Poor misguided men, you are in very truth my brothers, and I am your friend. I am the light, trying to illumine your ignorance. Light is the essence of brotherhood. Moreover, have we not all one common mother,—our native land? Then listen to me. Sooner or later, you—or at least your children or grandchildren—will know that every event of this present time is the result of the higher law, and that this revolution is the work of God himself. But while we wait for the time when, to the inner sense of every man, even unto yours, all these things will be made plain, and when all fanaticisms, including our own, will vanish before the powerful light that is to dawn, is there none to take pity on your ignorance? Behold, I come to you, and I offer you my head; more than this, I hold out my hand. I beg of you to take my life and spare your own. All power is vested in me, and what I promise I can fulfil. I make one final effort in this decisive moment. He who speaks to you is both citizen and priest. The citizen contends with you, but the priest implores you. I beseech you to hear me. Many among you have wives and children. It is in their behalf that I entreat you. Oh, my brothers—"

"Go on with your preaching!" sneered the Imânus.

Cimourdain continued:—

"My brethren, avert this fatal hour. There will be frightful slaughter here. Many of us who stand before you will not see tomorrow's sun; yes, many indeed will perish, and you,—you will all die. Have mercy on yourselves. Why shed all this blood to no avail? Why kill so many men when two would suffice?"

"Two?" asked the Imânus.

"Yes, two."

"Who are they?"

"Lantenac and myself."

Here Cimourdain raised his voice.

"We are the two men whose deaths would be most pleasing to our respective parties. This is my offer; accept it and you are saved. Give Lantenac to us and take me in his place; he will be guillotined, and with me you may do what you will."

"Priest," howled the Imânus, "if we but had you, we would roast you over a slow fire."

"So be it," said Cimourdain; and he went on:—

"You, the condemned who are in this tower, in one hour may all be safe and free. I offer you salvation. Will you accept?"

The Imânus burst out:—

"You are a fool as well as a villain. Why do you interfere with us? Who invited you to come here with your speeches? You expect us to deliver up Monseigneur, do you? What do you want to do with him?"

"I want his head, and I offer you—"

"Your skin, for we would flay you like a dog, curé; but no, your skin is not worth his head. Begone!"

"The slaughter will be terrible. Once more I beseech you to reflect."

Night had come on during the progress of this gloomy conference, which had been heard both within and without the tower. The Marquis de Lantenac listened in silence, letting the affair take its course; leaders sometimes exhibit this self-absorbed indifference, as a kind of prerogative of responsibility.

The Imânus raised his voice above that of Cimourdain, exclaiming:—

"You men who are about to attack us, we have declared our intentions. You have heard our offers; we shall make no change in them, and woe be unto you if you refuse them. But if you consent, we will give you back the three children whom we now hold, on condition that each one of us is allowed to depart in safety."

"You may all go free, save one," replied Cimourdain.

"Who is that?"

"Lantenac."

"Monseigneur! Deliver Monseigneur! Never!"

"We must have Lantenac."

"Never!"

"We can treat with you on no other condition."

"Then you had better begin the attack."

Silence ensued.

The Imânus having given the signal on his horn, came down, the Marquis grasped his sword, the nineteen besieged silently gathered in the lower hall behind the *retirade*, and fell upon their knees; they heard the measured tread of the attacking column as it advanced towards the tower, drawing nearer and nearer in the darkness, until suddenly the sound was close upon them, at the very mouth of the breach. Then every man knelt and adjusted his musket or blunderbuss in an opening of the retirade, while one of their number, Grand-Francoeur, the former priest Turmeau, rose, and holding in his right hand a drawn sabre, and in his left a crucifix, solemnly uttered the blessing.

"In the name of the Father, of the Son, and of the Holy Ghost!"

All fired at once, and the conflict began.

IX

Titans Against Giants

IT WAS INDEED A FEARFUL scene.

This hand-to-hand struggle surpassed all conception.

To find its parallel one must have recourse to the great duels of Æschylus, or to the butcheries of old feudal times; to those "attacks with short arms" that continued in vogue until the seventeenth century, when men penetrated into fortified places by way of concealed breaches; tragic assaults, where, says an old sergeant of the province of Alentejo, "the mines having done their work, the besiegers will now advance, carrying boards covered with sheets of tin, armed with round shields and bucklers, and supplied with an abundance of grenades; and as they force those who hold the intrenchments and *retirades* to give way, they will take possession of them, vigorously expelling the besieged."

The scene of the attack was terrible; it was one of those breaches technically termed "a covered breach," and was, it must be remembered, not a wide breach opened to daylight, but a mere crack, traversing the wall from side to side. The powder had worked like an auger. The effect of the explosion had been so tremendous that the tower was cracked for more than forty feet above the chamber of the mine; but it was only a fissure, and the practicable rent that served as a breach and afforded an entrance into the lower hall, had the effect of having been pierced by the thrust of a lance rather than cleft by a blow from an axe.

It was a puncture in the side of the tower, a long, deep cut, not unlike a well, horizontal with the ground, a narrow passage twisting and turning like an intestine through a wall fifteen feet thick, a shapeless cylinder, abounding in obstacles, pitfalls, and all the débris of past explosions, where a man, blinded by the darkness and stumbling over the rubbish beneath his feet, would surely dash his head against the granite rock.

Before the assailants yawned this black portal, like a cavernous mouth, whose upper and lower jaws, closely set with jagged rocks, rivalled a shark's mouth in the number of its teeth. This cavity was the only means of entrance or exit, and while the grape-shot was raining within, on the other side—that is to say, in the lower hall of the ground-floor—rose the *retirade*.

The ferocity of the encounter can only be compared with the encounters of sappers in underground passages when a counter-mine has just cut across a mine, or with the cutlass butcheries that take place when in a naval battle a man-of-war is boarded. Fighting in the depths of a grave reaches the very climax of all that is dreadful. The fact that a ceiling is overhead seems to increase the horror of human slaughter. Just as the first of the assailants came surging in, the *retirade* was wrapped in a sheet of lightning, and it seemed like the bursting of a subterranean thunder-clap, report answering report as the besiegers returned the thunder of the ambuscade. Above the uproar rose the voice of Gauvain, shouting, "Break them in!" then Lantenac's cry, "Stand firm against the enemy!" then the cry of the Imânus, "Stand by me, men of Maine!" then the clang of sabres clashing one against the other, and terrible discharges following in swift succession, dealing death on every hand. The torch fastened to the wall but dimly lighted this scene of horror. A lurid glare enveloped all objects, amid which nothing could be clearly distinguished; and those who entered were straightway struck deaf and blind,—deafened by the uproar, blinded by the smoke. The disabled lay here and there among the rubbish; while the combatants trampled upon the corpses, crushing the wounds and bruising the broken limbs of the injured men, who groaned aloud in their wild agony, and sometimes set their teeth in the feet of those who were torturing them. Now and then a silence more appalling than sound would settle over all. Men seized each other by the throat, and then were heard fierce pantings, followed by gnashings of teeth, death-rattles and imprecations, and directly all the din returned again. A stream of blood flowed through the breach in the tower, and spreading in the gloom, formed a dark, smoking pool outside upon the grass.

One might have said that the tower herself was bleeding like a wounded giantess.

Surprising to relate, all this tumult was hardly audible on the outside. The night was very dark, and around the besieged fortress an almost funereal sense of peace rested on forest and plain. Hell was within, a sepulchre without. This life-and-death struggle in the darkness, these volleys of musketry, this clamor and fury,—all this tumult and confusion was subdued by the massive walls and arches. There was not air enough for reverberation, and a sense of suffocation was added to the carnage. Outside the tower the noise was scarcely audible; and meanwhile the three little children still slumbered.

The fury of the combat deepened; the *retirade* held its own.

There is nothing more difficult to force than this kind of barricade, with a re-entering angle. If the besieged were at a disadvantage in numbers, their position was in their favor. The attacking column had suffered serious loss of men. Formed in a long line outside the tower, it gradually worked its way through the breach, shortening as it disappeared, like a snake twisting itself into its hole.

Gauvain, with the rashness peculiar to a youthful leader, was in the lower hall, in the thickest of the mêlée, with the bullets flying in all directions. Let us add, however, that he felt all the confidence of a man who had never been wounded.

As he turned to give an order, the flash from a volley of musketry lighted up a face close beside him.

"Cimourdain!" he-cried, "why are you here?"

"I came to be near you," replied the man, who was indeed Cimourdain.

"But you will be killed."

"What of that? Are you not in the same danger?"

"But I am needed here, and you are not."

"Since you are here, my place is by your side."

"No, my master."

"Yes, my child."

And Cimourdain remained near Gauvain.

The dead lay in heaps on the pavement of the lower hall. Although the *retirade* had not as yet been carried, the majority would sooner or later gain the day. The assailants, it is true, were not protected, while the assailed were under cover; and ten of the besiegers fell to one of the besieged; but the latter were constantly replaced.

In proportion as the besieged diminished the besiegers increased.

The nineteen besieged were collected behind the *retirade*, since that was the centre of attack; and among them were their dead and wounded; not more than fifteen of them were in fighting condition. One of the fiercest, Chante-en-hiver, had been fright-fully mutilated. He was a thick-set Breton, with curling hair, and short of stature, but full of life and energy. Although his jaw was broken and one of his eyes blown out, he could still walk, and he dragged himself up the winding staircase into the room on the first story, hoping there to be able to say his prayers and die.

He leaned against the wall near the loop-hole trying to get a breath of air.

The butchery down below in front of the *retirade* had grown more and more horrible. Once when there was a pause between two volleys Cimourdain raised his voice.

"Besieged," he cried, "why continue this bloodshed? You are conquered. Surrender! Remember we are four thousand five hundred against nineteen, which is over two hundred to one. Surrender!"

"Let us put an end to that idle babble," replied the Marquis de Lantenac.

And twenty balls responded to Cimourdain's appeal.

The *retirade* did not reach as high as the vaulted ceiling, thus the besieged were enabled to fire over it; but at the same time it presented to the besiegers an opportunity for an escalade.

"An assault on the *retirade*!" cried Gauvain. "Is there a man among you who will volunteer to scale it?"

"I," replied Sergeant Radoub.

X

Radoub

A SUDDEN STUPOR FELL UPON the assailants. Radoub had been the sixth to enter the breach at the head of the attacking column, and of these six men of the Parisian battalion four had already fallen. After uttering the exclamation "I," he was seen to draw back instead of advancing, and bending over, in a crouching attitude, he crawled between the legs of the combatants, until, reaching the opening of the breach, he rushed out. Was this flight? Was it possible for such a man to flee? What could it mean?

Having escaped from the breach, Radoub, still blinded by the smoke, rubbed his eyes, as though to dispel the horror and gloom of the night, and by the faint glimmer of the stars began to scrutinize the wall of the tower. He nodded with an air of satisfaction, as much as to say, "So I was not mistaken."

Radoub had noticed that the deep fissure caused by the explosion of the mine extended from the breach to that loop-hole on the first story whose iron grating had been shattered and partially torn off by a cannon-ball, and thus hanging, the network of broken bars left just room enough for a man to pass through,—provided he could climb up to it; and that was the question. Possibly it might be done by following the crack, supposing the man to be a cat; and Radoub was precisely like a cat. He was of the race which Pindar calls "the agile athletes." Although a man may be an old soldier, it by no means follows that he is no longer young. Radoub, who had been in the French Guards, was not yet forty years of age, and he was as active as Hercules.

Laying his musket on the ground, he removed his shoulder-belt, threw off his coat and waistcoat, keeping only his two pistols, which he stuck in the belt of his trousers, and his drawn sabre, which he held between his teeth. The butts of his pistols projected from above his belt.

Thus burdened by no unnecessary weight, and followed in the darkness by the eyes of all those of the attacking column who had not as yet entered the breach, he began the ascent, climbing the stones of the cracked wall as though they had been the steps of a staircase. It was an advantage to him that he wore no shoes; there is nothing like a naked foot for clinging, and he twisted his toes into the holes between the stones. While hoisting himself by means of his fists, he used his knees for support. It was a hard pull, not unlike climbing up the teeth of a saw. "Luckily," he thought to himself, "there is no one in the room on the first story; for if there were, I should never have been allowed to climb up in this way."

He had about forty feet to climb after this fashion, and, as he advanced, somewhat inconvenienced by the projecting butts of his pistols, the crack grew narrower and the ascent more and more difficult. The increasing depth of the precipice beneath his feet added constantly to the danger of a fall; but at last he reached the edge of the loop-hole, and on pushing aside the twisted and broken grating he found that he had ample room to pass through. Then raising himself by a powerful effort, he braced his knees against the cornices of the ledge, caught hold of a fragment of the grating on either hand, and holding his sabre between his teeth, he drew himself up as high as his waist in front of the embrasure of the loop-hole; there, with his entire weight resting on his two fists, he hung suspended over the abyss.

Now, with a single bound, he had but to leap into the hall of the first story.

Suddenly he beheld in the gloom a horrible object; a face appeared in the embrasure, like a bleeding mask with its jaw crushed and one eye torn out, and this one-eyed mask was gazing steadily at him.

The two hands belonging to this mask were seen to reach forth from the darkness in the direction of Radoub; one of them instantly caught the pistols from his belt, and the other pulled the sabre from his teeth, and thus Radoub was disarmed.

He felt his knee slipping from the sloping cornice, the grasp of his hands on fragments of the grating barely sufficed to support him, while behind him yawned an abyss of forty feet.

That mask and those hands belonged to Chante-en-hiver.

Suffocated by the smoke that rose from below, Chante-en-hiver had made his way into the embrasure of this loop-hole, where the out-door air had revived him, the freshness of the night had checked the bleeding of his wounds, and he had begun to feel somewhat stronger, when suddenly in the opening before him appeared the form of Radoub; then, while the latter hung there, clinging with both hands to the railing, with no choice but to drop or suffer himself to be disarmed, Chante-en-hiver, with an awful calmness, snatched the two pistols from big belt and the sabre from his teeth.

Whereupon ensued a duel between the unarmed and the wounded,—a duel without a parallel.

There could be no doubt that the dying man would come off victorious; one shot would be enough to hurl Radoub into the yawning gulf below.

Luckily for Radoub, Chante-en-hiver, in consequence of holding the two pistols in one hand, was unable to fire either, and was forced to use the sabre, with which he gave Radoub a thrust in the shoulder,—a blow which wounded him and at the same time saved his life.

Although unarmed, Radoub, in full possession of his strength and heedless of his injury, which was simply a flesh-wound, suddenly swung himself forward, and releasing his hold on the bars, leaped into the embrasure, where he found himself face to face with Chante-en-hiver, who had thrown the sabre behind him, as he knelt clutching a pistol in either hand.

As he took aim at Radoub, the muzzle of his pistol was so close as nearly to touch him; but his enfeebled arm trembled, and a minute passed before he could fire.

Radoub availed himself of this respite to burst out laughing.

"Look here, you hideous object!" he cried, "do you think you can frighten me with your jaw like beef *à la mode?* Sapristi! how they have spoiled your face for you."

Chante-en-hiver was aiming at him.

"I suppose it is rather rude to say so," continued Radoub, "but the grape-shot has made a pretty ragged piece of work of your head. Bellona spoiled your beauty, my poor fellow. Come, come, spit out your little pistol-shot, my friend."

The pistol went off, and the ball, grazing Radoub's head, tore away half his ear. Chante-en-hiver, still grasping the second pistol, raised his other arm, but Radoub gave him no time to take aim.

"It's quite enough to lose one ear," he cried. "You have wounded me twice, and now my turn has come."

Throwing himself on Chante-en-hiver, he gave his arm so powerful a blow that the pistol went off in the air; then seizing him by his wounded jaw, he twisted it until Chante-en-hiver uttered a howl of agony and fainted.

Radoub stepped over his prostrate form and left him lying in the embrasure.

"Now that I have made known to you my ultimatum, don't you dare to stir," he said. "Lie there, base reptile that you are! You may be very sure that I shall not amuse myself at present by killing you. Crawl at your leisure over the ground, under my feet You will have to die, anyhow. And then you will find out what nonsense your curé has been telling you. Away with you into the great mystery, peasant!"

And he sprang into the hall of the lower story.

"One can't see his hand before him," he grumbled.

Chante-en-hiver was convulsively writhing and moaning in his agony. Radoub looked back.

"Silence! Will you please to keep still, citizen without knowing it? I have nothing more to do with you; for I should scorn to put an end to your life. Now, leave me in peace."

And as he stood watching Chante-en-hiver, he plunged his hands restlessly into his hair.

"What am I to do? This is all very well, but here I am disarmed. I had two shots to fire, and you have wasted them, animal that you are. And besides, the smoke is so thick that it makes my eyes water;" and accidentally touching his tom ear, he cried out with pain.

"You have not gained much by getting my ear," he continued; "in fact, I would rather lose that than any other member; it's only an ornament, any way. You have scratched my shoulder, too, but that's of no consequence. You may die in peace, rustic; I forgive you."

He listened. The noise in the lower hall was frightful. The fight was raging more wildly than ever.

"Things are progressing downstairs. Hear them yelling 'Long live the King!' It must be acknowledged that they die nobly."

He stumbled over his sabre that lay on the floor, and as he picked it up, he said to Chante-en-hiver, who had ceased to moan, and who might very possibly be dead:—

"You see, man of the woods, my sabre is not of the slightest use for what I intended to do. However, I take it as a keepsake from you. But I needed my pistols. Devil take you, savage! What am I to do here? I am of no use at all."

As he advanced into the hall, tiding to see where he was and to get his bearings, he suddenly discovered in the shadow behind the central pillar a long table, and upon this table something faintly gleaming. He felt of the objects. They were muskets, pistols, and carbines, a whole row of fire-arms arranged in order and apparently only waiting for hands to seize them. This was the reserve prepared by the besieged for the second stage of the assault; indeed, it was a complete arsenal.

"This is a treasure indeed!" exclaimed Radoub; and half dazed with joy he flung himself upon them.

Then it was that he became formidable.

Near the table covered with fire-arms could be seen the wide-open door of the staircase leading to the upper and lower stories. Radoub dropped his sabre, seized a double-barrelled pistol in each hand, and instantly fired at random through the door leading to the spiral staircase; then he grasped a blunderbuss, firing that also, and directly afterwards a gun loaded with buckshot, whose fifteen balls made as much noise as a volley of grape-shot. After which, pausing to take breath, he shouted in thundering tones down the staircase, "Long live Paris!"

Seizing another blunderbuss bigger than the first he aimed it towards the vault of the winding staircase and paused again.

The uproar that ensued in the lower hall baffles description. Resistance is shattered by such unlooked for surprises.

Two of the balls of Radoub's triple discharge had taken effect, killing the older of the brothers Pique-en-bois and Houzard, who was M. de Quélen.

"They are upstairs," cried the Marquis.

At this exclamation; the men determined to abandon the *retirade* and no flock of birds could have surpassed the rapidity of their flight, as they rushed pell-mell towards the staircase, the Marquis urging them onward.

VICTOR HUGO

"Make haste!" he cried; "now we must show our courage by flight. Let us all go up to the second floor and there begin anew!"

He himself was the last man to leave the *retirade*, and to this act of bravery he owed his life.

Radoub, with his finger on the trigger, was concealed on the first landing of the staircase, watching the rout. The first men who appeared at the turn of the staircase received the discharge full in their faces and fell, and if the Marquis had been among them he would have been a dead man. Before Radoub had time to seize another weapon they had all passed, and the Marquis, moving more deliberately than the others, brought up the rear. Supposing as they did that the room on the first story was filled with the besiegers, they never paused until they reached the mirror room on the second story,—the room with the iron door and the sulphur match, where they must either capitulate or die.

Gauvain, quite as much surprised as any one of the besieged at the sound of the shots from the staircase, and having no idea of the source of this unexpected assistance, but availing himself of it without trying to understand, had leaped over the *retirade*, followed by his men, and, sword in hand, had driven the fugitives to the first story. There he found Radoub, who, with a military salute, said to him,—

"One moment, commander. It was I who did that. I had not forgotten Dol, so I followed your example, and took the enemy between two fires."

"You are a clever scholar," replied Gauvain with a smile.

One's eyes, like those of night birds, grow accustomed to a dim light after a certain time, and Gauvain discovered that Radoub was covered with blood.

"But you are wounded, comrade!"

"Oh, that is nothing, commander. What is an ear more or less? I got a sabre-thrust, too, but I don't mind it. When one breaks a pane of glass, of course one gets a few cuts; it is only a question of a little blood."

In the room in the first story conquered by Radoub the men halted. A lantern was brought, and Cimourdain rejoined Gauvain; whereupon they both took counsel together, and well they might. The besiegers were not in the confidence of the besieged; they had no means of knowing their scarcity of ammunition nor their want of powder; the second story was their very last intrenchment, and the assailants thought it not unlikely that the staircase might be mined.

One thing was certain,—the enemy could not escape. Those who were not killed, were like men locked in a prison. Lantenac was caught in the trap.

Resting upon this assurance, they felt that it would be well to devote a short time to considering the matter of bringing the affair to a crisis. Many of their men had already been killed. They must take measures to prevent too great a loss of life in the final assault.

There would be serious danger in this last attack. At the first onset they would no doubt find themselves exposed to a heavy fire.

Hostilities had ceased. The besiegers in possession of the ground-floor and the first story waited for orders from their chief to renew the fight. While Gauvain and Cimourdain held counsel together, Radoub listened in silence to their deliberations.

At last he timidly ventured another military salute.

"Commander!"

"What is it, Radoub?"

"Have I earned a small reward?"

"Certainly. Ask what you will."

"Then I ask to be the first one to go up."

It was impossible to refuse him; besides, he would have gone without permission.

XI

The Desperate

WHILE THESE DELIBERATIONS WERE IN progress on the first floor, a barricade was going up overhead. If success inspires fury, defeat fills men with rage. The two stories were about to clash in wild frenzy. There is a sense of intoxication in the assurance of victory. The assailants below were buoyed up by hope, that most powerful incentive to human effort when it is not counteracted by despair. All the despair was above,—calm, cold, and gloomy despair. When they reached this hall of refuge, their last resource, they proceeded first of all to bar the entrance, and in order to accomplish this object they decided that the blockading of the staircase would be more effectual than barring the door. Under such circumstances an obstacle through which one can both see what is going on and fight at the same time is a better defence than a closed door.

All the light they had, came from the torch which Imânus had stuck in the holder on the wall near the sulphur match.

One of those great heavy oaken chests such as formerly served the purpose of holding clothing and linen, before the invention of chests of drawers, stood in the hall, and this trunk they dragged out, and set up on end in the doorway of the staircase.

It fitted so closely into the space that it blocked up the entrance, leaving just room enough for the passage of a single man, thus affording them an excellent chance to kill their assailants one by one. It seemed somewhat doubtful whether any of them would attempt to enter.

Meanwhile, the obstructed entrance gave them a respite, during which they counted the men.

Of the original nineteen, but seven remained, including the Imânus; and he and the Marquis were the only ones who had not been wounded.

The five wounded men, who were still active,—for in the excitement of battle no man would succumb to anything less than a mortal wound,—were Chatenay, called Robi, Guinoiseau, Hoisnard, Branche-d'Or, Brin-d'Amour, and Grand-Francoeur. All the others were dead.

Their ammunition was exhausted, and their cartridge-boxes were empty. On counting the cartridges, they found that there were just four rounds apiece among the seven men.

Death was now their only resource. Behind them yawned the dreadful precipice. They could hardly have been nearer to the edge.

Meanwhile, the attack had just begun again,—slowly, it is true, but none the less determined. As the assailants advanced, they could hear the butt-end of their muskets strike on each stair by way of testing its security.

All means of escape were cut off. By way of the library? Six guns stood on the plateau, with matches lighted. Through the rooms overhead? To what avail? Opening on to the platform as they did, they simply offered an opportunity to hurl themselves from the summit of the tower into the depths below.

And now the seven survivors of this epic band realized the hopelessness of their position; within that solid wall, which, though protecting for the moment, would in the end betray, they were practically prisoners, although not as yet really captured.

The voice of the Marquis broke the silence.

"My friends, all is over," he said.

Then, after a pause, he added,—

"Grand-Francoeur will for the time being resume the duties of the Abbé Turmeau."

All knelt, rosary in hand. The sounds of the butt-ends of the besiegers' guns came nearer and nearer.

Grand-Francoeur, bleeding from a gunshot wound which had grazed his skull and torn away his hairy leathern cap, raised a crucifix in his right hand; the Marquis, a thorough sceptic, knelt on one knee.

"Let each one confess his sins aloud. Speak, Monseigneur."

And the Marquis replied, "I have killed my fellow-men."

"And I the same," said Hoisnard.

"And I," said Guinoiseau.

"And I," said Brin-d'Amour.

"And I," said Chatenay.

"And I," said the Imânus.

Then Grand-Francoeur repeated: "In the name of the Most Holy Trinity I absolve you. May your souls depart in peace."

"Amen!" replied all the voices.

The Marquis rose.

"Now let us die," he said.

"And kill, as well," said the Imânus.

The blows from the butt-ends of the muskets already shook the chest that stood within the door, barring the entrance.

"Turn your thoughts to God," said the priest; "earth no longer exists for you."

"Yes," rejoined the Marquis, "we are in the tomb."

All bowed their heads and smote their breasts. The priest and the Marquis alone remained standing. All eyes were fixed on the ground,— the priest and the peasants absorbed in prayer, the Marquis buried in his own thoughts. The chest, under the hammer-like strokes of the guns, sent forth its dismal reverberations.

At that moment a powerful, resonant voice suddenly rang out behind them, exclaiming,—

"I told you so, Monseigneur!"

All the heads turned in amazement.

A hole had just opened in the wall.

A stone, fitting perfectly with the others, but left without cement and provided with a pivot above and below, had revolved on itself like a turnstile, and, as it turned, had opened the wall. In revolving on its axis it opened a double passage to the right and left,—narrow, it is true, yet wide enough to allow a man to pass; and through this unexpected door could be seen the first steps of a spiral staircase. A man's face appeared in the opening, and the Marquis recognized Halmalo.

XII

The Deliverer

"Is that you, Halmalo?"

"It is I, Monseigneur. You see I was right about the turning stones, and that there is a way of escape. I have come just in time. But you must make haste; ten minutes more, and you will be in the heart of the forest."

"God is great!" said the priest.

"Save yourself, Monseigneur!" cried the men.

"Not until I have seen every one of you in safety," said the Marquis.

"But you must lead the way, Monseigneur," said the Abbé Turmeau.

"Not so," replied the Marquis; "I shall be the last man to leave."

And in a severe tone he continued:—

"Let there be no strife in this matter of generosity. We have no time for a display of magnanimity; your only chance for life is in escape. You hear my commands: make haste now, and take advantage of this outlet,—for which I thank you, Halmalo."

"Are we, then, to separate, Monsieur le Marquis?" asked the Abbé Turmeau.

"Certainly, after we have left the tower; otherwise, there would be small chance for escape."

"Will Monseigneur appoint some place of rendez-vous?"

"Yes; a glade in the forest,—the Pierre-Gauvaine. Do you know the spot?"

"We all know it."

"All those who are able to walk will find me there tomorrow at noonday."

"Every man will be on the spot."

"And then we will begin the war over again," said the Marquis.

Meanwhile Halmalo, bringing all his strength to bear on the turning stone, found that it would not stir, and therefore the opening could not be closed.

"Let us make haste, Monseigneur," he cried; "the stone will not move. I managed to open the passage, but now I cannot close it."

In fact, the stone, from a long disuse, had stiffened, so to speak, in its groove, and it was impossible to start it again.

"Monseigneur," said Halmalo, "I hoped to close the passage, so that when the Blues came in and found no one here they would not know what to make of it, and might imagine that you had all vanished in smoke. But the stone is not to be moved, and the enemy will find the outlet and probably pursue us; so let us lose not a minute, but reach the staircase as quickly as we can."

The Imânus laid his hand on Halmalo's shoulder.

"Comrade," he said, "how long will it take to go through this passage and reach the woods in safety?"

"Are any of the men seriously wounded?" asked Halmalo.

"None," they answered.

"In that case, a quarter of an hour will be sufficient."

"So if the enemy does not get in here for a quarter of an hour—" rejoined the Imânus.

"He might pursue, but he could not overtake us."

"But they will be upon us in five minutes," said the Marquis; "that old chest cannot keep them out much longer. A few blows from their muskets will settle the affair. A quarter of an hour! Who could hold them at bay for a quarter of an hour?"

"I," said the Imânus.

"You, Gouge-le-Bruant?"

"Yes, I, Monseigneur. Listen. Out of six men five of us are wounded. I have not even a scratch."

"Nor I either," said the Marquis.

"Yes, but you are the chief, Monseigneur. I am a soldier. The chief and the soldier are two different persons."

"Our duties are not alike, it is true."

"Monseigneur, at this moment we have but one duty between us, and that is to save your life."

The Imânus turned to his companions.

"Comrades," he said, "we must hold the enemy in check and delay pursuit until the last moment. Listen. I have not lost a drop of blood; not having been wounded, I am as strong as ever, and can hold out longer than any of the others. Go now, but leave me your weapons, and I promise to make good use of them. I will undertake to keep the enemy at bay a good half-hour. How many loaded pistols are there?"

"Four."

"Put them down on the floor."

They did as he required.

"That is well. I remain here, and they will find some one to entertain them. Now, get away as fast as you can."

In moments of imminent peril gratitude finds but brief expression. Hardly had they time to press his hand.

"We shall soon meet again," said the Marquis.

"I hope not, Monseigneur,—not quite at once, for I am about to die."

One by one they made their way down the narrow staircase, the wounded in advance; and as they went, the Marquis drew a pencil from his note-book and wrote a few words on the stone that, refusing to turn, had thus left an open passage-way.

"Come, Monseigneur, you are the only one left," said Halmalo, as he went down.

The Marquis followed him, and Imânus remained alone.

XIII

The Executioner

Upon the flagstones which formed the only floor of the hall the four pistols had been placed, and the Imânus, taking two of them, one in each hand, advanced stealthily towards the entrance of the staircase, obstructed and concealed by the chest.

The assailants evidently suspected a snare. They might be on the verge of one of those decisive explosions that overwhelm both conquerer and conquered in one common ruin. In proportion as the first attack had been impetuous, the last was cautious and deliberate. They could not, or perhaps did not care to batter down the chest by main force; they had destroyed the bottom of it with the butts of their muskets and pierced its lid with their bayonets; and now through these holes they attempted to see the interior of the hall before venturing within it.

The glimmer of the lanterns, by means of which the staircase was lighted, fell through these chinks, and the Imânus, catching sight of an eye peering through one of them, instantly adjusted the barrel of his pistol to the spot and pulled the trigger. No sooner had he fired than to his great joy he heard a terrible cry. The ball passed through the head by way of the eye, and the soldier, interrupted in his gazing, fell backward down the staircase. The assailants had broken open the lower part of the lid in two places, forming something not unlike loop-holes; and the Imânus, availing himself of one of these apertures, thrust his arm in it and fired his second pistol at random among the mass of the besiegers. The ball probably rebounded, for several cries were heard, as though three or four had been killed or wounded, and a great tumult ensued as the men, losing their footing, fell back in confusion. The Imânus threw down the two pistols which he had discharged, and caught up the remaining ones; grasping one in each hand, he peered through the holes in the chest and beheld the result of his first assault.

The besiegers had retreated down the stairs and the dying lay writhing in agony upon the steps; the form of the spiral staircase prevented him from seeing beyond three or four steps.

He paused.

"So much time gained," he thought to himself.

Meanwhile, he saw a man crawling up the steps flat on his stomach, and just at that moment, a little farther down, the head of a soldier emerged from behind the central pillar of the winding stairs. The Imânus aimed at this head and fired. The soldier fell back with a cry, and as the Imânus was transferring his last pistol from his left hand into his right, he himself felt a horrible pain, and in his turn uttered a yell of agony. Some tone had thrust a sabre into his vitals, and it was the very man whom he had seen crawling along the stair, whose hand, entering the other hole in the bottom of the chest, had plunged a sabre into the body of the Imânus.

The wound was frightful. The abdomen was pierced through and through.

The Imânus did not fall. He ground his teeth as he muttered, "That is good!"

Then, tottering, and with great effort, he dragged himself back to the torch still burning near the iron door; this he seized, after putting down his pistol, and then, supporting with his left hand the protruding intestines, with his right he lowered the torch until it touched the sulphur-match, which caught fire, and the wick blazed up in an instant.

Dropping the still burning torch upon the ground, he grasped his pistol, and although he had fallen on the flags, he lifted himself and used the scanty breath that was left him to fan the flame, which, starting, ran along until it passed under the iron door and reached the bridge-castle.

When he beheld the triumph of his villanous scheme, taking to himself more credit for this crime than for his self-sacrifice, the man who had acted the part of a hero and who now degraded himself to the level of an assassin smiled as he was about to die, and muttered:—

"They will remember me. I take vengeance on their little ones, in behalf of our own little king shut up in the Temple."

XIV

The Imânus also Escapes

AT THAT MOMENT A LOUD voice was heard, and the chest, violently hurled aside, was shattered into fragments,—giving passage to a man, who, sabre in hand, rushed into the hall.

"It is I, Radoub!" he cried. "Who wants to fight me? I am bored to death with waiting, and I must run the risk. I don't care what happens; at all events, I have disembowelled one of you, and now I come to attack you all. Follow me or not, as you like; but here I am. How many are you?"

It was indeed Radoub himself, and he alone. After the slaughter that the Imânus had made on the staircase, Gauvain, suspecting some hidden mine, had withdrawn his men and was taking counsel with Cimourdain.

Amid the darkness, where the expiring torch cast but a feeble glimmer, Radoub, sabre in hand, stood on the threshold and repeated his question,—

"I am alone. How many are you?"

Receiving no reply, he advanced. Just then one of those sudden flashes, emitted from time to time by a dying fire,—a kind of throbbing light, which might be compared with a human sob,—burst from the torch and illuminated the entire hall.

Radoub caught sight of one of the little mirrors hung on the wall, and approaching it, inspected his bloody face and lacerated ear, saying as he did so,—

"What a horrible mutilation!"

Then he turned, surprised to see the hall empty, and cried,—

"No one here! not a soul!"

His eyes lighted on the revolving stone, the passage, and the staircase.

"Ah, I understand! they have taken to their heels! Come on, comrades! come on! They have all run away; they have gone, evaporated, dissolved, vanished. There was a crack in this old jug of a tower; there is the hole through which they got out, the rascals! How are we ever to get the better of Pitt and Coburg, when men play tricks like these? The Devil himself must have come to their aid. There is no one here!"

A pistol-shot was fired, and a ball, grazing his elbow, flattened itself against the wall.

"Ah! some one is here, then! To whom do I owe this delicate attention?"

"To me," replied a voice.

Radoub, peering through the shadows, at last descried the form of Imânus.

"Aha!" he cried, "I have got one of you! The others have escaped, but you will not get off."

"Is that your opinion?" replied the Imânus. Radoub made one step forward and paused.

"Hey I who are you, lying on the ground there?"

"I am a man on the ground, who laughs at those who are on the feet."

"What is that in your right hand?"

"A pistol."

"And in your left hand?"

"My intestines."

"I take you prisoner."

"I defy you to do it."

And the Imânus, stooping over the burning wick, blew feebly upon its flame, and with that breath expired.

A few moments later, Gauvain and Cimourdain, followed by the others, entered the hall. They all saw the opening, and after searching every corner and exploring the staircase which led down into the ravine, they felt very sure that the enemy had escaped. They shook the Imânus, but he was dead. Gauvain, with lantern in hand, examined the stone which had furnished the fugitives with a means of escape. He had heard of this revolving stone, but he too had always regarded it as a fable. While he was examining the stone he noticed certain words written with a pencil; and holding the lantern nearer, he read as follows:—

"Au revoir, Monsieur le Vicomte.
"Lantenac."

Guéchamp had joined Gauvain. Pursuit was manifestly out of the question; the escape had been successful; everything was in favor of the fugitives,—the entire country, the underbrush, the ravines, the copses, and even the inhabitants themselves. No doubt they were far enough away by this time; there was no possibility of finding them, and the entire forest of Fougères was one vast hiding-place. What was to be done? They saw themselves forced to begin the whole affair over again. Gauvain and Guéchamp exchanged their regrets and conjectures.

Cimourdain listened gravely without uttering a word.

"By the way, Guéchamp, how was it about the ladder?"

"It has not come, commander."

"But we saw a wagon with an escort of gendarmes."

"It was not bringing the ladder," replied Guéchamp.

"What, then, was it bringing?"

"The guillotine," said Cimourdain.

XV

Never Put a Watch and Key in the Same Pocket

The Marquis de Lantenac was not so far away as they supposed, although he was in perfect safety, and beyond their reach.

He had followed Halmalo.

The staircase by which they had descended, following the other fugitives, ended in a narrow passage quite near the ravine and the arches of the bridge. This passage led into a deep natural fissure in the ground which formed a connecting link between the ravine and the forest. In this fissure, twisting and turning as it did through impenetrable thickets and utterly hidden from the human eye, no man could ever have been captured; he had but to follow the example of a snake, and his safety was assured. The entrance to this secret passage was so overgrown with brambles, that its constructors had deemed it unnecessary to provide it with any other screen.

The Marquis had now no further need even to consider the matter of disguise. Since his arrival in Brittany he had continued to wear the peasant dress, feeling himself to be more truly a grand seigneur when thus attired. He had contented himself with taking off his sword, unfastening and throwing aside the belt.

When Halmalo and the Marquis emerged from the passage into the fissure, nothing was to be seen of the five others,—Guinoiseau,

Hoisnard Branche-d'Or, Brin d'Amour, Chatenay, and the Abbé Turmeau.

"They have lost no time," said Halmalo.

"Follow their example," replied the Marquis.

"Does Monseigneur wish me to leave him?"

"Of course; I have told you so already. A man who is trying to escape must remain alone if he would insure success; one man can often pass where two would find it impossible. Were we together, we should attract attention and imperil each other."

"Does Monseigneur know the neighborhood?"

"Yes."

"And the rendez-vous is still to be the same,—at the Pierre-Gauvaine?"

"Tomorrow at noon."

"I will be there. We shall all be there."

Halmalo paused.

"Ah, Monseigneur, when I remember the time we were alone together on the open sea, when I wanted to kill you, you who were my lord and master and might have told me, but did not! What a man you are!"

The sole reply of the Marquis was, "England is our only resource. In fifteen days the English must be in France."

"I have a great many things to tell Monseigneur. I have given all his messages."

"We will attend to all that tomorrow."

"Farewell till then, Monseigneur."

"By the way, are you hungry?"

"Perhaps I am, Monseigneur. I was in such a hurry to get here, that I have forgotten whether I had anything to eat today or not."

The Marquis drew from his pocket a cake of chocolate, broke it in two, and giving one half to Halmalo, he began to eat the other himself.

"Monseigneur," said Halmalo, "you will find the ravine on your right, and the forest on your left."

"Very well. Leave me now. Go your own way."

Halmalo obeyed, and was at once lost in the darkness. At first there was a rustling of the underbrush soon followed by silence, and in a few moments every trace of his passage had disappeared. This land of the Bocage, bristling with forests and labyrinths, was the fugitives' best ally. Men vanished before one's very eyes. It was this facility for rapid disappearance that made our armies pause before this ever-retreating Vendée, and rendered its combatants so formidable in their flight.

The Marquis stood motionless. Although he was a man who kept his feelings under perfect control, he was not insensible to the joy of breathing the fresh air, after having lived so long in an atmosphere of blood and carnage. To be rescued at a moment when all seemed utterly lost, to find one's self in safety after gazing into one's own grave, to be snatched from death to life, is a severe shock even for such a man as Lantenac; and although this was by no means his only experience of the kind, he could not at once subdue his agitation. For a moment he admitted to himself his own satisfaction, but straightway suppressed an emotion that was akin to joy.

Drawing out his watch he struck the hour. He wondered what time it might be, and to his great surprise discovered that it was but ten o'clock.

When one has just passed through some terrible crisis wherein life and death have hung in the balance it is always astonishing to discover that those minutes so crowded with action were no longer than any others. The warning cannon had been fired shortly before sunset, and half an hour later, just at dusk, between seven and eight o'clock, the assault on the Tourgue began; hence this tremendous combat beginning at eight and ending at ten, this epic, as one might call it, had consumed just one hundred and twenty minutes. Catastrophes often descend like a flash of lightning, and events are marvellously fore-shortened, and when one pauses to reflect, it would be surprising were it otherwise; two hours' resistance offered by so small a band against a force vastly superior to itself was extraordinary, and this struggle of nineteen against four thousand could not be called a brief one.

But it was time to go. Halmalo must by this time be far away, and the Marquis felt that prudence no longer required him to remain there. He put his watch back into his waistcoat pocket, but not into the one from which he had taken it, for he noticed that in that one it came in contact with the key of the iron door which the Imânus had brought him, and there was danger of breaking the crystal. Just as he was on the point of taking the left-hand turning towards the forest, he fancied he saw a feint ray of light.

He turned, and through the underbrush which all at once stood out against a red background, thus revealing its minutest details with absolute distinctness, he beheld a bright glare along the ravine very near the spot where he was standing. At first, he turned in that direction, then changed his mind as the folly of exposing himself to that light occurred to him; whatever it might be, it was really no affair of his in any event. Once more he started to follow Halmalo's directions, and advanced several steps towards the forest.

All at once, buried and hidden by the brambles as he was, he heard above his head a terrible cry; it seemed to come from the very edge of the plateau, above the ravine. The Marquis raised his eyes and paused.

Book V

In Dæmone Deus

I

Found, but Lost

WHEN MICHELLE FLÉCHARD FIRST PERCEIVED the tower reddened by the rays of the setting sun, it was more than a league away; and this woman, nothing daunted by the distance, though scarcely able to put one foot before the other, kept bravely on her way. Women may be weak, but mothers are strong.

The sun had set: twilight came on, followed by the darkness of night; as she walked along, far away in the distance, from some invisible belfry, probably that of Parigné, she heard the clock strike eight, then nine. From time to time she paused to listen to something that sounded like heavy blows; but it might have been only the uncertain noises peculiar to the night.

She walked straight onward, crushing the furze and prickly heather beneath her bleeding feet. She was guided by a faint light issuing from the distant keep, which bathed the tower in a mysterious glow while it defined its outlines against the surrounding gloom. This light changed in measure as the sounds grew loud or faint.

The vast plateau across which Michelle Fléchard made her way was completely covered with grass and heather; neither house nor tree was to be seen. Its rise was almost imperceptible, and as far as the eye could reach, its long line was clearly defined against the dark horizon dotted with stars. She was supported, as she climbed, by the sight of the tower constantly before her eyes, and as she drew nearer, it gradually increased in size.

As we have just remarked, the muffled reports and the pallid gleams of light that issued from the tower were intermittent; dying away and then returning as they did, it seemed to the wretched mother in her distress like some agonizing enigma.

Suddenly they ceased, and with the sound, the light too died away; there was a moment of absolute silence, an appalling tranquillity, and then it was that Michelle Fléchard reached the edge of the plateau.

She saw beneath her feet a ravine, whose depths were hidden by the dim shadows of night; at a short distance, on the top of the plateau, the confused mass of wheels, slopes; and embrasures which formed the battery; and before her, indistinctly lighted by the burning matches of the guns, an enormous edifice that seemed built of shadows blacker than those that surrounded it.

This building consisted of a bridge, whose arches rested in the ravine, together with a kind of castle erected on the bridge, both castle and bridge supported by a round and lofty mass of masonry; this was the tower which had been that mother's distant goal. One could see the lights moving to and fro behind the loop-holes of the tower, and it was evident, from the noise issuing therefrom, that it was crowded with men, whose shadows were projected even as high as platform.

Michelle Fléchard could distinguish the vedettes of the camp near the battery, but the darkness and the underbrush concealed her from their view.

She had reached the edge of the plateau, and was so close to the bridge that it seemed as if she could almost touch it with her hand. The deep ravine alone separated her from it. She could distinguish even in the darkness the three stories of the bridge-castle.

She knew not how long she had been standing there, having lost all consciousness of time, absorbed in a silent contemplation of that yawning chasm and the gloomy building. What was it that was going on within. Was this the Tourgue? She felt that restless sense of expectation peculiar to travellers who have either just arrived or are on the eve of departure. As she stood listening and gazing around, she tried to think why she was there. Suddenly all objects vanished before her eyes.

A veil of smoke had suddenly obscured the object she was watching. A sharp pain forced her to close her eyes; but she had no sooner done so, than a light flashed upon them so intensely brilliant that her eyelids seemed transparent, and when she opened them again, the night had changed into day, but the light of that day, dreadful to look upon, was born of fire. What she saw was the outburst of a conflagration.

The smoke had changed from black to scarlet, from which at times a mighty flame leaped forth, with those fierce contortions peculiar to the lightning and the serpent. It darted forth like a tongue from some monstrous jaw; but it was really a window filled with fire, whose iron bars were already red hot,—a casement in the lower story of the bridge-castle, and the only part of the entire building that could now be seen. Even the plateau was shrouded in the smoke, and the edge of the ravine alone could be distinguished against the crimson flames.

Michelle Fléchard looked on in amazement. Smoke is a cloud; dreams come from the clouds; hardly realizing what she saw, she knew not what to do. Should she stay, or try to make her escape? She almost felt herself transported beyond the actual world.

There came a gust of wind, that rent the curtain of smoke and revealed through this gap the tragic Bastile, in all its grandeur, with its keep, its bridge, and its castle, dazzling and terrible, magnificently gilded by the light of the flames which were reflected upon it from summit to base. Michelle Fléchard could see everything by the awful glare of the flames.

Only the lower story of the bridge-castle was as yet burning.

Above it could be seen the two other stories, still intact, though resting as it were upon a bed of flames. From the edge of the plateau where she stood, through the smoke and fire, Michelle Fléchard caught an occasional glimpse of the interior. All the windows were open. Through those of the second story, which were very large, she could see cases along the walls, which seemed to her to be filled with books; and in front of one of the windows, lying on the floor in the shadow, she noticed a little group whose outline had no definite form; it lay in a heap, like a nest or brood of young birds, and from time to time she thought she saw it stir.

She watched it.

What could this little group of shadows be?

Sometimes she fancied it was composed of living forms. She was feverish and exhausted, for she had not eaten a mouthful since morning, had walked incessantly, and she felt as if she were the victim of some sort of hallucination which she instinctively mistrusted. But her eyes were now riveted upon this dark group of objects, whatsoever they might be; doubtless it was something inanimate lying there upon the floor in the hall directly over the conflagration.

Suddenly, as though inspired by a will of its own, the fire flung forth a jet of flame upon the dead ivy that mantled the very wall on which Michelle Fléchard stood gazing. It was as if it had just discovered this network of withered branches; a spark greedily seized upon it, and the fire began to rise from twig to twig with the frightful rapidity of a powder-train. In the twinkling of an eye the flame reached the second story, and from thence a light was thrown into the one below. A vivid glare brought into instantaneous relief three little sleeping children.

It was a charming group, their little legs and arms intertwined, their eyelids closed, their faces sweetly smiling.

The mother knew her children.

She uttered a terrible cry.

That cry of inexpressible anguish is given only to mothers. No sound can be more savage and yet pathetic. Uttered by a woman, it is like the cry of a she-wolf; and when one hears it from a wolf it might well come from a woman.

This cry of Michelle Fléchard was a howl. Hecuba howled, Homer tells us.

And this was the cry just heard by the Marquis de Lantenac.

We saw him pause to listen.

He was between the outlet of the passage through which Halmalo had guided him in his escape, and the ravine. Through the tangled wildwood about him he saw the burning bridge, and the Tourgue reddened by the reflection; he pushed aside the branches, and discovered on the opposite side, above his head, on the edge of the plateau, in front of the burning castle, and in the full light of the conflagration, the haggard and woful face of a woman bending over the ravine.

This face was no longer the face of Michelle Fléchard; it was a Medusa. There is something formidable in intense agony. This peasant woman had changed into one of the Eumenides. The unknown rustic, low, ignorant, stupid, had suddenly taken on the epic proportions of despair. Great sorrows expand the soul to gigantic proportions. This mother was the embodiment of maternity. A summary of humanity rises to the superhuman; she stood towering above the edge of the ravine, within sight of the conflagration, in presence of that crime like a power from beyond the grave. Moaning like a wild beast, she stood in the attitude of a goddess, with a countenance like a flaming mask, hurling forth imprecations. Nothing could have been more imperious than the lightning that flashed from those eyes drowned in tears; her look was like a thunderbolt hurled against the conflagration.

The Marquis listened. These reproaches fell upon his head; he heard her inarticulate, heart-rending cries, more like sobs than words:—

"My children, oh, my Lord! They are my children! Help! Fire! Fire! Fire! You must be brigands! Is there no one here? But my children will be burned to death! Such doings! Georgette! My children! Gros-Alain! René-Jean! What can this mean? Who put my children there? They are sleeping. I am mad! Oh, this is impossible! Help!"

Meanwhile, a great commotion was going on in the Tourgue and on the plateau. The whole camp had rushed to the fire, which had just broken out. The besiegers, after encountering the grape-shot, had now to struggle against the fire. Gauvain, Cimourdain, and Guéchamp were giving orders. What could be done? A few buckets of water might possibly be drawn from the slender stream in the ravine. The edge of the plateau was covered with terrified faces, gazing at the sight with ever-increasing distress; and it was an awful scene.

There they stood looking on, but none could lend a helping hand.

By way of the ivy the flames had risen to the upper story, and finding there a granary filled with straw had rushed upon it; and that entire granary was now on fire, the flames merrily dancing. A dreadful sight is the glee of a fire! It was like the breath of fiends fanning a funereal pile. One could fancy that the terrible Imânus was in person there, metamorphosed into a whirlwind of sparks, living in this cruel life of flame, and that his horrible soul had been transformed into a conflagration. The flames had not yet reached the library story; its lofty ceiling and massive walls had retarded the fatal moment that was now drawing near. The flames, like tongues of fire, darted upward from the story below; while the flames from above touched the stones, as if carressing them with the dread kiss of death. Beneath it lay a cave of lava, above an arch of fiery coals. Were the floor to cave in, all would be precipitated into a bed of red-hot ashes; were the ceiling to give way, they would be buried beneath the glowing coals. René-Jean, Gros-Alain, and Georgette had not yet waked; they were sleeping the sound and innocent sleep of childhood; and through the sheets of flame and smoke which now hid, now revealed the windows, they could be seen in this fiery grotto against a background of meteoric light, calm, graceful, and motionless, like three heavenly cherubs confidingly slumbering in hell. A tiger might have wept to see such blossoms in that furnace,— their cradles in the grave.

Meanwhile the mother wrung her hands:—

"Fire! Fire! I am crying fire! Are they all deaf, that no one comes? They are burning up my children! Come, you men over yonder! To think of the days and days I have walked, and to find them like this! Fire! Help! They are angels, nothing short of angels! What have those innocents done? They shot me, and now they are burning them! Who does such things as these? Help! Save my children! Don't you hear me? If I were a dog, you would have pity on me! My children! They are asleep! Ah, Georgette, I see her dear little body! René-Jean! Gros-Alain! Those are their names. You can see well enough that I am their mother. Such abominable doings go on in these days! I have walked for days and nights. Why, I talked about them this very morning to a woman. Help! Help! Fire! They must be monsters! This is horrible! The oldest one is not five years old and the baby not two. I can see their little naked legs. They are asleep. Holy Virgin! Heaven gives them to me and Hell snatches them back again. Just think how far I have walked! The children that I fed with my milk,—I who felt so wretched because I couldn't find them! Have pity on me! I want my children; I must have them! And to think of them there in the fire! See my poor bleeding feet. Help! It cannot be that there are men on earth who would let those poor little creatures die like that! Help! Murder! Who ever saw the like? Ah, the brigands! What is that dreadful house? They stole them from me to murder them. Merciful Jesus! I want my children. Oh, I don't know what to do! They must not die! Help! Help! Help! Oh, I shall curse Heaven if they die like that!"

Simultaneously with the mother's entreaty other voices rang out on the plateau and the ravine.

"A ladder!"

"There is none."

"Water!"

"None to be had!"

"Up in the tower there, in the second story, there is a door."

"It is iron."

"Break it in!"

"Impossible."

Here the mother redoubled her desperate appeals.

"Fire! Help! Make haste, or kill me at once! My children! My children! Oh, that terrible fire! Throw me into the fire, but save their lives!"

In the intervals between her cries could be heard the constant crackling of the flames.

The Marquis felt in his pocket and his hand met the key to the iron door. Then stooping below the arch, through which he had just escaped, he re-entered the passage from which he had so lately emerged.

II

From the Door of Stone to that of Iron

A WHOLE ARMY DRIVEN HALF wild by its enforced inaction in the presence of danger; four thousand men unable to save three children,—such was the situation.

In point of fact, they had no ladder; the one sent from Javené had not arrived; the flames spread as from a yawning crater; it was simply absurd to attempt to extinguish them with the water from the half-dried brook in the ravine; one might as well empty a glass of water into a volcano.

Cimourdain, Guéchamp, and Radoub had gone down into the ravine. Gauvain had returned to the hall on the second story of the Tourgue, where the turning stone, the secret passage, and the iron door of the library were to be found; it was there that the sulphur match had been lighted by the Imânus, and there the fire had originated.

Gauvain had brought with him twenty sappers. Their last resource was to force open the iron door. Its fastenings were terribly strong.

They went at it with their axes, dealing violent blows. The axes broke. One of the sappers exclaimed,—

"Steel shivers like glass against that iron."

In fact, the door was composed of double sheets of wrought-iron bolted together, each sheet three inches thick.

Then they took iron bars and tried to pry the door open from below. The iron bars broke.

"One would think they were matches," said the sapper.

"Nothing less than a cannon-ball could open that door," muttered Gauvain, gloomily. "We should have to mount a field-piece up here."

"But even then—" replied the sapper.

For a moment they stood in despair, and their arms fell helpless by their sides. With a sense of defeat, these men stood in speechless dismay, gazing upon that door so awful in its immobility. They caught a glimpse of the red reflection from beneath it. Behind them, the fire was spreading.

The frightful body of the Imânus was there, dread victor that he was.

But a few minutes more, and the entire building might fall into ruins.

What could they do? The last ray of hope was gone.

Gauvain, whose eyes were riveted on the revolving stone and the opening through which the escape had been made, cried in the bitterness of his exasperation,—

"And yet the Marquis de Lantenac escaped through that door!"

"And returns," said a voice.

Against the stone setting of the secret passage appeared a white head. It was the Marquis.

It was many a year since Gauvain had seen him so close at hand. He drew back.

Every man present stood as if petrified.

The Marquis held a large key in his hand; with one haughty glance he compelled the sappers who stood in his path to make way for him, walked at once to the iron door, stooped beneath the arch, and put the key into the lock.

It creaked in the lock, the door opened, they saw the fiery gulf; the Marquis entered it.

With head erect and steady step he strode forward. And those who looked on shuddered as their eyes followed his receding form.

He had barely taken a few steps in the burning hall, before the inlaid floor, undermined by the fire and shaken by his tread, gave way behind him, setting a chasm between him and the door. The Marquis pursued his way, never once turning his head, and vanished in the smoke.

Nothing more was seen.

Had he succeeded in making his way; or had another fiery chasm opened under his feet; or had he but ended his own life? No one could tell. A wall of smoke and flames rose before them. Whether dead or alive, the Marquis was on the other side.

III

Where the Sleeping Children Wake

MEANWHILE, THE LITTLE ONES HAD at last opened their eyes.

The fire, although it had not yet reached the library, cast a red reflection on the ceiling. It was not the kind of dawn the children knew. They were gazing at it,—Georgette utterly absorbed.

The conflagration showed forth all its glories; the black hydra and the scarlet dragon appeared amid the smoke-wreaths in all their sombre and vermilion hues. Great sparks shot out into the distance, lighting up the gloom like contending comets pursuing one another. Fire is a prodigal; its furnaces abound in jewels which they scatter to the winds; and it is to some purpose that charcoal is identical with the diamond. From the fissures opened in the wall of the third story, the embers were showering down into the ravine like cascades of jewels; the heaps of straw and oats burning in the granary began to pour in a stream through the windows like avalanches of gold-dust,—the oats changing to amethysts, and the straw to carbuncles.

"Pretty!" cried Georgette.

All three were now sitting up.

"Ah!" cried the mother, "they are awake!"

When René-Jean rose, then Gros-Alain rose also, and Georgette followed.

René-Jean stretched himself, and going towards the window, exclaimed, "I am hot!"

"Me hot!" repeated Georgette.

The mother called them.

"Children! René! Alain! Georgette!"

The children looked round. They were trying to find out what it all meant. Where men feel terrified, children are simply curious; he who is open to surprise is not easily alarmed; ignorance is closely allied to intrepidity. Children have so little claim upon hell, that were they to behold it, it would but excite their admiration.

The mother kept repeating,—

"René! Alain! Georgette!"

René-Jean turned; that voice roused him from his reverie. Children have short memories, but their recollections are swift; the entire past is for them but as yesterday. When René-Jean saw his mother, it seemed to him the most natural thing that could happen, surrounded as he was by strange things; and with a dim consciousness of needing support, he called, "Mamma!"

"Mamma!" said Gros-Alain.

"M'ma!" repeated Georgette.

And she stretched out her little arms.

The mother shrieked, "My children!"

The three children came to the window-ledge; fortunately, the conflagration was not on this side.

"I am too warm," said René-Jean; then added, "it burns"! and he looked for his mother.

"Why don't you come, mamma?" he said.

"Tum, m'ma," repeated Georgette.

The mother, with her hair streaming, torn and bleeding as she was, let herself roll from bush to bush, down into the ravine. There stood Cimourdain and Guéchamp, as powerless in their position as Gauvain was in his. The soldiers, in despair at their helplessness, were swarming around them. The heat would have seemed unbearable, had any one noticed it. They were discussing the escarpment of the bridge, the height of the arches and of the different stories, the inaccessible windows, and the necessity for speedy action. Three stories to climb, with no means of access. Radoub, wounded by a sabre-thrust in the shoulder, his ear lacerated, dripping with sweat and blood, had appeared upon the scene. He saw Michelle Fléchard.

"What have we here,—the woman who was shot come to life again?"

"My children!" cried the mother.

"You are right!" replied Radoub; "this is no time to inquire about ghosts." And he started to scale the bridge,—a useless attempt. He dug his nails into the stone, clung thus for a few seconds, but the smooth layers of stone offered neither cleft nor projection; they were as accurately fitted one upon the other as if the wall had just been built, and Radoub fell back. The fire was still increasing, terrible to behold. They could see the three fair heads framed in the window lighted by the glowing flames. Then Radoub shook his fist towards Heaven as though he beheld some one, and exclaimed,—

"Has Almighty God no mercy?"

The mother, kneeling, clasped her arms around one of the piers of the bridge, crying, "Mercy!"

The hollow sound of crashing timbers mingled with the crackling of the flames. The glass doors of the bookcases in the library cracked and fell with a crash. There could be no doubt that the woodwork was giving way. Human strength was of no avail. One moment, and the entire building would be swallowed up in the abyss. They were only waiting for the final catastrophe. The little voices could be heard repeating, "Mamma, mamma!" They were in paroxysms of terror.

Suddenly against the crimson background of the flames a tall figure came into view standing in the window next to the one where the children stood.

All heads were raised, all eyes were riveted upon the spot. A man up there, in the hall of the library,—a man in that furnace! His face looked black against the flames, but his hair was white. They recognized the Marquis de Lantenac.

He vanished, but only to appear again.

This appalling old man stood in the window, managing an enormous ladder. It was the escape-ladder, which had been lying along the library wall, and which he had dragged to the window. He seized one end of it, and with the masterly agility of an athlete he let it slip out of the window over the outer ledge down into the depths of the ravine. Radoub, standing below, wild with excitement, received the ladder in his outstretched arms, and clasping it to his breast, cried,—

"Long live the Republic!"

"Long live the King!" replied the Marquis.

"You may cry what you please," muttered Radoub, "and talk all the nonsense you like; you are a very angel of mercy."

The ladder was firmly planted, and communication thereby established between the burning hall and the ground. Twenty men, led by Radoub, rushed forward, and in the twinkling of an eye grouped themselves on the ladder from top to bottom, leaning back against the rungs, like masons carrying stones up and down, thus forming a human ladder over the wooden one. Radoub, standing on the uppermost rung, facing towards the fire, was just on a level with the window.

The little army, dispersed across the heath and along the slopes, overcome by contending emotions, hastened towards the plateau down into the ravine and up to the platform of the tower. Again they lost sight of the Marquis, but he reappeared, carrying a child in his arms.

The applause was tremendous.

He had caught up the first child that came within his reach, and it chanced to be Gros-Alain, who cried out,—

"I am frightened!"

The Marquis handed him to Radoub, who passed him on to a soldier standing just behind him, a little farther down, who in his turn delivered him to the next one; and while Gros-Alain, screaming with terror, was thus transferred from hand to hand until he reached the bottom of the ladder, the Marquis, disappearing for a moment, returned to the window with René-Jean, who, struggling and crying, slapped Radoub just as the Marquis handed him to the sergeant.

Again the Marquis went back into the burning room. Georgette was the only one left. She smiled, and this man of granite felt the tears spring to his eyes. "What is your name?" he asked.

"'Orgette," she said.

He took her still smiling in his arms, and as he gave her to Radoub his conscience, austerely pure, albeit darkened, succumbed to the overpowering charm of innocence, and the old man kissed the child.

"It is the little midget!" exclaimed the soldiers; and so Georgette in her turn, amid the cries of admiration, was also passed from hand to hand till she reached the ground. The soldiers clapped their hands and stamped their feet. The old grenadiers sobbed aloud as she smiled upon them.

The mother stood at the foot of the ladder, panting, frantic, intoxicated by this sudden transition from hell to paradise. Excess of joy tears the heart in a fashion of its own. She held out her arms, first receiving Gros-Alain, then René-Jean, then Georgette. She covered them with frenzied kisses; then bursting into a laugh she fell swooning to the ground.

Then rose a loud cry,—

"All are saved!"

And so indeed they were, except the old man.

But no one thought of him, not even he himself perhaps. For several instants he stood dreamily near the window-ledge, as though he would give the fiery abyss time to make up its mind; then deliberately, slowly, and proudly he stepped over the window-sill, and without turning, holding himself upright and perfectly erect, with his back towards the rungs, the conflagration behind and the precipice before and beneath him, with all the majesty of a supernatural being he proceeded to descend the ladder in silence. Those who were on the ladder rushed down; a thrill ran through the witnesses, and they drew back in holy horror before this man who was approaching them like a vision. But stately and grave he continued his descent into the darkness before him, drawing nearer and nearer as they recoiled before his approach. His marble pallor revealed not a wrinkle; his ghost-like eyes, cold as steel, neither glittered nor flashed. As he drew near these men, whose startled eyes were fixed upon him in the darkness, he seemed to grow at every step; the ladder shook and echoed beneath his ominous tread; he might have been compared to the statue of the commander returning to his tomb.

When he reached the bottom and had stepped from the last rung of the ladder to the ground, a hand seized him by the collar. He turned.

"I arrest you," said Cimourdain.

"I approve," replied Lantenac.

Book VI

After Victory, Struggle Begins

I

Lantenac Taken

THE MARQUIS HAD INDEED DESCENDED into his tomb.

They led him away.

The oubliette dungeon on the ground-floor of the Tourgue was forthwith reopened under Cimourdain's severe superintendence; a lamp was placed there, a jug of water, and a loaf of soldier's bread; a bundle of straw was flung in; and in less than a quarter of an hour from the instant when the priest's hand had seized upon him, the dungeon door closed upon Lantenac.

This done, Cimourdain joined Gauvain; at that moment the clock from the distant church of Parigné struck eleven: Cimourdain said to Gauvain:—

"I am about to summon a court-martial. You will not join it; you are a Gauvain as well as Lantenac. You are too nearly related to be a judge; and I do not approve of Égalité sitting in judgment upon Capet. The court-martial will consist of three judges,—one officer, Captain Guéchamp, one non-commissioned officer, Sergeant Radoub, and myself, who will preside. You need have no further concern in the matter. We shall be governed by the decree of the Convention; all we have to do is simply to prove the identity of the ci-devant Marquis de Lantenac. Tomorrow the court-martial, the day after tomorrow the guillotine. The Vendée is dead."

Gauvain made no reply; and Cimourdain, preoccupied with the important business that lay before him, departed. He now had to appoint the hour and select the place. Like Lequinio at Granville, Talien at Bordeaux, Châlier at Lyons, and Saint-Just at Strasbourg, he had made a practice of superintending executions in person. It was regarded as an excellent example, this supervision on the part of the judge of the executioner's work,—a custom borrowed by the Terror of '93 from the parliaments of France and the Spanish Inquisition.

Gauvain himself was preoccupied.

A cold wind blew from the forest. He left Guéchamp to give the necessary orders, went into his tent, which was in the meadow on the outskirts of the wood at the foot of the Tourgue, and taking his hooded cloak wrapped himself in it. This cloak was trimmed with that simple galoon which in accordance with the republican fashion, averse to decoration, designated the commander-in-chief. He began to pace up and down this bloody field where the assault was begun. There he was alone. The fire, though scarcely heeded, had not yet ceased to burn. Radoub was with the mother and children, almost as motherly as she herself; the bridge-castle was nearly consumed, the sappers completing the work of the flames; they dug ditches, buried the dead, cared for the wounded, demolished the *retirade,* and removed the dead bodies from the rooms and the staircases; the men were at work purifying the scene of carnage, sweeping away the mass of horrible filth, and setting matters in order after the battle with military rapidity. Gauvain took no note of all this activity.

Absorbed in his own thoughts, he hardly glanced at the sentries guarding the breach, doubled by the order of Cimourdain.

He could distinguish this breach amid the darkness, about two hundred paces from that part of the field in which he had found refuge. He saw that black opening. There the attack began three hours ago; this was the breach through which Gauvain had made his way into the tower; there was the ground-floor, with the *retirade;* the Marquis's dungeon-door opened on to that floor. The sentries posted near the breach guarded the dungeon.

While thus he gazed absently upon it, these words returned confusedly to his ears, like the tolling of a funeral knell: "The court-martial tomorrow; the guillotine the day after tomorrow."

The fire, which had been isolated, and upon which the sappers had dashed all the water that they could obtain, still resisted their efforts to extinguish it, and continued to shoot forth occasional jets of flame. Now and then was heard the cracking of the ceilings and the crashing of the stories as they fell one upon another; then showers of sparks flew about as from a whirling torch, revealing like a flash of lightning the extreme limit of the horizon; and the shadow cast by the Tourgue would grow to colossal size, extending to the very edge of the forest.

Gauvain walked slowly back and forth in this shadow in front of the breach. Now and then he clasped both his hands behind his head, covered by his military hood. He was thinking.

II

Gauvain Meditating

HIS REVERIE WAS FATHOMLESS.

An unheard of change had taken place.

The Marquis de Lantenac had been transfigured, and Gauvain had seen it with his own eyes.

He would never have believed it possible that such a state of things could have come to pass from any complication of events whatsoever. Even in a dream he could not have imagined such a condition of affairs.

The Unforeseen, that inexplicable force that makes a man the plaything of its capricious will, had seized Gauvain and held him fast.

Before his eyes he beheld the realization of the impossible,—visible, palpable, inevitable, inexorable.

And what did he think of it? This was no time for evasion; he must make up his mind. A question had been presented to him; he must meet it fairly.

Who had asked this question?

It had come to him in the course of events, but not through events alone.

For when events, which are ever changing, ask us a question, immutable justice summons us to answer.

Behind the cloud that casts the shadow is the star that sheds the light.

We can no more escape the light than the shadow.

Gauvain was undergoing an interrogatory.

He had been arraigned before a judge.

An awe-inspiring presence.

His own conscience.

His entire being was vacillating within him; his firmest resolutions, his most solemn promises, his most irrevocable determinations, were all shaken to their foundations. The soul has its earthquakes.

The more he reflected upon what he had just witnessed, the more confused he grew.

Gauvain, Republican as he was, believed himself to be and was just; but a superior law had been revealed.

Human law takes a higher stand than the law of revolutions. This affair now in progress could not be evaded; it was a serious matter, and Gauvain formed a part of it; he was involved in it, and could not extricate himself; and however much Cimourdain might say, "This matter no longer concerns you," he felt all the sensations of a tree torn up by its roots.

Every man has a basis; a shock to this basis produces a serious disturbance; and this was what Gauvain now felt. He pressed his head between his hands, as if to express from it the truth. It was no easy task to gain a clear idea of a situation like his: nothing could be more uncomfortable; he saw before him a formidable array of ciphers to be added up. To add up the columns of human destiny! The bare thought made him dizzy. And yet he was endeavoring to do this; he was trying to explain matters to himself, to collect his ideas, to subdue the resistance that he felt within him, and to review the facts. He revolved them again and again in his mind.

Is there one among us who has not been called upon to consider some important subject in all its bearings, or has not asked himself at a serious crisis which road to follow,—whether to advance or to retreat?

Gauvain had been witness to a miracle.

While the earthly combat was still in progress, a celestial one had begun.

A contest between good and evil.

A merciless heart had just been conquered.

In the man before him, with all the evil inherent to his nature, violence, error, blindness, an unwholesome obstinacy, selfishness, and pride, Gauvain had witnessed a miracle. A victory won by humanity over the man.

The human victorious over the inhuman.

And by what means? How was it achieved? How had it overthrown a colossus of anger and hatred? What weapons had it used? What machinery of warfare? Simply the cradle.

To Gauvain it was positively bewildering. To the very midst of civil war, at the climax of hostility and vengeance, in the darkest and fiercest moment of the tumult, when crime lent all its fires, and hatred all its blackness, at the very crisis of the struggle when anything may serve for a missile, when the mêlée is so direful that man is lost to every sense of justice, honesty, and truth, suddenly from the Unknown, that mysterious monitor of the human soul, overpowering all the lights and shadows of humanity, came one broad flash of the everlasting light.

Above that fatal duel between falsehood and comparative truth, the face of absolute truth had suddenly risen from the depths.

The strength of the weak had suddenly intervened.

The triumph of three poor little beings, but lately born into the world, unconscious of wrong, orphans, forsaken, and alone, lisping and smiling, with all the Gorgons of civil war, retaliation, the terrible logic of reprisals, murder, carnage, fratricide, wrath, and malice, had just been witnessed, together with the failure and defeat of an infamous conflagration kindled with criminal intent; cruelty had been frustrated and baffled; ancient feudal ferocity, inexorable disdain, the professed experience of the necessities of war, reasons of State, all the arrogant resolves of savage old age vanished before the innocent blue eyes of infant life; and what could be more simple? The infant whose little life has just begun, has done no evil; it is the embodiment of justice, truth, and innocence; the highest angels of heaven dwell in little children.

And truly it was an edifying sight; these frenzied combatants in a merciless war had, in the face of all their evil deeds, their crimes, fanaticism, and murder, vengeance fanning the funeral piles, death advancing torch in hand, suddenly seen Innocence rise in its omnipotence above this countless legion of crimes.

And Innocence had won the day.

One might well say, No; civil war has no existence; there are no such evils as barbarism, hatred, or crime; there is no darkness; the divine dawn of infancy has but to rise, and all these spectres will straightway vanish.

Never in any struggle had the presence of Satan and of Almighty God been more plainly visible.

A conscience had furnished the arena for this combat. It was the conscience of Lantenac.

And again it was renewed, more desperate, and possibly more decisively than ever, in another conscience,—in the conscience of Gauvain.

What a battle-field is the mind of man!

Our thoughts, like gods, monsters, or giants, hold us in their power.

Sometimes those terrible wrestlers trample our very soul beneath their feet.

Gauvain was thinking.

The Marquis de Lantenac, hemmed in, blockaded, condemned, outlawed, confined like a wild beast in a circus, held like a nail in a vice, immured in his own home that had changed into a prison, encompassed on every side by a wall of iron and fire, had eluded his enemies and stolen away. He had effected a miraculous escape. He had achieved a masterpiece,—the most difficult of all accomplishments in a war like this,—flight. He had regained possession of the forest to intrench himself therein, of the district where he would renew the combat, and of the impenetrable shadows among which he might vanish from sight. Once more he had become formidable, ever on the wing, a knight-errant whose presence boded evil; the captain of invisible forces, the leader of men who dwell beneath the ground, the master of the woods. Gauvain was victorious, but Lantenac was free. Henceforth Lantenac was safe, his career unfettered, asylums without number from which to choose. He was intangible, unapproachable, inaccessible. This lion, caught in a snare, had forced his way out, and now behold he had come back to it.

The Marquis de Lantenac had voluntarily, impelled only by his free will, left the shades of the forest, where safety and freedom awaited him, to return to the most frightful danger; first, Gauvain had seen it himself, rushing with fearless spirit into the flames that threatened to engulf him, and again descending that ladder that was to deliver him into the hands of his enemies,—the same ladder that offered escape to others, but to him absolute ruin.

And why had he done this?

To save three children.

And what were they now about to do with this man?

Guillotine him.

And so, this man, for the sake of three children,—his own? No; of his kin perhaps? Not at all; belonging to his own rank in life? By no means; for three little beggars, chance children, foundlings, unknown to him, ragged and barefooted, this nobleman, this prince, this old man, who had made his escape, who was both a free man and a victor, for escape is a triumph in itself,—had risked everything, compromised his own safety, imperilled the cause, and while restoring the children, he offered up his own head, this head hitherto terrible, but now august.

And what were they about to do with it?

To accept it.

The Marquis de Lantenac had had the opportunity to choose

between the life of others and his own; and when this splendid option lay before him, he chose his death.

And it was to be granted him.

They would put him to death.

What a reward for heroism!—To return a generous action by a deed of barbarity!

To cast this reproach upon the Revolution!

Thus to humiliate the Republic!

While he, a man still in the bondage of prejudices and slavery, suddenly assumed another form and re-entered the lists of humanity, they, the champions of deliverance and freedom, would still remain plunged in civil war, with its routine of blood and fratricide!

And they who fought on the side of error respected the supreme law of divine forgiveness, of abnegation, of redemption, and of sacrifice, while for the soldiers of truth it had apparently ceased to exist!

What! Was there to be no rivalry in magnanimity? Were they, who were now in the ascendant, to resign themselves to defeat, to acknowledge their weakness, to take advantage of their victory, to commit murder, and to allow men to say that while the defenders of monarchy save little children, Republicans kill old men!

This grand soldier, this powerful octogenarian, this disarmed warrior, betrayed rather than captured, seized in the very act of doing a good deed, bound by his own consent, with the moisture of a superb devotion still upon his brow, would be seen mounting the steps of the scaffold as if borne upward in an apotheosis; and they would offer to the knife that head round which the three souls of the little angels he had saved would hover in supplication! And standing face to face with a death so infamous for the executioners, a smile would be seen on the face of that man, while a blush of shame would overspread that of the Republic!

And that was to take place in the presence of Gauvain, the chief!

And he, possessing the power to prevent this,—was he to hold his peace? Was he to content himself with that haughty dismissal, "You have no further concern in this matter," and not to realize that in a case like this, abdication of authority was equivalent to complicity? And could he not see that in a deed so outrageous, the coward who allows the act is worse than the man who commits it? But had he not promised that this death should take place? Had not he, Gauvain the merciful, declared that Lantenac was to be excluded from mercy, and that he would deliver him to Cimourdain?

This head was a debt which he owed, and he paid it That was all.

But was this indeed the same head?

Hitherto Gauvain had seen in Lantenac nothing but a barbarous warrior, enslaved by the fanaticisms of royalty and feudality, the murderer of prisoners, an assassin let loose by war, a man of blood,—and of that man he felt no fear; this proscriber of others he would himself proscribe; this relentless man would find him relentless also. Nothing could be more simple; the road was already mapped out and terribly plain to follow; all had been anticipated; he who had killed others was now to suffer the same fate; they were in the direct path of the horrible. Suddenly this straight line changed; an unlooked for turn revealed a new horizon, a transformation had been effected. Lantenac had appeared on the scene in an unexpected character. A hero had come forth from the monster; yea, one greater than a hero,—a man. Something higher than a mind,—a heart. He stood before Gauvain no longer a murderer, but a saviour. Gauvain was overwhelmed by a flood of celestial light. Lantenac had felled him to the ground by a thunderbolt of virtue.

And had not this transfigured Lantenac in his turn the power to transfigure Gauvain? What! Was this flood of light to meet with no responsive flash? Was the man of the past to lead the van of progress, and the man of the future to fall back to the rear? Was the man of barbarism and superstition suddenly to spread his wings and soar upward, all the while gazing down at the man with the lofty ideal, groping below him in the mire amid the murky shadows of the night? Gauvain would lie prostrate in the savage old rut, while Lantenac soared higher and higher in his new career!

And another thing must be considered,—the family!

This blood that he was about to shed,—for to allow its shedding amounted to the same as shedding it himself,—was not this his own blood? His grandfather was dead, it is true, but his great-uncle still lived in the person of the Marquis de Lantenac. Would not he, who already rested in the grave, rise to bar the entrance against his brother? Would he not lay his command upon his grandson henceforth to pay the same veneration to that crown of white hair as to his own halo? Would not the indignant glance of a departed spirit rise between Gauvain and Lantenac?

Was it then the object of Revolution to destroy the natural affections, to sever all family ties, and to stifle every sense of humanity? Far from it. The dawn of '89 came to affirm those higher truths, and not to deny them. The destruction of bastilles signified the deliverance of humanity; the overthrow of feudalism was the signal for the building up of the family. Since authority takes rise from and is centred in its author, there can be no real authority save in fatherhood; thus we see the legitimacy of the queen-bee who gives birth to her subjects and combines the mother with the queen; and also the absurdity of the king-man, who not being the father, has no right to be the master; hence the suppression of the king, and the rise of the Republic. And what is the meaning of all this? It is family, humanity, revolution. Revolution is the accession of the people, and in reality The People is Man.

It had now become important to ascertain whether, since Lantenac had returned to humanity, Gauvain would return to the family.

The question was whether the uncle and the nephew would meet again in the higher light, or whether the decline of the nephew would correspond to the progress of the uncle.

In this pathetic struggle between Gauvain and his conscience the question thus presented itself, and the answer seemed instinctive,—Lantenac must be saved.

Yes—but France?

Here the puzzling problem suddenly assumed a different aspect.

What! France, at the last extremity, betrayed, exposed to attack on all sides, dismantled! Her moat was gone; Germany could cross the Rhine: her walls were overthrown; Italy might leap over the Alps, and Spain over the Pyrenees. All that was left to her was the ocean, whose infinite abyss was on her side. She could lean against it, and, giantess as she was, supported by the expanse of the sea, fight the whole world,—an invincible position one might well call it. But no: she was on the point of losing this position. The ocean was no longer her own: England lay in this sea, though she knew not how to cross it. Well, there stood a man ready to throw a bridge across, to lend her a helping hand,—a man who was about to say to Pitt, to Cornwallis, to Dundas, to the pirates, "Come!" a man who would cry out, "England, come over and seize upon France!" and this man was the Marquis de Lantenac, whom they now held in their grasp.

After three months of an eager, passionate chase they had finally seized him. The hand of Revolution had swooped down upon the accursed one, the clenched fist of '93 grasped the Royalist murderer by the collar; and by one of those mysterious dispensations of Providence which enter into human affairs, it was in his own family dungeon that the parricide now awaited his punishment,—the feudal lord lay in the feudal oubliette; the stones of his own castle had risen and closed upon him. Thus he who would have betrayed his country was himself betrayed by his own castle. God had visibly ordained all this; the hour of doom had struck, and Revolution had turned the key upon the public enemy. He could no longer fight, neither could he struggle nor work further harm. Of that Vendée, where there was no lack of arms, his alone was the brain: his death would be the signal for the close of the war,—tragic climax ardently desired. After all the massacre and carnage he had caused, the murderer was in their power, and doomed in his turn to die.

And was there a man who could wish to save him?

Cimourdain in the person of '93 held Lantenac, or, as one might call him, the spirit of monarchy; and could a man be found to snatch that prey from these brazen talons? Lantenac, around whose name was bound that sheaf of scourges which men call the past, the Marquis de Lantenac, was in the tomb; the heavy door of eternity had closed upon him, and would one appear from without to draw back the bolt? This social malefactor was dead, and with him had perished revolt, the fratricidal struggle, the brutal war; and conceive of a man who would bring him back to life!

Oh, how that death's-head would laugh!

The spectre would exclaim, "Good! I am still alive, you fools."

With what zeal he would begin his hideous work all over again! With what implacable rejoicing would he plunge again into the abyss of hatred and war! Not a day would pass before houses would be in flames, prisoners massacred, the wounded slain, women shot.

And, after all, was it not possible that Gauvain exaggerated the deed that so fascinated his imagination?

Three children were in danger of death: Lantenac had saved them.

But who had imperilled their lives?

Was it not Lantenac?

Who had put their cradles in the fire?

Was it not the Imânus?

Who was the Imânus?

The lieutenant of the Marquis.

It is the chief who bears the responsibility.

Hence Lantenac was both the incendiary and the assassin.

Why then was his deed so admirable?

He had simply desisted from evil,—nothing more.

Having conceived the crime, he had recoiled before its presence; he was horrified at himself. The mother's shriek had stirred within him the dregs of human pity,—the deposit of universal life which exists in every soul, even in the most cruel. At this cry he had retraced his steps; from the darkness towards which he was plunging he had turned back towards the light. Having committed the crime, he made haste to retrieve it. He had not continued a monster to the very end; herein lay all his merit.

And in return for so small a thing was all to be restored to him,—his liberty, the fields and plains, the open air, daylight, the forest, which he would use for brigandage; his own freedom, that he might use it to plunge others into slavery; his own life, which he would devote to the death of his fellow-men?

As for trying to come to an understanding with him, as for attempting to treat with this arrogant soul, offering to save his life under conditions, to ask him whether he would agree, provided his life were spared, to abstain henceforth from hostility and revolt,—what a mistake would such an offer be, what an advantage it would give him, with what scorn would he greet the proposal, how he would scourge the question by the answer! Hear him exclaim: "Keep such indignities for yourselves! For my part, give me death!"

Nothing could be done with such a man; he must either be set free or put to death. His was a rugged, inaccessible nature; ready for flight, ready for sacrifice,—it mattered not which. His strange soul displayed the characteristics of the eagle as well as of the precipice.

To kill him? Dreadful to contemplate! To set him free? What a responsibility!

Suppose Lantenac were saved, it would simply be a return to the beginning of the Vendée, like a struggle with a hydra, whose head is not yet severed. In the twinkling of an eye, like the flash of a meteor, all the flames which expired when this man vanished, would be rekindled. Lantenac would never rest until he had effected his detestable plan,—to establish Monarchy like the lid of a tomb over the Republic, and to give England control over France! He who would save Lantenac must sacrifice France; Lantenac's life would be death to a multitude of innocent creatures,—men, women, and children,—who would again become the prey of civil war; it meant the landing of the English, the Revolution retarded, the cities sacked, the inhabitants distracted, Brittany torn and bleeding; in short, it would be like tossing back his prey to the tiger's claws. And Gauvain, amid all this uncertain glimmering of cross-lights,—Gauvain, in-his reverie, caught a vague glimpse of the problem as it gradually took form in his mind: the setting at liberty of a tiger.

And then the question resumed its former aspect; the stone of Sisyphus, which is nothing less than the conflict of man with his own conscience, recoiled upon him. Was Lantenac then a tiger?

Once he may have been; but was he a tiger still? Gauvain grew dizzy with conflicting thoughts,—thoughts which coiled themselves around one another after the fashion of a snake. Could one, after mature consideration, really deny the devotion of Lantenac, his stoical self-abnegation, his sublime disinterestedness? What! after he had shown his humanity in the very jaws of civil war? What! when in the conflict between inferior truths he had shown forth the truth that stands above all others? What! when he had proved that the deep tenderness of human nature, the protection that strength owes to weakness, the duty which binds every man who is saved to lend a helping hand to his perishing brother, the fatherhood which every old man owes to every little child, are above all principalities and revolutions, above all earthly questions whatsoever,—when he had proved the truth of all these grand things, and proved it by the gift of his own head? What! general as he was, to have renounced strategy, battle, and revenge? What! he, being a Royalist, had taken the scales, and placing in one end the King of France, the monarchy fifteen centuries old, the restoration of ancient laws and the re-establishment of an old society, and in the other, three little unknown peasants, and had found the king, the throne, the sceptre, and the fifteen centuries of monarchy out-weighed by those innocent creatures?

Could it be possible that all this was to count for nothing? Was he who had done this to remain a tiger and be treated like a wild beast? No, no, no! He was no monster, the man whose divine action had just illumined the abyss of civil war! The sword-bearer had been transformed into a messenger of light. The infernal Satan had become once more the heavenly Lucifer. Lantenac had expiated all his cruel deeds by one act of sacrifice; his moral salvation had been attained by way of his material ruin; he had returned to a state of innocence; he had signed his own pardon. Does Hot the right of self-forgiveness exist? Henceforth he was an object for veneration.

Lantenac had just proved himself a remarkable man. It was now Gauvain's turn to make fitting response.

The struggle between the passions of good and evil was fast converting the world into chaos; Lantenac, dominating this same chaos, had set humanity free, and now it was left for Gauvain to assert the rights of the family.

What was he about to do?

Was he to betray God's trust?

No. And he muttered to himself: Lantenac must be saved.

Well, then, go your way; connive with the English, desert your country, ally yourself with her enemy! Save Lantenac and betray France!

Here he shuddered.

Dreamer that thou art, this is no solution! and Gauvain fancied he saw in the shadow the baleful smile of the sphinx.

This combination of circumstances was like a platform whereon conflicting truths had taken their stand, ready for the encounter, and where the three loftiest principles of mankind—humanity, family, and country—stood face to face.

Each of these voices spoke in turn, and each one spoke the truth. How was a man to choose? Each one by turns seemed to have discovered the point of union between justice and wisdom, and said, "Act thus." Must he obey this voice? Yes. No. Reason suggested one thing, sentiment another; and their counsels were diametrically opposed. Logic is nothing more than reason; sentiment is often the voice of the conscience: the one comes from man, the other from above.

Hence the perceptions of sentiment are less clear, but wield a stronger influence.

But what a power dwells in stern reason!

Gauvain hesitated.

Torturing perplexities!

Two abysses opened before Gauvain,—to destroy the Marquis, or to save him? Into one or the other he must needs plunge. Towards which of these two did duty call him?

III

The Commander's Hood

THE QUESTION HAD INDEED RESOLVED itself in a matter of duty.

Duty arose stem-visaged and immutable before the spirit of Cimourdain, and terrible before that of Gauvain.

Simple to the one; complex, many-sided, devious, to the other.

The hour of midnight sounded; then one o'clock.

Without realizing where he was going, Gauvain had unconsciously approached the entrance of the breach.

The light of the expiring fire cast now but a dim reflection. The plateau on the other side of the tower caught the light and became visible for an instant only, to vanish as the clouds of smoke obscured the flames. This light, with its unexpected flashes and sudden darkening shadows, exaggerated the surrounding objects and gave to the sentinels of the camp the effect of phantoms. Gauvain, lost in thought, unconsciously watched the alternations of smoke and flame. There seemed to him a strange analogy between these changes of light and shade and the varied phases of truth in his own mind.

Suddenly, between two clouds of smoke, a flame burst forth from the bed of dying coals, threw a brilliant light on the summit of the plateau, and revealed the red outlines of a wagon. Gauvain gazed upon it. It was surrounded by horsemen wearing the hats of gendarmes. He concluded that this must be the same one that he had seen through Guéchamp's spy-glass against the horizon a few hours before, just as the sun was setting. There were men on the wagon who appeared to be unloading it. The object which they were removing seemed heavy, and at times the clanking of iron could be heard; it would have been difficult to say what it was. It seemed to be wood-work; two of the men lowered from the wagon and placed on the ground a case, which, judging from its shape, might contain some triangular object. The flame died out, and everything was dark again; Gauvain, wrapped in thought, gazed steadily before him upon that object now hidden by the darkness.

Lanterns were lighted, and men could be seen moving to and fro on the plateau; but the outlines were indistinct, and moreover, Gauvain, standing as he did, and on the opposite side of the ravine, could only discern those objects which were close to the edge.

He could hear the voices, but not the words. Now and then he caught the echo of hammering upon the wood. He could also hear a grinding, metallic sound, like the sharpening of a scythe.

It struck two.

Slowly, and like one who would from choice take two steps forward and three back, Gauvain advanced towards the breach. On his approach, the sentinel, recognizing in the dusk the commander's cloak and braided hood, presented arms. Gauvain entered the hall on the lower floor, which had been transformed into a guard-room. A lantern hung from the ceiling, and cast just light enough so that one could cross the hall without treading on the men, most of whom lay upon the straw, sound asleep.

There they lay, on the spot where but a few hours since they had been fighting. The grape-shot, from the careless sweeping, still lay scattered about beneath them, and was not very comfortable to sleep on; but weary as they were, they could sleep in spite of it This hall had been the terrible spot: here the assault had been made; yonder men had roared, howled, gnashed their teeth, given blow for blow, struck down the enemy, and in their turn expired; many of their men had fallen dead upon this floor where they were now slumbering; the same straw on which they slept had been drenched with the blood of their comrades. Now all was ended; all the blood was stanched and the sabres dried, the dead were dead, peacefully slumbering. Such is war; and it may be no longer than tomorrow before every man among them will sleep the same sleep. On Gauvain's entrance some of the sleepers rose, among them the officer in command. Pointing to the door of the dungeon, Gauvain said to him,—

"Open it."

The bolts were drawn, and the door opened.

Gauvain entered the dungeon.

The door closed behind him.

Book VII

Feudality and Revolution

I

The Ancestor

A LAMP STOOD ON THE flags of the dungeon, beside the square air-hole of the oubliette.

There was also to be seen a jug of water, a loaf of army bread, and a truss of straw. As the dungeon was cut out of solid rock, any prisoner who conceived the idea of setting the straw on fire would have had his labor for his pains,—no risk of a conflagration for the prison, and certain suffocation for the prisoner.

When the door turned on its hinges, the Marquis was walking up and down in his prison, with that mechanical pacing to and fro peculiar to caged wild animals.

At the sound of the opening and closing door, he looked up, and the light from the lamp that stood on the floor between Gauvain and himself struck full upon the faces of both men.

They looked at each other with such an expression that each stood there as if transfixed.

The Marquis burst out laughing and exclaimed:

"Good-evening, sir. Many years have passed since I have had the pleasure of meeting you. You honor me by your visit. I thank you. Nothing could please me more than a little conversation, for I was beginning, to be bored. Your friends are wasting their time,—proofs of identity, court-martials, all those ceremonies are tedious. Were it my affair I should proceed more rapidly. I am at home here. Will you be good enough to come in. Well, what do you think of the present state of affairs? It is original, is it not? Once upon a time there was a king and queen in France; the king was the king; France herself was the queen. They have cut off the king's head and married the queen to Robespierre; and to this pair a daughter has been born,—they call her Guillotine, and it seems that I am to make her acquaintance tomorrow morning. I shall be as pleased to meet her as I am to meet you. Is that perchance the object of your visit? Have you been promoted? Shall you officiate as headsman? But if this be simply a visit of friendship, I feel grateful. You may perhaps have forgotten, Viscount, what a nobleman is? Allow me to present you to one. Behold me; it has become a rare specimen; it believes in God, in tradition, and in the family; it believes in its ancestors, in the example of its father, in fidelity, in loyalty, in its duty towards its princes, in reverence for ancient laws, in virtue and in justice; and it would order you to be shot with much pleasure. Will you do me the favor to take a seat? I must ask you to sit upon the floor, since there is no arm-chair in this salon; but he who dwells in the mire may well sit upon the ground. I do not say this to offend you, for that which is mire in our esteem, represents the nation in your eyes. You will not, of course, require me to shout for Liberty, Equality, and Fraternity? This is an old room in my house, where in former times the lords used to imprison their peasants; nowadays, it is the peasants who imprison the lords. And these follies men call revolution! It seems that my head is to be cut off in thirty-six hours. I have no objection to offer; still, had they been well-bred they would have sent me my snuff-box, which is upstairs in the mirror-chamber, where you used to play when you were a child, and where I have dandled you on my knee. Sir, let me tell you one thing: your name is Gauvain, and strange as it may seem, you have noble blood in your veins,—yes, *pardieu*! the very same blood that flows in mine; and this blood which has made a man of honor of me, has made of you a scoundrel. Such are the idiosyncrasies of the human race! You will tell me that it is not your fault. Nor is it mine. *Parbleu*! one may be a rascal unconsciously. It depends upon the air one breathes. In times like ours, no man is responsible for what he does; revolution is the scapegoat for all mankind, for your great criminals are supreme innocents. What blockheads! To begin with yourself. Allow me to admire you. Yes, I admire a youth like yourself, who, well-born, with an excellent position in State affairs, possessing noble blood fit to be shed in a noble cause, Viscount of this Tower-Gauvain, Prince of Brittany, a duke in his own right, belonging to the hereditary peerage of France,—which is about all that a sensible man can desire here below,—a youth who, being such as he is, amuses himself by playing a part like yours, until his enemies believe him a scoundrel, and his friends regard him as an idiot! By the way, give my regards to the Abbé Cimourdain."

Perfectly at his ease, the Marquis spoke slowly and calmly, without emphasis, in his society voice, his eyes clear and tranquil, and with both hands in his waistcoat pockets. He paused, took a long breath, and then continued:—

"I do not conceal from you that I have done all in my power to kill you. As I stand before you, I have three times in person aimed a cannon at you. A discourteous proceeding, I confess, but it would be relying upon a false maxim did we allow ourselves to fancy that in time of war the enemy proposes to make himself agreeable. For we are in a state of war, nephew. Everything is put to fire and sword, and they have killed the king besides. A fine century!"

He paused again, then continued:—

"And when one thinks that none of these things would have happened if they had hung Voltaire and sent Rousseau to the galleys! Ah, those men of intellect! What a scourge they were! For what crime did you reproach the Monarchy? The Abbé Pucelle was sent to his Abbey of Corbigny, it is true, allowing him the choice of conveyance and as much time as he required in the journey; and as for your Monsieur Titon, who was—begging your pardon—a wretched libertine, who visited abandoned women before going to the miracles of Deacon Pâris, he was transferred from Vincennes to the fortress of Ham in Picardy, which is, I admit, rather a disagreeable place. Those are your grievances; I remember them, for I too inveighed against them in my day. I have been as stupid as you."

The Marquis fumbled in his pocket as though he expected to find his snuff-box; then he continued:

"But not so wicked. We talked for the sake of talking. There was, moreover, the mutiny of demands and petitions; and then those gentlemen the philosophers appeared upon the scene, whose works they burned,—they would have done better had they burned the authors: Court intrigues were mixed up in the affair. Then came all the dunces, Turgot, Quesnay, Malesherbes, the physiocratists, and so forth, and the wrangling began. All this was the work of scribblers and rhymsters. The Encyclopædia! Diderot! D'Alembert! Ah! the malicious scamps! Fancy a well-born man like the King of Prussia joining hands with them! I would have made short work with all those paper-scribblers. Ah! we know how to administer justice; you can see here, on this wall, the mark of the quartering-wheels. There was no jesting in the matter. No, no; let us abolish scribblers! So long as there are Arouets there will be Marats. So long as there are men who scribble, there will be wretches who murder; while there is ink, there will be black stains; so long as men's claws can hold a goose-quill, frivolous nonsense will engender atrocious follies. Books are the authors of crime. The word 'chimera' has a double signification,—it means a dream and it means a monster. What a price one pays for all this idle nonsense! What is it you keep repeating to us about your rights,—the rights of man, the rights of the people! Has it any sense whatever? Could anything be more stupid, utterly imaginary, and devoid of meaning! When I state the fact that Havoise, the sister of Conan II, brought the Comté of Bretagne to Hoël, Count of Nantes and of Cornwall, from whom the estate descended to Alain Fergant, the uncle of that Bertha who married Alain le Noir, lord of Roche-sur-Yon, and bore unto him Conan le Petit, grandfather of Guy or Gauvain de Thouars our ancestor,—I make a plain statement, and claim my rights. But the knaves, the rascals, the scoundrels of your party, what rights do they claim? Deicide and regicide. Is it not frightful? Ah! the ragamuffins! I am sorry for you, sir; still, you come of that proud Breton blood; you and I have a Gauvain de Thouars for our grandfather, and furthermore we have an ancestor in that famous Duke de Montbazon, a peer of France and decorated with the Grand Collar, who attacked the Faubourg de Tours and was wounded at the battle of Arques, and who died Grand-veneur of France in his house of Couzières in Touraine at the age of eighty-six. I could tell you of the Duke of Laudunois, son of the Lady de la Garnache, of Claude de Lorraine, of the Duke de Chevreuse, of Henri do Lenoncourt, and of Françoise de Laval-Boisdauphin. But to what purpose? Monsieur has the honor of being an idiot, and he delights to lower himself to the level of my groom. Learn this: I was already an old man when you were still a nursing infant. I watched you, and I would watch you still. As you grew up you succeeded in degrading yourself. Since we ceased to meet, each of us has followed his inclinations; mine have led me in the direction of honesty, while your course has been the very reverse. Ah! I know not how all this will end; but your friends are consummate villains. Oh, yes, I acknowledge it is all very fine, the progress is marvellous; they have done away in the army with the punishment of the pint of water, inflicted for three days in succession, on drunken soldiers; they have the maximum, the Convention, Bishop Gobel, Monsieur Chaumette, and Monsieur Hébert; there has been a wholesale extermination of the past, from the Bastille to the calendar. The saints are replaced by vegetables. Very well, citizens; be our masters if you will, reign over us, take your ease, act your good pleasure, stand upon no ceremony. All that will not prevent religion from being religion, nor alter the fact that royalty has occupied fifteen hundred years of our history, and that the old French nobility, even though beheaded, stands higher than you. And as to your sophistries concerning the historical right of royal races, what care we for that matter? Chilpéric was really nothing but a monk by the name of Daniel; it was Rainfroi who invented Chilpéric to annoy Charles Martel,—we know that as well as you. That is not the question. The question is this: that there shall be a great kingdom, old France, a well-regulated country, where men consider first the sacred person of the monarchs, absolute rulers of the State, then the princes, then the officers of the crown, naval and military, as well as the controllers of finance. Then there are the officers of justice of the different grades, followed by those of the salt-tax and the general receipts, and finally the police of the kingdom in its three orders. All this was fine and well-regulated; you have destroyed it. You have destroyed the provinces, without even understanding—so great was your ignorance,—what the provinces were. The genius of France was made up from that of the entire continent, and each of its provinces represents a special virtue of Europe; the frankness of Germany is to be found in Picardy, the generosity of Sweden in Champagne, the industry of Holland in Burgundy, the activity of Poland in Languedoc, the grave dignity of Spain in Gascony, the wisdom of Italy in Provence, the subtlety of Greece in Normandy, the fidelity of Switzerland in Dauphiny. You knew nothing of all this; you have broken, shattered, crushed, demolished, behaving like stupid beasts of the field. So you wish to have no more nobles? Very well, you shall have none. Prepare your mourning. Your paladins and heroes have departed. Bid farewell to all the ancient glories. Find me a D'Assas at the present time, if you can! You are all trembling for your skins. You will have no more Chevaliers de Fontenoy who saluted the enemy before killing him; you will have no more combatants in silk stockings like those at the siege of Lérida; you will have no more of those days of military glory when plumes flashed by like meteors; your days are numbered; the outrage of invasion will descend upon you. If Alain II were to return, he would no longer find a Clovis to confront him; if Abdérame were to come back, he would encounter no such foe as Charles Martel; neither would the Saxons find a Pépin waiting for them. You will have no Agnadel, Rocroy, Lens, Staffarde, Nerwinde, Steinkerque, La Marsaille, Raucoux, Lawfeld, Mahon; you will never have another Marignan with Francis I; nor a Bouvines with Philip-

Augustus, who took Renaud, Count of Boulogne, prisoner with one hand, while with the other he held Ferrand, Count of Flanders. You will have Agincourt, but you will not have the great standard-bearer, the Sieur de Bacqueville, wrapping himself in his banner to die. Go on, go on, accomplish your work! Be the new men. Dwarf yourselves!"

Here the Marquis paused a moment; then he continued:—

"But leave to us our greatness. Kill the kings, kill nobles and priests, if you will; sow broadcast over the land destruction, ruin, and death; trample all things under foot; set your heel upon the ancient laws, overthrow the throne, stamp upon the altar of your God, and dance over the ruins. All rests with you, cowards and traitors as you are, incapable of self-devotion and sacrifice. I have said all that I have to say. Now have me guillotined, Monsieur le Vicomte. I have the honor to be your most humble servant."

Then he added,—

"It is but the truth. What difference can it make to me? I am dead."

"You are free," said Gauvain.

And he advanced towards the Marquis, unfastened his commander's-cloak, and throwing it over the shoulders of the latter, he drew the hood down over his eyes. Both men were of the same height.

"What is this that you are doing?" said the Marquis.

Gauvain raised his voice and called out,—

"Lieutenant, open to me!"

The door was opened.

Gauvain cried,—

"You will be careful to close the door behind me."

And he pushed the astonished Marquis across the threshold.

It must be remembered that the low hall which had been turned into a guard-room was lighted by a horn lantern, whose dim rays served only to deepen the shadows; it threw an uncertain glimmer on the surrounding objects, and in this indistinct light those of the soldiers who were not sleeping saw a tall man walk past them towards the entrance, wrapped in the cloak and braided hood of the commander-in-chief. The soldiers saluted him as he passed out.

The Marquis slowly crossed the guard-room and the breach,—not without hitting his head more than once,—and went out. The sentinel, supposing that it was Gauvain whom he saw, presented arms.

Once outside, within two hundred steps of the forest, feeling the turf beneath his feet, and space, the protecting night, liberty, and life before him, he paused and stood for a moment motionless, like a man who has allowed himself to be influenced, has been overcome by surprise, and who, having taken advantage of an open door, asks himself whether he has acted nobly or ignobly, and hesitates before going on,—giving ear, as it were, to an afterthought. After some moments of deep reverie, he raised his right hand, and snapping his thumb and finger, cried,—

"Faith!"

And he went on.

The door of the prison had closed again, and this time it was upon Gauvain.

II

The Court-Martial

Nearly all the court-martials of this period were arbitrary tribunals. In the Legislative Assembly, Dumas had drawn up a rough plan of military legislation, afterwards improved by Talbot in the Council of the Five Hundred, but the final code of councils of war was not drawn up until the time of the Empire. From that time also, be it mentioned by way of parenthesis, dates the law imposed on military tribunals in regard to the taking of votes, that of beginning with the lower grade. This law was not in existence during the Revolution.

In 1793, the president of a military tribunal might almost be said to personify the tribunal itself; he elected the members, arranged the order of the ranks and regulated the method of voting; he was master as well as judge.

Cimourdain had selected the identical room on the ground-floor where the *retirade* had been, and where the guard was now posted, for the judgment-hall of the court-martial. He was anxious to shorten everything,—the road from the prison to the tribunal, and the passage from the tribunal to the scaffold.

In accordance with his orders, the court opened its session at noon with no more display of ceremonial than three straw chairs, a pine table, two lighted candies, and a stool placed in front of the table.

The chairs were for the judges and the stool was for the prisoner. At each end of the table stood another stool, one for the commissioner-auditor, who was a quartermaster, and the other for the clerk, who was a corporal.

On the table there was a stick of red sealing-wax, a copper seal of the Republic, two inkstands, bundles of white paper, and two printed placards, spread wide open,—one containing the sentence of outlawry, the other, the decree of the Convention.

The middle chair was pushed back against a group of tricolored flags; in those times of rude simplicity, decorations were quickly arranged, and but little time was needed to change a guard-hall into a court of justice. The middle chair, intended for the president, faced the prison door.

The audience was composed of soldiers.

Two gendarmes stood on guard beside the stool.

Cimourdain was seated in the middle chair, with Captain Guéchamp, the first judge, on his right, and Sergeant Radoub, the second, on his left.

He wore a hat with tricolored plumes, a sabre by his side, and two pistols on his belt. His scar, of a vivid red, increased the ferocity of his appearance.

Radoub had at last consented to allow his wounds to be dressed. He wore a handkerchief tied round his head, on which a blood-stain was gradually extending.

At noon, before the Court opened, a messenger stood beside the table of the tribunal, while his horse impatiently pawed the ground outside. Cimourdain was writing; and this was what he wrote:—

"Citizen members of the Com. of Public Safety:"

"Lantenac is taken. He will be executed tomorrow."

After dating and signing the despatch he folded and sealed it, and then handed it to the messenger, who took his leave.

Whereupon Cimourdain said in a loud voice,—

"Open the dungeon."

Two gendarmes drew back the bolts, opened the dungeon, and went in.

Cimourdain raised his head, crossed his arms, glanced at the door, and exclaimed:—

"Bring forth the prisoner!"

Beneath the archway of the open door appeared a man between the two gendarmes.

It was Gauvain.

Cimourdain started.

"Gauvain!" he cried

Then continued:—

"I demand the prisoner."

"It is I," said Gauvain.

"Thou?"

"I."

"And Lantenac?"

"He is free."

"Free?"

"Yes."

"Escaped?"

"Escaped."

Cimourdain trembled as he murmured:—

"True, it is his own castle, he is familiar with all its outlets; the crypt perhaps communicates with one of them. I ought to have thought of this; he probably found means of escape; he would need no help."

"He has been helped," said Gauvain.

"To escape?"

"To escape."

"Who helped him?"

"I."

"Thou?"

"I."

"Thou art dreaming."

"I went into the dungeon, I was alone with the prisoner, I took off my cloak and wrapped it about him, I drew the hood over his face; he went out in my stead, while I remained in his. Here I am."

"Thou hast not done this?"

"I have."

"It is impossible."

"It is true."

"Bring me Lantenac."

"He is no longer here. The soldiers, seeing the commander's-cloak, took him for me and allowed him to pass. It was still dark."

"Thou art mad."

"I tell you what happened."

A silence ensued. Cimourdain stammered:—

"Then thou deservest—"

"Death," said Gauvain.

Cimourdain was as pale as a corpse, and as motionless as a man who has been struck by lightning. He seemed to have lost the power of breathing. A great drop of sweat formed upon his forehead.

He controlled his voice, forcing himself to speak firmly as he said:—

"Gendarmes, seat the accused."

Gauvain took his seat on the stool.

Cimourdain continued:—

"Gendarmes, draw your sabres."

This was the usual formula when the accused was under sentence of death.

The gendarmes bared their sabres.

Cimourdain's voice regained its ordinary tone.

"Accused," he said, "rise."

He no longer used the familiar "thee" and "thou."

III

The Votes

GAUVAIN ROSE.

"What is your name?" asked Cimourdain.

"Gauvain," was the reply.

Cimourdain went on with the interrogatory:—

"Who are you?"

"I am commander-in-chief of the expeditionary column of the Côtes-du-Nord."

"Are you a kinsman or connection of the man who has escaped?"

"I am his great-nephew."

"Are you acquainted with the decree of the Convention?"

"I see the placard on your table."

"What have you to say in regard to this decree?"

"That I have countersigned it, and have ordered its execution; that it was I who had that placard written, to which my name is affixed."

"Choose your defender."

"I will defend myself."

"You may speak."

Cimourdain had become impassible. Only his impassibility was more like the calmness of a rock than that of a man.

For a moment Gauvain remained silent and thoughtful.

Cimourdain continued:—

"What have you to say in your defence?"

Gauvain slowly raised his head, and without looking at any one, replied:—

"This: one thing has prevented me from seeing another. A good deed, viewed too near at hand, hid from my sight hundreds of criminal actions; on the one side, an aged man, on the other, children,—all this interfered between me and my duty. I forgot the burning villages, the ravaged fields, the massacred prisoners, the wounded cruelly put to death, the women shot; I forgot France betrayed to England: I have set at liberty the country's murderer. I am guilty. When I speak thus I seem to speak against myself, but it is not so; I am speaking in my own behalf. When he who is guilty acknowledges his fault, he saves the only thing worth saving—honor."

"Is this all you have to say in your defence?" returned Cimourdain.

"I will add, that being the commander I should have set an example, and that you in turn as judges must offer one."

"What example do you require of us?"

"My death."

"You think it just?"

"And necessary."

"Take your seat."

The quartermaster, who was commissioner-auditor, rose and read, first the decree pronouncing the sentence of outlawry against the ci-devant Marquis de Lantenac; second, that of the Convention sentencing to death any one whomsoever who should aid or abet the escape of a rebel prisoner. He ended with the few lines printed at the bottom of the placard, forbidding men to "aid or abet" the rebel aforesaid, "under penalty of death," and signed: "Commander-in-chief of the expeditionary column, GAUVAIN." The reading ended, the auditor-commissioner again took his scat.

Cimourdain, crossing his arms, said:—

"Attention, accused, and let the public listen, look on, and keep silence. The law lies before you. It will be put to vote. The sentence will be determined by the vote of the majority. Each judge will in turn pronounce his decision aloud, in the presence of the accused; for justice has nothing to conceal."

Cimourdain continued,—

"Let the first judge cast his vote. Speak, Captain Guéchamp."

Captain Guéchamp seemed unconscious of the presence either

of Gauvain or Cimourdain. His eyes, riveted upon the placard of the decree, as if he were absorbed in the contemplation of an abyss, were hidden by his downcast lids. He said:—

"The law is clearly defined. The judge is more and less than a man,—less than a man, inasmuch as he has no heart; more than a man, in that he wields the sword. In the year 414 of the building of the city of Rome, Manlius put his son to death because he gained a victory without waiting for orders. That infraction of discipline required an expiation. Here, the law has been violated; and the law stands higher than discipline. A man has been overcome by the emotion of pity, and the country is once more endangered. Pity may rise to the level of a crime. Commander Gauvain has connived at the escape of the rebel Lantenac. Gauvain is guilty. I vote for death."

"Write it down, clerk," said Cimourdain.

The clerk wrote, "Captain Guéchamp: death."

Gauvain said in a firm voice,—

"Guéchamp, you have voted well; I thank you."

Cimourdain continued,—

"It is the turn of the second judge. Speak, Sergeant Radoub."

Radoub rose, and turning towards Gauvain, he made the military salute, exclaiming,—

"If that is the way things are going, then guillotine me; for upon my most sacred word of honor, I would like to have done, first, what the old man did, and then what my commander did. When I beheld that man of eighty rushing into the flames to save the three midgets, I said to myself, 'Good man, you are a brave fellow!' And since I hear that it was my commander who saved this old man from your beastly guillotine, by all that is holy, I say, 'Commander, you ought to be the general; and you are a true man; and by thunder, I would give you the Cross of Saint-Louis if there were any crosses or saints or Louises left!' Are we going to make idiots of ourselves, for pity's sake? I should say so, if this is to be the result of winning the battles of Jemmapes, Valmy, Fleurus, and Wattignies. What! here is Commander Gauvain, who for these four months past has been driving those donkeys of Royalists to the sound of the drum, who saves the Republic by his sword, and who did something at Dol that needed brains to accomplish it; and when you have a man like that, you try to get rid of him, and instead of making him your general you propose to cut his throat! I say that it is enough to make one throw one's self head-foremost from the Pont-Neuf! and if you, citizen

Gauvain, were only a corporal instead of being my commander, I would tell you that you talked a heap of nonsense just now. The old man did well when he saved the children, you did well to save the old man; and if men are to be guillotined for their good actions, then we might as well go to the deuce; and I am sure I don't know what it all means. There is nothing to depend upon. This must be a sort of dream, isn't it? I pinch myself to see if I am really awake. I don't understand. So the old man ought to have let the midgets burn alive, and my commander did wrong to save the old man's head? See here! guillotine me; I wish you would! Suppose the midgets had died; then the battalion of the Bonnet-Rouge would have been dishonored. Is that what they wanted? If that is the case, then let us destroy one another. I know as much about politics as you do, for I belonged to the Club of the Section of the Pikes. Sapristi! we are getting to be no better than the brutes! In a word, this is the way I look at it. I don't like such an upsetting state of affairs. Why the devil do we risk our lives? So that our chief may be put to death. None of that, Lisette! I want my chief; I must have my chief. I love him better today than I did yesterday. You make me laugh when you say that he is to be guillotined. We'll have nothing of the sort. I have listened. You may say what you please; but let me tell you in the first place, it is impossible."

And Radoub took his seat. His wound had reopened. A thin stream of blood oozed from under the bandage, from the place where his ear had been, and ran along his neck.

Cimourdain turned towards Radoub.

"You vote that the accused be acquitted?"

"I vote to have him made general," replied Radoub.

"I ask you whether you vote for his acquittal."

"I vote that he be made the head of the Republic."

"Sergeant Radoub, do you, or do you not, vote for Captain Gauvain's acquittal? Yes, or no?"

"I vote that you behead me in his place."

"Acquittal," said Cimourdain. "Write it down, clerk."

Then the clerk announced,—

"One vote for death, one for acquittal: a tie."

It was Cimourdain's turn to vote.

He rose, took off his hat, and placed it on the table. He was no longer pale or livid; his face was the color of clay.

Had every man present been lying in his shroud, the silence could not have been more profound.

VICTOR HUGO

In solemn, measured tones Cimourdain said,—

"Gauvain, the accused, your case has been heard. The court-martial, in the name of the Republic, by a majority of two against one—"

He broke off; he seemed to pause. Was he still doubtful whether to vote for death or for life? The audience was breathless. Cimourdain went on,—

"—condemns you to the penalty of death."

His face revealed the torture of an awful triumph. When Jacob in the darkness forced a blessing from the angel whom he had overthrown, he must have worn the same terrible smile.

It passed like a flash, however, and Cimourdain again became marble. He took his seat, replaced his hat on his head, and added,—

"Gauvain, you will be executed tomorrow at sunrise."

Gauvain rose, bowed, and said,—

"I thank the court."

"Remove the prisoner," said Cimourdain; and at a sign from him the door of the dungeon was reopened, Gauvain entered, and it closed behind him. Two gendarmes with drawn sabres were stationed on each side of the door.

Radoub, who had just fallen senseless, was carried away.

IV

After Cimourdain the Judge, Cimourdain the Master

A CAMP IS A WASPS nest, especially in time of revolution. The civic sting which exists in the soldier darts forth at a moments notice, and after driving out the enemy, will often turn without ceremony upon its own chief. The brave army which had taken the Tourgue was alive with conflicting rumors. When first the escape of Lantenac was discovered, it was all against Gauvain; but when the latter was seen coming out of the dungeon where they had supposed Lantenac to be imprisoned, it was like the transmission of an electric spark, and in less than a minute the whole army knew of it. A murmur broke forth from the little band; at first it ran: "They are getting ready to try Gauvain. But it is all a farce. He is a fool who trusts these ci-devants and calotins! We have just seen a Viscount save a Marquis, and presently we shall see a priest acquit a noble!"

When the condemnation of Gauvain became known, there was a second murmur: "That is an outrage! Our chief, our brave chief, our young commander, a hero! He is a Viscount, to be sure, but so much more to his credit that he is also a Republican! What, he, the liberator of Pontorson, of Villedieu, of Pont-au-Beau: the conqueror of Dol and of the Tourgue! the man who has made us invincible! the sword of the Republic in the Vendée,—he who for five months holds his own against the Chouans, and corrects all the blunders of Léchelle and others! And Cimourdain dares to condemn him! Wherefore? Because he saved an old man who had rescued three children! Does it become a priest to put a soldier to death?"

Thus murmured the victorious and dissatisfied camp. On every side a dull sense of anger prevailed against Cimourdain. Four thousand men against one might be supposed to constitute a power; but it does not. These four thousand men were nothing more than a crowd; Cimourdain was a will. They all knew that his frown was easily provoked, and this knowledge sufficed to hold the army in awe. In those times it needed but the shadow of the Committee of Public Safety behind a man to make him formidable, and to convert an imprecation into a whisper, and that whisper into silence. Before, as well as after their murmuring, Cimourdain was absolute master of the fate of all, as well as of that of Gauvain. They knew that it would be vain to entreat him; that he would listen only to his conscience,—that superhuman voice audible to himself alone. Everything depended upon him. What he had done simply in his capacity of military judge, he could undo as civil delegate. He alone could pardon; there were no limits to his authority; it needed but a sign from him to set Gauvain at liberty; life and death were in his hands; the guillotine was at his command. In this tragic moment he held supreme authority.

There was no resource but to wait.

The night came.

V

The Dungeon

Once more the hall of justice was changed into a guard-room; and as on the previous evening, the sentinels were doubled, two of whom guarded the door of the closed dungeon.

Toward midnight, a man, bearing a lantern in his hand, crossed the guard-room, where he made himself known, and ordered the dungeon to be opened. It was Cimourdain. He entered, leaving the door half open behind him. The dungeon was dark and silent. Taking one step forward in the gloom, he placed the lantern on the ground and stood still. The even breathing of a sleeping man could be heard through the darkness. Cimourdain stood dreamily listening to this peaceful sound.

On the truss of straw at the farther end of the dungeon lay Gauvain sound asleep. It was his breathing that he heard.

Cimourdain moved as noiselessly as possible, and when he had drawn near, he fixed his eyes upon Gauvain; no mother gazing upon her sleeping infant could have worn a look more unutterably tender. The expression was probably beyond his control; he pressed his clenched hands against his eyes as children sometimes do, and for a moment stood perfectly still. Then he knelt, gently lifted Gauvain's hand, and carried it to his lips.

Gauvain stirred. He opened his eyes, with the vague surprise of sudden waking. The feeble glimmer of a lantern dimly lighted the dungeon. He recognized Cimourdain.

"Ah, is that you, master?" he said.

Then he added,—

"I dreamed that Death was kissing my hand."

A sudden influx of thoughts will now and then startle a man, and so it was with Cimourdain; at times this wave rolls in so tumultuously that it threatens to submerge the soul. But Cimourdain's deep soul gave forth no sign; he could but utter the word "Gauvain!"

And the two men stood gazing at each other—Cimourdain's eyes alight with flames that scorched his tears, Gauvain with his sweetest smile.

Gauvain raised himself on one elbow, and said:—

"That scar I see on your face is the sabre-cut you received in my stead. It was but yesterday you stood beside me in the mêlée, and all for my sake. If Providence had not placed you by my cradle, where should I be today? In ignorance. If I have any sense of duty, it is to you that I owe it. I was born in fetters,—I mean the bonds of prejudice,—which you have loosened; you promoted my free development, and from the mummy you have created a child. You have implanted a conscience in a being who bade fair to prove an abortion. Without you my growth would have been cramped; it is through your influence that I live. I was but a lord, you have made of me a citizen; I was only a citizen, you have made of me a mind; you have fitted me to lead the life of a man upon the earth, and have shown my soul the way to heaven. It is you who placed in my hands the key of truth that unlocks the domain wherein we find the realities of human life, and the key of light to the realms above. I thank you, my master! To you I owe my life."

Cimourdain, seating himself on the straw beside Gauvain, said,—

"I have come to sup with you."

Gauvain broke the black bread and offered it to him. After Cimourdain had taken a piece, Gauvain handed him the jug of water.

"Drink first yourself," said Cimourdain.

Gauvain drank, and then passed the jug to Cimourdain, who drank after him.

Gauvain had taken but a swallow.

Cimourdain took deep draughts.

During this supper Gauvain ate, and Cimourdain drank,—a proof of the calmness of the one, and of the burning fever of the other.

A certain awful tranquillity pervaded this dungeon. The two men conversed.

"Gauvain was saying,—

"Grand events are taking form. No one can comprehend the mysterious workings of revolution at the present time. Behind the visible achievement rests the invisible, the one concealing the other. The visible work seems cruel; the invisible is sublime. At this moment I can see it all very clearly. It is strange and beautiful. We have been forced to use the materials of the Past. Hence this wonderful '93. Beneath a scaffolding of barbarism we are building the temple of civilization.

"Yes," replied Cimourdain, "these temporary expedients pave the way for the final adjustment, wherein justice and duty stand side by side, where taxation will be proportionate and progressive, and military service compulsory; where there is to be absolute equality in rank; and where, above all things else, the straight line of the Law is to be maintained,—the republic of the absolute."

"I prefer the republic of the ideal," said Gauvain.

He broke off, then continued:—

"But, oh, my master, where in the picture you have just drawn in words do you place devotion, sacrifice, abnegation, the sweet intermingling of kindliness and love? An accurate adjustment of proportions is a good thing, but harmony is still better. The lyre stands higher than the scales. Your republic deals with the material interest of man; mine transports him to the skies: it is like the difference between a theorem and an eagle."

"You are lost in the clouds."

"And you in your calculations."

"There is an element of dreaminess in harmony."

"So there is in algebra."

"I would have man fashioned according to Euclid."

"And I like him better as described by Homer."

The stern smile of Cimourdain rested on Gauvain as though to stay the flight of his soul.

"Poetry. Beware of poets!"

"Yes; that is a familiar warning: beware zephyrs, beware of sunbeams, beware of perfumes, beware of flowers, beware of the stars."

"That sort of thing can never supply us with food."

"How can you tell? There is mental nourishment: a man finds food in thought."

"Let us indulge in no abstractions! The republic is like two and two in mathematics: two and two make four. When I have given to each man his due—"

"Then your duty is to give him what does not revert to him as a right."

"What do you mean by that?"

"I mean those mutual concessions which each man owes his neighbor, and which go to make up the sum of social life."

"There is nothing beyond the just limits of the law."

"Ah, but there is—everything!"

"I see nothing but justice."

"I look higher."

"What stands higher than justice?"

"Equity."

Now and then both paused, as though a sudden light had flashed across their minds.

Cimourdain continued,—

"Explain your assertion. I challenge you to do it."

"Very well, then. You demand compulsory military service. Against whom? Against mankind. I object to military service; I would have peace. You desire to help the wretched; what I wish is the abolition of their misery. You demand proportionate taxation; I would have no taxes whatsoever. I would have the public expenses reduced to the lowest level, and paid for by the social surplus."

"What do you mean by that?"

"This: In the first place, it is for you to suppress sycophancy,—that of the priest, the soldier, and the judge. Then, use your wealth to the best advantage; distribute over your furrows all that fertilizing matter which is now thrown into your sewers. Three quarters of the soil lies fallow; plough it up; redeem the waste pastures; divide the communal lands; let each man have a farm, and each farm a man. You will increase a hundredfold the social product. At the present time, France affords her peasants meat but four times a year; well cultivated, she could feed three millions of men, all Europe. Utilize nature, that gigantic auxiliary; enlist every breeze, every waterfall, every magnetic current, in your service. This globe has a subterranean network of veins, through which flows a marvellous circulation of water, oil, and fire; pierce this vein of the globe, and let the water feed your fountains, the oil your lamps, and the fire your hearths. Consider the action of the waves,—the ebb and flow of the tides. What is the ocean? A prodigious force wasted. How stupid is the earth, to make no use of the ocean!"

"There you go, in full career with your dreams!"

"You mean with my realities."

Gauvain continued,—

"And woman,—how do you dispose of her?"

Cimourdain replied,—

"Leave her as she is,—the servant of man."

"Yes, under one condition."

"What is that?"

"That man shall be the servant of woman."

"What are you thinking of?" exclaimed Cimourdain. "Man a servant? Never! Man is the master. I admit but one kingdom,—that of the fire-side. Man is king in his own home."

"Yes, on one condition."

"What is that?"

"That woman shall be its queen."

"You mean that you demand for both man and woman—"

"Equality."

"'Equality'! Can you dream of such a thing? The two beings are so entirely unlike!"

"I said equality, not identity."

There was another pause, a sort of truce as it were, between these two minds exchanging their lightning flashes. Cimourdain broke it.

"And the child? To whose care would you intrust that?"

"First to the father who begets, then to the mother who gives him birth, later to the master who educates, and to the city that makes a man of him, then to the country which is his supreme mother, and lastly to humanity which is his great ancestress."

"You have not mentioned God."

"Each step—father, mother, master, city, country, humanity—is but a rung in the ladder that leads to God."

Cimourdain was silent, while Gauvain continued:

"When one climbs to the top of the ladder one has reached God. God is revealed, and one has but to enter into heaven."

Cimourdain made the gesture of one who calls another back: "Gauvain, return to earth. We want to realize the possible."

"Do not begin then by making it impossible."

"The possible may always be realized."

"Not always. Rough usage destroys Utopia. Nothing is more defenceless than the egg."

"Still, Utopia must be seized and forced to wear the yoke of reality; she must be circumscribed by a system of actual facts. The abstract must be resolved into the concrete: what it loses in beauty it gains in usefulness; although contracted, it is improved. Justice must enter into law; and when justice has become law, it is absolute. That is what I call the possible."

"The possible includes more than that."

"Ah, there you go again, soaring away into the land of dreams!"

"The possible is a mysterious bird, always hovering above the head of man."

"We must catch it."

"And take it alive too."

Gauvain continued:—

"My idea is this: Ever onward. If God had intended that man should go backwards He would have given him an eye in the back of his head. Let us look always towards the dawn, the blossom-time, the hour of birth. Those things which are falling to decay encourage the new springing life. In the splitting of the old tree may be heard a summons to the new one. Each century will do its work,—civic, today; humane, tomorrow: today, the question of justice; tomorrow, that of compensation. Wages and Justice are in point of fact synonymous terms. Man's life is not to be spent without a suitable compensation. When

He bestows life, God contracts thereby a debt: justice is the inherent compensation; remuneration is the acquirement thereof."

Gauvain spoke with the calm serenity of a prophet; Cimourdain listened. The parts were changed, and now it seemed as if it were the pupil who had become the master.

Cimourdain murmured,—

"You go at a rapid rate."

"Perhaps because I have no time to lose," replied Gauvain with a smile.

He continued:—

"Ah, master, here is the difference between our two utopias. You would have military service obligatory; I demand the same for education. You dream of man the soldier; I, of man the citizen. You wish him to strike terror; I would have him thoughtful. You establish a republic of swords, while I desire to found—"

He broke off.

"I should like to establish a republic of minds."

Cimourdain looked down on the flag-stones of the dungeon.

"And in the mean time what would you have?" he asked.

"The existing condition of things."

"Then you absolve the present moment."

"Yes."

"Why?"

"Because it is a tempest. A tempest always knows what it is about. For every oak that is struck by lightning, how many forests are purified! Civilization has a plague; a strong wind is sent to expel it from the land. It may not choose its methods wisely, perhaps, but can it do otherwise? Its task is no light one. Viewing the horror of the miasma, I can understand the fury of the wind."

Gauvain went on:—

"But what matters the storm to me, if I have a compass; and what power can events gain over me, if I have my conscience?"

And he added in that undertone which produces so solemn an effect:—

"There is One to whose will we must always yield."

"Who is that?" asked Cimourdain.

Gauvain pointed upwards. Cimourdain looked in the direction of the uplifted finger, and it seemed to him that he could see the starry sky through the dungeon vault.

Once more they relapsed into silence.

Cimourdain continued:—

"A supernatural state of society; I tell you it is no longer possible,—it is a mere dream."

"It is a goal; otherwise, of what use is society? Better remain in a state of nature; be like the savages. Otaheite is a paradise, only in that paradise no one thinks. Better an intelligent hell than a stupid heaven. But, no,—we will have no hell whatever. Let us be a human society. Super-natural? Yes. But if you are to add nothing to Nature, why leave her? In that case you may as well content yourself with work like the ant, and with honey like the bee. Rest content among the laboring classes, instead of rising to the ranks of superior intelligence. If you add anything to Nature, you must of necessity rise above her: to add is to augment; to augment is to increase. Society is the exaltation of Nature. I would have what bee-hives and ant-hills lack,—monuments, arts, poetry, heroes, men of genius. To bear eternal burdens is no fit law for man. No, no, no! let us have no more pariahs, no more slaves, no more convicts, no more lost souls! I would have every attribute of man a symbol of civilization and an example of progress; I would present liberty to the intellect, equality to the heart, fraternity to the soul. Away with the yoke! Man is not made for dragging chains, but that he may spread his wings. Let us have no more of the reptile. Let the larva turn into a butterfly; let the grub change into a living flower and fly away. I wish—"

He broke off. His eyes shone, his lips moved, he said no more.

The door had remained open. Sounds from without penetrated into the dungeon. The distant echo of a trumpet reached their ears,— probably the réveille; then, when the guard was relieved, they heard the butt-ends of the sentinels' muskets striking the ground; again, apparently quite near the tower, so far as the darkness allowed one to judge, a noise like the moving of planks and beams, accompanied by muffled and intermittent sounds resembling the blows of a hammer. Cimourdain turned pale as he listened. Gauvain heard nothing. Deeper and deeper grew his reverie. Hardly did he seem to breathe, so absorbed was he in the visions of his brain. Now and then he moved, like one slightly startled. A gathering brightness shone in his eyes, like the light of dawn.

Some time passed thus.

"Of what are you thinking?" asked Cimourdain.

"Of the future," replied Gauvain.

And he fell back again into his meditation. Unobserved by the latter, Cimourdain rose from the bed of straw whereon they had both been sitting. His eyes rested yearningly upon the young dreamer, while he slowly moved backward towards the door. He went out. The dungeon was again closed.

VI

Still the Sun Rises

It was not long before day began to dawn on the horizon; and together with the day there sprang to light upon the plateau of the Tourgue, above the forest of Fougères, a strange, stationary, and wonderful object, unfamiliar to the birds of heaven.

It had been placed there during the night,—set up rather than built. From a distance, against the horizon, it presented a profile composed of straight and rigid lines, resembling a Hebrew letter, or one of those Egyptian hieroglyphics which formed part of the alphabet of the ancient enigma.

The first thought that entered the mind at the sight of this object was its uselessness. There it stood, among the blossoming heather. Then came the question, could it be used; and for what purpose? Then came a shudder. It was a sort of trestle-work, supported by four posts. At one end were two long upright beams, united at the top by a cross-beam, from which hung a triangle that looked black against the pale blue of the morning sky. At the other end of this trestle stood a ladder. Between these two beams, beneath the triangle, could be distinguished a sort of panel composed of two movable sections, which, fitting into one another, offered to the eye a round hole about the size of a man's neck. The upper section of the panel ran in a groove, by means of which it could be raised or lowered. For the moment the two semicircles that formed the collar were drawn apart. At the foot of the two pillars supporting the triangle was seen a plank that moved on hinges like a see-saw. Beside the plank stood a long basket, and in front, between the two posts at the end of the staging, a square one. This object was painted red, and made entirely of wood, except the triangle, which was of iron. One might know that it was built by men, so ugly, sordid, and contemptible did it look; and yet so formidable was it that it might well have been transported hither by genii.

This shapeless structure was the guillotine.

In front of it, a few paces off, in the ravine, was another monster, La Tourgue,—a stone monster, companion-piece to the monster of wood. And let us add, that after wood and stone have been manipulated by man they lose something of their original substance, taking on a certain similitude to man himself. A building is a dogma; a machine is an idea.

The Tourgue was that fatal product of the past called in Paris the Bastille, in England the Tower of London, in Germany the Fortress of Spielberg, in Spain the Escurial, in Moscow the Kremlin, and in Rome the Castle of Saint-Angelo.

The Tourgue was the condensation of fifteen hundred years,—the period of the Middle Ages, with its vassalage, its servitude, and its feudality. The guillotine showed forth but one year,—'93; but these twelve months were a fitting counterpoise for those fifteen centuries.

The Tourgue was the personification of monarchy; the guillotine, of revolution.

A tragic encounter.

On the one hand, the debt; on the other, the requirement thereof. All the hopeless entanglement of the Gothic period—the serf, the lord, the slave, the master, the plebeian, the nobility, a complex code with all the ramifications of practice, the coalition of judge and priest, the infinite variety of shackles, fiscal duties, the salt-tax, the mortmain, the poll-tax, the exception, the prerogatives, the prejudices, the fanaticisms, the royal privilege of bankruptcy, the sceptre, the throne, the arbitrary will, the divine right—opposed to that simple thing, a knife.

On one side, a knot; on the other, the axe.

For many a year the Tourgue had stood alone in this desert, and from its battlements had rained the boiling oil, the burning pitch, and the melted lead; there it stood, with its dungeons paved with human bones, its torture-chamber alive with memories of its tragic past. For fifteen centuries of savage tranquillity its gloomy front had towered above the shades of the forest; it had been the only power in the land,— the one thing respected and feared; its reign had been supreme, without a rival in its wild barbarity, when it suddenly saw rising before it, with an aspect of hostility, a thing,—nay, more than a thing; a creature as hideous as itself,—the guillotine.

Stone seems at times endowed with the sense of sight. A statue observes, a tower watches, the front of a building contemplates. The Tourgue seemed to be examining the guillotine.

It was as if questioning itself,—

"What can this object be?"

One might fancy it to have sprung from the soil.

And so, indeed, it had.

Like a poisonous tree it had sprouted from a fatal soil. From that soil so plentifully watered by human sweat, by tears, and by blood, from the soil wherein men had dug countless graves, tombs, caves, and ambushes, from the same soil wherein had rotted the innumerable victims of every kind of tyranny, from that soil covering so great a multitude of crimes, buried like frightful germs in the depths below, had sprung forth, on the appointed day, this stranger, this avenging goddess, this fierce sword-bearing instrument; and '93 cried out to the Old World,—

"Behold me!"

The guillotine had a right to say to the dungeon: "I am thy daughter."

And yet at the same time the keep—for these fatal objects live a certain obscure life—recognized its own death-warrant.

At the sight of this formidable apparition the Tourgue seemed bewildered. One might have called it terror. The immense mass of granite was both majestic and infamous; that plank with its triangle was still more dreadful. Deposed omnipotence felt a horror of the rising power. It was criminal history studying judicial history. The violence of former days was comparing itself with the violence of the present time; the ancient fortress, both the prison and the dwelling of the lords, where the tortured victims had shrieked aloud, this structure devoted to war and murder, now useless and defenceless, violated, dismantled, discrowned, a pile of stones no better than a heap of cinders, hideous to look upon, magnificent in death, dizzy with the vertigo of those terrible centuries, stood watching the passage of the awful living hour. Yesterday shuddered in the presence of Today. The old ferocity beheld and did homage to the new terror, and that which was mere Nothingness unclosed its spectral eyes before the Terror, and the phantom gazed upon the ghost. Nature is pitiless; she never withholds her flowers, her melodies, her perfumes, her sunbeams, from human abominations. She overwhelms man by the contrast between divine beauty and social ugliness; she spares him nothing, neither the wing of butterfly, nor song of bird; on the verge of murder, in the act of vengeance or barbarity, she brings him face to face with those holy things; nowhere can he escape the eternal reproach of universal benevolence and the implacable serenity of the sky. Human law in all its hideous deformity must stand forth naked in the presence of the eternal radiance. Man breaks and crushes, lays waste, destroys; but the summer, the lily, and the star remain ever the same.

Never had the fair sky of early dawn seemed lovelier than on that morning. A soft breeze stirred the heather, the mist floated lightly among the branches, the forest of Fougères, suffused with the breath of running brooks, smoked in the dawn like a gigantic censer filled with incense; the blue sky, the snowy clouds, the clear transparency of the streams, the verdure, with its harmonious scale of color, from the aqua-marine to the emerald, the social groups of trees, the grassy glades, the far-reaching plains,—all revealed that purity which is Nature's eternal precept unto man. In the midst of all this appeared the awful depravity of man; there stood the fortress and the scaffold, war and punishment, the two representatives of this sanguinary epoch and moment, the screech-owl of the gloomy night of the Past and the bat of the twilight of the Future. In the presence of a world all flowery and fragrant, tender and charming, the glorious sky bathed both the Tourgue and the guillotine with the light of dawn, as though it said to man: "Behold my work, and yours."

The sun wields a formidable weapon in its light.

This spectacle had its spectators.

The four thousand men of the expeditionary army were drawn up on the plateau in battle array. They surrounded the guillotine on three sides, forming themselves around it after a geometrical fashion in the shape of the letter E; the battery placed against the centre of the longest line made the notch of the E. The red machine was, if we may so express it, shut in by these three battle fronts, a wall of soldiers, extending in a sort of coil and spreading as far as the edge of the escarpment of the plateau; the fourth side, left open, was the ravine itself, which looked upon the Tourgue.

This formed an oblong square, in the centre of which stood the scaffold. The shadow cast upon the grass by the guillotine lessened as the sun rose. The gunners with lighted matches stood by their pieces. A faint blue smoke curled upward from the ravine,—the last breath of the dying fire on the bridge.

This smoke obscured without veiling the Tourgue, whose lofty platform overlooked the entire horizon. Only the width of the ravine separated the platform from the guillotine, and voices could easily have been heard between them.

The table of the tribunal and the chair shaded by the tricolored flags had been conveyed to this platform. The sun rising behind the Tourgue brought into relief the black mass of the fortress, and upon its summit, seated on the chair of the tribunal, beneath the group of flags, the figure of a man, motionless, his arms crossed upon his breast.

This man was Cimourdain. He wore, as on the previous evening, his civil delegate's uniform, a hat with the tricolored cockade upon his head, a sabre by his side, and pistols in his belt.

He was silent. The entire assembly was silent likewise. The soldiers, their eyes downcast, stood at order-arms. They touched elbows, but no one spoke. They were thinking vaguely about this war,—the numerous battles, the hedge fusillades so valiantly faced, of the hosts of furious peasants scattered by their prowess, the citadels conquered, the engagements won, the victories; and now it seemed as though all this glory were turned to their shame. A gloomy expectation oppressed every breast. They could see the executioner walking up and down the platform of the guillotine. The growing light of day deepened until it filled the sky with its majestic presence.

Suddenly was heard that muffled sound peculiar to crape-covered drums; nearer and nearer came their funereal roll; the ranks opened, and the procession, entering the square, moved towards the scaffold.

First came the black' drums, then a company of grenadiers with lowered muskets, then a platoon of gendarmes with drawn sabres, then the prisoner, Gauvain.

Gauvain walked without constraint. Neither hands nor feet were bound. He was in undress uniform, and wore his sword.

Behind him marched another platoon of gendarmes.

The same pensive joy that had lighted his face when he said to Cimourdain, "I am thinking of the future," still rested upon it. Nothing could be more sublime and touching than this continued smile.

When he reached the fatal spot, his first glance was turned to the summit of the tower. He disdained the guillotine. He knew that Cimourdain would feel it his duty to be present at the execution; his eyes sought him on the platform and found him there.

Cimourdain was ghastly pale and cold. Even those who stood nearest heard no sound of his breathing.

When he caught sight of Gauvain not a quiver passed over his face; and yet he knew that every step brought him nearer to the scaffold.

As he advanced, Gauvain looked at Cimourdain, and Cimourdain

VICTOR HUGO

looked at him. It seemed as though Cimourdain found support in that glance.

Gauvain reached the foot of the scaffold. He ascended it, followed by the officer in command of the grenadiers. He unbelted his sword and handed it to this officer; then he loosened his cravat and gave it to the headsman. He was like a vision. Never had he looked more beautiful: his brown locks floated in the wind (at that time they did not cut the hair of those about to be executed); his fair throat reminded one of a woman's; his heroic and commanding expression gave the idea of an arch-angel. He stood upon the scaffold, lost in reverie. There, too, was a height. Gauvain stood upon it stately and calm. The sun streamed about him, crowning him, as it were, with a halo. Still, the prisoner must be bound. Rope in hand, the executioner advanced.

At that moment, when the soldiers saw their young leader so near the knife, they could no longer restrain themselves; the hearts of those warriors burst forth. Then was heard a startling sound,—the sobs of an entire army. A clamor arose: "Mercy! mercy!" Some fell on their knees, others threw down their muskets, stretching their arms towards the platform where Cimourdain stood. One grenadier, pointing to the guillotine, cried, "Here I am; will you not take me as a substitute?" All repeated frantically, "Mercy! mercy!" The very lions would have been moved or terrified; for the tears of soldiers are terrible.

The headsman paused, uncertain what to do.

Then a voice, quick and low, and yet in its ominous severity distinctly heard by all, cried from the top of the tower,—

"Execute the law!"

They recognized the inexorable tone. Cimourdain had spoken. The army shuddered.

The executioner hesitated no longer. He moved forward, holding out the cord.

"Wait," said Gauvain.

And turning towards Cimourdain, he waved his free right hand in token of farewell; then he allowed himself to be bound.

When he was tied he said to the executioner,—

"Pardon,—one moment more. Long live the Republic!" he cried.

He was laid upon the plank. The infamous collar clasped that charming and noble head. The executioner gently lifted his hair, then pressed the spring; the triangle detached itself, gliding first slowly, then rapidly: a frightful blow was heard.

At the same instant another report sounded; the stroke of the axe was answered by a pistol-shot. Cimourdain had just seized one of the pistols that he wore in his belt; and as Gauvain's head rolled into the basket, Cimourdain sent a bullet through his own heart. A stream of blood gushed from his mouth, and he fell dead.

Thus these twin souls, united in the tragic death, rose together,—the shadow of the one blending with the radiance of the other.

THE END